THE EMPEROR OF EARTH-ABOVE

Also by Sheila Gilluly

Greenbriar Queen
The Crystal Keep
Ritnym's Daughter
The Boy from the Burren
The Giant of Inishkerry

THE EMPEROR OF EARTH-ABOVE

Sheila Gilluly

HEADLINE

First published in 1993 by
HEADLINE BOOK PUBLISHING PLC

10 9 8 7 6 5 4 3 2 1

British Library Cataloguing in Publication Data

Gilluly, Sheila
The Emperor of Earth-Above
I. Title
813.54 [F]

ISBN 0–7472–0676–7

Royal Paperback ISBN 0 7472 7913 6

Phototypeset by Intype, London
Printed and bound in Great Britain by
Mackays of Chatham PLC, Chatham, Kent

HEADLINE BOOK PUBLISHING PLC
Headline House
79 Great Titchfield Street
London W1P 7FN

THE EMPEROR OF EARTH-ABOVE

PROLOGUE

It happened again this morning and right in the middle of an attack by those cess-eating renegades from Dun Aghadoe, too.

You'd think a good pirate would have his mind fully on the business of ducking arrows and helping his mates to swing out the grappling boom. Yet for a moment – longer, if truth be told – the faces sighting in along their shafts on the other boat weren't the bearded, hardened countenances of our foes in this war, the priests of the Wolf. For a moment, there was a warm, flower-scented breeze in my nostrils, and the colored sands spread quickly on the painting floor of my mind . . .

The enemy were dark-skinned men, fierce of eye beneath the snouts of their jag'har helmets. One of them raised his spear on its throwing stick and cocked his arm. I followed the direction of his murderous stare and yelled to Grumahu to save himself, but the giant calmly made the horizontal wave with his hand that meant, Relax, Runt Mage. I knew he hadn't seen the other one, though. 'Duck!' I screamed at him . . .

The dwarf's cutlass flashed in the sunlight as he expertly sliced the shaft out of the air – a pirate trick one learns very quickly. Timbertoe cast a disgusted look up at me. 'I saw him, I saw him,' he snarled. 'If ye're going to stand there like a moonstruck calf, get yourself below where ye'll be out of the way, at least. Too busy to look after a mage with the vapors.'

It was the rankest kind of insult from one pirate to another, and it worked. I grabbed hold of a line, paused to snarl back, 'Right, save your own damn arse next time, then!' and launched myself. I swung over the gap of water, cleared the rail of the enemy ship by a good two feet, and with one to-and-fro swing of my sword dropped the first two astonished Dinan in their tracks. The blood beat in my ears, nearly drowning out the sound of the cheer from the pirate ship, and then the lads were following my lead. Many of the Dinan never even had time to fling away their bows and draw their swords. Once we landed on that deck, it was short work.

The victory cost us two men, but we put a dent in their attack plan and gained a fine ship that we can use hereafter as a decoy. I suppose you could say it was worth it, but I tell you, I kenned the two dead dwarves before Timbertoe gave the solemn nod and the shrouded forms slid down the plank into the sea. I had to be sure they were dead, you see. I had to be sure of it and I never am, now.

There has been some talk among the crew about my odd moments, but I always had black moods, and they don't dare say what they really think in front of Timbertoe. The skipper feels so guilty about the whole affair that he lashed out with his crutch at the only man who has ventured to raise the topic, and the fellow was left with ringing in his ears and double vision for a week. But I can tell from their looks, from the way they keep their hands behind them to make the sign, and I can hear the thought plainly though no one gives it voice: *Lost it, he has, poor sod.*

There is quite a lot of sympathy in their eyes, though like all dwarves, they cover it with a kind of cheerful malignancy. They were all aboard the *Inishkerry Gem* that overcast day when Timbertoe cut the tow line to let my funeral ship float free upon the ocean, and they all know – or think they know – what it must have been like to wake in the wooden coffin sometime later, weakened by the long coma, and find yourself absolutely alone on a featureless sea with no food, no water, and the shroud a mildewed weight of tattered canvas upon your face. Aye, who wouldn't be mad, their eyes say.

They don't know the half of it.

Actually I'm not sure I know the half of it, but I had a long time on the drifting hulk to try to piece it out, and as nearly as I can tell, it must have had something to do with the dose of Hag's Embrace I took at Cnoch Aneil.

Together with Rose, the Maid of the Vale, I had gone into the labyrinth beneath the sacred mountain to try to paint the ritual scenes which would unlock the Realm of the Dead and free Ritnym, the Power of the Earth herself, from the Warding of her evil brother Tydranth, Lord of the Wild Fire. We had planned to make the mystical journey to Mother's Realm and return, at the dawn of a new day, with the symbolic seed given by Ritnym to the rightful King of the Burren. Thus we hoped at one stroke both to put right the havoc Tydranth had wrought in unbalancing the Realms, and to legitimize our friend and king, Jamie the Gentle.

However, we had reckoned without Jorem, archpriest of the Dinan an Lupus, the Brotherhood of the Wolf. I thought him dead, but suddenly he was there, at the head of the stairs leading down into the crypt, black against the torch-light behind him. I flung up my ring hand, intending to burn him with my fire, but he hurled a poisoned bone dart that transfixed my hand, and then Rose pulled me away down into the safety of the labyrinth, and Jorem's men levered the mountain down to seal the entrance.

After that, the images in my mind are confusing. I know I painted with Rose's voice chanting beside me the whole time. And I recall that the scenes I painted were from the life of my ancestor, Colin Mariner, the first bearer of the ring I inherited from my grandfather, Bruchan, the master of Skellig Inishbuffin. They were vivid scenes of the life the

Mariner had in the Burren with his wife and children, and scenes also of that other life, the one he shared with a foreign woman he called Tanu, which means Beloved. So compelling were these scenes to me that it seemed I was the man with the wife and sons and also with the one woman in my life who would always have first claim upon my soul. And when I roused from the trance, there she lay beside me on the bank of the river that had carried us out of the mountain: Rose, the woman I loved, who loved another.

I suppose the spell of Colin's story still held me in its grip, as the new day dawned over the shoulder of the mountain. I realized that only one course of action stood even the remotest chance of saving Rose and me, for we were both grievously wounded. I treated her with some of my last remaining dose of the Hag's Embrace, a powerful and dangerous drug to be used only in extremity, to put her into a coma until Neilan, the excellent surgeon at the Vale, might heal her. I remember horses skidding to a stop in the gravel, and I remember telling King Beod of Ilyria, my stalwart ally and rival for Rose's love, not to let some idiot cut through my ring to get it off my grossly swollen finger. He nodded firmly, and then, as the battlefield surgeon seemed determined to prod at my agonized hand, I stuck myself with the drugged needle I had just used on Rose and welcomed the blackness.

It all worked well enough, except for one thing: I forgot that no one else had ever taken *two* doses of the stuff in one lifetime, and that this would be my second.

CHAPTER ONE

I had the damnedest dream.

I was in a dark place, but not the dark of deepest night or of a nightmare, more like the silvered darkness just before the sky lightens towards dawn. The air was cool, but I was snug in warm blankets that had been kept in a cedar chest; they smelled sweet and woody. A nightingale was caroling somewhere nearby, and I smiled even in my sleep.

I knew in the way of a dreamer that I was in a room of the house of healing at the Vale, safe, swimming up out of the counterfeited death of the Hag's Embrace potion. My hand hurt, but not as much as it had – Neilan, extraordinary physician that she was, must have managed another triumph of the healer's art. I'd thought for sure I'd lose the hand at least, maybe the whole arm, to the bone dart.

Memory began to return. *A blackness like this one . . . swirling colors blooming across the sand floor of the labyrinth on Cnoch Aneil . . . 'Stop,' I told the Dark Fire. 'The Gate is open. Get out.' . . . The Power's eyes, widening like the jaws of a snake. 'You're mine, Painter, you're marked with my Sign.' 'And you're marked with mine, my lord. Leave now, or there will be no place left for you, I promise it, by the Five.'* I groaned in my sleep, held by the dream.

There was cold now, real cold, and the sweet singer beyond my window stopped between one sliding note and the next. It became unearthly quiet.

Somewhere in the silence of the sleeping hospital

someone laughed, not loudly, but very clearly, a sly, insinuating laugh. If wolves laugh when the pack has a stag cornered, they laugh like that. It raised gooseflesh, and I reached to draw the blankets up, but it was no good, I was still cold. In fact, I was so cold I couldn't move.

The floors here were stone-flagged, the better to clean, and the siochlas wore soft slippers as a consequence, not to disturb the patients as they tended their ills and hurts. It struck me as odd, then, that I could hear this one's footfalls so clearly, striking the stone – clicking, actually, I amended as I lay listening to the approach down the corridor outside, as though she wore nailed . . . no, clicking like a dog's paws on marble. That was it. Someone's herd dog had slipped in at the portico past the portress and was prowling for supper scraps. Neilan wouldn't like that at all. A dog is a good enough beast and a fine companion, but she kept a clean hospital. She'd given even Timbertoe a bath, a rare thing for the pirate. Oh ho, pup, I thought, you're in trouble.

The laugh was much closer this time, only a few rooms away, and, cold as I was, I was nettled that the inconsiderate bastard should disturb the slumbers of the sick and dying.

Symon was there suddenly, in my dream, though I couldn't see his face clearly for the shadowed dark. His huge bicep flexed under the leather jerkin he always wore for practice workouts. He was tossing a dagger up in the air, end over end, catching it as he spoke. The other indentured boys and I used to be fascinated when he did that during lectures. We'd bet sometimes on when he would miss. He never did. I was so mesmerized by the knife that his voice startled me a little. *'The first rule I taught you, Aengus. What was it?'*

'Be prepared,' I answered, quoting from memory. 'Never be taken unaware.'

His shadowed head moved. *'Aye.'* The dagger suddenly arced towards me, hilt first for me to catch it out of the air, but I was so cold that I couldn't move in time. The knife clattered under my wooden cot.

'Sorry, Sy,' I apologized. 'I've been sleeping for a long time and I'm so c—'

'*Wake up, Aengus!*' my weaponsmaster commanded sharply.

I turned my head a little from him to hear the dog's padding out in the hall. Closer now; I could hear it pause and sniff the air, questing a scent. When I looked for Symon again he had gone, the way people do in a dream, with no apology.

'*Grandson, thee's slept too long.*' Bruchan sounded sharp, irritated. I saw him in the darkness a few feet away, near the unshuttered window that would look out onto the terrace above the harbor in the daytime. '*Rouse thyself, and look to the ring!*' His white hair blew a little in the wind that was starting to come in strongly. I saw stars behind him, a kind of cowl of silvery pinpoints.

Obediently, I moved my hand where it rested on my chest. Under the heavy bindings, I could tell: 'She had to take my finger off, master. It was all poisoned. It's all right, though. Neilan will have put my ring on the table here by the bedside so I can see it when I wake up.'

'*Haste, boy! Put it on!*'

'No, it won't fit over the bandages, you see,' I objected drowsily. 'It's all right,' I answered his impatient movement towards the table. 'It isn't as though anybody in the Vale would steal it anyway. You don't have to keep an eye on witches as you do on pirates.'

'*Wake, Aengus! Thee's in danger! Symon, stand by the door!*'

'*Aye, master,*' I heard the weaponsmaster say, though he'd been gone a moment before. I heard his sword ring from its sheath.

The beast had caught scent of me. It was loping now, nails clicking on the floor, panting breath bulging the walls a little. It was heavy, too, a very heavy dog, because the floor was shaking under its feet. The vibration was making my hand start to throb.

'Get your arse out of bed, Giant,' Timbertoe growled calmly. He was balanced on his pegleg and crutch, cutlass in hand, by the foot of my bed. '*There's no ruby chalcedon big enough to lure this bastard off the trail.*'

'Oh, all *right,*' I told them all. 'But I wish you'd let a fellow sleep.' I pushed the covers aside and extended my left hand awkwardly over my body, searching on the bedside table in the darkness for the chalcedon ring. Some of their tension had infected me. That damned dog was coming at a full run. If it jumped on my bed, my hand would be hurt again. I brushed the ring, but it rolled away from my clumsy fingers. I swore and turned a little on my side, reaching—

The door burst, shattered, from its hinges. I raised my swathed hand to block some of the flying debris, and a heavy piece of iron lock struck it, sending a roaring cataract of pain up my arm. The bed was rocking wildly, pitching like the deck of a ship in a storm, and the beast filled the doorway and the corridor, its sapphire eyes gleaming above the sable muzzle. It grinned, red tongue lolling between huge canines, and laughed its sinister-sly laugh once more. '*I told you you were mine, Painter,*' the Dark Fire said. He started to advance into the room, and flagstones sank beneath the tremendous weight of his paws at each step.

I dived over the side of the lurching bed and caught the ring as it rolled off the table. 'Stop!' I gasped, fumbling it with my good hand against the bandages, frantic to slip it on my finger – any finger would do. Part of my mind wondered where Symon, Bruchan, and Timbertoe had got to, and why they weren't helping, but I knew even in the nightmare that their part had been only to rouse me out of the Hag's Embrace; they could not fight the Wolf for me. The chalcedon signet slipped on my left forefinger. I rose on my right elbow, holding it up like a torch. 'Stop,' I repeated firmly. Only that. I could feel the Rainbow Light of the ring beginning to crackle.

Beldis, the Wolf incarnation of the Dark Fire, halted,

forepaw raised in mid-stride, and its features shifted into those of a man dark of hair, red of lips, with impossibly pointed canines. Jorem, archpriest of the Wolf whom I had killed by the river, leered. '*Really, pickpocket, you disappoint time after time, don't you? You might want to think a bit before throwing that Fire at me. Look.*' He jerked his head, pointing with his chin at the pendant hanging round his wolf's neck. I held him at bay with my Fire and glanced into it.

The crystal was black, black as despair, and in its dark depths I saw for one brief instant Rose's terrified face. She was impossibly far away, and very alone.

'*She's quite beautiful, isn't she? I find I've taken a fancy to her. Now, now, Painter, mustn't be jealous.*'

'Let her go, my lord.'

'*Give me the ring.*'

'Impossible.'

'*I thought you might say that. But I felt obliged to give you the chance to give it up before I took it by force.*'

I looked into Rose's fearful and despairing eyes. 'Fight me for it,' I challenged the Dark Fire.

He laughed with genuine humor. '*We played this wager once before, Colin, my friend, and you won.*' The beast's eyes narrowed, blank as an adder's. '*I do not intend to lose a second time, I assure you. Still, if you wish it, I'll enter the tile game gladly. You'll find me waiting at our accustomed place. Oh, by the way, I think you should know before we start that I have this.*' His lips snarled back to show me a wrinkled seed about the size and shape of a pea clenched between his teeth. My heart went cold. It was the seed from Earth-Below that Ritnym had given Rose and me to give to Jamie. The Wolf saw my despair and snickered. '*Surely you didn't think I'd give up my claim on the Realm of the Dead just because you did some painting, did you?*' His voice dripped sarcasm like venom. '*Fight me for it,*' he mocked.

'I will!' I vowed. *'And this time there will be nothing left for you, my lord, not so much as a dark corner to hide yourself.'* My hand was shaking, though, the Fire of the ring flaring and dying like a torch in a draft, and he smiled.

'*Really? I'll look forward to the combat, then. The first move is mine as usual, I believe, so I'll take this.*' With a quick slash of his fangs, he cut the chalcedon in my ring in half. '*I may not take it all, according to the rules, but I've always fancied it.*'

'*Give it back,*' I demanded.

'*Come and collect it, if you dare.*' His wolf's tongue lolled as he laughed. '*Here, I'll even give you something to help.*'

He thrust his black muzzle skyward, and the roof of the hospital collapsed. I saw a single star for a moment in the hole where he had been before the hewn ceiling beam crashed down upon my head and crushed me. I did not feel the pain, but looking down as I floated away, up through the tangle of splintered timbers and broken clay roofing tiles, I saw the blood spreading in a quick gush through the gray jelly and the shards of the shattered ring striking glints of fading Fire.

How odd, I thought. *I've always heard you can't dream your own death.* The screams and cries for help grew fainter below me as I spiraled upward into the darkness. *Well, I don't think much of that dream. It ended badly, and Rose looked so alone.*

Let's have another.

Again, I was somewhere above, looking down, as the procession paced slowly down to the harbor from the knoll on which the Motherhouse stood. The grayness of the open sky was smudged with lavender and rose at the eastern horizon over the water. It would be one of these inbetween days when the weather doesn't know whether to rain or clear. Usually in those conditions there is good wind for sailing, so I was happy. I watched the torches bob, approaching the wharf, keeping pace with the muffled thump of a single drum. Most unusually, no mounted outriders headed the long line. Instead, the banner was borne by a man who strode along lightly to the front of the procession, a Yoriandir, one of the green-complected servants of the Vanui. He had a harp case slung on his back, and by that I knew him as Dlietrian. He looked very grave, and I could see why: he'd forgotten to untie the lacings and let the flag wave; it was still furled tightly about the standard. That marred the solemnity of the ritual, whatever it was.

The procession jammed up for a moment passing through the small village that lay at the head of the harbor, and I lost sight of Dlietrian and the first rank who followed him as they wound among the red-tiled roofs of the cottages, some of which showed mending with thatch. The Vale must have had quite a gale recently if it ripped the roofs right off. No doubt this ritual was a solemn thanksgiving for having weathered the storm. The drum beat slowly.

No, I was wrong. It was a funeral, I saw that as the cart with its team of matched grays paused beyond the last cottage, held up for a moment by the press of people going before through the narrow street. The coffin showed in the torchlight, beautifully carved and glowing softly with beeswax well rubbed in. Flowers bedecked the cart round it, heaped high in what seemed extravagant abandon, as though the siochlas had each thrown a blossom as the cart passed, for remembrance and grief. The dead person was well known to them, and liked, apparently; no doubt someone who had died in the storm. The people marching to the front of the line got themselves sorted out, and the siochlas leading the team clucked softly to get the horses moving again. I lost sight of them in the village.

Where the road opened from the village to cross the narrow beach before the pier, Dlietrian appeared, bearing the furled banner at a measured walk; then, a few paces behind him, the first rank of mourners cleared the village. From above, I watched.

It was quite a distinguished assemblage. Beod, Crown Prince of Ilyria, resplendent in royal scarlet and gold, the black sash of mourning no darker than his hair and the new beard that gave his face a surprising maturity, marched with the automatic tread of a soldier, pain in his gray eyes. On his arm, Mistress Caitlin, once wife to the late Diarmuid ap Gryffyn, King of the Burren, and mother to Jamie the Gentle, for whose sake Rose and I had risked the labyrinth on Cnoch Aneil. Caitlin was dressed from head to foot in black, signaling complete mourning, and I was surprised at that, because her husband had already been dead awhile and she had suffered no other deaths in her immediate family. In my dream, I frowned. If Beod was here, Jamie might have been as well. But I could not see him.

On Caitlin's other side walked the Shimarrat king, Ja-Solem, magnificent in his outlandish flowing robes, jeweled and twinkling like a star, but his dark face was still and set, and for the most part he looked straight ahead, out to sea, except once, when the woman beside him stumbled a step on the cobbles and he courteously gave her his arm. The woman who nodded her thanks wore the siochlas' hooded green mantle, making her age difficult to tell, but she seemed a little unsure on her feet and there were deep crow's-feet around her eyes, so I guessed her to be one of the senior Vanui. When the torchbearer moved up at her signal and the light on her face strengthened, I recognized her slightly, though I could not place her name. She seemed to be acting as head of the community in this funeral, for she was carrying a wand of office showing the double-sided skull and maid's face that I had seen at a ritual in a chamber below the knoll. Freezing fear shot through me suddenly. Where was Rose, who should have been here in her office of Reverend Daughter, the Maid of the Vale?

I looked over the mourners, but I could not see the face

of the woman I loved. I found Comfrey Lichen, though. The little man, whom I had seen only once in the meeting of the Privy Council where the invasion of the Burren had been planned over my protests, was riding on the caisson itself, nearly buried in the flowers. The dead person had quite an honor guard.

Only as the procession clattered over the cobbles of the beach road onto the pier did I realize the oddity: the crypts of the dead here in the Vale were tunneled into the knoll itself, a mile distant. Why were they all headed *away* from the burial place?

The first ray of the rising sun struck low over the gray water of the harbor, illumining Dlietrian's beech-green face. He lifted his head to greet the light and inhaled a breath of the morning air, but the standard in his hands did not waver as he led them onto the wharf itself. Drawn by the gleam of sunlight, I turned to the dawn.

I was looking down on a pirate ship rising easily at anchor, trim lines and reefed sails neatly black against the wash of apricot light cast by the rising sun. The light flared for a moment, gilding the ship briefly as the orb climbed free of the earth, then the colors died to be replaced by gray as the cloud cover swallowed the sun. As I had thought, it would be an inbetween day.

The flag at the mast, half down the halyards in respect, showed the Guildmaster's dagger and sash, and beneath it a single white gem rippled on its field of burgundy as the master's own flag ran up and broke open to the dawn wind: the *Inishkerry Gem*. It was Timbertoe's ship. My mates had come to pay their respects.

Jamie, or Rose? Which of them had died and occasioned such a profound outpouring of honor from this noble company?

Tied up at the end of the pier were two small boats, linked, I saw, by a towing rope. In the lead dory was a complement of dwarven pirates, scrubbed for once, trimmed up, every beard neatly braided, every short jacket clean, every sash knotted just so about their waists. They sat at the oars, waiting. Amidships, Timbertoe balanced on his pegleg and crutch. I scarcely recognized him in the new linen shirt, fine velvet jacket with silver buttons, and neatly oiled hair. He bore himself as straight as ever, but the customary glint of combined mischief and malice was gone from his eye. He turned his head slightly, gave some quiet order that I could not catch, and the last two rowers left their seats to hop across the small open water into the boat at the end of the tow line. They took up stations, one in the bow, one in the stern, at either end of the bier that had been nailed across the thwarts.

Without thought, I went closer to see more clearly. Yes, it was a dragon-prow. A funeral ship. It must be Jamie who was dead, then, and they were sending him the same way his father had gone. Grief as pure and piercing as the first frost of autumn flooded through me. He'd been a good man, and I had known very few of them.

Upon reaching the end of the pier, Dlietrian dipped the standard, and the dwarf in the bow reached to unclip the furled flag from the pole. This he carried to the single mast, where his mate helped him attach it to the halyard rings. Slowly, with ceremony, they raised it to the masthead, but did not slip the thongs that bound it yet. Dlietrian bowed and stepped aside, unslinging his harp case.

The assembled nobles divided on some signal I didn't see to line the wharf, forming a lane for the pallbearers. Beod handed Caitlin off to Ja-Solem and went down the pier to be one of them. The Yoriandirkin and the Ilyrian prince hoisted the coffin to their shoulders and, in cadence with the drum, marched it down to the dwarven ships. Comfrey followed. The drummer beat a tattoo, and they handed the casket down to the dwarves waiting in the dragon-prow, who laid it on the bier and drove in the wooden retaining pegs on all sides that would prevent it from sliding with the action of the waves at sea.

The drum stopped.

The witch who bore the staff of office raised it high in the profound silence. 'Fly, shade, straight to Mother's lap,' she intoned. 'Be welcomed to the rest She has prepared for thee, and do not trouble the living lands in thy passage. Peace be thine, now and for ever.'

'Be it so,' the assembled company answered in the ritual response. From above, I could see that most of the dwarves, including Timbertoe, had one hand out of sight of the pier, and I knew they were making the sign. A witch in full regalia is enough to give any man the collywobbles.

The crone lowered the staff to horizontal, pointing straight at Timbertoe. The old seadog didn't flinch, but it must have taken all the bravado he'd acquired in his long life not to. 'We entrust him to your care, Captain. See that you sail well and truly. I bind you under a geis to see him fairly on his way.'

Several of the dwarves blanched, but Timbertoe met her eye to eye. 'I never intended otherwise, mistress. It's what he would have chosen.'

She nodded, satisfied, and stepped back. I got a little angry, not at the slight to Timbertoe – imagine anyone's having the gall to instruct a pirate captain how to sail! – but because they were apparently going to send off James ap Gryffyn, King of the Burren and Lord of the Isles of Wyvin, without a single mark of honor befitting his rank. There was nothing in the boat except the ritual meal, a loaf and a cup of wine set in an open box to hold them. No gilded sword or shield marked with the Gryffyn; no casks of precious gems and gold; not even a fine fleece to warm his voyage. Nothing but a few flower petals that had stuck to the coffin. Of course, I reflected, being Jamie the Gentle, maybe he ordered the money that might have been spent on his funeral to be spent on the poor people of his kingdom instead. That would have been like him. Still, you'd have thought the siochlas could have done better by him than this, especially with his mother watching. I could see Caitlin, outwardly composed, standing next to Ja-Solem.

Now Dlietrian set himself to make music, the sweetest air I had ever heard. He'd saved my life with an impossible shot once; now it seemed he was as much a master of the harp as he was of a bow. The melody, clear and unexpectedly sprightly in the gray morning, told somehow of sea birds nesting by the hundreds in high cliffs, of peace and plenty that had survived through grief, of distant things seen and dimly understood. It was a pretty song, but I wouldn't have said it fitted Jamie very well, the hunchback having been more a man of the land than of the sea and no notable traveler.

Beod turned to his equerry to reclaim and set on his black hair the royal circlet that would not have been meet to wear during the ritual, then gird on the sword the man handed to him. He bent to kiss the skull when the crone lowered it, then wordlessly climbed down the short ladder from the pier and dropped into Timbertoe's boat, where the dwarves had made room for him. This was a rare mark of distinction for the deceased, to be accompanied on the first part of his journey by a prince.

When the Ilyrian was seated, Timbertoe looked over his head and nodded to the two dwarves in the dragon-prow. One stood on the thwart amidships, steadied by his mate, and flicked the blade of his dagger through the thongs that bound the flag. The banner fluttered limply for a moment, then lifted to snap in the freshening breeze. On a field of midnight blue, the Swan floated, the insignia of the Master of Inishbuffin. It was my own flag flying from that masthead.

No, I thought. *I* said *I didn't like this dream. Let's have another!*

But in the way of nightmares, this one carried me along with it regardless of my protests. I watched as the dwarves climbed back aboard the dory and flung the mooring lines up onto the wharf. Timbertoe's hand lifted, and the oars went out over the sides smartly, held poised just above the water, waiting. The captain nodded to the helmsman, the hammer clanked, and the blades bit into the water. Slowly, they towed my funeral ship away from the pier.

The pegleg remained standing, balancing easily, and the boat lifted and dipped, lifted and dipped with the men's rowing. He looked back once, to be sure the towing line had not fouled, and met Beod's eyes. Neither of them said anything.

We drew up to the side of the *Inishkerry Gem*, where the crew left aboard already had the rope ladders down over the sides for the dory team. Timbertoe looked back at the prince then. 'There's the swing, if ye'd rather.'

Beod shook his head. 'I'll manage the ladder.'

'Right. Up ye go then, lads, and don't anybody wind up in the drink. We want to look sharp for the eyes on shore who'd just love to see pirates muck it up at something as important as this.'

The subdued crew swarmed up the ladders with Beod more surefooted on the ropes than landsmen usually were, though Arni had to reach a hand to help the prince over the rail when he got to the top. Timbertoe had lowered himself to a seat in the dory, and it was winched aboard the *Gem* and swung into its place. By the time the captain took his place on the quarterdeck, the towing line had been secured. Timbertoe looked over the aft rail for a moment at my casket rocking gently below in the dragon-prow that reached only halfway up the larger ship's side. 'Ries, take us out nice and steady,' he ordered the bo's'n quietly.

'Aye, Skipper. Up anchor!' Ries Nieboldson sang out. The heavy winch creaked protestingly.

'Anchor weighed!' came the report.

'All hands to sailing stations! Stand by!'

'Standing by!' came the shout from several quarters.

'Boost the mains'l!' Ries ordered.

Immediately teams of dwarves lined on both sides of the deck with the ends of the mainsail lines in their hands broke into a pounding run the length of the deck towards the bow. When they reached the end of the ropes a couple of feet from the very bowsprit, each in turn leaped over the side clinging to his knotted rope end, like very heavy necklace beads sliding down a fat lady's bosom, to be brought up sharp a scant meter or so above the water. The mainsail rose as though shot on the point of an arrow to the top of the mast, the canvas bellied with a sound like a lightning strike, and the *Gem* raced from her anchorage like a greyhound. It is the standard pirate trick for making a quick getaway.

'Dammit, Ries, I said nice and steady!' Timbertoe exploded, grabbing the rail and whacking the bo's'n with his crutch.

'It *was* nice and steady! I didn't know you wanted it *slow* too!' Ries yelled back, offended that his helmsmanship was being questioned.

Even in my dream, I laughed.

The two of them glared at each other for a moment until Timbertoe rubbed his nose and sighed. 'Ah, codswallop. It's a proper enough beginning to a pirate's sending-off, I guess.' He nailed Ries with an icy look. 'But any more moves like that and I'll have your liver and lights fried for breakfast. Clear?'

'Of course, Skipper.' The old bo's'n had sailed with the pegleg for years, and they got on well. For dwarves.

Timbertoe squinted to check the bearing for the harbor mouth, nodded, and spat over the side, glancing to make sure he'd missed my dragon-prow. I thought it was considerate of him. He looked to Beod, who was regarding them with a mixture of amusement and some surprise that even on this occasion, pirates could not act with seemliness. The pegleg read that look for what it was, and for an instant he grinned a feral grin, as though he'd got a rich merchantman centered off his port bow and a favoring wind for an attack. Then he shook himself a little. 'Invite ye below, Prince?'

'Below' was his own cabin, and the stocks of flotjin. Below was also private for talking. Beod stood away from the rail and inclined his head graciously. 'Thank you, Captain.'

The Ilyrian was a familiar figure to the crew. He'd chartered the ship on several occasions. As odd as it may seem, a pirate crew is absolutely trustworthy once you've purchased their silence, and Beod and Rose's business had been the most private a man and woman have together. I had sailed with Timbertoe for four years before I'd found out about the couple's assignations, and then I'd discovered the secret only by accident and not from any of the dwarves. Maybe in their own rough way, the pirates were sympathetic to a pair who would be doomed if their love were known.

I followed when Beod and Timbertoe swung themselves through the hatch and made their way along to the captain's cabin. In another time, Neddy, our mute cabin boy, would have been there, with a beaker of flotjin already pulled, guessing his master's need for the release of the liquor on a day such as this. But Neddy was gone, of course. Timbertoe waved the prince ahead of him, gesturing he should take a seat on the bunk. The pegleg shut the door, dropped the bolt, and pulled open his liquor locker. Only when he had poured a brimming mugful for Beod and a tankard for himself did he look at the Ilyrian.

'Early for it,' Beod ventured as he accepted the drink.

'Drink up, Prince. You'll want it before this day is out, I'll venture.' He raised the tankard. 'To Aengus, a stout mate and a good enough lad even if he was a Burrener.'

Beod looked away for a moment, swallowed, and raised his own cup. 'To Aengus Gill Fisher, King of the Burren and Lord of the Isles of Wyvin, Lord Protector of the Vale, and Master of Inishbuffin: all hail!' At Timbertoe's raised eyebrow, the Ilyrian prince said quietly, 'Well, why not? With Jamie gone, Aengus would have been next in precedence to the throne if he had wakened. I'd have backed him in a claim, and so would Ja-Solem, to say nothing of Queen Caitlin and Lady Sive Mac Maille.'

Timbertoe pursed his lips, considering, then nodded. 'Fair enough,' he said. They touched cups and drank. I hardly heard Beod's coughing. Jamie *was* dead, then. Powers, what had happened?

Beod caught his breath and wiped a hand across his mouth, wincing at the fire of the dwarvish liquor. 'How could something so well begun end so badly? First Jamie gets killed in a hunting accident, gored by a boar, because his nobles wanted the king to go hunting and the poor man had never held a boar spear in his life! Then an earthquake hits the Vale, and Aengus—' He broke off and looked suddenly up at Timbertoe. 'Sorry. I know you two were friends.'

The old seadog's face was unreadable. 'Aye,' he said shortly and drained the rest of his tankard. Beod took another swallow of his own. In the silence I thought I could still hear a whisper of Dlietrian's song, borne on the wind through the open porthole. The pegleg studied the prince's bowed head as Beod sat forward, elbows braced on his knees, looking down into his mug. 'I was glad to hear your sweetheart wasn't hurt when the roof of the hospital wing came down. Slept right through it, they say.'

Beod sighed. 'Yes,' he said. 'She's still sleeping. Neilan keeps telling me to be patient, even though it's been three months already; she says the effect of the Hag's Embrace is probably deepened by how deep the bone point went, and how near her heart it was. The surgery to remove it was quite dangerous in itself.'

'Mistress Neilan's a fair hand with a knife, though,' Timbertoe said judiciously.

Beod's glance went involuntarily to the pirate's empty

trouser leg. 'I suppose so,' he said, and drank another swallow of flotjin. His lips tightened. 'I hope so. Because she's going to have to deliver my son that way if Rose is still sleeping six months from now.'

Timbertoe wasn't very often lost for words, but he was now. I was, myself. I could not have spoken even if I hadn't been dreaming, remembering a scene I had 'lived' in the entranced hours on Cnoch Aneil. I was Colin . . . *The sand warm under my naked back, the sound of waves lapping, Tanu's eyes like the summer sea watching me. 'Maybe Marner too tired go in morning, hey?' she teased.*

And the painting on the floor when I awoke and found Rose asleep beside me on the floor of the labyrinth, the painting I had not wanted her to see. *Powers!* I thought as I realized, shock and joy commingled, and then dread and loss coming hard on their heels, because in my dream I was dead in my casket aboard the dragon-prow.

Mutely the pirate tipped more flotjin into his cup and took a long pull at it. 'I hadn't heard that,' he admitted, probably nettled that the Guildmaster's spy network did not extend to the Vale.

The Ilyrian prince gave him a sharp look. 'I should hope not! As of this moment, only three people in the world know: you, me, and Neilan.'

Four, mate, I told him silently. *And don't think you can take my son just because you're a live prince and I'm a dead king.*

'How—?' Timbertoe pulled at the braids of his beard, then went straight at it, which was the only way he ever went at anything. 'How d'ye know it's yours, boy? She was held by the Wolfhounds for quite a little time, is all I mean. And that damned arch-mucking-priest of theirs might have . . . Well, he hated all the wise women, you know that. Your Rose most of all.'

Beod's chin firmed under the new black beard. 'The same way I know it's a boy: Neilan told me. She has ways, you understand?' Witch ways, he meant.

But Neilan didn't know about the painting under Cnoch Aneil. It was my child, all right. It must be.

Timbertoe accepted the explanation, nodding, then regarded the foreign prince from under his bushy eyebrows. 'The penalty for the Maid who takes a lover is death, I know that much about those women back there and their way towards men. And, like you said, there's three of us that know now. I'm assuming you're wanting to charter, else you'd not have told me that little girl was in the family way. So what's your deal, Prince?'

Beod gave him a small appreciative salute for his quickness. 'I may need to hire a fast ship and a crew that wouldn't be afraid of a witch's curse, if Neilan can't convince them to delay the punishment until Rose wakes.'

'The ship is no problem. I don't fancy making any of those old girls angry at me, though. Where's this fast ship to go once you've stolen Rose out of their hospital?'

'Past the Wyvins, round the Horn, and up a river that isn't marked on any map, according to Comfrey Lichen. The Folk will be waiting there to carry Rose up into their mountains. The place has magic of its own, he tells me, and is far from the Vale in any case.' He looked at Timbertoe hopefully. 'Will you help me, old friend?'

'You haven't named a price yet.'

Beod smiled. 'There isn't much that could tempt a pirate who owns a chalcedon mine, I think.'

'*Half* owns a chalcedon mine,' the pegleg corrected quickly, then checked himself and pulled at his beard roughly. He'd forgotten for a moment that I was dead, and he owned the whole thing now. 'Right,' he continued after a pause. 'Money won't do this time. Well, since you're so sure its a boy she's carrying, here's the price: send your little prince to us dwarves for fostering. Aye, other jaws than yours will drop, I don't doubt, but we'll do right by him. You won't find better weaponsmasters than pirates, and we'll teach him to make better bargains than his father.' Timbertoe spat in his palm and offered his hand to Beod, eyeing him steadily.

The Ilyrian closed his mouth and thought about it briefly. Then he spat in his own palm, and they shook on it. I smiled. My son would be well looked after until I woke up. As nightmares went, this one was turning out all right.

'Time, Skipper,' Arni's voice called from topside.

Both Beod and Timbertoe looked a little ashamed, as though they had momentarily forgotten why they were here. 'Guess it's time,' the pegleg said, quietly closing the liquor locker. Beod stood up, straightening his black sash. We went up on deck.

The crew was lining the rails, waiting. Ries made way for Timbertoe at the cleat where the tow line was tied off, and handed the pegleg a knife. 'Ready for you, Skipper.' Beod folded his arms to hide the slight shaking of his hands.

All eyes went to the funeral ship, to the softly polished casket.

Timbertoe was facing away from all of them, so they never saw, but I did. As far as I know, he never shed another tear in his life. The knife flashed down to slice the tow rope. 'May ye go safe upon the deeps, lad,' he whispered.

And beat you home to port, Skipper, I answered in my dream. It is the traditional leavetaking between pirates.

I watched from above as the dragon-prow slowed, propelled now only by her one small sail. The *Gem*, its yards of canvas sheeting billowing like a thundercloud, bore downwind, swiftly growing smaller until it was just a dot on the horizon, just another seabird winging over the ocean. I was alone.

Well, you can wake up now, I told myself.

A sudden wind came up, no more than a good sailing breeze at first, and the dragon-prow responded like a willing horse to a rider's knee. I was borne along, somewhere on that boat or maybe a little above it, but I knew even in the dream that some other power than mine was steering it.

When the swells became heavier I grew a little alarmed, because water began to gather in the bottom of the boat, dashed off the tops of the sliding waves. But it was only a dream, so I rode the heaving ship where it wanted to go, the sail straining, the lines humming.

Night came, and day, and sometimes I wasn't sure in the odd gray light which was which. The carved casket grew weathered by the salt water, and the Swan banner frayed at the end where the wind whipped it. But it was still all right, because the caulking of the planks was tight, and, anyway, it was only a dream.

Then the gale began to shriek and the waves became rank after rank of mountainous seas. The sail let go with a great tearing sound, but even then the boat was pushed on nearly as fast as it had been. I looked for a rudder, but there wasn't one, and I could not have steered in this gale in any event. The sea broke over the casket again and again, but the stout dwarven pegging held it secure to the dying ship, and the lid didn't come off, though I thought it might. The Swan above my head set her neck into the wind, and we sailed on.

Came a time when the sound of a great cataract was carried on the shrieking wind, and then I knew. I had come to the Falls at World's Edge. *No, I knew I didn't like this dream*, I said. *Let's have another.* But the dragon-prow canted abruptly, and I was looking down over my bow at the stars.

Then I went over.

CHAPTER TWO

There was blood in my mouth, a copper taste mixed with salt, and my hands were cut with razors. My head was being slowly slammed again and again into something that slithered and slipped under my cheek. It stank like the bottom of a chum bucket, reeking of fish offal. I retched and brought up seawater.

When I opened my eyes, everything was lit by an eerie, dull green light, a moving light that surged and trickled—

Oh, I realized, and lifted my head. The surf broke over me again, and instinctively I held my breath, grasping for a hold, but I got cut again and the seawater burned. I scissored a kick, and an astonishingly sharp pain from my right leg exploded lights in my skull. I retched once more, bile mixed with seawater this time, and for a while was too sick to care.

At some time I became aware of another light, outside my skull and not the phosphorescence of the sea. Torchlight, near enough for me to see a slight reflection of it in the water. I turned my head, my cheek sliding over the disgustingly slippery clump of seaweed. A procession of torches was coming closer. *The thump of a single drum, and a green-skinned man . . .* The thought flashed through my mind, leaving a wake of the sea's phantom light for a moment, then vanished. From below, I watched the torches approach.

They were spreading out, it seemed to me, some ranging

to my left out of sight, and some to my right. The lights bobbed as they came. I tried to raise a hand to signal whoever was carrying them, but my arms were too heavy to move, so I puffed a breath out of my salt-swollen lips, and lay watching, waiting for someone to come close enough to hail. I tried to grasp something, and this time got a hold with my left hand that didn't cut too much. That helped steady my head. My leg was really starting to hurt.

A torch was coming, streaming a little in the night's small breeze, the figure under it showing only one browned arm and a head that was white on top and oddly swollen. But I could see the other hand, poised at his shoulder, and the spear he held, clearly enough. Maybe I wouldn't hail him, after all. I shut my mouth on the sounds of pain that wanted to get past my teeth, and hoped I wasn't showing much above the sharp rocks.

The torchlight came closer, my man walking slowly, picking a way, pausing sometimes as the waves surged through channels in what seemed to be a rock causeway against which I was being held by the press of the tide at my back. The fellow was close enough now for me to see that he was nearly naked but for a cloth wrapped round his waist that reached just to mid-thigh, and a close-fitting headgear of some kind. Slick black hair escaped from under this, and the rest of him was as brown as his hands. He was peering intently into the water, the spear motionless.

Suddenly it flashed down into the water on the other side of the causeway, and he drew it back up by the line attached to the butt end. A fat fish was impaled on the point. He smiled at the size of it, stuck the torch into the rocks, and wrested the flapping fish off his spear, stuffing it into a woven creel slung at his back.

'Hey, give us a hand, mate?' I called weakly.

He whipped round, hissing something I didn't catch, and drew back his spear. I could see the whites of his eyes showing in the dark.

'Peace!' I tried to yell, but it came out as more of a croak.

The fisherman stared for a moment. He was breathing heavily.

'Peace,' I repeated. 'I mean thee no harm, friend.' The tide must have been on the turn, flooding towards the high-water mark, because just then a master wave crashed over my head. My hand slipped, the ring clicking on the sharp coral, and I kicked instinctively to keep near the wall. I heard someone cry out hoarsely, and dimly realized the voice was my own.

He seized one of my hands, but our grips slid and broke. My head cracked against the razor rocks. My fisherman grasped me firmly under the armpits. 'Olowai!' he said sharply and jerked his head. He obviously meant something like 'Climb out!' or maybe 'Hang on!' but I was too far gone to do either. He muttered something else that I could not hear through the roaring in my ears, then strained, trying to drag me over the top of the causeway.

That was when my leg came apart. I actually felt the bones separate for an instant before I screamed. He was so surprised he let me go and I slid under the dark water. At the time, it seemed a relief.

A rhythmic slapping sound woke me. I opened my eyes, squinted in the filtered sunlight, and was looking up at roof poles lashed together like the hub of a wheel. The roof itself was woven, not thatched, of some stuff that let a speckled sunlight through. I turned my head to the source of the sound.

A few feet away a scantily dressed woman knelt over a small fire that had burnt down to coals glowing redly under a flat rock. Her black hair had been bound up with wooden pins, but some strands had escaped as she went about her work. She was flattening dough of some kind between her slapping palms. I watched as she set the thin cake on the griddle rock and pinched off another lump of dough from the wooden bowl by her knee. Slap-slap, slap-slap-slap. I tried not to stare at her swaying breasts.

Her attention was outside. The wall, which was woven like the roof, was rolled halfway up and tied. This allowed the sweet-smelling breeze to carry off the cooking smoke. There was a clay pot near my head; I couldn't see beyond it much, but I could hear light, running feet out there, and the muffled laughter of children trying to play quietly. One of them whooped delightedly, and the woman leaned across the griddle to hiss, 'Tiwi! Te nalawai!'

'It's all right,' I said. 'I'm awake.'

She looked over to me, startled, but then her eyebrows went up. 'Ah?' she said as if to herself, then nodded to me and smiled. That smile transformed her face, which was round with flattened cheekbones and oddly set eyes, into such an expression of jolly warmth that I smiled back instantly. She laughed throatily, heaved herself to her feet – she was a large woman – and crossed the floor to kneel at my side. She reached one well-muscled arm and felt my forehead. I tried not to stare at her breasts, but as they hung only inches from my face, this was difficult. 'Nai?' she asked softly.

'Sorry. I don't know the customs here. What's your husband going to think?'

She understood me no more than I understood her, apparently, for a small frown appeared between her peat-dark eyes, but she patted my shoulder reassuringly and went to the open side of the tent. 'Tiwi, te bai-bai maluwai!'

The game outside was broken off in mid-shout, and a boy peered in. I had an impression of dark hair cut straight above wide, questioning eyes, a slim, straight body. He glanced at the woman, then raced past the open wall.

She suddenly remembered the cakes and bent to flip them off the stone, waving away the smoke. She'd burned them. 'Cacamalu!'

That was clear enough in any language, and I closed my eyes, smiling a little. I was aware of the throbbing in my leg and the stiffness in my muscles, but I was comfortable enough and did not try to stir.

A step brought me out of the drowse. The old man who stood just outside the tent was someone important, I could tell that immediately. His slave or manservant, a huge mountain of a man, stood back. The woman was half-bowed to the visitor, palms placed flat together, thumbs resting on her forehead. He was very thin, emaciated I might have said, shaved bald but for a single lock of gray hair at the crown of his head, and dressed in the same kind of short kilt as my fisherman, with the addition of a cloak of white material that he had looped over his skinny arm. The other hand held a walking stick. He ducked a little to peer in under the flap at me, then his voice lifted in a soft question, and the woman bowed lower, waving him in. He turned for a word to his man, who nodded and left. Then the old one carefully kicked off the sandals he wore before stepping up onto the hut's floor.

He propped his stick against the wall and eased himself down on one knee by my mat. Putting his palms together at his forehead, he smiled a little, and nodded. I nodded back. He reached to brush back my hair and finger some bruised places. I winced, and he made a small sound of sympathy, but his hands did not leave off their deft examination. He fingered up my eyelids, felt the pulses under my jawline, and lifted my bandaged hands one by one to unwrap them. They were nearly as raw as newly slaughtered meat, but none of the cuts was very deep, and the salt water had helped them to begin closing already. The healer nodded and replaced the bandages. He paused to point at the mat by my pillow, and I saw my ring. I thanked him with a nod.

As his hands compressed my ribs I coughed and got a taste of salt in my mouth. They must have rolled me over a barrel the night before to clear my lungs of the seawater.

I wiped my mouth on a bandaged hand, and the old man turned his attention to my leg. But even his careful touch at the broken place in my right thigh was too much, and I struck his hand away. 'Ow, shit, cacamalu!' I gasped.

The old healer's eyebrows shot up, the woman covered her mouth with her hands, and the flock of children squatting on the open side of the tent burst into laughter.

He began to laugh, too, with his lips together, nearly silently, the way some old people do, his eyes shining like two polished beads of rare and precious wood. Then he laid a finger across my lips and raised it to shake at me. Not a word one said in polite company, I guessed. I nodded. 'Sorry. It hurt.'

He patted my stomach and pantomimed eating, raising an eyebrow.

I nodded vigorously. 'Yes, please.'

The healer nodded, and then nodded more vigorously, saying, 'Zai.'

'Zai,' I repeated. Yes.

He struck his hands together delightedly, grinned broadly, revealing an excellent set of teeth which surprised me in one so obviously old. He beckoned to the woman. She hurried over with a stack of cakes piled on a leaf, and a small bowl. These she handed to the old man while she returned to her griddle stone for an earthenware pitcher set in the outermost embers to warm.

He set the food by me and helped me sit up a little, propped by a bolster that seemed to be a rolled fleece, though from what kind of sheep I couldn't guess, as it was long, silky, and the color of goatskin. The doctor handed me the stack of cakes. They were round, nearly as thin as paper, and soft, still warm from the griddle stone. I tore a piece out of one of them awkwardly with my bandaged hands and nibbled cautiously. The flavor was a little nutty, a little sweet, very toothsome. 'Mm. That's good.' I took a mouthful and asked through it, 'How do you say that?' I rubbed my belly in a circular motion and smacked my lips appreciatively. 'Good!' Then I cocked an eyebrow at the healer.

He was a sharp old fellow, he got it on the first try. 'Doh-wan!'

'Zai, doh-wan.'

The woman smiled, pleased, and invited me by gesture to try the food in the bowl. The children were mesmerized, watching me as though they'd never seen anyone eat before. I smacked my lips and waggled my eyebrows at them, and they screamed with laughter. The old man clapped his hands at them gently and shooed them away.

The bowl contained a brightly colored stew, chopped yellow, green, and red bits. There was no meat in it that I could see, and it didn't smell of fish, so I assumed these were the fruits or maybe vegetables of the place. Emboldened by the goodness of the cakes, I scooped up some of the mixture with one forefinger and popped it into my mouth.

'Aashis' balls!' I was seized by a coughing spell, and my eyes and nose streamed from the fierce heat. I struggled to throw off the healer's restraining hand. If they were going to poison me, I'd take them with me if I could!

I heard him snap something to the woman. She pushed what I recognized as a cup shape into my hand, but I resisted as long as I could before the burning demanded something, anything, to put it out. I took a swallow, expecting it to be my last.

It was a heated drink, smooth and sweet, and it quenched the fire with the first sip, lingering on the lips with a bouquet of spicy richness after I had swallowed it. I wiped my tearing eyes, sniffed, and drank some more of the dark brown liquid.

The healer and the woman were regarding me anxiously. 'I guess it isn't poisoned after all, is it?' I said, a little hoarse from the coughing. Oddly enough, my ferociously empty belly was begging for more of the fiery stew. I sniffed and was about to oblige, when the doctor stopped me for a moment. He took one of the cakes, spooned some of the stew into the middle of it with his finger, folded one end, then flapped the two sides one over the other to make a sort of envelope. This he handed to me.

I was ready for the burn this time, but it wasn't as bad. The cake seemed to damp it down somehow. I sipped the brown drink and relaxed. 'Doh-wan.'

The old one eased himself to a seat on the floor, and the woman went back to her cooking. Slap-slap. Slap-slap-slap. I ate everything and finished off the drink, savoring the last swallow, then stifled a belch and lay back. When I glanced at him, his eyes were thoughtful.

He tapped his own skinny chest. 'Bai Nati.' He gestured to me inquiringly.

'Pleased to meet you, sir. My name's . . . my name is . . .'

And it was only then that I realized I had absolutely no idea who I was.

The tent swam suddenly, and a scalding sweat broke on my body. My heart pounded and I sat up much too fast. He caught my shoulders, firmly pushed me down, and touched a place on the back of my neck.

I think only a few minutes had passed when I woke again. The boy was sitting cross-legged on the floor near the cooking fire, hungrily consuming cakes and stew. He had a smear of yellow and red on his chin, which he wiped off with the back of his hand as he saw my eyes open. The woman, obviously his mother, was scouring her cooking pot with sand. She glanced at me, murmured something to him, and he swung his gaze outside guiltily.

The old man was still there by my side, one foot drawn up and his arms encircling that knee. His head was tilted back, and his lips were moving soundlessly, too rapidly to be an idle conversation with himself. An incantation or prayer, I guessed, but it did not frighten me. He obviously meant me no harm. Still, I'd have liked to know how he'd knocked me out without a blow.

A flicker of panic returned. 'I can't remember anything,' I said with as much control as I could manage.

The healer's lips stopped, and he looked down at me. 'Nai?' When I raised my bandaged hand to my head, his expression cleared somewhat, and he did not try to prevent my exploration of my skull for lumps.

I found an odd thing with the fingertips that were exposed, and probed there, but it did not hurt. 'There's a dent,' I said, amazed for a moment that it was so deep, but even without the way it didn't hurt and wasn't an open wound, I knew that it had been there for a long time. It was familiar.

Bai Nati was watching and must have divined something of my thoughts, because he guided my hand to touch my jaw. It was crooked. I knew that, too. 'Something damned near killed me once,' I said, but I was only stating the obvious. I had no memory of how I'd acquired the terrible wounds.

He saw me frowning. The healer shook his head a little, waving his hands horizontally. Don't think about it, don't worry about it, he seemed to be saying. *Some degree of temporary memory loss is not uncommon in cases of concussion or overbearing shock*, I told myself. I knew that, but did not know *how* I knew it. With the thought, I found the panic held at bay, but the unknowing was still worrisome.

Bai Nati tapped my arm to get my attention. He pulled a lock of my red hair free of the bolster behind me and brought it before my eyes. 'Pel,' he said.

'Hair?' I asked, reaching to brush his single lock of gray.

He waved a hand horizontally, shaking his head. 'M-zai.' No, not hair. Casting his eye around the tent, he pointed at a string of red fruit of some kind that was hanging from the roof poles to dry. 'Pel.' He lifted my hair again. 'Pel.'

'Oh. Red.' I pointed to a net bag stuffed with brilliant red feathers tipped at the ends with bands of black and white. 'Pel.'

'Zai.' Now he put both his hands together and made a rapid, graceful zigzagging motion. 'Kinu.' He pointed through the open wall towards the sea.

'Fish.' Without thought I rose on an elbow and traced the outline of one with my finger on the floor mat. 'Kinu.'

Bai Nati looked surprised and glanced quickly at the woman and the boy. Both of them were looking at the mat as though the fish were visible there. The boy slowly looked up at me. His hands came together, and he made the sign at his forehead, staring all the while. Puzzled, I nodded to him in friendly fashion. His mother abruptly poked him between the shoulder blades, and he jumped. From the wall she took down a flattish basket, gave it to him, and pushed him out wordlessly. He disappeared round the other side of the hut.

'Sorry, what's wrong? What did I do?' I turned a palm up and frowned.

Bai Nati patted my hand gently with his own skinny one. Nothing, he seemed to say. It's all right. He pointed at me. 'Pel Kinu.' I frowned. He pointed to himself, 'Bai Nati,' then to me once more. 'Pel Kinu.'

'Red Fish, eh? Your big red fish that came out of the sea. Well, it will do for now, I suppose. All right, master. Zai, Pel Kinu.' I smiled.

'Ah,' the old one said in a satisfied tone.

I gestured straight hair across my forehead, and pointed the way the boy had gone. 'Tiwi, zai?'

The woman made a sound, an exclamation of dismay, I thought, but bit it back when Bai Nati's calm eyes went to her. Looking at her, he said steadily, 'Zai. Tiwi.'

'And you, goodwife? What's your name?' I smiled at her and lifted an eyebrow. I pointed at her.

'La-lini.' She answered reluctantly it seemed to me.

'La-lini, who has been very good to me.' I put my bandaged hands together at my forehead. Her face relaxed a little. She drew a breath, took down another net bag, an empty one, and slipped out of the hut, moving gracefully for so big a woman.

'Bai Nati, I need a pot.' I made him understand. His old face split in a grin, then he carefully unfolded his thin legs and got up to bring me a necked vessel. When I was done, he took it, stepped into his sandals, and walked briskly down to the beach with a swinging, ground-eating stride that surprised me. This was a man who did a lot of walking.

He returned with the rinsed jug and set it where I could reach it. Then he went prowling about the hut, searching for something. Evidently he felt he had a perfect right to look through everything, though from the signs of respect they had paid him and the way he had asked if he could come in, he didn't seem to be a member of the immediate family. Healers must be high-ranking folk hereabouts.

The old man finally found what he was looking for, a small leather pouch holding something that rattled. He tucked this into the waist of his garment for a moment while he prepared another jug of the brown drink and set it to warm in the ashes of the fire. Making a sign to me, he went out again and returned in a matter of moments with a handful of leaves. Then he came and sat down.

Taking one of the leaves, he put it into his mouth and let me see that he was holding it there, rather than swallowing it. He offered one to me. Wary of the fiery bite of the food in this place, I cautiously tasted it. It was bitter, but not unpleasantly so. I sucked on it and watched the healer roll his leaf into a wad with his tongue and hold it in the side of his mouth while he undid the knot on the pouch. I did the same with my leaf and discovered that my lips and tongue were a little numb. It was a drug, then. He saw that I was aware, and pointed to my leg, making quelling motions with his hands. For the pain, he was gesturing, to keep the broken bone from throbbing so much. I nodded, swallowing some of the juice. 'What's it called?' I asked. 'Nai?' I pointed to my bulging cheek.

'Kalan-kalan.'

The name sounded oddly familiar, but I tried not to push for a memory and start the panic off again. Bai Nati pulled the drawcord of the pouch and spilled out the contents between us. 'Tiles! You play that here?' He was setting up the first rank. I quickly began building the second. 'Is that how you do it here, too?'

'Zai!' he said delightedly and clasped his hands together, chortling.

I had a little trouble at first making out the symbols – some of them were different from those I knew – but the game itself told me a few interesting things. They had no Thistle, for instance, yet the image of that tile was one I knew well, and when I thought of the flower, I thought of rocky ground, wet with rain. On the other hand, some of their symbols meant little to me; there was the familiar Gull, but also another bird, long-tailed, that I didn't recognize at all. Binoyr, the old healer called it when I asked what it was. It was a high-ranking, valuable tile, next in importance only to the familiar T'ing. This seemed the same as we drew it at home: horned hackles, a longish snout, wings.

Bai Nati and I played at tiles all that afternoon, while I chewed kalan-kalan leaf, and we shared the brown drink, which he named for me: pilchu. The sun shifted round, and the hut grew warm. The old man rolled up the other side as well, and then the breeze blew right through, making it very comfortable.

Late in the day, La-lini returned, the string bag bulging with muddy roots. Her apprehension seemed to have passed, and she said something quick to the old man that he answered with a laugh. I think she asked him how much he had lost, and he told her he was down to his kilt.

Tiwi came back with the flat basket covered with petals of some bright orange flower, and a long bluish-gray feather that his mother seemed glad to have. His legs were covered with scrapes, so I gathered he'd been foraging in thorny thickets all day. La-lini made some comment about these scratches, because the boy craned to see how bad the ones on the backs of his legs were, then gestured towards the water. His mother nodded, and the boy raced for the beach, pitching aside his kilt as he went and whooping.

We laughed, and I said, 'I always liked to go swimming on a warm day when I was a lad, too.' I had an image . . . *bright water sparkling at the bottom of a round well and boys splashing like otters . . . a black bird that stared at me, beak parted . . . cliffs*. I came out of it to find my hand pressed to my head, over the dent. 'I fell off those cliffs once, I think. Don't let Tiwi . . .' But there weren't any cliffs here, only a long sweep of sand and the turquoise sea. 'Don't let him play on the cliffs,' I finished anyway, lamely.

They had picked up the boy's name and looked after him, then at each other. The old man shrugged. La-lini gave me a sharp look, then settled herself to cleaning and scraping the roots she had dug. When Bai Nati shook the dice again questioningly, I shook my head. 'No, thanks. I'll sleep a bit now, if that's all right.' I feigned closed eyes and snoring.

'Ah.' The healer got to his feet, flexing his knees to get the kinks out. Then, with a nod to La-lini and a wave to me, he said, 'Ndoh!' and stepped into his sandals.

'Ndoh!' La-lini called after him.

'Come back tomorrow, and I'll win that walking stick of yours, mate!' I called, shaking the tiles in their pouch. 'Ndoh!' Goodbye!

He waggled a finger at me, swung the walking stick jauntily over his shoulder, and strode down to the beach, where he kicked out of his sandals, stuck the stick in the sand, dropped the cloak beside it, and waded out into the water. I saw him duck his shaven head into the water and begin his ablutions, and then I turned to face the cool green foliage on the other side of the hut and went to sleep.

The smell of good food woke me. I rubbed my eyes and rose on an elbow. My fisherman was sitting near the fire, sipping from a bowl and smoking a carved pipe, while Lalini plucked a brilliantly golden-plumed bird. They were talking quietly. The boy had his arms wrapped round his knees, listening to his father. He heard me first. 'Ah, Pel Kinu!' Then to his father, 'Papu, Pel Kinu nisa.'

My rescuer put his hands together at his forehead. 'Pel Kinu,' he acknowledged, squinting through the smoke. His teeth gripped the pipe, and he smiled round it suddenly. 'Kinu.' He pantomimed the fish as Bai Nati had done.

I nodded. 'Yes. You caught me.' I mimed him with his spear and torch.

He laughed. 'Mocu,' he said, pointing to himself. 'Mocu Pel Kinu,' he mimed casting a net and pulling it in, 'sahdonni.'

Mocu Red Fish caught, I translated. Something close to that, anyway. 'Zai,' I agreed. 'Doh-wan!' I put my hands together and thanked him, but I wished I knew how to say it.

He looked at his wife, amazed that the stranger should know even a few of his words, and she explained. I caught the old man's name mentioned. 'Ah,' he said.

'Papu,' Tiwi chimed in, 'Pel Kinu ne-harno!' He was tracing a fish on the mat at his feet, as I had done earlier.

'Nalawai!' his mother commanded, cuffing him sharply. The lad ducked his head so I wouldn't see his shame and sprang up to run out of the hut. I heard him running away.

I was embarrassed and lay back down with my forearm over my eyes. Something about that innocent sketch had upset her twice now, and startled even the old healer. Well, I wouldn't do it again, by the Powers! *Now, why did I say that?* I asked myself. The oath had sprung naturally to my mind, but I didn't know what it meant.

My arm was nudged. I found Mocu offering a bowl. 'Thanks,' I said. 'I'm hungry.' I propped myself, tasted the white paste in the bowl, and found it bland, but nothing unpleasant. On a flat clay platter by my side, fried yellow blossoms were sizzling among strips of fish with the scales still attached. Mocu handed me a sort of short, two-pronged pick not unlike a fork, and I began to eat. He sat smoking and watching me. 'Pilchu?' I asked. He obligingly got up to get me the hot drink pitcher. 'Thanks.' I've got to know how to say that, I told myself in frustration. Putting down the platter, I made the gesture, asking, 'Nai?' He looked blank. I did it again, pointing to my mouth and showing something coming out of it. 'Nai?'

Mocu was lost, but from beyond the fire La-lini's soft voice answered, 'Te janni.'

'Ah, te janni, La-lini.' I sat up a bit more to see her more clearly and hissed at the sudden jolt of pain in my legs as the bones were disturbed. I fumbled one of the kalan-kalan leaves into my mouth, wincing at the angry throb. My one brief glance at what she was doing had been interesting, though. 'La-lini?' When she looked up from her stitching, I indicated the material spread over her knees. Hold it up, let me see, I motioned.

She secured the needle and carefully unfolded one side to show me a cape or blanket made entirely from feathers stitched onto some coarse material backing. Against a gray-blue background, she was stitching in a red stepped design that might have represented a thundercloud. 'Doh-wan,' I told her appreciatively.

'Te janni, Pel Kinu,' she said, pleased.

'Huh,' her husband grunted. He left his pipe smoking and went to drag a bundle out into the center of the room. Quickly untying the laces that held it together, he rolled out a long mantle or train. I caught my breath.

Against a background of mixed grays and blues that seemed to suggest clouds in mountain passes, he had worked a huge scarlet and gold t'ing, wings cupped to hover, claws extended like an eagle's stooping to strike. The creature's mouth spewed smoke like a fire mountain. I whistled slowly, and Mocu laughed proudly and tapped his chest. 'Doh-wan, eh?'

I nodded emphatically. 'Doh-wan.'

Someone hailed him from outside and he yelled back, hurriedly rerolling the feather embroidery. La-lini tucked her own piece into a sort of satchel woven of leaves and said something to him. He smiled, pinched her cheek affectionately, and strutted out, yelling again as soon as he was out the door. Torches were gathering down there on the beach. I thought they were going spear fishing again.

The woman brought the pilchu pitcher to set by my arm, then nodded, gathered her work satchel, and followed him out. After a moment, she came back in muttering what sounded like a reproach to herself, and quickly rolled up the side of the hut again so I could see out into the lingering sunset where the people were gathering. 'Te janni,' I told her, and she smiled and left once more.

I turned as much on my side as I could and pillowed my head on my arm to watch.

Down on the damp sand where the footing was firm but not splashy, the men had stuck some long fronds in the sand to describe an open oblong some one hundred yards long by fifty yards wide. At either end of this at about the midpoint stood a tall pole with a crossarm. I watched as some very fragile object – it looked like a gull's egg – was placed atop the end of each crossarm by one man sitting on the shoulders of another to reach it.

The men ranged themselves into two teams, equal numbers on a side, facing off on either side of the center court line scraped in the sand. The ball was tossed by one of the watching women to a tall man, and amid some friendly jeering from the other team, he took his place at the rear of the righthand court from me. I looked for Mocu and thought I recognized him among those on the lefthand team.

The ball handler stood studying the array before him, then tossed the ball to one of his team. This one lightly pitched it up in an arc, and as it descended, the tall man suddenly sprang into a handstand and caught the ball with a powerful kick that sent it smashing across the centerline. There was a warning shout from someone on Mocu's team, and a man caught the ball on his hip, twisting to bump it up into the air, setting it up. Mocu ran up lightly, flipped to a handstand, and powered the ball back across the line. A man on the righthand team managed to dive under the low ball and deflect its arc, but he couldn't bump it high enough in the air for any one of his own men to make the return kick. The ball thudded into the sand. There was shouting from his team, probably comic curses, and some laughter. I saw some fists shaken at Mocu's team, but the rivalry was good-natured. While all but one of his teammates cleared off his side of the court, Mocu took his place on the back line of his own court. On the other side, the opposing team had formed a line facing him. One man took his mark at the sideline exactly on the centerline, facing away from Mocu, but looking back at him.

There was a moment of quiet, and then one of the children shouted something from the sideline, and the players laughed. Mocu waved away the distraction with a smile. He studied the array, and nodded to his ball setter. The ball arced towards him slowly. He ran forward, dropped to a handstand, and smashed a kick straight at the other team's goal. At the same time, the receiver sprinted towards his own line of men, gauging his spot with a quick glance back at Mocu. As the ball left Mocu's foot and shot towards the goal, the receiver leaped up on the waiting linked hands of his mates who spun him into the air with a powerful heave, and he caught the ball in mid-air with his feet.

'Cacamalu, that was great!' I roared.

Fortunately, no one heard me. There was a cheer from his supporters and a groan from Mocu's, and I saw my fisherman make a laughing palms-up shrug as the teams rearranged themselves into their original positions.

I had forgotten my leg for a moment, but it had not forgotten me, so I dug another kalan-kalan leaf from the dwindling pile old Bai Nati had left for me, tucked it into my cheek, and poured myself a drink of pilchu. The game began again, Mocu's team serving this time. The ball went smashing the length of the court, the dark men twisted to intercept it and keep it in play. It was exciting stuff, and I don't know how long the boy had been sitting at the door before I noticed him.

'Tiwi? Want some pilchu?'

He got up slowly and came in. I pointed to the cup the old healer had used, and he handed it over for me to pour. When we were both sipping, I said, 'Your father, Papu Mocu, is quite a player. Don't you want to go down and watch?' I motioned him inquiringly towards the beach. Moodily he shook his head, picking at the scab on one of his day's scratches. 'I'm sorry, I won't get you in trouble again,' I promised.

'Nai?' he murmured politely, squinting up past the black bangs.

'Mothers do that sometimes, cuff you one. It doesn't mean they don't love you.'

He was frowning, trying to understand. I shifted the kalan-kalan with my tongue and pointed to the two cakes his mother had burned that morning and left sitting by the fire. He got up and brought them over. I motioned him to bring me a blackened stick from the banked fire. Again, the boy did so without question, though his eyes widened. Until the stub was in my hand, I didn't know myself what I was going to do with it.

I arranged the cakes side by side to form a small surface,

reached for the image in my mind, and swiftly drew straight bangs, the rounded shape of his head, and her hands gently placed to either side of it. Then I sketched just her lips, barely touching the top of his head.

I looked up at him where he bent with his hands braced on his scratched knees. His lip trembled for just a moment at the truth of the sketch, then his eyes met mine. One hand came out tentatively to touch my hair. 'Pel,' he said. His eyes went to the cakes with their tracing of charcoal as if he were questioning something in his own mind. When his gaze swung up to me again, it seemed he'd arrived at an answer. He knelt slowly and touched his forehead to the mat, holding the bow.

I was hoping nobody from the beach was watching, else he'd be in trouble again. 'Hey, none of that, matey,' I said softly. Giving him one cake, I took the other myself. He understood immediately, and we ate in companionable silence, washing down the evidence with the rest of the pilchu. He licked crumbs from his lips, watching me. 'Papu Mocu,' I reminded him. I smiled a little, and indicated the shouting spectators with my chin. Then I shooed him away with my hands.

Tiwi nodded and jumped up. He made me the sign of respect and left with a bound. I saw him drop to a handstand and flip a little way down towards the beach, and then he ran on.

Mocu's team won that night, but I missed the final shot on the goal that sent the gull's egg smashing to the ground. Long after the family returned to the hut and lay down on their sleeping mats, I was awake, twisting my ring, trying to remember where and when I had learned to paint.

It rained sometime during the night, and I suppose that is what woke me. The pattering on the roof mats was something like a horde of mice in the thatch of a tumbledown hut, and I thought foggily that the place must be overrun with them and we ought to get a cat. I came awake enough to realize that it was rain, and the hut was blowing a little with it, the woven walls swelling and sucking with the draughts. My leg felt tremendously swollen, pressing against the flat wooden splints that had been bound to it, and was throbbing painfully.

I reached to adjust the end of a splint where it seemed to be pressing particularly, and my fingers encountered a heavy, smooth rope *that moved.*

I mustn't yell, it'll strike me in the eyes. Powers, won't somebody come*! Gwynt's asleep right there, and Geri beyond him. Wake up, Geri, wake up this time and mind your face. Where's the* mucking *water bucket?* I inched my hand off my chest and reached up to find the bucket. Cold water. Cold water would make it move.

The snake felt my movement and, so quickly I hadn't time to fend it off, threw a coil of its sinuous body round my arm, and trailed across my chest. It began to tighten its coils. I knew it was probably poisonous and would strike, but it was so heavy that I could not simply lie still and let it twine about me. I counted three and drove the hand that was still free towards where I thought its head might be. My slicing palm crunched something, and then the serpent began to whip and coil convulsively, dragging me with it under the back wall of the hut. My leg was being racked, and I was being tossed around like a sailor in a maelstrom.

Mocu was there suddenly; I felt him fumble a grip as the snake thrashed. 'Its head is here, no, *here*!' I gasped. 'Hold it!' He found it, throwing all his weight into straightening the first coil by stretching the damned thing out. But it was taking too long – Powers, it was an eternity! – and I struck again at the only thing I could see in the dark, the twin shining points of its eyes. There was a snap as I connected, the sound of bone breaking, and the lights went out.

Even in death, the thing was still trying to coil, and it

took Mocu and another man who had by then been shouted into the hut by La-lini to prise the coils away and drag it off me. I was all right till then, until La-lini stirred up the fire and I saw the rope as thick as a man's thigh that the men draped over their shoulders to haul out of the hut.

I began to scream.

Even while the shrieks boiled out of me I was ashamed of myself, but I couldn't stop, though Tiwi was staring amidst the knot of villagers in the doorway, and his mother and father tried to gentle me by touch and quiet words, the way one does a foaming, roll-eyed horse. Bai Nati was there suddenly, his eyes lowered to hold mine, his hands firmly on either side of my face. Through everything else – the smell of my own sweat, the murmuring of the villagers, the rain sluicing on the roof mats, the *thing*, the *damned* thing over there outside on the floor – I was conscious most of all of the master's eyes, one blue, one brown. 'The snake was meant for me, I found it in my blankets,' I babbled.

Alin, he said in my mind, and I understood him perfectly: *Peace*.

At once, I could breathe again without gasping, and the horror was washed away by cleansing calm. I looked into his wood-brown eyes. Without thinking, I replied in the same mind-talk: *Thee's much a mage, are thee not, old master?*

Bai Nati's lips parted in surprise. Then a slow smile lit his features, dawn over a mountain lake. *Hush. Sleep*.

And I did.

CHAPTER THREE

They moved me while I slept. Maybe Mocu and La-lini had found my night-time experience too harrowing, or maybe the old healer decided my leg could better be looked after nearer to hand because it had broken again in the fight with the serpent. In any event, the hut of woven mats was no longer around me when I woke. Instead, I was in a cave.

The place was not large, but easily accommodated my full length and left room for a fire circle and the old man's sleeping mat. The rock arching overhead a few feet higher than his head seemed as though it might be the same stuff as the causeway on which I had snagged the night Mocu found me, for it was sharp and dry. Some of the rougher edges had been filed off to be less dangerous to the head, and the floor was sand, so I was comfortable lying on it. He saw me dig my fingers into it a little.

Better, eh? They don't like this stuff – it's too sharp for them, he kenned.

That was thoughtful of you. Thanks.

Grumahu did the work. No, he is not here just now. Do you hunger?

No, not very much. I feel a little woozy, actually.

He nodded. *You have fever. Until it breaks, you'll probably only want something to drink. Here, try this.* Bai Nati poured from a beautifully turned wooden pitcher, then held my shoulders up while I sipped from a matching bowl. The stuff was clear as spring water, deliciously cool, and smelled of summer somehow. The only way I knew it wasn't plain water was the tiny bubbles in it, and the euphoria that it produced nearly as soon as I swallowed it. I wasn't drunk, but I was very, very relaxed.

You could make a fortune shipping this stuff! I told him.

The old one smiled. *What would this worthless person do with a fortune? The sea is free, the morning costs nothing, and Bai Nati's people provide food for him. A fortune would be nothing to this insignificant man.* He wrapped his hands round his knee. *What would* you *do with one, Kinu?*

I smiled. *You're trying to jog my memory, aren't you? If I could say what to buy with a fortune, it might tell us where I'm from.*

His teeth showed. *Indeed. Forgive my presumption.*

No, it's all right. Can you see anything in my mind?

Alas, no. Can you?

I looked into the fire. *Almost. It's like having something on the tip of your tongue but not being able to say it.*

Very frustrating. But as your body becomes strong, doubtless your mind will also. There is no damage to your head to account for your inability to remember; therefore, this old one judges that you must have had some great shock, something so terrible that you do not want *to remember it. Perhaps it has to do with how your ring got broken.*

I sighed. *Yes, I thought so myself.* It was too much to think on, so I changed the subject. *I'm sorry about last night – that damned thing threw me into a fit. I hate snakes.*

Yet you carry one in your skin. He drew my arm out and indicated the serpent tattooed on my right forearm. *It is an important sign to you.* My face must have mirrored my confusion, for he patted my wrist in his old man's way. *Well, no matter. Perhaps it is a protection against the creatures.*

It didn't work last night!

Bai Nati met my eye. *Assuredly, it did. Many and many are the stories told from village to village about people who have been killed in their sleep by just such a snake as that kind. You had a narrow escape, Kinu.*

I know. If Mocu hadn't been there—

Mocu says that he did not kill the snake. He says you hit it with one hand and the life went out from it. He says it was Kinu who killed the snake that would have killed Kinu. We have not heard of such a thing before, that a man may kill this kind of snake with a blow from his hand.

He was waiting expectantly, but I didn't know how to account for it either. *Just luck, I guess.*

Thee's had much luck in thy life, then, my friend, the old healer commented dryly. He leaned a little forward and indicated my hand. *Please?* Puzzled, I extended it to him, and he set about unwrapping the bandage. The cuts looked surprisingly better than they had the day before, but that wasn't what he wanted me to see. He turned my hand so that the outer edge of the palm was exposed. There was a deepish slice in it, but he ignored this and ran his finger lightly over the callus that ran the length of my hand. The ridge spoke of many hours of pounding against some rough or hard surface. Useful training for killing snakes, maybe, but not much else.

I looked up at Bai Nati. *What kind of trade would make your hands look like this?*

Assuredly, I know not. I have not seen the like before. I think no one I know does such work, not the fisherman, nor the potters; not those who till the earth, or those who stitch the feathers. I cannot think of it at all.

I asked the question that had been nagging me since I woke to see La-lini's dark skin and black hair. *Bai Nati, do you know where people who look like me come from?*

I have never in my life seen anyone who looks like you, Kinu, he replied simply. But that wasn't all of it; I could see something else in his face.

'Nai?' I demanded.

'M-zai.' *No, I will not speak of it,* he said quietly, and it wasn't just pique, althought I suppose not many people spoke in such a way to so respected a figure.

But you, of all people, have to help me! I pleaded desperately.

Assuredly, I of all people must. The lot has fallen to this worthless one, and I will help you in every way I am able, Red Fish. He nodded at some private thought and smiled. 'Pel Kinu.'

He poured once again from the wooden pitcher, and I drank thirstily. I noticed that not only did the bubbling water seem to help the fever, but it also eased my throbbing leg better than the kalan-kalan leaf had. I mentioned this to Bai Nati, and he told me that the drink was the juice of the leaf added to the water of a spring he knew. It was most beneficial, he assured me, and I would soon be up and about.

I was skeptical about that. The leg was badly broken, and although the bone had not come through and he had set it with all his skill, the twisting it had suffered both in the sea and from the snake had left the muscles torn and weak. I did not think it would be straight again.

As it seemed I would need a walking staff if I were ever going to leave the cave, I set myself to carving one. By the third time I cut myself with the sharp shell knife, it was obvious to both Bai Nati and me that this was not a skill with which I had been very familiar in my former life. He turned the stick this way and that, rubbed a thumb over the hacked bits, and gracefully volunteered his man, Grumahu, to finish it for me. I gracefully let him tell the big man when he returned to the cave a few hours later with a couple of nice fish. The giant glowered at the stick, then at me, and went outside in the sunshine to work.

So much for carving to take up the time. The three of us played at tiles until we were sick of it, and Bai Nati taught me some of the language of the place so that I could make a beginning at talking to people besides himself. Grumahu would not be one of them, I quickly found. 'Do not be offended,' the old man counseled. 'Walking Thunder does not speak many wasted words to anyone.'

'Walking Thunder?'

'It is what his name would mean to you.'

I grinned. 'It fits.'

The old man handed me one of the fruits the giant had picked for us. 'He is a good man and carries burdens you cannot know, Kinu. Be content to accept his presence, asking no more companionship than he can give.'

I was embarrassed and changed the subject. I asked for a smooth piece of bark or wood or leather, anything to write on. He was mystified at the marks I made on the hide he brought me, but the dictionary helped. Now when he was gone from the cave for longish hours tending to other patients or collecting his herbs, I could study and record some of my thoughts. I took to trying for an entry each day, mentioning the weather and any unusual or interesting thing I had seen or heard that day. This procedure seemed very familiar to me and helped me order my days. When I explained it to the old man, he brought me several more hides so that I wouldn't run out of writing material. I found later this was extravagantly wasteful of him. Leather was a precious commodity, because they had very few large animals.

When my leg healed enough to be able to sit propped up without too much pain, Bai Nati suggested some sunshine would do me good, and Grumahu helped me inch my way out of the cave onto the shelf of rock that fronted it. I gingerly got myself turned round, leaned back against the sun-warmed rock at the cave's mouth, and my spirits shot up with a bound at the sight spread below my feet.

We were not so high above the village, probably no more than seventy or eighty feet, but this was enough to clear the fringed canopy of vegetation that sheltered the woven huts and give an unobstructed view of the beach and the turquoise stretch of calm water to this side of what I had taken for a causeway in the darkness that night, but now realized was a reef. On the ocean side of the reef, the surf boomed, white spray flying; beyond that, the water shaded from teal in the middle distance to the dark blue that told of deep seas further out. I took a lungful of the salty air. 'The sunny weather will hold for a day or two more, but then the wind will swing round, and we're in for a bit of a blow,' I said with assurance.

'Nai?'

I repeated it for him in kenning. *Ah*, he said, and added, *Kinu was a fisherman.*

It was a relief to have that decided. 'Zai,' I told him. I shaded my eyes. 'Look, dolphins.'

The old man followed my pointing finger. 'Zai, Tiwi.'

'M-zai,' I said a little impatiently. 'The lad's there, on the beach, see him? I was talking about the dolphins.'

He must have followed my meaning even without the kenning, for he smiled. *Yes, I see them. The boy is named for that fish.*

Ah? Tiwi and Kinu, two brothers of the sea, I mused.

He shot me a look, then took up his walking stick. *Grumahu and I must go to the spring for more of the water you like. Here, I will set the bowl of cryl by you.* He brought out the bowl of green, juicy fruit from the cave, and stood looking down at me over his stick. *Maybe I will send the boy up.*

If his mother will let him come, it would be good to have a visitor.

Bai Nati nodded and took the trail down to the village, the big man striding a little behind him. I saw him call the boy to him, then Tiwi's head lifted and he looked up to where I watched. He hit the path up to the cave at a jogging run, leaving his collecting basket where it had dropped. I noticed that the old healer did not go towards the tent where Mocu and La-lini lived to ask her permission, and Grumahu did not have the water pitcher with him.

Tiwi broke from the opening in the trees, hopped up to the stone shelf, and made the gesture of respect, grinning. 'Welcome, Dolphin,' I told him, returning the gesture.

He looked pleased. 'Bai Nati told you I am named for Fish-That-Stands-On-His-Tail.'

'Aye. That means "Zai" in my language,' I answered his inquiring look. 'It makes us brothers, I think.'

Now he was beaming. He sat at my waved invitation and nodded at my leg. 'You heal well, Elder Brother?'

'Well enough, Small Brother. Soon I will be able to go on a stick. Grumahu has already made one for me.' My words were halting enough, as I was having to pick between what I wanted to say, and what I knew how to say, but the boy was surprisingly patient. I did not know whether this was just Tiwi's own way, or whether the children here were always so respectful.

'What are you doing?'

I'm drawing a map of this coastline, at least as much as I can see of it from here. That's what I wanted to say, but I had no words in his language for map or coastline. 'I am making a picture-cloth to teach myself this land – all that I can see from here.' I swept a hand side to side from one horizon to the other. He was fascinated but puzzled, looking first down at the leather scroll, then up at the ocean, as I was doing. 'It's a rutter,' I said, using my word because it was the only one I had for the thing. 'Mariners use them to navigate, to find their way.'

'Marner? This is something of Marner?'

'Yes, a thing of mariners,' I confirmed, busily sketching the jutting headland to the east.

'Ah,' Tiwi said. He fell silent, watching interestedly.

'You can talk, it won't bother me,' I told him after several minutes.

'Is Elder Brother sure? Papu does not like me to be around when he stitches the feathers.'

'Well, you can see the reason for that, Dolphin. The

feathers blow around easily, and if you run through the house, Papu Mocu's work could follow you out to the sea. You run quickly, Small Brother,' I said, smiling.

'Aye,' he agreed, eyes bright, very proud of himself for speaking my language.

To please him, I drew a leaping porpoise off the coastline of my map, in the wide, blank space where I had written 'This is unknown territory'. Tiwi struck his hands together and laughed. As he raised his eyes to me, something out in the water caught his eye, and I saw the laughter die in an instant.

Startled, I followed his intent stare. A craft the likes of which I was sure I had not seen before was edging into sight round the headland. It was low in the water, powered by pairs of oarsmen, and had a peculiar boom of some kind riding parallel to it in the waves. Eyes, glaring topaz eyes, were painted on either side of the high prow. 'They come again,' Tiwi breathed beside me. Small pebbles skittered on the rock shelf as he sprang up. 'Hide in the cave, Kinu! They must not see you! *Hurry!*' he urged frantically.

When someone is as afraid as the boy was, you don't stop to question whether there is reason for it or not. I dragged myself into the dim interior of the cave after him. Tiwi had run to the natural shelf of rock where the old man kept his medicine pots, a couple of baskets, the bow-like affair with which he made fire, and a large pink shell. The boy was familiar with the place; he went right to it and lifted down the shell.

Stepping to the cave entrance, but keeping himself out of sight in the shade, he raised the shell to his lips and blew. At first nothing much came out, but then a long, low note swelled and held in the warm air. The cave amplified the sound and sent it in a strong blast down over the village. Startled birds set up a screech and rose in a cloud out of the trees. On the beach below, a woman stripping leaves to use for weaving jerked her head up to look to the cave, then stood and peered out to sea, shading her eyes. An instant later she scooped up the child playing naked in the surf and ran towards the woven huts scattered at the edge of the jungle. Her mouth was open, and I am sure she screamed, although I could not hear her for the shell's warning note.

Pirates! I thought.

The boy lowered the shell, clutching it to his bare chest, rigid with tension. I dragged myself to the fire circle and began smearing my pale skin with the ashes. 'Bring me the knife, would you? And the shell?' Tiwi's eyes widened when he saw what I was doing, but he moved to obey. 'Do they know about this cave?'

He got it then. 'Cacamalu! I never thought! Bai Nati and Grumahu always go away into the jungle after they have made the shell sound!'

'No, you did well, Small Brother. The people must be warned of danger, and that was the only way. Those ones of the boat may not even come here if they know the old man always goes away. But you must go now. Go quietly, and watch that your footmarks do not make a trail. I will be well. Do not come out of the trees even if you see those ones come in here. I have ways to make them hurt.'

He nodded. 'I believe it, Kinu. I saw what you did to the snake. I will fetch Bai Nati now from the place where he sometimes goes.' He touched his hands to his forehead, crouched, and bolted from the cave.

I could not have said how I knew what to do, and one part of my mind was amazed, observing my methodical actions. After darkening my skin, I took handfuls of the ash and rubbed it into my hair. I did not want them to see me in the darkness of the cave by a glint of red hair or flounder-white skin. This hasty darkening completed, I paused to listen, and then I thought of my ring. Hurriedly I twisted it around so that no gleam of light would catch the gem.

The birds had stopped squawking but had not resumed their normal songs, and there was no sound from the village. I hoped the women and children had all escaped into the forest. The men, I knew from my daily observations, would be occupied with their day's work elsewhere.

I drew my walking staff to me, considered lashing the shell knife at the end of it for a spear, but decided against it. It is too easy to disarm a man who has only a spear for a weapon. I preferred my hands as the primary weapon, the knife as reserve, and the staff itself would give me a third. Because I wasn't able to move much, I must put my opponent in a situation where his advantage of mobility would be nullified. (*How do you know this?* one part of my mind wanted to know.)

Having had days in which to do nothing much but stare at the walls of the cave, I knew that it narrowed towards the back. The firelight never penetrated much back there, but I thought there might be at least a shallow apse. If I crawled back, drew matting over me, and set a pot or two in the sand at arm's length for warning, I should have time enough. An attacker would be silhouetted against the sky, while I would be nothing but a shadow, black against black.

Painfully, and as quickly as my splinted leg would allow, I gathered the shell to me, pitched the staff down into the apse, and followed, covering the trail I made in the sand by brushing it with my sleeping mat. I set my pots to serve as a warning signal and hauled myself backwards into the apse, feeling cautiously with my hands. Despite what Bai Nati had said, I didn't fancy finding a serpent back there.

It was, as I had thought, a low niche in the back cave wall. Better yet, it bent in a dog leg to the left, forming a blind corner. If an intruder took a notion to prod with a spear into the back of a cave, he'd hit nothing. That made things infinitely easier. It was a narrow fit, but I worked my way into the little niche and sat up against the wall of it, my knife hand free, though I could not use the staff because of the scant room. It lay at my feet. I tucked the shell safely out of the way. If the sound of it was the only chance these poor folk had to defend themselves, I'd save it for them if I could.

I turned my head to the comparatively lighter main cave and watched for a shadow to darken the entrance by the rock shelf.

That was when the screaming started.

It was a woman's voice, rising up and up in pitch until my nails drew blood in the palms of my hands to hear it, that impossibly high, impossibly drawn-out cry of pain. There came a silence in which I heard the beating of my heart and the rasp when I passed my tongue over my dry lips. Then she screamed again, once, as piercing and sharp as a sword thrust. After that, I strained to hear, though I dreaded what might come next, but there was nothing.

Until his foot scuffed on the rock shelf outside. The back wall of the cave showed a vague shadow, big-headed, swollen about the knees and lower legs. He was listening. I opened my mouth to breathe more silently and readied the knife. He came in, I heard a step on the rock and then none on the sand.

'Cacamalu!' he snarled quietly, drawing out the syllables. There was something foreign in the way he said it. I heard the smash and scattering of things against the cave wall as he swept the shelf. I did not know the next words he said, but the 'old man' was part of it, and I imagined he was cursing Bai Nati.

Someone outside called a question, and he answered, 'M-zai, he's gone again, the old [another word I didn't know, but could guess]. Let's go. What? No, leave it – there's nothing here worth taking anyway. We'll go up the coast a little and maybe have better luck.'

Although I still held the knife ready, I relaxed slightly. The next instant the force of his mind-shout pounded me like a towering wave. *Old man, do not think you can avoid your duty much longer! I, Denjar a Tchlaxi, will catch you!*

I gasped aloud with the sheer *pressure* of it.

He stopped stock-still, then I saw the slim, pointed shadow of the spear lift. I did not realize he had thrown it until its point struck the back of the cave wall. When he came down to retrieve it, he would have only to look a little to his left to see me. Soundlessly I flexed the muscles of my hand and shoulder, pumping the humors of my blood through them, getting ready. (*And how do you know how to do this?*)

I heard his footsteps cautiously creeping towards me, the slight check as his probing foot discovered the pots, dismissed them as unimportant, and came on. I shrank into the wall behind me to get a firm platform to launch myself in a strike with the knife towards where his eyes would be, my empty left hand dancing over the rock slightly, seeking a purchase.

I saw his foot come into view, sandal, broad foot, above it a shin guard made of some tawny yellow pelt with black spots, the animal's foot, claws still attached. His hand came down, closed over the spear shaft. Then his head. *Powers, he was a beast himself – no, a headdress, jackass, a snarling animal's head, a huge cat of some kind and he was turning to look in here.*

My left hand brushed a deeply scored section of rock, but nothing protruded, there was no grip and his eyes were swinging to me.

'Denjar, come here quickly! Binoyr! Look, can you see it?' his companion yelled excitedly from outside the cave.

'Where?' His head swung the other way, looking back at the cave opening, and he rose from his crouch, taking his spear with him. 'It can't be a Binoyr, we're too far—'

'I can see the green tail feathers, I'm telling you! Look, down there!'

'Ah. Give me your sling, will you?'

'It's too far, my lord. You'll never—'

'Give me the sling.'

A moment later I heard what sounded like a whir, then silence broken by a whoop from the other man. 'Well done, my lord!'

Denjar sounded bored, but I could hear the pride, too. 'It wasn't hard. She was sitting right out on the branch. Go down and get it, and be careful not to hurt her when you unwind the sling from her legs. At least we'll have *something* to give my lord from this miserable trip. I'm going back to the boat.'

I heard them both step down off the rock shelf onto the path and tramp away, sliding a little on the stones.

I leaned my head back against the cool rock wall of the niche and fought to keep my stomach from heaving. There was an acid taste in the back of my throat.

After a time, when I felt stronger – my small store of strength having been taxed to its limit – I squirmed out of the niche and dragged myself to the cave mouth. The marauders' ship was pulling out of sight downwind to the left of my vantage. I dropped my head to the sand and rested. Her screams rang yet in my ears. Whatever they had done, I couldn't see it from up here. I hoped it wasn't Lalini.

That thought made me grasp the staff, lever myself off the shelf onto my rear end, and inch my way down the path through the trees until the surface flattened as it left the hillside. I broke a sweat just trying to stand, using a tree trunk and the staff for help, but finally I was up, though I did not try to put my foot down. Even my good leg seemed weak after lying around so much. I took a breath, grasped the staff as an oversized crutch, and started off in a crazy zigzagging way, falling from tree trunk to tree trunk.

My leg set up a roaring protest, but I knew Bai Nati would have kalan-kalan and spring water for it, so I gritted my teeth and went on. No one else was on the path, and I heard no sound from the village ahead. The birds, however, flitted over my head, chirping and calling once more.

I came upon a string bag of smashed fruit and a broken pottery crock from which ground grain spilled, the ants already busily swarming over the food, carrying it off. My head was beginning to swim a bit, and I rested, one arm encircling a smooth tree trunk, jointed every few feet. B'mbu, Bai Nati had named it. There was a grove of it just here, but he said it did not grow well towards the beach, so I must still be a little out of the village. I caught my breath and went on. Still there was no sound other than the raucous calling of the birds.

Not long after, the first woven hut appeared through the trees ahead, its mats slashed and flapping in the ocean breeze. I approached cautiously although I was fairly certain none of the marauders had stayed behind. Pirates do not leave shore parties to suffer the vengeance of the victims of a raid. (*How do you know that?*)

The casting net was still slung over the conical roof of the house to dry, but the stones that weighted it clunked hollowly against the b'mbu poles, slashed and ripped beyond any reweaving. I cursed, scanned the smashed storage jars, the pulp of fruit and vegetable mess trampled into the floor mats, and moved on up the beach. I found pretty much what I expected: wanton destruction. One odd thing that did not occur to me until I had looked through most of the huts was that there were no bags of feathers and no stitched tapestries of them. The marauders had taken them all, including Mocu's glorious scarlet and gold t'ing cloak. A few red fluffs still blew about the ground outside his hut, with some gray-blue ones from La-lini's work bag. Of the family itself, there was no sign, and I was glad of that. As yet I had seen none of my people. If it hadn't been for the woman's screams, I could have cursed the vermin pirates for the destruction they had wrought to the property and blessed our luck that the people had been spared.

I was bending to search among the rubble of Mocu's house for a container of water or of drink, the only house where I'd felt I had the right to do that, when a vicious squabbling of birds broke out. I raised my head to see what they were fighting over and saw a perfect blizzard of winged black forms darting about the ball court. That would be where they had left her, then. I seized Mocu's fishing spear, evidently too poor a thing for the pirates to trouble themselves with, and using it and my staff for support went down there.

As I labored through the tough grass at the verge of the beach, I could see the naked victim was positioned so that she faced the village, although, thankfully, her head had fallen forward and the concealing long hair hid her face. My first thought was that they had hanged her from one of the goal posts. She was a slight woman with the full breasts of a young mother, not La-lini, and I was ashamed at the relief that washed through me.

My bad foot wanted to twist in the loose sand, and until I got onto the firmer footing where the village men had beaten the surface to compact if for the game, I was occupied with keeping myself upright. When I looked up again, the first thing that struck me was that the goal post was a good deal shorter than I had thought when I watched Mocu from the hut. The top of it was only three feet or so above my head, her dangling legs close to touching firm ground. The second was that there was a lot of blood for a hanging, the pole black with gouts, the sand carved into runnels by it.

I had instinctively backed off a little and circled slightly to my right. Maybe I was feverish again or maybe only so sickened with the thing that my mind refused for a moment to function, but it was not until I saw the bloodstained spear tip of the pole thrusting up between her shoulder blades that I realized what the animals had done to her. I heard again that long, drawn-out scream, and my stomach turned itself inside out. I stumbled away from the impaled woman, my injured leg forgotten for the first step, and then fell full length and retched.

I never thought to try to keep the birds off her, I am not

sure I could have done it anyway, but the clean aqua water drew me, and I dragged myself into the lagoon. Swilling water over my ash-streaked face and neck, I welcomed the sting as the salt found the few scrapes I had acquired on the trip down the hillside, the pain some kind of small expiation for being alive when she was so horribly dead.

When I was clean again and somewhat calmer, I remained sitting in the water, leaning back on my hands for a long time, watching the sea birds skim and dip. I heard the villagers calling cautiously to one another as they came out of hiding, and the cries as her body was discovered. I heard them digging the shaft end of the pole out of the ground to lower her, the women keening softly, the men's grunts of exertion, the thump of the digging sticks.

A small, cold body burrowed against my side, and I put my arm round Tiwi's shoulders. 'Thy family is well, Dolphin?'

'Zai, we are all well, Elder Brother. I went to the cave, and my heart was sick when I could not find you.'

His sandal-shod foot, the animal's claws still attached, his head just coming into sight . . . 'I should have killed the bastard when I had the chance.'

'What does Kinu say?'

I heard the pole creak as the weight came off, the quiet chant, one, two, three, and the ripping as it came out of her. Gripping Tiwi's shoulder, I kept him facing the lagoon. 'Did you find Bai Nati?'

'Yes,' he said, eyes steadily fixed on the reef birds, as mine were. 'I went to the place I told you about, the place the old one goes sometimes, and he was there with Grumahu. We came back together, hurrying, but—' For the first time he faltered and swallowed hard.

'In a little while, when the thing up there on the ball court is done, I would like you to ask the old one to come down here, if he can take the time.'

'Assuredly.' We watched the birds awhile. 'She was my

mother's younger sister,' he said suddenly. 'I have been set to mind her baby many times. Sometimes it made me angry, because I would rather have been playing.'

Powers, his aunt . . . 'Where is the baby now?'

'Femati was watching him today. She will take him as a breast-son now until he is old enough not to need milk. Then he will come into our house.' He looked at me. 'Then we will have a Smallest Brother, you and I. His name is Monkey, though. He is not a fish, like us.'

'Not many people are fish like us, Dolphin. It is probably a good thing, too.' I glanced back over my shoulder. His aunt's body was decently covered with matting, and the men were scooping sand to bury the blood. The b'mbu post had been dragged into the water to our left, floated out across the lagoon, and then flung over the reef to be cleansed and broken up by the pounding surf. The carrion birds were screaming their disappointment, and the clouds of flies had started to disperse.

'I will fetch Bai Nati now,' the boy said and slipped from under my arm.

A few minutes later, the old man walked into the water behind me, stripped off his clothes, and washed himself as I had done. He swam a little, slowly but with a smooth stroke, and then he rested at my side. 'Tiwi is with his mother,' he reported. 'We can mind-speak, if you would find it easier.'

'Only if I need a new word, master. I must learn to speak the language of this place quickly and well.'

'As you wish. They went into the cave, the boy tells me.'

Tiwi must have seen the broken pots and litter from the shelf. 'I hid in the small place at the back,' I answered his implied question. 'It might have been good to know it was there.' I had not intended it to sound like an accusation.

The old mage's cheeks reddened slightly. *I forgot. Stupid of me.*

I shook my head wordlessly and made the horizontal

hand motion that meant it doesn't matter, don't trouble yourself about it.

I indicated the left horizon with my chin. 'Those that came in the boat . . .'

'We call them rinnun a jag'har.'

Sons of the something, the final word completely unfamiliar to me. 'Say it in mind-talk, please.'

Sons of the jaguar. It is a kind of large cat, a wild one.

Tawny, marked with dark spots?

The common ones are. We have them around here sometimes. But the rarer one is the black jaguar. That we do not have, and it is good, because that beast is a killer.

'You had it here today, old one.'

His lips came together. 'Zai.'

'These rinnun a jag'har must pay for what they did.'

Bai Nati scooped some sand from the bottom of the lagoon and let the gentle action of the water sift the sand from the tiny shells. 'There is no payment for what they did. Too, the rinnun are very strong, and their numbers are many more than one boatful. No one can make them pay.'

I turned to look full at him. 'I can,' I said.

It seemed he caught his breath and held it for a moment. His eyes were on the shells in his hand. *Is it thy will I should help thee in this?*

In truth, I would have no other, old master. I will need someone to help me talk to the men.

It is my duty to aid you, and I will do my duty.

I had forgotten it till then. 'That's what he said.' His eyes came up to mine, puzzled. 'The rinu – that's right, isn't it? Rinu would be a single one of the rinnun? Yes, I thought so. The rinu shouted at you with his mind, there in the cave.'

'At me?'

'Aye. He said, "Old Man, do not think you can avoid your duty much longer! I, Denjar a-something – I can't remember the other name – will catch you!" '

Bai Nati opened his fingers and let the shells fall into the water. 'Denjar a Tchlaxi. Our enemy summons me.' He seemed troubled, and his eyes watched the b'mbu pole tossed by the surf. 'I did not know it was Denjar who was here today.'

'I see you know him well, master. It grieves you that this man is the way he is.' *Sick, twisted, I mean.*

'Assuredly. He was once a gifted student of the Way.'

'He has much power; his mind-shout nearly split my head.'

'It has split others,' he murmured.

'Can you teach it to me, old friend?'

A slight smile drew up the corners of his lips. 'You have much power, too, Kinu. You do not know how loud your own voice is.'

'Good,' I said grimly in my own language. 'I'll blow the bugger's brains out of his arsehole with it.'

Although I had not kenned it, some thought, some image must have flown from my angry thoughts to the mage, for his eyes widened for a moment before his brows drew down. 'M-zai, you must not make your heart dirty with it. If this thing is done, it must not be done in anger, but only as a hard task one man must do so that others may have peace. It is the only way.'

I didn't care for the lecture. 'Look, you can't expect these people to be safe by running off into the forest each time the rinnun come here. You have to be prepared to fight, you have to build a skellig to protect them, you need walls.' *A gate, sagging off its hinges, a tower jutting against the sky, smoke billowing from the open windows at the top.* I shook my head, and the lagoon was before me once more. 'And even then, he'll come through.' I switched back to his language. 'Sorry. A picture made itself in my mind.' My leg was aching inside its splints, and he saw me rub it absently.

'Pel Kinu, you are tired, and getting redder in the sun. It

would be well to go back up to the cave now.'

I squinted up at the sun falling rapidly down the western horizon. 'The rinnun have gone up the coast to raid another village. Will they have to come back this way when they are done?'

'Assuredly.'

'When? How much time do we have?'

'Maybe two days, maybe three. Not longer. They will want to get home before the moon disappears.'

I nodded, splashing salt water over my shoulders absently. 'They travel at night, then, by moonlight? Good. Do we have any boats of that kind?'

'Zai. Smaller ones, of course, not so fast as that boat. What are you thinking?'

I fingered a piece of sharp rock that had broken off the reef and been caught in the sand under my hands. When I chucked it out into the water, it wouldn't skip at all. I hadn't really expected it would. 'I am thinking maybe the rinnun are not very good sailors.'

He put a hand on my elbow. 'We must not put the villagers in danger.'

'But if the rinnun have left the villages up the coast and passed by here, and then are never seen by eyes again . . .' I shrugged expressively.

Bai Nati nodded once, bringing himself to accept the risk, I could see that, and then again, the tip of his tongue caught between his teeth as he thought. 'There is a channel through which they must go.'

I chucked another rock. 'Channels are hard for any mariner to navigate in the dark, sometimes.'

CHAPTER FOUR

'All right, mates. Let's see if the bugger works,' I called in a low voice. I had said most of it in their language, and after a night and a day working together, they were getting the drift of the other words I used more and more frequently as the sun got hotter, the rocks heavier, and the time shorter. They grinned tiredly up at me where I stood a little above on the promontory some three miles down the coast from our village of Anazi.

I waved to the corresponding team opposite us, and Bai Nati acknowledged the signal. On the islet across the fifty-foot channel, his men gripped the b'mbu pole. 'Ready, Mocu?' I asked.

'Ready, Kinu,' he replied.

Now! I kenned to the old man. His hand dropped, and his team broke into a run. 'Now!' I commanded my own, and Mocu gave a cry and leaped forward, the men bending their backs into pushing the pole.

The counterweighted pivots turned smoothly, the two booms swept in their arcs over the water, and the nets of heavy stones – first one, and then, a second later, the other – crashed into the anchored boat, or proa in their language, we were using for a target. The first battering ram neatly took out the supports for the outrigger, and the second heavy netful of rocks crushed into the canoe itself, lifted the bow, and swept it end over end in splinters.

The men lifted their fists in a cheer. 'GRAB THE

BOOM!' I yelled. The net full of rocks, like a giant whirled mace, was still moving. If it hit the braking pole full tilt, the boom would break. I had told them that, but in the excitement of the moment, they had forgotten.

Alerted by my shout, even though he did not understand the words, Mocu jumped for the boom, grasped it, and clung, his feet plowing the sand. Another man dived for the braking line and got dragged, but the boom slowed its arc, and the other men finally woke up. They slowed it, but it still thumped off the retaining pole with a lurch, the net bag swinging dangerously and the long b'mbu tree trunk bobbing like a fishing pole with a whale on the end of the line.

The net let go. The rocks splashed into the channel, the suddenly released boom sprang up in the air, and the counterweight grounded itself in the sand. The men stared, sweat streaming off their backs.

Bai Nati looked across the channel to me. 'Pretty good, eh?' he called jauntily.

I raised my eyes to him. I could have killed him cheerfully.

'Oh, the net is nothing.' He made the horizontal wave with his hand. 'Assuredly, we can have that fixed before the birds go home to roost. But didn't it work well!' he said with relish, twirling his walking stick and watching the flotsam of the proa surging in the channel.

The men's eyes went from the old man to me. They had worked hard, they had worked their guts out, and we were maybe an hour's work away from their revenge for the murdered woman. I bit back the curses, grinned, and raised a fist in the air.

Mocu vaulted the grounded boom, ran some steps on the beach, dropped into a handstand and kicked the hell out of an imaginary ball. The men stomped their feet and cheered, slapping each other on the back. 'All right, lads,' I called. 'Let's finish this, and then eat and rest awhile.'

'Aye,' Mocu called. 'And then we will show the mucking ugly cats some Marner magic, by Powers!'

I had to laugh, the mixed languages sounded so oddly from him.

Bai Nati's team secured their boom and swam the channel to help us. Some of the men made the collection of heavy stones a race, while others went up into the verge of the forest where we had left the gear. I was glad Bai Nati had thought to include an extra net. Lifting the counterweight and swinging the boom onshore turned out to be the hard part, and in the end Grumahu the Walking Thunder had to wade out into the channel, throw his sling over the boom, and hang on it to bring it down near the water. Then it was easy to pivot the pole ashore and attach the new net.

It took a little longer than I expected, but there was still some sun left in the sky when it was finished. We ate tiredly, cold cakes and hot stew that Bai Nati had kindled a small fire to reheat. The pilchu jug went from hand to hand, and then the old man passed round the stoppered container made from a dried vegetable, which had replaced the wooden pitcher as the bottle for my spring water and kalan-kalan mixture. The men drank a swallow or two each to ease their aching muscles, and then lay on the warm sand to play tiles or talk quietly, resting. I lost at tiles to Grumahu, who seemed to take that as a matter of course.

Bai Nati cast a glance up at the graying sky, lifted an eyebrow to me, and I nodded. He led his team back across the channel, the lookout fingered his b'mbu whistle and loped off in the direction of the village, and the men began to daub their dark skins with a paste of chalk and grease, giving themselves gray-white spots. I darkened my hair and spotted my light skin with ash from the fire. In the moon-light on the silver-and-shadow rocks, none of us should be too visible until we moved. Across the channel we could see Bai Nati's men only because we knew they were there.

We settled in the lee of the promontory to wait, the men

whispering, although it was unlikely anyone more than a few feet away could have heard us talking above the waves quietly lapping the rocks at our feet. To pass the time, they began to tell stories. I was invited to join in, but I hadn't enough words to make a decent job of it, so I waved them off and listened. One in particular was a well-told tale. An older man named S'lolo spoke.

In an age before ages, man was a poor thing, witless and sightless. The world was dead to him, though he trod its hills and valleys, and its rain fell upon his head. He was, thee may say, a little stupid, as younglings often are.

The dolphin and gull took council together, and the mouse and hare also were with them. Gull was shrill, crying out, 'I don't like him. He steals my eggs!'

And Mouse, too, had a tale. 'He's made friends with Cat. It's a bad pairing. Mark my words, trouble will come of it, oh yes, it will. I'm very much troubled by it.'

Hare was hurt most, perhaps. 'He wears my mother's skin,' she said softly.

Dolphin lolled in the shallow water near the strand on which they met, four friends with a problem. 'Haa!' he said, which for him was not making a joke, but simply his way of clearing his mind. 'Haa!' he repeated more quietly. 'Well then, we must find who has charge of this youngling, and see that Man gets straightened out.' He rose half out of the wave, head cocked to look at his friends on the beach. 'He looks something like Pig might if piggy went upright – all pink, thee knows. I'll have a word with Pig. Go home, friends, and let us meet again next moontime.' They agreed, relieved that Dolphin would take the job of finding out Man's guardian, for Dolphin was the wisest of them, and the best speaker, and if thee will tell a parent a bad thing about his child, thee must needs be a good speaker.

So they parted for that time, and Dolphin, going by the

seaways, called Pig down to a tide pool to have a chat about Pig's wayward youngling. 'Now, Pig,' Dolphin began, 'thee and I have been friends a long time, and I know thee to be a good and loving parent to thy litter, and—'

Pig sat down with a grunt, there amidst the seaweed and old barnacles. 'What's on thy mind, Dolphin?' she asked wryly. Old Dolphin was nearly standing on his tail with some favor he did not want to ask.

Dolphin's snout was a little pink. Never had he gone to any animal with such a request. 'Haa! Well, Pig, there seems to be a problem with this youngling called Man. He talks to no one, poisons the ear of Cat against our friend Mouse, steals Gull's eggs, and Hare . . . well, it is too terrible to tell that. I will just say that he is altogether an obnoxious animal, and we all wish thee would have a word with him about it, if thee please.'

Pig's snout wrinkled. 'I, talk to Man? Why, Dolphin? I am not his guardian.'

'Oh? Haa, well, we thought he looks a bit like thee,' Dolphin said apologetically. 'Thy pardon. I didn't think thee'd have such an ill-mannered lout for a piglet of thine,' he added.

Pig rooted through the seaweed, tossing it aside. 'Talk to Seal. I wouldn't be surprised if there's a relationship there, they laugh so much alike, he and Man.'

'Haa! An excellent idea! Of course! Seal!' Dolphin threw a back somersault in excitement. He sped back to the strand to meet his friends. 'Hello, Mouse, Hare, and Gull! Thee's about, friends?'

Gull glided along the rocky sand, looking watchfully about before she perched on a stone at the water's edge. 'Man's been here today,' she reported. 'I saw him with Hare.'

'Haa! Talking?' Dolphin inquired eagerly.

Her black eye was ringed with yellow. 'No, Dolphin. Not talking.' She had no need to say more.

Dolphin went under the water and stayed there a time, washing away the grief. Hare had been a good friend, and he had loved her well. When he came up, Mouse was wringing his little hands at the terrible news. 'Did thee talk to Pig?' he called when he saw Dolphin's nose break the water.

'Pig does not know him,' the Dolphin reported shortly, because he was angry, and he had never been angry before. 'I will see Seal. Pig thinks our slick black friend may know Man.'

Mouse cast a glance over his shoulder. 'Hurry, then. I'm afraid, and my missus is home alone with the children.'

'Stay, then. I will return.' So saying, Dolphin swam like a silver streak in the water. When he neared certain rocks, he called, 'Seal? Thee's home?'

A sleek head popped up near him in the water. 'Come play, Dolphin, heh, heh!'

'There is no playing today, my friend. This animal Man, is he *thy* charge?'

'No, and am I glad of it! Heh, heh.' Seal noticed something was greatly amiss with Dolphin. 'I think thee wants to talk to Chipmunk. Chipmunk's hands are something like Man's, thee thinks?'

'I'll talk to Chipmunk.' And Dolphin, who was never rude, left without saying so much as goodbye. 'Hello, Gull and Mouse? Come out onto the beach.'

But only Gull was there, and she would not land. 'Out to the rocks in the bay,' she called down to him. 'I feel safer there.'

When they met safely out from shore, Dolphin asked, 'Where is Mouse?'

'The cat got him. I have never seen her act that way before. Dolphin, thee must do something more!'

'What, then? Where is there to go? Seal sends me to Chipmunk, but one can see at a glance that Man is no kin to him, and Chipmunk with his temper would be offended if I suggested it.'

They thought, Gull standing on one leg and Dolphin wallowing in the shallows near the ledge. 'Well, I see no other way,' the bird said finally.

'Yes,' agreed the sea creature. 'I shall have to take the case to Lady Swan.'

'I will go with thee,' Gull said, and so they set off, flying and swimming, to the island where the Swan dwelt, fairest of all animals.

She received them kindly, and they talked as old friends, and finally the talk came round to Man and his bad behavior. 'So do thee think thee could talk to him, Lady?' asked Dolphin anxiously.

'Indeed,' Swan answered. 'I will. Come, if thee's not too tired, friends, we should go now rather than later.'

So back they went to the place where Man was making trouble, there to see what Swan could do. She floated close to the cave where he lived. 'Ho, there! Man!' she called. 'Come out. I have something to say to thee.'

But Man went stolidly about his work, weaving a net out of vines.

Cat sat up at the mouth of the cave, curling her tail about her toes. 'He can't hear you, Lady.'

'Hmm,' said Swan, dipping her head to think. 'Cat, since thee has turned against the company of thine own and holds now with Man, thee shall be his guardian, for it is apparent he has need of one.'

At this Cat washed her face. She did not like the command, but she could not say so to Lady Swan.

Swan, knowing what Cat thought, smiled a little to herself. 'Now I will open his eyes and ears, for there is something wrong with them, I perceive.' She took wing and circled overhead, the wind making music in her feathers. The man looked up, amazed.

And then he flung the net.

So unexpected was his action, and so quick, that neither Dolphin for all his wisdom, nor Gull for all her shrill tongue, could do more than gasp for shock as Lady Swan tumbled to the ground, all gyved in the net of vines. This youngling's stupidity was of a spectacularly dangerous sort. Swan was cruelly trapped, and some of her pinions were damaged.

Even Cat was ashamed for him. 'Yeow fool! Let her go!' she hissed urgently.

For the first time, Man heard one of the other animals. He looked at Cat, surprised not so much that she spoke to him, but at what she had said. 'Why should I let her go? She's the most beautiful thing I've ever seen, and makes the prettiest song. I'll put a ring round her neck with a bit of line on it and keep her for a pet, as I keep you, kitten.'

Well, thee can imagine how Cat took this effrontery. She arched and spat, 'Yeow are more stupid even than Dog, and that is saying a deal!'

'Hush, Cat,' Lady Swan finally said after catching her breath from the fall. 'Would slap a little one of thine that had chewed thy tail?'

'Yes,' Cat answered promptly.

'I can hear that!' Man interrupted. 'I can hear you both talking!'

Lady Swan fixed him with her bright black eye, peering through the lattice of his net. 'Thee's late come to it, Man, so hark, and listen well: no more shall thee tread the breast of earth without giving proper respect to the others who were here before thee and shall remain after. Thy ears shall be opened to them, and they, because they are wise and forgiving, shall teach thee what thee has the wit to learn.'

'Which won't be much, I warrant,' Gull whispered to Dolphin.

If Lady Swan heard this, she paid it no mind. 'Open thy ears and eyes, Man, the world is bigger than thee suspects. Learn the Way of it, that thy years may be numbered as the stars, and thy days filled with the music that does not end.' So saying, she burnt his net to ash in the winking of an eye by the power that was in her and leaped from earth. Up and up she circled and all earth rang with the music of the wind across her feathers, and the flowers bowed and nodded to see her go.

Man sat for a long time silent, so long that the sky went light and dark many, many times, and his hair was white when he stirred. Rising stiffly, he went into the cave. The other animals looked at each other, but only Cat, who was his guardian, followed him inside. She saw him take a piece of the rock of the cave and begin to work it, heating it in the fire. Man blew on the rock, and Cat saw colors in it, all the colors of the rainbow. 'It is pretty, Man,' she purred.

'It is nothing, Cat. But it will remind me of Lady Swan, and I will learn my lessons well for remembering her.' Then Man set the rock on a ring about his finger and went out of the cave. He sat down once more. 'I think I am ready to learn now, friends, if thee will teach me.'

And so, each in turn, they taught him, Dolphin and Gull, Cat and Seal, Pig and Chipmunk, who was irritated at being left out when Man was still young but taught him the lore of the trees anyway. And Man wept over Hare, whom he had killed, and from whose gentle ways he might have learned much. As each lesson was done, Man breathed it into the rock, so that he should not forget.

He learned much, but he could not learn everything, because Man had been too deaf for too long. By and by, when the hairs of his head had all fallen out except for a long white strand at the top. Man rose once more. He took the rock from his finger, kissed it, and put it in the cave. 'I have learned what I could,' he said. 'I am too stupid to learn more, and I am tired now. Let us walk awhile, Cat.'

So Cat and Man walked, and everywhere they walked the flowers nodded after them. When Man came to the edge of the sea, he walked out into the water, and Dolphin and he spoke together. What they said, no one knows, but Dolphin helped him swim away, and Man was not seen again.

His son inherited the cave, but the animals could not

teach that one, and he did not listen to the rock. He was a stupid man.

S'lolo finished.

'Ah,' murmured the men appreciatively, nodding.

'That's a good story,' I whispered. 'I liked the part—'

From up the coast, the whistle sounded, low and fluting like a nightbird.

At once the men were utterly silent, scrambling to their stations. *The whistle*. Bai Nati kenned to me across the water, his mind-voice very quiet.

Yes, I heard it, I replied quietly. We had agreed to ken only that warning and then the final signal, because Denjar might catch a whisper of the mind-talk as his boat reached the channel between us. Normally, no one could hear the kenning except the person to whom it was directed, but we wanted to take no chances.

I stretched a little, careful to keep my head below the top of the promontory, to see through the cleft in the rocks that I had already picked as my vantage. I knew that the old man on the islet was doing the same.

The moonlight was bright, showing everything in stark black and silver contrasts, the sliding sea and the black foliage blowing in the night wind the only movement. That should work to our advantage: we were in deep shadow here in the channel, and our eyes were adjusted to it, but the men in the proa would be coming out of that silver radiance into the darkness, and for a few moments they should be nearly blind to our movements.

I held my breath, willing them to hold course for the channel and not tack to take the longer but safer way. They were confident sailors, though; they had their single sail fully up, and they bore right for the channel. I smiled, giving the lads at the boom a thumbs-up gesture to let them know the enemy approached our ambush. I saw Mocu's lips move in a whisper I could not hear above the water, and the men worked their toes in the sand to get a good first running step, put their hands lightly to the beam, and looked back at me.

I stole another peek through the cleft in the rocks. The proa was making spanking time, the sail augmented by paddlers. I could see the dip and flash of their paddles now. Denjar must be a hard taskmaster to work his men like this with a good enough wind at his back to have enabled an easy sail if he'd chosen. I glanced down at the current in the channel, gauging it for only the twentieth time that night. The timing was so critical. My stomach began to flutter a little with nerves, but my hands were steady as I gave the signal that dropped my team into their starting positions. *One*, I kenned across the channel.

The proa straightened her line a little, the helmsman wanting to be sure they entered the channel exactly in the middle. The sleek dart of the boat crossed the imaginary line I had set. *Two*, I told Bai Nati, then gave the second signal to my own lads. A shell knife slashed the rope that had secured the boom, and it swung free. The men poised, muscles tensed.

The enemy ship crossed the shadow line into the channel. *Three*, I whispered across to the old man. I counted two beats of my heart, then dropped my hand. Mocu and his men strained against the boom, broke to a walk, then to a trot, and then raced round the arc, pushing the boom on its pivot.

The proa cleared the promontory, the light-colored matting of her sail visible in the darkness, the paddlers showing as glistening shapes that bent and straightened, bent and straightened. From the boat a voice suddenly said, 'What—?'

The next instant the giant ball of the first boom crashed through the outrigger and took the mainsail. The boat slewed, and the boom from our side of the channel stopped her bow dead in the water, so that the stern rose almost to vertical, crushing the crew between the rushing ball and the exploding splinters of the proa. I saw a man tossed in the air to be transfixed by the flying debris, and then the giant rock maces shuddered against their braking poles and the nets of rocks burst, spilling the gore-spattered stones into the channel. The water heaved greasily between the islet and the shore. We saw a broken body roll slowly to the top and then be sucked under again while the tangle of wood and sail drifted apart. Nothing living moved, and then a triangular fin broke the surface.

'Powers,' I murmured, sickened.

And then I remembered the dead woman and Smallest Brother. 'It is done,' I said quietly to my men, who were standing or leaning on their knees, silently staring, still gasping for air from their exertion.

Mocu looked up at me. 'I do not like this, Kinu.'

'That is because thee's a good man, my friend. I am not a good man, and remember, it was my idea. Thee has little guilt in it.'

'I have enough,' he said and began unlashing the counterweight from the boom, dismantling the instrument of death. Most of the others joined him, speaking very little, keeping their backs to the water. One or two broke for the verge of the forest and did not come back that night.

Old master, thee was right. My heart is filthy with this, and I have made the men dirty, too. They keep their backs to me.

A sigh carried through the kenning. *And yet by our action tonight, how many people have been spared Denjar's cruelty? We do not know. So I say perhaps we have stitched some blood-red feathers into a tapestry we did not design. It does not mean the whole cloak is wasted, Kinu.*

He meant it as comfort, but no one was meeting my eye. *We will join you at the other landing place*, I told him. I knew he had seen the sharks, too, so his team would dismantle its own boom and then take the fishing proa in which we'd earlier transported the equipment. The alternative landing place – a precaution in case the enemy boat had only capsized and we'd had a fight on our hands – was a mile towards the village in a small lagoon with a freshwater stream emptying into it.

Let us make haste. This has become an evil place.

Assuredly. I picked my way down the rocks of the promontory, fitted under my arms the crutches I had made while the teams worked that afternoon, and walked up the beach alone, unburdening the men of my company.

We spent the next day fishing out beyond the reef, which was what we had given as the reason for our trip. I think the women and old men had guessed what we were about when we left the village with three heavy nets and every coil of rope we could appropriate, but the children were not to know, lest their innocent babbling should let the secret out to a stranger sometime in the future. The killing of a proa full of rinnun was a dangerous affair. So we fished to give the children something to talk about, and to provide the food for the dead woman's funeral feast.

The weather was beautiful – it had been beautiful every day, discounting a few late afternoon rain showers – and the camaraderie of fishing together seemed to ease the dark memory of what we had done back at the channel. In fact, once or twice the pride of having vanquished a deadly enemy surfaced. When Bai Nati made no reprimand, the lads began to talk of the ingenuity of the thing, of the straining run together, of Grumahu the Walking Thunder casually pitting himself against the counterweight and winning. I got a new, sly nickname: Tewinu, He of the Long Stick.

We drifted over a rich fishing ground, some of the men sitting on the outrigger, dangling their feet in the cooler water, the rest of us in the proa itself, trolling the net and chatting. When we hauled in the catch, the wide-mesh net held some excellent fish, big, solid-fleshed, very beautiful with their olive bodies and yellow stripes. They were good eating, the men said, and would make a fine feast. We took as many as would fit in the boat, covering them with dampened mats to keep the flesh from going bad in the sun. Then they brought out the paddles, hoisted the sail, and started up the coast.

It was all so familiar to me. I squinted up at the sail and pulled the line to trim a little, gauging the wind and handling the line so automatically I knew I had done it many times before. I was a sailor, I thought. I am a sailor, and I got washed overboard, that's all. I'll remember soon, and I'll make a boat and sail home, and the Sons of the Jaguar can dress themselves in animal clothes and sail blind into channels at night all they want, sod the bastards.

'. . . must be the son of a t'ing, he's so red!' Mocu was saying, and they laughed and looked at me, grinning.

It took me a minute to realize what he must have said. My sunburn was getting past the joking stage, actually, as I discovered when I moved automatically to cuff him.

'Yes,' agreed another man. 'Truly, he is Lord of the S—'

'*M-zai*.' Bai Nati ordered sharply, and the man sucked in his breath.

'Lord of the what?' I demanded, looking from the old mage to the man he had rebuked. 'What's worse than He of the Long Stick, eh?' I added, trying to pass it off as a joke.

The man cooled his forehead with some water. 'That's what I was going to say – Lord of the Stick. Say, S'lolo, can't I borrow your headcloth? I'm too hot.'

Bai Nati dipped his cloak in the water, wrung it, and offered it to me. 'Here, T'ing Kinu, Dragon Fish, before steam starts coming out of your mouth.'

I laughed with them and accepted the wet cloak, draping it over my head and back. *What was he going to say?* I kenned to the old man.

Not now, my friend. We are nearly home, and our coming

in must be seemly. A woman has died, and this fish is dedicated to her.

The rest of the village gathered on the beach when the first child shrilled and pointed at our proa coming in through the channel in the reef. Rafan, the bereaved husband, waited at the water's edge, a lonely figure, smeared dark with ashes, wearing a shredded cloak as a token of his mourning.

Mocu, as the closest kinsman, jumped out of the proa and waded ashore, making the sign of respect. The two men gripped each other's biceps while Rafan's eyes asked the question. Mocu nodded slightly, saying, 'Brother, it is done.'

Rafan inhaled, held it until he had his composure, then nodded back. He could not speak, but he nodded again, then turned and hurried back to the hut set apart and his imposed solitude. In that moment, I was almost at ease about the death we had given them.

The proa was dragged ashore, the children set to unloading the catch, and the men stretched, scanning the line of huts in the trees to gauge how much damage had been done. The women, old men, and children had worked as hard as we had, if not harder, and in many ways they had had the tougher job, because they had stayed where the atrocity had been done, they could not get away from the body wrapped in its pitch-sealed funeral mat or the grieving, silent husband. So it was with a general sigh of relief that the families assembled once more, even though the huts were patched with hastily laid fronds and the women had to cook at a central fire because so many clay cooking vessels had been smashed. Grumahu promised he would get right to work. I had not guessed him for the potter, but he was. He was clever with his hands, it seemed. Some withdrawn men are like that.

They would send her by fire. I guessed as much when I saw the huge pile of driftwood the children had collected, much more than would be needed to cook the fish. This made sense to me, for one could not bury a body in the forest without erecting a cairn over it to keep the animals off, and the sandy beach would give up its dead in a bad gale.

We all gathered round the cooking fire to take a spare meal. The children were children, inquisitive about the fishing expedition, but the men were properly somber and said there were no stories to tell. I saw one or two of the women exchange glances with their husbands, and surmised there might be some whispered talk on the sleeping mats that night.

When the men were done eating, they split naturally into two work teams: one to dig the baking pit for the feast and get the fire going there; the other to prepare the cremation itself. Mocu, as the murdered woman's brother-in-law, had the responsibility for this. Bai Nati left to tend the husband after quiet advice to me to stay covered against the sun, Grumahu led the digging team; I walked on my crutches over to Mocu while the men chopped down the other goal post, the one that had not . . .

'I cannot walk into the forest and back to bring wood, but I would like to help,' I told him. I gestured where some of the men had begun work, sinking four corner posts into the sand over the very place where she had died.

'It is good of you, Kinu,' he replied gravely. 'This will truly make you one of Anazi village. Come.'

The b'mbu frame for the raised floor was soon up, and we lashed stringers across it to hold the floor mats while the poles for the side walls were fitted into place by others of the team. I could not drag the wood into place and also hold myself on my crutches, but I could lash easily, for the floor stood nearly breast-high to accommodate the driftwood that would be stuffed underneath to make the pyre. I was busy with my own thoughts, reliving the ambush, my hands moving automatically, knotting the rough fiber rope about the stringer, tugging it tight, and hobbling the step to the next, when S'lolo said, 'Dragon Fish's hands are very skilled in this work. That is a knot quick to make, but I have been watching, and I cannot get it right. How is it done?'

Now that he drew my attention to it, I couldn't tell him, it was so automatic. I demonstrated, fumbling a little because I was trying to do it slowly to show him. 'Ah,' he said, and copied my movements. 'Ah,' he said again, pleased when his fell into place. 'Thank you. It is good to learn a new thing.'

'You are welcome. I learned a new thing from you, S'lolo, and I was just thinking about it.'

'Yes? What was that?' Our hands moved together, lashing the poles.

'The story you told at that place in the night, while we waited. I had not heard it before.' I wasn't sure I hadn't, but it didn't seem familiar, and an artist is never immune to praise.

He nodded, but did not break a smile. The work we were doing was too serious for that. 'I am pleased you liked it. It is an old, old story. I can remember sitting at my grandfather's feet to hear it. He told it better than I can,' he added with disarming modesty.

'Maybe, but I do not know it,' I replied in the ways of this place. His eyes came up, and he gave me a nod of thanks. We lashed for a moment, and then I said, 'I have seen no seals or chipmunks or hares, or any mice, for that matter. I didn't know you had them here.'

He waved a hand horizontally. 'Oh, it is an old story, as I said. There were more people in those days; one can find their villages covered over in the forest. Probably those old ones killed all those big creatures for much meat.'

I nearly chuckled, but recollected the solemnity of our task in time. 'Oh, I don't think so, my friend. You wouldn't want to feed a village off chipmunks.'

Mocu was lashing a roof rafter into place. He looked down over his shoulder. 'Why not, Kinu? Is their flesh not good to eat?'

I held up a hand, measuring off a space between my thumb and forefinger. 'They're only about this big.'

'Ah?' He considered a moment, absently finishing off his knot. 'Hmm. Well, maybe the ones in your land are runts, and the ones we used to have here were bigger. But I do not know it at all.' He mopped his brow and went back to work.

I said no more about it, but I kept trying to picture hares or chipmunks in the kind of warm, damp forest they had here, and I could not do it, though the dolphins were right and the gulls swooped over the reef. A wave of homesickness swept over me for a place I could not even picture in my mind. I pushed my way through the mood resolutely. One man's private confusion and longing was nothing in the face of what had happened to the woman whose funeral we were preparing, and, as Mocu had said, I was truly becoming a man of Anazi. I had a place.

La-lini bore the leaf platter, heaped high with tender chunks of fish and fruit and adorned with flowers, to her sister's funeral hut. She reached to set it on the floor next to the dead woman's grave goods: a string of pink shells, a fine grinding trough and her favorite griddle stone, her carved wooden hairpins. Then Mocu rolled down the mat walls and tied them to give the deceased a little quiet time to herself before the final farewell. Both of them made the palms-together gesture of respect and returned to the fire pit, and the feast in honor of Wainoni – Tiwi had told me his aunt's name – began.

You would think it might have been very quiet, a subdued affair, with everyone taking just a little food to show respect, though their stomachs really had no desire for it, but it wasn't that way at all. Though not riotous as a marriage feast would have been, the funeral meal was not grim. In fact, there was animated chatter, and everyone ate until they were patting their stomachs and groaning while the smallest children toddled over outstretched legs and screamed when they were imprisoned for a couple of minutes on someone's lap. The idea, S'lolo explained to me, was to set the dead spirit on its path with as light a heart as possible. I stole some glances at the widower, who was finally allowed to cry publicly, and forced myself to eat.

At length, Bai Nati gave the man a cup to drink from, and I was glad of it. Whatever the drug was, it hit him hard and nearly immediately. His sobs stopped, his features went slack. Mocu put an arm round him to steady him.

The old man began the ritual, speaking in much more formalized language than any I had learned, so I could not follow much of it. It was blessedly brief. Then he kindled a torch from the embers of the fire pit, walked to the funeral hut, and touched off the pyre. The people rose to their feet and filed down to pay their respects, La-lini, Tiwi, and Mocu at the head of the line, the bereaved husband at the rear.

As La-lini stood before the fire, she took from round her neck a pretty string of polished stones and shells. She held it up a moment. 'This is my gift to my sister,' she said, and tossed it into the pyre. The mat walls and roof of the funeral hut had caught, and the flames were beginning to roar.

Mocu stepped up, drawing from the waist of his kilt a carved dough paddle. 'This is Mocu's gift to Wainoni.' When he had thrown it onto the fire, he took La-lini's hand.

Tiwi offered a small toy proa. 'I hope you like this, my aunt.' Mocu's hand rested on his head a moment, and then the family withdrew a little apart.

I wondered whether I should step out of the line. I had nothing to give. Bai Nati must have read my hesitation from his position near the pyre. *Stay, Kinu. I will say a thing when you come up.*

The few people between me and the funeral pyre offered their small gifts, and then it was my turn. The mats were burnt away now, the sheets of flame almost, but not quite, hiding the rolled, black mat in the middle of the floor. Unbidden, the sight that had met my horrified gaze when I had come down to the ball court two days before was suddenly vivid before me again, and I closed my eyes for a moment. Bai Nati said, 'Kinu's gift to Wainoni has already been given.' He meant the ambush. I opened my eyes and glanced at him. Mocu was nodding beside him, and Tiwi tugged his father's hand. Though I couldn't hear him over the crackling. I knew he was asking what Kinu's gift had been.

'I would give something else,' I said. 'It is a poor thing, but all I have.'

I stepped out of the line of mourners, smoothed a place in the sand with my good foot, and eased myself down. The picture came to my mind, and having nothing else with which to sketch it, I used my finger. Send the spirit on its way with as light a heart as possible, S'lolo had said. The flower shapes grew under my hand, lilac, rose, snapdragon, a carpet of flowers spreading to the shores of a little pond, dotted with water lilies. The islet in the middle where the huge tree cast a soft and dappled light. The Power with her girdle of woven plaits, and the woman staring at me, waiting behind the shut and lichened gate of the garden. My hand described an arc over the picture, a rainbow network crackled over the broken stone of my ring, and for an instant I saw colors in it: the rose and white of the cherries blossomed; the lavender sweet peas were gilded with dew; her sea-green eyes smiled.

The ridge pole of the hut crashed into the pyre in a shower of sparks. I came back to find them all staring, utterly silent. I heaved myself up with my crutches. 'This is Kinu's gift to Wainoni.'

S'lolo was the first to kneel and put his forehead to the

sand, and then all of them were prostrate. I was embarrassed, but it must be part of the ritual to show reverence for the finest gift. I looked over them to Bai Nati.

The old man made me the gesture of respect, then drew a shell knife from beneath the folds of his cloak. 'Thy pardon a moment, so that the ritual may be consummated.' Gently he stretched the drugged husband's right hand over the stone at his feet.

The man was staring at me, slack-jawed. He flinched when the knife took off the first joint of his ring finger, but his eyes never left mine, and he showed no other sign of pain. Bai Nati guided him in the words, threw the most precious sacrifice in the fire to go with his beloved's smoke, and cauterized the wound. The old mage had to clap his hands twice before anyone heard him, then the four oldest women of the village took the husband into the lagoon and washed him clean, the ashes and the grief coming off together. The joints of the b'mbu poles in the fire began to explode, sending fountains of sparks in every direction, and Wainoni's spirit flew with them into the night.

After that, people sat at the borders of the picture I had made, sipping pilchu and talking very little, keeping vigil. I thought it a little odd that they were not ringed round the pyre, but perhaps it was too hot for that.

It was not borne home to me for several hours what they were waiting for, not until the tide turned, and the water edged up the beach to lap up my picture. When it was gone, the adults took the sleeping children on their shoulders and went to Bai Nati and the widower to bid them a weary good night. Several of them paused and looked uncertainly across the former ball court to me. The old man said something too softly for me to catch, and I heard a soft chorus of assent. Mocu lifted a hand. 'Ndoh, Kinu. Yours was a good gift. Both of them were.'

'Maybe, friend, but I do not know it. Good night.'

At last only Bai Nati, Rafan, Grumahu, and I were left

on the beach. The widower's eyes were clearing from the drug, and he was going a little pale with the pain, but he moved the kalan-kalan leaf into his cheeks to say, 'My wife was honored at your presence, Lord Kinu.'

The poor man, searching for words good enough at a time like this. Impulsively I held out my hand and moved to grip his bicep as I had seen Mocu do. To my surprise, Rafan grasped my hand awkwardly and brought it to his lips to kiss. Then he turned without another word and walked up alone to his empty tent.

'Let us go home,' Bai Nati murmured to the giant and me, and we walked through the ageing night together up to the cave. We were on the rock shelf when an unearthly screech rent the night. I jumped and went off balance, but the giant steadied me. 'Jag'har,' he said.

'It is hunting,' the old man explained. 'As I said, we have them here sometimes. Come, Grumahu will make a fire here on the ledge to keep him away, and I have a lotion to soothe your red skin.'

Every time I slept that night, I kept seeing topaz eyes beyond the fire, topaz eyes that changed to sapphire and burned.

CHAPTER FIVE

The old man was sitting on the rock shelf when I woke the next morning. Grumahu must be out rustling up some breakfast. 'Didn't you sleep at all?' I said, making my way out.

'I have been thinking.'

'They must have been heavy thoughts. You look tired, old one.'

He nodded. 'I have been thinking that I was wrong, and that will make anyone tired.'

My sunburn protested when I drew the cloak round me. 'Wrong about what?'

His eyes slid past me down to the still sleeping village. Though he did not answer directly, I had the feeling he wasn't avoiding the question when he said, 'There is a place we must go. It is some distance from here, and I wanted to wait until your leg healed, but I think we should go now.'

My heart sank. I felt as though I'd like to sleep for a week, and the old man wanted to go walking! However, I had enough respect for him both as a healer and as a mage to realize he wasn't an idle jester. 'My leg is feeling much better, master, but it is far from well yet. This walk, will it be hard?'

He knew what I was really asking: is it worth my risking a crippled leg for the rest of my life? He was silent for a time, then one hand came out to rub his bony ankle thoughtfully. 'Some of it is hard, but Grumahu is very strong, and at the end of the journey there is the pool with the water that you like. It is good to drink it, but it is immeasurably better to bathe in it. Indeed, it is our chief purpose in going there, to bathe you in that pool, Kinu. Your leg needs to be well quickly.'

Good enough, I thought. I'm fair sick of being stove up like a dinghy on a reef. 'I will try this walk with you, then.'

He slapped his hands briskly on his knees. 'Good! Then I think we may go as soon as Grumahu returns. It would be well to begin walking before the sun grows too hot.'

'First things first, mate,' I told him in my own language, slipping awkwardly off the shelf.

'I will get some kalan-kalan and fetch Walking Thunder while you are watering the cryl tree, then.' He stuck his walking stick over his shoulder and strode off down the path, whistling to the birds.

I admit I looked for tracks, but if the jag'har had come prowling about the cave in the night, I could find no sign of it. I went back in, munched a couple of cold cakes, washed them down with the last of the water in the gourd, and straightened the mats and doused the fire with sand. The shell was still securely hidden in the niche.

By the time I was done, the old man was back. I didn't know where he had found a travelling pouch and another gourd, but I didn't think anyone would begrudge them. Nobody seemed to begrudge Bai Nati much of anything. Grumahu returned, emerging from the jungle further up the hill laden with a net bag of rough-husked brown fruit. We stopped at the stream that ran down to the village to fill the water gourds, then I tucked a kalan-kalan leaf in my cheek, and we started off. The first smoke of the cooking fires in the village curled toward us, and then the morning breeze rose with the dawn and blew it away.

We went slowly enough, the old man accommodating his ground-eating stride to my painful hobbling, the giant gripping my elbow in what he evidently thought was a helpful way. I tried not to think about the cloak rubbing my blistered skin, the crutches bruising my palms and armpits, the steady ache in my leg. Instead, as often as I could, I looked up to see the birds.

They were marvellous to see. I suppose I had thought, when I saw the feather stitchings in Mocu and La-lini's hut, that some of the feathers were dyed, but I realized now that the colors were natural. Brilliant flashes of blue, startling reds, a clear gold – all these were visible without even leaving the path to seek out the shyer birds. As we walked along, Bai Nati bent every so often to pick up a fallen feather and put it into his bag to give to someone back at the village. They were valuable, he told me, for the birds were not so plentiful everywhere in the land, and so our folk were able to make a decent living selling the feather tapestries to those further inland.

I was curious. 'How does this land go?' I asked, pausing for a moment to lean on my crutches and get my breath. 'How big is it? Who is the king, and what is he like?'

The mage and the giant exchanged a look, and I got the distinct impression some message passed between them. Grumahu unslung a water gourd and served the old man first. Bai Nati scratched the back of his leg thoughtfully. 'How big it is I do not know. I journeyed a little when I was a young man, but I did not see every part of it. In those days one could walk the length of one moon in the direction of the sunset and not come to the other beach of it. I knew a man who walked it once, and he did not return for two years.'

I knew without knowing that this information jibed with no rutter I had ever seen. Even allowing for exaggeration, this was still a huge kingdom. 'And one king holds all of it?' I asked incredulously.

'Oh, yes, I think so. Except, what do you mean by "king"?'

I snorted. 'The fellow in charge. You know, the one

who,' I waved a hand in exasperation, 'the one who owns everything, or at least has the right to collect taxes on it; the leader of the army, the one everybody else looks up to. The one who takes care of the people.'

'Emperor,' Grumahu grunted.

'Ah,' the old man said. 'Is that what a king is?' He sipped a little of the bubbly pool water and took a kalan-kalan leaf when I offered him one. He gestured me to walk on with him. 'Yes, we have a king. He is called Teotl, the Feathered Serpent.' He passed the gourd bottle to me.

I swatted away a fly. 'Feathered Serpent? That's a hell of a name for a king!'

Bai Nati shrugged. 'The creature is powerful, quick, and subtle, and it sheds its skin, so it can live for ever. Maybe these are good things in an emperor king.'

'I'd say you'd want compassion and wisdom over any of those traits,' I rejoined. 'And the snake isn't a sign of those things.'

'No,' Bai Nati murmured. 'For wisdom and compassion, one must look to a t'ing. Dragon – now that would be a good name for a king, don't you think? Names are important. They define a thing, make it real,' he mused.

I must not be real, then, I thought. I have no name.

The old mage tilted his head to the sound of the bird song over our heads. 'Bird names are the best,' he said softly. 'But only women are gentle enough and wise enough to bear them.'

I got an image of a baby girl, himself tucking a blanket of soft feathers round the infant. 'What did you name her, master?'

His eyes found me, briefly surprised, and then he looked up again at the bright flitting colors. 'I named her Binoyr,' he said.

Grumahu wiped the sweat from his broad forehead and looked off into the jungle, his jaw clenched. He wasn't the patient type, and it was hot.

'Will you tell me the reason for it?' I asked, giving the old man a little time to enjoy the memory. 'All I know of this bird is that its name is used in the tile game.'

'It is a very rare bird, white as sea foam with a green tail. It can be found hopping about during the day from tree to tree, but it only sings at night, and then everything else quiets to hear, for the voice of the binoyr is very beautiful.' He looked at me then and smiled an inward, gentle smile. 'I gave her this name because all through the day my baby daughter would be awake, but she only cried at night. My wife grew very tired of it, but I was enchanted that so small a creature could make the entire village listen in their sleep!'

The giant took up the net bag of fruit and the water bottles and stalked off down the path ahead. I smiled with Bai Nati at his memory, but I did not ask him what had happened to his wife and daughter.

I took another kalan-kalan leaf from the traveling pouch, and we went on, but we did not talk much for a while. The path was narrow, yet it seemed fairly well traveled. Bai Nati was not the only one who used it, surely. My crutches caught in the vines to either side of the path, and at times I had to hop without them to get through at all. Twice we had to climb up hills, the second of which was so steep that I had to let the giant help me. No doubt he meant well, but my leg still got dragged more than I wanted. My temper was as frayed as a three-year-old sail when I got to the top of it. 'How much f—'

'See.'

We were looking down into a narrow forested valley. At first I saw only some high outcroppings of rock piercing the forest roof, but then with a start I realized these were actually the ruined towers and walls of a building so ancient the trees and vines had reclaimed it. I hoisted myself to my crutches next to the old man. 'What is this place?'

'It is one of our old holy places, Kinu, a place from the

time before the Nightlanders invaded our land.'

'The Nightlanders?'

'The Emperor's servants. They came from the Forbidden City many lifetimes ago. Being very fierce, they quickly killed our own king and helped themselves to whatever they desired. They went over these old places of ours like those highest waves that come sometimes with the shaking of the earth, and when the Nightlanders went away from here again the holy place was empty.'

'But some of the holy men were left,' I guessed. 'Some of them escaped.'

His eyes flashed. 'Assuredly. And each of them trained some young man to take his place when he should go into his cocoon.'

It was a quaint way of referring to a funeral shroud, but my mind was on Denjar, who was 'once a gifted student of the Way'. He was supposed to have been Bai Nati's apprentice priest, I guessed. I nodded, surveying the ruined skellig. (*Where did that word come from?* my mind whispered.) 'How many of you are left, master?'

'I think I may be the only one, Kinu, but I do not know it. Maybe some others live yet in other parts of the land. Yet here I am the only one.'

'The Nightlanders are such enemies that they are still hunting down mages such as yourself?'

'They are the People of the Night, my friend, and we are the People of the Morning. Midnight has always been jealous of the dawn.'

It was the priest's answer, but behind it I could see the outlines of the conflict as clearly as the shape of the building below was emerging from the trees, now that I knew what I was looking for. 'What is this duty that Denjar summoned you to do, master?'

He shifted his walking stick to his other hand and started down the path to the ruined skellig. 'Come, Kinu. The waters are cool, and we are almost there. Mind your step over this root.'

I thought I could guess well enough what the duty was, and I was glad to have saved the last Mage of Morning from Denjar's fanatic hunt. Sometimes it's good to have a filthy heart.

The water was exquisitely cool against my sunburned skin. I submerged again, and let the subtle bubbling of the spring which fed the pool massage my face. Then I rose to the surface and simply floated for a while, utterly relaxed. 'How does the leg feel?' Bai Nati called from the rock ledge that ran round the perimeter.

'Hmm? Nai?' I murmured, the soothing bubbles filling my ears.

The old man flicked water with one dangling foot to splash me awake.

'Oh. The leg? It feels fine.' A moment later it hit me. It *did* feel fine, not a trace of an ache. I drank some of the water in my surprise.

'You might leave some in the pool for other sufferers, please.'

I was standing by then, thigh deep in the pool, reaching for the knots that bound the splints.

'Not yet, Kinu. The water helps, but a broken bone is still a broken bone. Leave the wood that straightens in place for now. We will be here for seven days. At that time, you may try standing without help. Ah, I see you do not think so.' He paddled his feet contentedly in the water, like a little child. 'Well, then, I shall make a bet with you, hmm? If the leg does not bear you seven days from now without pain, I shall carry you on my back to Anazi.'

And him so skinny, if he turned sideways you couldn't see him. I grinned. 'It would almost be worth it to cheat, master, and say that it hurt like hell. What do you get if you win?'

He turned one hand palm up. 'If I win, I don't have to carry you home. This is a very good bet, zai?'

'I'd like to get you into a dice game, mate,' I said in my

own language. On second thoughts, though, it wouldn't be worth it. The poor old fellow had nothing to put up for a pot anyway but the cloak, the walking stick, and his sandals. He was rubbing his bony knees with the water. 'If other people know about this place,' I said as I hoisted myself onto the smooth rock coping, maneuvering the splinted leg out straight, 'I'm surprised there's any water left.'

He looked across the pool to the hut where Grumahu had a small fire going. The sound of rhythmic slapping told me he was making cakes. 'Some people know, but only the ones who have been trained can come up the path. Others who want to come here cannot find the way.'

I toweled myself with my cloak. 'The path seems pretty plain to see, and the climb isn't so bad, really.'

Bai Nati drew his wet feet up and sat cross-legged in a patch of shade. 'No, but that is not the way of it, you see. The path was plain for *us*, but it is not always to be found where one expects to find it.'

I frowned. 'It grows over with vines, you mean?'

He gave up trying to express it in speech. *No, I mean the trees close in, so that if one looks ahead the path is not there, nor on the sides, nor behind one. For the untrained, there is no path*. He could see he'd lost me completely. Jumping up, he beckoned.

I followed him comfortably, so comfortably I only realized I'd left the crutches behind when we began climbing the path to the lip of the valley. I was about to say something about it when Bai Nati put a hand on my arm to halt. He gestured. 'A path, plain to see, zai? A child could follow this path and not have to have his mother come looking for him.'

'Right,' I agreed.

His hand turned me to face the way we had come. 'And it goes down into the valley, also very plain. In fact, there are our footprints and the marks of your crutches from before.'

'Yes, all right, it's the path,' I agreed again, a little impatiently because I thought he was joking, and I don't like being the butt of fun.

'Now, look again up the path.'

I turned obediently. There was no path. The trees and vines made one interwoven wall, like some vast tent braided of living materials. I blinked, then whirled to look, the old man steadying me as I stumbled a bit on the splints. 'Bugger me!'

His mouth was moving in his tight-lipped laugh. 'So, Dragon Fish, let us return to the pool. You lead!'

I was damned if I was going to look like the village idiot who can't find his way to the well and back, so I rubbed my nose, growled a curse under my breath, and bent to scan the ground. A little way back there was a scrape and the clear impress of my good foot. I slowly moved down the valley, feeling the slope of the ground under me, working my way from one faint track to another. Here the end of the crutch had dragged, there the old man's sandal left an indentation in the ground cover over the moist earth. Bai Nati said nothing, merely following, with his walking stick clasped in both hands behind him.

Finally the trail ran out. Cast back and forth as I might, I could find no sign that we had passed this way. I straightened, scanning the dimly sunlit forest ahead. Insects hummed in the air, a violet-black bird arrowed surely through the trees, a little green lizard no longer than my thumb bobbed on a vine at nearly eye level and puffed out his melon-colored throat, proudly claiming his territory. For a moment I glimpsed something else, green and white or gold, moving beyond the trunk of a tree some distance away. I shook my head. 'You win,' I told the mage. 'I'm lost.'

At once, though I had not moved at all – I was *sure* I hadn't moved – the path was ahead of me. I looked for the lizard, but couldn't even be sure what tree he'd been clinging to. I turned to the old man with an accusing glare, but the words died on my lips. I was looking over his head down into the valley. We were at the rim wall, and I'd been going *backwards* all this time!

The walking stick was over his shoulder, and his bead eyes shone. I shook my head, laughing with him. 'You did this thing,' I accused. 'You made my eyes not see!'

'I did not, Dragon Fish. In fact, I was most impressed with the way you went about tracking us. It was a much better display than I made when my master showed me the secret of the trees.' He gestured me back towards the ruined skellig. 'Only I was more stubborn than you: I did not give it up for half of one day, and by the time I told my master I was lost, even he had a hard time finding the way back to the house of studies!' He reached to pick a few of a pink-orange fruit that dangled over the path. 'So now you see it is as I said: though other people may have heard of the pool, none can find his or her way to it unless trained in the lore of the trees.' He offered me a fruit.

I copied his action in stripping the rough peel off it with my teeth, though I had no idea what it was. I had not seen any in La-lini's hut, and there had been none of it served at the funeral feast. I spat the peel away. 'But—'

A movement at the corner of vision drew my eyes off the path. I found myself looking into the handsome countenance of a *green* man. His dark green eyes, the color of fir trees, smiled at my shock, then he stepped out onto the path, making the sign of respect, palms to his forehead. 'Ah, it is thee, Mulib Nati. The trees spoke of two who passed this way, and I came to see whether help might be needed.'

'Thank you, Imlaud, but we are well. I closed the path and reopened it only to demonstrate the mystery to our friend here. I am sorry to have taken you from your work for naught. Perhaps you and your people might join us for a meal tonight.'

'Excellent! I would like thy opinion on a new song. It is good to see thee come to thy own again, my lord T'ing Kinu,' he added, smiling at me. Once more, he made the gesture and bowed.

'Wait! What do you mean?' I called after him, but he was gone. The dappled forest was empty.

The mage bit into his fruit and moved towards the skellig in the valley. I caught up with him. 'What did that fellow mean, "It is good to see thee come to thy own, my lord"?'

Bai Nati swallowed. 'I told you, Kinu, your mind-voice is very strong. Imlaud is one who can hear it. He knows, therefore, that you are one of us.'

'I'm no mage!'

The blue and brown eyes turned to me. 'Assuredly, you are, my friend.'

Well, that took a bit of digesting. I jerked a thumb over my shoulder. 'He's *green*.'

The old man laid his skinny arm alongside mine. 'As you are red, and I am earth color.' He shrugged. 'Birds have different colors, fish have different colors. Why not people?'

I rubbed my nose and sighed. 'What's his job, the one we took him away from?'

'Imlaud and his folk, the Yoriandirkin, are wardens here in the forest. They take care of the birds and the trees, healing their hurts, making sure the forest is protected from those who would abuse it.'

I snorted, juice running down my chin from the sweet fruit. 'How can you abuse trees?'

Bai Nati turned his head to look back at me. 'The Night-landers can,' he said shortly.

'I'm sorry,' I offered after several moments of silence, during which the old man's stride lengthened until I lagged behind.

He seemed to pull himself up sharply, stopping in his tracks, then turning to me slowly. He waited until I eased myself down the last bit of slope onto the broken flagstones of the terrace round the pool. 'M-zai,' he murmured. 'It is mine to make the sorry sound. I have treated my guest badly.'

I made the horizontal gesture with my hand.

He smiled a little, and we fell into step towards the low stone shed, open on one side and thatched with fronds, that he had earlier pointed out to me as the guest chamber for pilgrims to the pool. He and Grumahu had rebuilt it after the earth shook the last time, he told me, so that those who suffered might at least have a way to keep the rain off their heads while they waited for the healing to be complete.

'But there can't be many who come,' I reasoned, 'if it takes a mage to open the path for them.'

'For the truly needy, Imlaud's folk will speak the mind-word.'

Yes, I admit I was dying to know it, but I restrained myself. Instinctively, I knew that Bai Nati would tell me in his own time if he thought me worthy of knowing the secret. Maybe the old man intends to keep you here, a dark voice whispered in my mind, maybe he won't say the word to let you out. After all, how much do you actually know about him? What does he *really* feel about suddenly having another mage around?

Belt up, I told the voice sternly. He's a good enough little mate, for all he's earth-colored and doesn't eat anything but fruit.

Then why, asked the dark voice, didn't he bring you here to the pool straightaway, the night you washed ashore?

I couldn't walk.

That wouldn't have mattered; they could have carried you on a litter, or the giant could have managed it all by himself. Why did Bai Nati wait? *What doesn't he want you to know?*

Belt *up*! I roared to myself.

'Eat as soon as the wardens get here,' Grumahu was

saying, kneeling at the fire pit and laying out his cakes on the griddle stone. He looked up through a curl of smoke that spiralled up towards the roof thatch. 'Cryl?'

The mage struck his forehead. 'I forgot! I was showing Kinu the tao-ti.'

For an instant the giant met my eyes with a flat, malevolent stare, and then he handed the stack of unbaked cakes to the old man to cook and left without another word. We heard him cross the terrace and head into the forest. I ducked out of the hut. 'I want to find a patch of sunshine and sit awhile to dry these splints.'

Bai Nati squinted up at me through the smoke, his head cocked to one side, and nodded. 'We shall call you when the meal is ready.'

I walked round the hut, away from the pool, and followed a narrow path through the trees that had seeded themselves all through the tumbled walls of the skellig. When I judged I had gone far enough to have some privacy, I stopped. The knots of the splints were still damp from my immersion in the pool, but I worked at them steadily. The leg hadn't hurt at all since I came out of the water, and the blisters on my sunburned skin were healed. Had he lied about how quickly the leg would heal under the water's influence? There was a simple way to find out. If I caught him out in a lie concerning that, I'd have some idea how far I could trust him.

Keeping an ear cocked, I undid the splints. If I'd been in a better mood, the sharp red-and-white striping of my leg where the splints had kept my skin from reddening with the sun might have been amusing. As it was, I barely paid it heed. I cast aside the wooden slats and the material that had bound them.

Pursing my lips, I held my breath and gingerly shifted some of my weight to the bad leg. A warning twinge made me shift again quickly and rest. But the pain had been nothing like what I'd expected, and I was emboldened to try it again. Yes, there was a creak in the bone, like a soft floorboard trod upon, but it held my weight. Bai Nati had not lied, but he had not quite told the truth, either. The leg would be well in seven days, as he had promised, but I might easily have dispensed with the splints after this morning's immersion. Had he stopped my removing them as a precaution to be sure the leg was not stressed prematurely? Or had he not wanted me to be too mobile, too quickly? If the latter, then why not? Obviously, he wasn't concerned that I might go into the forest: he knew the path wouldn't open for me, and in any event if I did wander off, Imlaud's warden folk would simply guide me back here.

So there was something *here* he did not want me to find. Further, I guessed, this something was probably either up or down a flight of steps, because that would be one place a man with a leg splinted straight out would be unlikely to go, even if he did take to rambling about. I stooped to pick up a fallen branch to use for a walking stick.

My leg protested a little as I limped on into an enclosed space that might once have been a walled garden or courtyard. It was now thickly overgrown, the forest trees and vines having seeded themselves in the very paving stones and heaved them. The wall, too, had been breached at several points, and I surmised this might be the result of the earthquake of which the old man had spoken. There were no steps here. I moved on, following one of the well-established paths he had made in his sojourns here, a lonely old ghost in a roofless hall of magicks.

The place was a regular warren. Though largely tumbled down, the intersecting walls told of a once large community with a thriving life. I recognized the beehive shapes of outdoor kilns, and there were numerous small sheds, some of which still held traces of broken storage jars, though the grain that had spilled out of them had been carried off by the industrious – and huge – ants. Some of this had sprouted into short, spindly plants that might be bigger with more sun, coarse narrow leaves surrounding a central cane, a tasseled seed head. I took some of the seeds, tested them with my teeth, and found them edible, though I did not recognize the taste.

I angled through the close tree trunks towards a gap where large blocks of stone had slid down a hillside to fetch up against the courtyard wall. If I got to the other side of that mess, I thought I might see a clearer way, easier for my leg. I had to hop up on the first block on my good foot, and then make my way up slowly, swinging myself from one to another. No good, I thought, there's no opening on the other side. In fact . . .

In fact, it was a huge stairway. I tilted my head up to try to see where it led, but the top disappeared into the trees. I debated briefly the wisdom of trying to climb, but my leg was holding up well, and it didn't seem so far. If I could just get above the trees, maybe I could see something. I turned round, sat down on the first step, and hiked myself up.

In places, the steps were tilted with the heaving of the earthquakes or the settling of time, and I was forced to detour a little. In other places they were fouled with bird slime or moldy moss, and as I was wearing only a short kilt, this was not a comfortable feeling. But I set my teeth and forced myself upwards, taking heart from brief glimpses up from time to time at the tree tops steadily coming down to meet me. I wondered what Bai Nati thought when I did not return to the pilgrims' shelter. Probably he would call Grumahu to help him search. I wasn't sure I wanted the taciturn giant to find me before the old man did. I tried to hasten, but my leg had begun to ache, the weak muscles twitching with the sudden exercise.

'If you break on me again, you bastard, I'll never forgive you,' I promised my thigh.

Just to show me who was head dwarf on this ship, it cramped. I rubbed it in agony and rued my hasty words.

After a time, I was forced to stand on it to try to straighten the knot. Thankfully, I felt it loosen somewhat, and after that I went more slowly.

I began to see a level place at about the height of the tree canopy. I put my head down and my back into it, and resolutely climbed the remaining stairs on my backside. Last step but one. I turned to look over the top.

'I was afraid you would do this, Dragon Fish.'

His walking stick was grounded on the block level with my head, and I couldn't read what was in his peat-colored eyes. *Grab his ankle and heave him down the steps while you have the chance*, the dark voice in me said.

Maybe he read some trace of kenning, or maybe my face was an open parchment, but Bai Nati knew what I was thinking. He bit his lip, backing up until he was no longer a threat, or threatened. Then he folded himself down on the pavement, sitting to watch me hoist myself gingerly over the top step to the broad terrace.

We were at the top of one of the buildings which broke through the forest roof. Now that I could get my bearings I recognized it from the view I'd had at the top of the path leading down to the healing pool. A large, tapering man-made mountain with a terrace on top and a smaller building square amidships. A sanctuary, I realized. The holy place of the holy valley.

I moved away from the edge, hobbling, but too fascinated to pay attention to my leg. I looked down at the old man and told him carefully, 'I intended no desecration.'

'It is not the building that is desecrated, Kinu, it is the friendship, which I have much valued.' He looked down, tracing the crack in the paving stone at his feet with one finger.

His sadness seemed genuine. I was beginning to feel guilty and foolish, and that made me truculent. 'I got to wondering why, if you were so worried about healing my leg, you hadn't asked Grumahu or Mocu and some of the other lads to carry me here before this. Why did it have to wait until we could walk it?'

He nodded, as though saying, fair enough. 'Because I was afraid if you went in the pool . . .' He sighed and shook himself. 'I was afraid your head would be made well again. Then you would remember whatever this thing was that made you like a fish in the sea for Mocu to find, and you would go home.'

Powers, was it as simple as that? The poor old blighter just wanted to find an apprentice to pass on the mysteries to before he died, to keep alive one tiny spark of the traditions? To leave a Mage of Morning in his place?

'Master, I am not the man you think,' I told him gently. 'I am not one capable of standing in your place to the people. You must look for another apprentice.'

Incredibly, he laughed. At least I thought he was shaken by mirth, but maybe it was something else, because his eyes were wet. He sniffed and struck himself on the forehead. 'Ah, Nati. Assuredly you are a foolish man to meddle in things you do not understand! That is not the Way!' He drew a steadying breath. 'I did not think of you as an apprentice, Dragon Fish. I told you I was to be your helper, and I am sorry I have done my task so poorly that your heart turned against me. Surely that was never meant to happen. It was just that I was not expecting you to come to me as a man with a broken leg, a bad sunburn, and a gift for violence. Forgive me.'

He'd lost me. 'You were expecting me? What do you mean?'

He raised the walking stick so quickly I had my forearm up to deflect the blow. He paused in scratching his back with the tip of it, and looked surprised, then sadness flooded through him again and made his straight back sag. 'Come, Kinu.' He beckoned. 'There is a thing for you to see.'

Half hopping, half hobbling, I followed. At the open archway leading into the sanctuary, he made the gesture of respect, adding a deep bow to whatever Power resided within, then kicked off his sandals, put aside his stick, and stepped up over the high threshold into the dim interior.

We were in a kind of vestibule. Before us was a pair of heavy doors. They looked like wood, grained and carved, but my incredulous touch confirmed they were bronze. Bai Nati said quietly, 'I try to keep them nice, but the rain makes them green very quickly. Look, here near the hinge, you can see a little of how they used to look.' I moved out of the light a little, and looked where he had indicated. The door showed a faded blue color. *A blue wooden door, carved with the Hag's Plait, wet with rain . . .*

Without thought, I raised my fingers to search the middle panel. Under the crusted green verdigris I could still trace the curves of the knot. 'Sanctuary,' I said aloud. I felt to the right of the door for the cord or knocker. It was a cord, and I pulled it. A bell rang within.

'Yes,' the old man said. 'That is the ritual. Now let us go in.' He pulled at one of the bronze latches, lifted it, and slowly swung the door open.

My immediate thought was that I was facing a mirror, polished and angled to catch the light from the open doorway behind me. I saw a young man with fiery red hair, blue eyes, and the sun- and salt-reddened cheeks of a sailor. But then I realized the clothing was wrong: he wore a short midnight-blue cloak, a tunic, and cross-gartered breeches; I wore my dirt-stained kilt and cloak. I raised my shaking hand to touch the wall painting, and flecks of the gold background came off on my fingers.

'Yes,' Bai Nati said as if in agreement with my thought. 'It is old, and I have not the skill to keep it nice. Some of it comes off when you touch it.'

I found my voice, but my breath was tight in my chest. 'Who . . . who is this?'

'This is Marner. He came to us in the time of our need and said he would return when we needed him again.' The old man turned his shining eyes on me. 'And now it is the end of days and, see, you have come to us, my friend. Assuredly, you are the King-Come-Again.'

'No, I'm—' The denial spun like flotsam on the whirlpool of confusion in my mind. Yes? the dark voice prompted. Just exactly who are you? Colors flowed over the black sand floor behind my eyes . . . *bright ruby eyes flashing against the stars, the graceful dragon-prow arching over my head . . . the woman beside me on the sand, her long black hair tangled with wind and the love we had made. 'Marner come back again, Tanu say.' I turned to take her in my arms and brush away her tears and—*

The sanctuary spun suddenly. The roaring of water filled my mind, and I was swept under its dark surge.

CHAPTER SIX

'He came to us out of a storm, they say, a storm the likes of which we have not seen before or since, and it was from an unusual direction that the winds blew that time.' The firelight sparkled off the water of the pool to animate Bai Nati's face. The vision I'd had in the sanctuary having upset me so badly, Imlaud and his folk had carried me down to the pilgrims' hut by the healing pool, where the old man had fed me some of the water of the spring. When I woke there were green-skinned people all around me, watching with concern. Even Grumahu seemed vaguely upset, though his customary impassive expression settled over his features when he realized I was awake and in my senses.

The hut was too cramped for all of us, so we had moved out onto the terrace to eat and talk. The old mage was telling the story of Marner to the accompaniment of a flute that Imlaud played with consummate skill. In spite of the gnawing fear the sight of the painting in the sanctuary had induced, I found myself listening to them with pleasure.

'A fisherman cut the vines with which he had lashed himself to a tree top during the storm. He climbed down, and went back to his village. But there was no village any more. The waters had eaten it. There was nothing there, only broken shells where his hut had stood, where his babies had been born, where he had played the ball game.' Bai Nati paused for a moment, wetting his throat with a swallow of water supped from his hand, and Imlaud's flute told of the fisherman's loss and his sorrow, himself as hollow as the shells on the sand.

The flute blew a low, sustained note. 'And then,' said Bai Nati, 'the fisherman looked out to the reef and he saw a boat there. No kind of boat like that had he ever seen before. It was high in the front and the back, and it had no outrigger. It was not a proa. The fisherman forgot his sorrow a little and swam out to have a look at the strange boat. When he got near, he could see that the boat was broken and could not go. Its mast had snapped off, and there was a hole in its side. It was caught on the sharp edges of the reef.' Imlaud made the sound of the sea surge, and the surf after the storm.

The old man continued. 'Then the fisherman had a great fright, and this fright was worse to him than the jag'har-shrieking winds of the storm had been. For there was a man all tied up in a knot of rope in the back of the strange boat, a man with skin like the inside of the b'mbu tree, a man with hair like fire, a man who was nearly as tall as the goal post for a ball game, so long were his legs, so long his body. And this man was dead.' Bai Nati paused to let Imlaud's music say that the fisherman was a little glad that the strange man was dead, because he would have been greatly afraid if the man had been alive.

'Assuredly he was dead, for he did not move even when the fisherman climbed up on his boat and knelt down to see him more closely, as close as we are sitting. And then, while the fisherman was looking curiously at him, the red man burped seawater and opened his eyes the color of the sky.' The sudden spiking pip of the flute made us all jump, as the fisherman had jumped. Imlaud's folk laughed a little, appreciatively. It was an old story to them, and they greeted each turn of the plot with smiling approval. A few glanced at me to see how I was taking it. I wasn't taking it well, in truth, but I hid my unease.

'Seeing that the strange man was alive after all, the

fisherman cut through the knots of the rope. They were big knots, and it took a little time. Once or twice the strange man said something, but the fisherman did not understand that talk; no, he did not understand it at all. The talk was as strange as the man, as strange as the boat, as strange as the storm.

'So he cut him free. Then they swam ashore together, the stranger and the fisherman, and they became good friends. The fisherman's name was Ikulu. The red man told Ikulu he was called Marner. So Marner and Ikulu were friends. Ikulu found them something to eat, although much of the fruit of the forest had been blown down and made bad by the storm. Then they were going to pull Marner's boat off the reef, but it was not there when they went back for it. Probably the hole in its side got bigger, and it drowned. Marner was very sad, like Ikulu had been when he saw only shells where his hut had stood.' Here Imlaud's flute spoke of a man sundered from his own home by a wide, gull-crying sea, too wide ever to cross again. The melody haunted me while Bai Nati wet his throat again.

'Then for a time Ikulu and Marner were the only two men of their village. There were no other men, there were no women, there were no children. There weren't even any snakes or snails. Assuredly, it was a poor life.' Here the flute wove under his words a sense of anticipation. 'So Ikulu and Marner made a thought together, and their thought was to go looking for some other people, to see whether the great storm might have left anyone else alive. They wove mats to sleep on, and made gourd bottles for water, and took some fruit with them. Then Marner and Ikulu began to walk.'

While Imlaud trilled the bird calls in the forest, Bai Nati motioned the tramping of their feet, brisk at first, two young men stepping out on an adventure, but lagging after a while, growing footsore. 'And this was how they went. First they went to Morningstar Mountain, but there was no one there.

Then they went to Ahimo, the city in the plain, but the people there drove them away with slingstones. So finally Ikulu and Marner went to Oaxacu, the city of the river, and there they found the gates opened to them. Assuredly the gates were open, and there was a warrior standing there with his bone lance. "Come in, friends," this one told Ikulu and Marner. "You are welcome here." '

Imlaud's folk nodded and exchanged significant glances, as if to say, be careful now, Ikulu and Marner. Now you are in trouble. Someone reached to add another chunk of stone fuel to the fire, and the flame leaped suddenly, staining Bai Nati's face nearly as red as my own. Imlaud piped caution.

'Marner did not want to go through the gates. "Let us stay out here," he said to Ikulu. "I do not like this man, no, I do not like this one of the bone lance at all. He grins like a skull. Do not, I ask you, go through the gates." But Ikulu was tired of being alone, the last man of his village. "I will go in," he said. Marner would not let him go alone, so together they went through the jag'har gates of Oaxacu.'

The flute shrilled. 'Now the men of Oaxacu in that time are the same as the men of Oaxacu now: one cannot trust them, and they do not know the Way. They hit Marner and Ikulu many times with their fists and with their war clubs. Blood came out of Ikulu's mouth, and something was broken in his chest. He could not breathe well. But Marner fought well, he made some of the warriors of Oaxacu feel hurt too. Many people came to look at Marner fighting because he fought so well. Finally, though, many of the warriors jumped on him all at the same time, and one of them got his stone knife ready to kill Marner. Then a man said, "Stop." That was all he said, but everyone stopped, because that one man was the Celestial Son of Night, the Emperor of Earth-Above.' Imlaud's flute went silent, and somehow the tension thickened. I found my hands were fisted on my knees.

'The Son of Night said to Marner, "If you will give me

the stone that hangs round your neck, I will give you your life back, and that of your friend." And Ikulu thought maybe Marner would fall, but he did not. "Sod off," Marner said to the Son of Night, which in the talk of his land meant that he would not give up the stone. Then the Son of Night tried to kill them both. But Marner took a woman of Oaxacu, and he said, "Stop," only that, but all the warriors stopped, because she was the daughter of the Son of Night, and they were afraid Marner would kill her. Then Marner and Ikulu and the girl, Nephali, went out through the jag'har gate together.'

Imlaud's music grew triumphant, and Bai Nati nodded confidentially to his audience. 'The three of them came at last to the valley of Molucca where the spring is.' He smiled and we all smiled back. The pool rippled quietly, bubbles rising from the spring that fed it, the very spring of the story. 'Nephali was happy to be out of Oaxacu. She was not like a woman of that evil place at all. She knew some of her father's power, but she was wise with it, harming no one. Marner called her Tanu, Beloved, and they were as husband and wife. She helped Marner and Ikulu, whose mouth no longer spat blood, to make the holy place. And Nephali put the tree there to guard the people from her father. Then they all had a good life.'

Bai Nati's quiet voice ended the tale, and Imlaud's flute drew it to a close with the sound of sparkling water under a dappled tree.

The warden folk applauded, and I joined in.

The tale-teller and the musician acknowledged the praise modestly and took some of the food that was pressed upon them. Bai Nati nibbled a corner of a triangular cake filled with a smooth fruity paste. Imlaud drank water from a pottery cup. It took me a moment to realize their eyes were on me. The old mage put his cake down on a leaf plate and clasped his hands in his lap. 'Well, that is our story of Marner, Kinu. Had you heard it before?'

Many people were watching me now, hushing to hear what I would say. I swallowed a sudden dryness in my throat. 'I don't think so. It did not seem familiar to me,' I lied. A murmur passed through the warden folk, and I added hastily, 'But that is the fault of my head, not of your telling. Your telling and playing were excellent.'

Imlaud polished his pipe, and the old man smiled a little. 'I thought while I was telling it that you might make a picture with a firestick, the way you did the other night on the beach.'

Seawater got as far as the back of my throat. I swallowed it. I did not want to paint that dragon-prow, and I did not want to look into the eyes of the Son of Night. Most of all, I did not want to see Tanu. I made the dismissing motion with my hand. 'I could not do it well enough. Some other time perhaps I will try.' To forestall any more talk of it, I got to my feet as quickly as I could and balanced on my crutches, which Grumahu pressed on me insistently. 'It's probably all the good food, but I'm tired now, and would like to sleep. Ndoh, everyone.'

If they thought me rude, no one remarked on it. 'Good-night, Kinu,' they called as I made my way to the pilgrims' hut.

Imlaud passed his pipe to another player after I left, and people began singing to the music which, though good, was nowhere near Imlaud's quality. Still, the singing was sweet, and I stretched out with my hands behind my head, staring up at the dark frond thatching.

Sometime later, a dark form was silhouetted for a moment in the door opening. 'Kinu, if thee's wakeful, maybe I could come in?' Imlaud inquired.

I turned my head to him. 'Please do. I was lying here in the dark, enjoying the singing.'

'I will tell my people they eased thee. They will be glad of it.' He seated himself against the door jamb. 'Mahib Nati feels badly that the Marner story upset thee.'

I asked the question their story had left stuck in my heart like a thorn: 'Didn't he ever get to go home, Imlaud?'

'Oh yes, assuredly,' the warden of the trees answered. 'Many are the stories we tell of Marner's life here, but after a time he grew restless for his own folk. He made another boat and sailed away home. Then, when he was an old man, he came back once more to drink the water of the spring. It was only a short time that he was with us then before he died of some sickness in his blood that the spring could not cure, a sickness he said his brother had given him. Just before he died, he told those who were waiting with him that he would return when the people had greatest need of him.'

His words were balm. I thanked him for coming to talk to me, he made the palms-to-forehead gesture, and went back to the fire.

So there *was* a way back to my own land! If Marner could sail it, so could I, even if, as it seemed, Bai Nati and everyone else I'd met had other plans for me. Well, no matter, I thought to myself. I would give them some plan like the pivoting giant maces with which to fight these Nightlanders, and that ought to square the debt I owed them for taking care of me since I washed ashore. Then I'd get busy on my boat. If I could make it to a port, any port, I could inquire after people who looked like me, and join up with some foreign crew to get home.

Feeling better, I buffed my ring lightly, stretched, and soon after fell asleep to the hushed music of the green people.

Later in the night I woke. Moonlight streamed in through the doorway, its silver radiance illuminating the half-burnt pieces of wood in the cooking fire circle, the tight weave of the sleeping mats, the frayed edges of the old man's cloak where he snored gently to my right. Grumahu's mat, spread outside the door, was empty. I was thirsty and the trickling of the pool drew me.

I crossed the terrace, which was heavily dappled with the shadows of the overarching trees. The air had cooled from its daytime heaviness, and the night-blooming flowers scented the breeze with spicy perfume. I lowered myself to the coping and supped water from my hand, the bubbles tickling my nose.

The water felt good, a little warmer now than the air, and I put my feet into the pool, letting the spring massage them while I leaned back on my hands. The solitude was delicious. I lifted my face to the moonlight and watched the shifting rustle of the leaves.

Something white flitted up there. *Swan*, my mind said, but a moment later I got a clear view of it as it settled on a lower branch. No, not a swan. It was a white bird, all right, but lacked the swan's arching neck. The tail feathers were long and looked dark in the shadows. They might have been green. A smile came to my face, and I waited to see whether the binoyr would sing.

A moment later I was rewarded for my stillness: a fluting call with a lovely husky quality about it went through the sleeping forest. The old man had given his daughter a beautiful name.

Only that once did the white bird give voice. It sat as still as I was for several moments. Just as I concluded it had gone to roost for the night, it glided down to the side of the pool opposite me. I could see the emerald sheen of its tail feathers now, the shine of its eyes as it turned its head this way and that, craning a little to see whether I might pose a threat. I sat very still, hardly breathing. The bird dipped its bill to the water, then raised it quickly, drinking. It peered up into the trees and fluted again.

I did not know where Grumahu had come from.

It annoyed me that he should intrude on my privacy, and I would have told him to piss off except that he was so quiet, crossing the broken paving stones noiselessly, with a smile on his face as if he, too, had been drawn by the binoyr's enchanting music.

He passed in and out of shadow, his short cloak floating behind him on the night wind, walking with the rolling gait of a sailor. No, it was not Grumahu, not with that walk. At the man's approach the bird cocked its head, and then suddenly it was no bird at all, but a beautiful woman who stood on the coping of the pool to await him, her head tilted to one side, glossy dark hair tumbling down her back, her eyes the binoyr's eyes, shining.

The tree above her head showered down petals, white petals, and I knew I had seen that tree before, though I could not remember where. The woman smiled and reached one brown hand towards him. The man's smile broadened, and he hastened to close the last few steps that separated them.

The sky blew up.

I saw the burning fragments come crashing down, splintering the heavy fruiting boughs of the huge tree and setting it alight, all the more eerie for being a silent conflagration. The man, dazed and scorched, reeled dangerously close to the burning tree. The woman moved to save him, and I myself moved to cross the pool and save her. But we all three froze at the warning crack, thunderous in that silence, and then it was too late. The massive tree toppled.

The man threw himself backwards, and the woman's shape flowed into the binoyr's vaulting wing beats, while I felt the branches graze me on every side, and closed my eyes, expecting to die. When I did not die, I opened my eyes once more.

The man had risen to his feet, though one of his legs was twisted with a break, and he was staring across the smoldering log that was all that was left of the beautiful tree. The binoyr could not cross it, for the embers would have set her feathers alight. She looked over it at the man, and fluted a quiet, despairing call. Then she flitted into the shadow of the forest, crying her grief until we could hear her no more.

The man looked around him desperately. His eyes, shadowed now in smoke, came to rest on me. I saw the hope spring vividly to his face, and he beckoned urgently, swinging his gaze to look for the white bird somewhere off in the forest.

I held back a moment, chilled, and his eyes sought mine again. He thrust a finger, pointing at the burnt tree. His voice could not carry so far, though, and seeing that I did not understand him, he clawed with scorched hands at the cord round his neck. He got the crystal pendant free. I stretched out my hands for it.

The night air dashed over my goosepoxed skin, and I came to myself clutching nothing more than shining droplets of water. I was standing thigh-deep in the pool, the moonlit night around me. The bird was gone.

There was a quiet scuff of sandals behind me. 'Did you see Marner?'

'And Tanu.' I swung my head to look at him. 'You've seen them before, master?'

'Only him, never her. I have seen the bird, though. It comes almost every night.' He reached a hand to help me out of the pool.

'The tree,' I said.

The old mage looked up at the space where it should have stood in the moonlight, and the shadows of the branches patterned his face. 'Ah, yes, the tree. I told you the Nightlanders abused the forest. They took Nilarion.'

I did not know the word. 'Nai?'

'The tree has a name, Kinu. All things have names. If you learn the true-name of a thing, you can talk to it, and understand its talk. That is the Way.'

You're a little daft, mate, I thought, watching his one lock of hair swing silver in the night breeze.

'Assuredly, it is true,' Bai Nati said quietly in the face

of my skepticism. 'Here, I will show you.' He turned a little this way and that, evidently trying to decide what he would use for his demonstration. *Be careful, now,* the voice whispered in my mind. *He's a mage, remember. He may have powers that could hurt you.*

He was pointing with his stick. 'Do you see that little tree, there, the one with its toe in the pool?'

I looked where he pointed. 'The one growing between the pavers.'

'Indeed. That is a gentle little thing. Let us talk to it awhile. Here, sit down.' He patted the terrace, and I joined him. 'Now, that type of tree is called soldida in mouth-talk, but in mind-talk the true name of its family is Wei-yiti, the Butterfly Bark Ones.' He gestured towards it. 'Call to it by its true-name.'

I rubbed my nose, cocked an eyebrow doubtfully, and decided it wouldn't hurt anything to humor the poor old blighter. *Ahoy, there, Wei-yiti*, I kenned.

Bai Nati clapped his hands to his ears and ducked, and the sapling shuddered as if at some gale wind. One of its twigs dropped. 'I did not say to shout at it!' the mage snapped disgustedly, the first sign of anger I had seen from him. He jumped up and trotted round the pool.

I was taken aback, but I really thought it was a trick, some effect that Bai Nati himself had produced to hoodwink me. I got up and walked slowly round to where he bent, dipping water with his hands to sprinkle over the tree. In his hands the droplets looked like gems, and the sapling seemed mantled in a winking net of light. In spite of myself, I thought at it, *Pretty one.*

At once, the tree seemed to straighten, rustling a little. I heard a young voice, almost a child's, say reproachfully, *Thee's too noisy, Loud Wind*, and I was splattered with drops.

Patience, little one. He meant no harm, Bai Nati murmured soothingly.

'I heard that! It said I was too noisy!'

'It also called you a fart,' the old man observed with satisfaction. He straightened and put his fists on his hips. 'Now, again. And please to be careful this time.'

Good evening, Miss Butterfly Bark.

Bid thee good evening, Loud Wind. Would thee mind just moving off that stone? My toe is under it.

Without thinking, I took a step back.

Ah, that is better.

I seem to have caused thee much trouble, Butterfly Bark. Pardon my ignorance.

Oh, thee's not ignorant, just a little clumsy. All thee two-leggeds are, till thee's taught differently. Isn't the moonlight pretty on the water?

Bai Nati was smiling at me. I kenned to the tree, *It is, indeed. No prettier than thee, however.*

The sapling rustled contentedly, the moving slim trunk catching the light in velvet iridescent colors, indigo, violet, and black. I caught my breath, the awareness of other life, of many other lives, other voices wakening in me as though sensation had returned to a paralyzed limb. When I swung my dazzled eyes to Bai Nati, he seemed limned in silver, cowled with stars. 'I want . . . please, will you teach me?'

He took my elbow and led me through the forest, opening the path by calling that space its true-name: Tao-ti, Way Between. It had not quite a voice, but rather a sound, a hum. Maybe it is the way bees find their way back to the hive, but I do not know it.

All through that enchanted night we walked, and everywhere Bai Nati spoke to things in their true-names, inviting me to join in the conversations. I was aware of Imlaud's folk, an approving glance in a moonlit glade, a green shadow that glided ahead and held the branches carefully aside, a hummed bit of music bringing sleep to the birds startled awake by our kenned voices.

The silver moonlight paled, melting into the jonquil glow of morning. When finally we returned to the pool, I was so exhausted I immediately slipped into the chill water to bathe. I splashed water on my face, sputtering a little with the cold of it. 'What's the pool's name?' I croaked to Bai Nati, my voice strained with all the talking we'd done that night.

When he did not answer immediately, I wiped the water out of my eyes and turned. 'Master, what's—' He was not at the side of the pool. His stick was leaning against the outside wall of the pilgrims' shelter. Poor old fellow, I thought, he must be even more tired than I am. I sent a light thought of peace for his sleep and talked to Butterfly Bark for a few moments as I rubbed myself briskly with my cloak. Feeling relaxed and pleasantly sleepy, I made my way to the hut, walking quietly not to wake Bai Nati.

I needn't have worried about that. I fell to my knees beside him, checked and rechecked to be sure, and gently closed his eyes. Powers, Grumahu is going to kill me! I thought. Better get Imlaud . . .

I stepped to the door of the hut and sent a mind-call up the valley. Within moments the warden and several of his folk appeared, consternation on their handsome faces, the women's hands flying to their mouths to stifle their cries. But after that first shock, there came an ordered calm that made me think of autumn leaves sifting slowly down to settle on rusty moss. Someone, perhaps Imlaud himself, began to sing. I left the hut and went out to stand under the open sky, listening idly to the murmur of the trees as they passed the news.

Grumahu came striding down the path, a string of fish in one hand, spear in the other. 'Happened?' he demanded, letting his night's catch fall to the terrace.

'Master's . . . dead,' I told him clumsily.

His face showed no surprise, but he suddenly hurled the spear into the pool and brushed past me. I felt coldness radiating from him.

After a time, Imlaud came out to find me. He took a breath of the sweet air. 'Did you know last night what master was doing?' I asked.

His fir eyes rested on me. 'I guessed it,' he answered honestly. 'No, thee must not reproach thyself, Kinu. Mulib Nati could not have lived much longer in any case, and he has been in pain for some time now. Thy initiation did not hasten his end; it only enabled him to lay down his burden peacefully. Thee saw the smile on his face.'

I nodded. So I had been mistaken: he had not been an ascetic, after all. Probably a canker of the stomach had been eating him alive, and the fruit had been all he could manage, that and a little kalan-kalan water. I sighed and looked away. 'I was a tardy pupil.'

'Hardly that, my friend. In truth, I have never known one to learn so quickly. The Way is a lifetime's learning, as thee will discover, but already thee's much advanced in it.'

'I don't feel it. In fact, I feel adrift without a rudder again.'

'I have no boat craft. What does it mean to be adrift without rudder?'

I searched for words to convey it. 'I feel as though my mind is broken, and Bai Nati was my crutch.'

'Ah. Well, if it is a stick thee needs, Kinu . . .' He had Bai Nati's walking stick tucked in the crook of his elbow. I saw him rub his thumb lightly over the carving for a moment, and then he held it out to me.

They must have known each other a long time, the warden and the mage. 'Thank you,' I said, not meaning the stick alone. I touched my hands to my forehead.

We fell into step together back towards the hut. 'I'd like to help build his funeral hut,' I said.

He turned startled green eyes on me. 'Oh no. There is no fire in this valley, ever – save for small camp fires. The mages are not sent that way.' He gestured towards the rough steps of the sanctuary pyramid. 'There is a crypt.'

I stopped short. 'A crypt?'

'Yes.' His brow smoothed as he thought he understood. 'There will be light from the lamps,' he said gently, 'but thee needs not go in if it will be a trial to thee to be in that enclosed place.'

My right hand had clenched with a memory of pain. I stared down at it, and after a moment, the sensation passed. 'No, I . . . it isn't that.' I raised my head. 'I'll go with master. And I'll try to give him a gift worthy of him.'

The Yoriandir smiled. 'Thy presence was that to him, Kinu.'

Maybe, friend, but I do not know it, I thought.

My heart had swelled into my throat by the time the slow procession made its way along the path Imlaud's mind-word had opened, past the courtyards and storage sheds, past the foot of the pyramid on the side where I had climbed it, past the neat herb garden – the only part of the skellig that Bai Nati had been able to keep clear – finally to arrive at the bottom of a ramp built into the south-facing side of the sanctuary mountain. I looked up along the moderate incline to the wide door that opened off a small platform about halfway up. I did not want to go in there.

I set my crooked jaw and took a firmer grasp on the limber pole that swung between my shoulder and Grumahu's, who walked steadily forward ahead of me. Suspended from this pole was a lattice basket woven of green vines and covered with silky fiber, and within this cocoon slept the dead mage, his skinny knees drawn to his chest as he had come from his mother's womb.

The Yoriandirkin went before and behind us with music and petals of many different kinds of flowers. All these had been donated by the plants for Bai Nati's funeral.

Grumahu reached the top of the ramp, drew on to the flat terrace, and gave me time to catch up. Between us the wickerwork cocoon swung gently, the old man's husk nearly as light as feathers. The lamp bearers awaited us at the portal. I had a moment of almost overwhelming terror, but then the giant stepped out again, and I perforce followed. We entered the crypt.

To my surprise, it was dry and airy, a vaulted room that leapt high above our heads. I could see no window slits, but there were currents of air moving that could not all be accounted for by the open door. By the slanting lamplight, I could see the rounded oblongs of the mages' cocoons, hundreds of them, hanging along the walls in orderly tiers. Powers, I thought, this must have been the biggest skellig in the world in its time.

So absorbed was I in my own thoughts that I missed Imlaud's gesture telling me we would take the righthand ramp, and had to hasten a couple of steps when Grumahu started up. It was an eerie experience, winding steadily upwards past the regularly spaced wooden poles hanging between bronze brackets in the wall, the shadows of the cocoons – some with their fiber shrouds long ago fallen to shreds, and the white bones visible through the dried vines – looming and then shrinking as we passed them. Oddly enough, however, it did not have the feel of a charnel house, and I was trying to figure out why not when Imlaud drew to a stop. 'Just here, I think,' he said softly.

I stood ready by the bracket he indicated. He nodded, and together the giant and I carefully swung the pole over the wall of the ramp, lowering it horizontally until the two ends of the pole slotted securely in the brackets. Bai Nati's cocoon scraped a little against the wall, then settled, the pole flexing. Imlaud nodded, satisfied, and regarded the rounded shape for a moment. 'Sleep well, Mulib, and fly free when the time comes,' he murmured. He patted the coping of the ramp wall as though touching the basket itself, and turned back down the ramp, leaving Grumahu and me in relative privacy, except for the lamp bearers.

The giant had known him longer, so I would leave the

final words to him, if he chose to break his customary silence. Now that it had come to it, a wave of sadness swept through me, a searing grief, all the griefs I had ever known. My eyes were blinded with tears. 'Warmth of the Fire, master,' I said, and stumbled after Imlaud down the ramp.

What Grumahu may have said, I did not know, but his face looked tired when he came out of the crypt. Imlaud's folk played music and the trees all about rustled as the great bronze doors were sealed.

And so passed the last Mage of Morning.

Next morning I rolled and tied my sleeping mat neatly, stowing it in the rafters of the pilgrims' shelter, as Bai Nati and I had found them. Grumahu silently indicated the cakes he had made and a pitcher of pilchu, and I as silently ate the light breakfast. Then I picked up master's walking stick and a water gourd.

'Going?' the giant asked, startled.

'The folk of Anazi will want to know. Also, this place is yours, Walking Thunder. I won't stay where I'm not welcome.' He made no reply, only sitting on his mat, huge hands stiffly on his knees.

When I went out to fill the water gourd, Butterfly Bark dabbled a toe shyly in the pool. *Thee's going journeying?* she asked.

Aye, little one. There are people I must tell of Bai Nati's passing. They will want to do him honor after their own fashion.

Will thee come back, Loud Wind?

Assuredly. There is much yet to learn, and thee and thine will have to teach me, now that master is gone.

She lifted a branch, questing the breeze. *Go, and return swiftly, then. I don't like this air. There is something wrong with it.*

I corked the gourd bottle and listened. Near at hand, I heard an ant complain that his mates weren't working a full shift; at the lip of the valley a small yellow bird flew wing to wing with her chick. *No*, up, *dear*; further off, a large b'mbu tree chuckled to himself in the sun. I heard nothing alarming.

Drink from the pool, pretty one, and grow tall. I'll look forward to thy shade upon my return. I slung the gourd over my shoulder, dipped myself a drink from my hand, and started back for the hut.

At first I thought it was far-off thunder, but then the ground bucked sharply under me. I teetered and lowered myself quickly to all fours, wary of injuring my leg again, and ducked my head into the protection of an upraised arm. Sweat broke on my skin, and my knees were scraped by the rocking pavement stones. Grumahu fought his way out of the hut, sighted me, and ran to land by my side.

As quickly as it had begun, the shaking ended. A medium-sized bough dangling over my head cracked and let go, landing half in the pool, showering me with leaves and water. The tree muttered something to himself, shaking his stump as though it pained. *Sorry, Loud Wind.*

It is nothing, friend. Thee's hurt much? Shall I fetch the Yoriandirkin for thee?

Nay, no need. There's worse hurt than I. Let them be looked to first, he said stoutly.

I tugged the fallen branch out of the pool, Grumahu lending a hand. *Thee's well, Butterfly Bark?*

Yes, but I told thee I did not like the feel of the air. Her voice shook.

Now, now, Little Sister, the larger tree said. *Let's brace up. We've known shakings before. Relax, and drink the water of the pool. Why, that was nothing compared to the shake fourteen seasons ago. I remember . . .*

I looked up at the giant. 'Are you all right?'

'Fine. Pool water for those.' He pointed to the scrapes on my knees.

I made the horizontal wave with my left hand. 'You want

to be sure to check the walls of the hut for cracks before you go in,' I advised.

He nodded. I slung the gourd over my shoulder and picked up the stick. 'Go with you,' Grumahu said.

He would be a doughty ally, and his eyes were as hollow with grief as my own felt. 'All right. Come on, Giant.'

'Right behind you, Runt Mage.'

I snorted, stepping to the head of the trail. *Tao-ti, please.*

The space rolled itself out, and we climbed out of the valley.

I asked a nling-ling, a Sweet Dew tree, if she might spare a few fruits, and was perfectly showered with the round little produce. As we stooped to gather them all – you cannot leave a gift to rot on the forest floor, especially where she can see it, Bai Nati had told me – I reflected wryly that from now on, I would be sure to specify how many 'a few' was.

I straightened, my collecting pouch bulging, and made the sign of respect to Mistress Nling-ling. All around us suddenly there was rustling. The giant looked up. *Loud Wind? Anybody know Loud Wind? Mage, they say, over to the valley. Right, pass it on, pass it on.*

Master Kinu? The voice was courteous, and right behind me. I whirled to find a Yoriandir youth stepping out of a thicket.

'Yes.'

His features were grave. 'If thee will follow me, sir. A call has gone out for thee.'

He ran like a deer. Grumahu snarled at him to slow down, and then the Yoriandir youth realized I could not keep up and slowed to pace me. I panted, 'Where?'

'I'm not quite sure, sir, but it seems to be coming from the region of Mulib Nati's cave. It is a single voice, not very loud, and I think she has only the one mind-word besides your name, for she keeps repeating it. As I am the boundary warden for this section, the call came to me first.'

Cold dread seized me. 'What is she calling?'

'She keeps saying . . .' his young eyes were shadowed, 'sanctuary.'

CHAPTER SEVEN

Even before we broke out of the overarching canopy of the trees, I smelled smoke. So did the young warden, for his mouth wrinkled with disgust. He paused at the verge of the wood to send an urgent call for more Yoriandirkin to help him.

I hobbled on ahead, Grumahu with me as I broke from the dim forest on Bai Nati's hillside above the village and took in the blackened huts, still smoldering, and the heavily flapping birds down there on the beach. I spat the bile out of my mouth and stopped, listening.

Kinuu . . .

'Her voice is coming from the cave,' I told Grumahu. Sprinting the few feet up the path, the giant jumped for the rock shelf, gave me a hand up, and paused as I signaled him back. 'She's hurt, we'll frighten her if we charge in.'

He nodded. 'Careful.'

We ducked into the dimness. I forced my voice to a whisper, going slowly towards the niche. She would be mindless with pain and fear. *I am here, La-lini, I am here now.*

A small sound of pain, not in the mind-talk.

I found her foot and touched it gently until she knew I was real, was there. The Yoriandir youth's shadow darkened the opening. 'Get me a healer,' I told him.

'I have done so already, sir.'

'See whether there's anyone else.'

He left, sliding down the path at a run.

'Kinuu . . . they took . . . Tiwi . . .'

'I'll find him, La-lini. I'll bring him back to you. Ssh, be easy.'

'They said . . . old man's magic . . . proaa . . .'

Grumahu and I looked at each other. 'It must have washed ashore,' I said. 'Still, it should have looked like an accident, unless—' The thought hit me like a mace. 'La-lini, was their leader wearing the skin of a jag'har, a tall man with a flat nose?'

'Denjar,' the giant growled.

'*Him*.' The hatred in the one word drained her, I heard it in the bubbling sigh. I reached for her hand and in doing so found the shaft. She gulped a breath, and her body clenched.

By the time the Yoriandir healer came running, we had eased her out of the niche and arranged her body neatly on the sand floor of the cave. The elderly green man halted when he saw me sitting there beside the giant who held the pulled shaft in his hand. 'Are there any living?' I asked.

'I think not, Kinu. At least, none had been found before I came up here.'

An entire village, massacred because of my clever trick. 'Bring her down to the beach,' I told the giant. I bolted out into the sunshine and strode down the path, heedless of the stones hurting my feet, heedless of the creeper tendrils I was tearing, forgetting the word that would have opened the space. I was too angry even to grieve.

When I reached the strip of village on the shore, I walked right through the knots of Yoriandirkin who labored to extinguish the blazes, through the teams of searchers who were carrying the dead to lie side by side on the beach grass, through the blood-warm waters of the lagoon. When I got to the reef, I threw aside my cloak and cast myself into the water.

But the churning surf fought my efforts to sink down beneath it, raising me to the surface to be scrubbed against the sharp rocks. I fought the sea, I wrestled it, I punched it in its frothing mouth. As it always does, the sea won.

When the salt in me was spent, I climbed out, the surf giving me a final quick lift to a handhold. Imlaud rose from where he crouched on the reef, and took my cloak from over his shoulder. 'Thanks,' I told him.

There was a wry wrinkle at the corner of his mouth. 'Did the sea tell thee its true name, Kinu?'

'Aye, but I can't pronounce it.'

He might have smiled, some other time. We stood looking in across the lagoon together, the small surf swirling around our ankles. Grumahu stood on the beach, his fists on his hips. I waved. The giant turned and went up to help with the search for survivors. 'If it will ease thee to know it, the attack was sudden, and most of them were not made to suffer,' the warden told me.

I flicked into the sea a few drops from a cut in my palm. 'Except La-lini. Denjar took her son.'

'All the girls and boys are taken. Forgive me, I see thee did not know this is the way of the rinnun. When they raid, they customarily kill whatever men, women, and young children are not needed for slaves. But the girls and boys are taken to die on the stone.'

My breath stopped. 'They're to be *sacrificed*?'

'Indeed. Their blood will feed Nilarion and the Tchlaxi on the Day the Sun is eaten.'

The obscenity of it was an actual taste in my mouth. 'Not mucking likely, mate. When is this ritual?'

'The sun will darken in one ten of days, and two days more. That is the Day. This year the ritual will be much bigger than usual. The Emperor is in failing health. The trees tell us he will pass out of his old body and take a new one on that night if the Tchlaxi cannot feed him enough spirits.'

For a moment I thought he meant whisky, but then I realized he meant actual spirits, ghosts. 'Your Emperor feeds on dead people's spirits?'

'Oh no, Kinu. On living ones! Then, when he has pithed

the spirit so the body is hollow, the body is given to the Tchlaxi priests to kill. Some of the blood then feeds the Tree, Nilarion. She cannot get sustenance any other way, because they keep her cruelly imprisoned in a pot. Each time she sends forth a root to seek nourishment from the soil, the Emperor clips it off. They practice foul ways in Oaxacu.'

Bai Nati had told me as much. A tree bathed in blood and a king so mad he had them convinced he ate people's spirits right out of their bodies . . . 'How does the Emperor separate the spirit from the body?' I asked.

'He sends his Nightlanders to wound the victim with a bone dart, then the spirit is caught in a crystal trap when it departs the failing body.'

I swung my head to him. My heart began to thud hollowly in my chest. 'Bone darts? These Nightlanders – are they living men?'

'No,' he answered, puzzled. 'They are shades themselves.'

I was chilled, the wind off the sea suddenly much colder. 'Walkers.'

'They are called that sometimes. In fact, the Emperor is one himself. He takes a new body from time to time, but he himself cannot die, of course. The elixir made from the berries of Nilarion strengthens the body he wears, and makes it possible for it to last many times longer than its natural life. Eventually, though, it fails, and then he must seek a new one.'

My hands were like ice. 'Is that what he wanted Bai Nati for?'

'No, the Mulib's body was too old to serve as the Flayed One: the victim whose skin will clothe the Emperor for his next life.' The warden looked in towards the beach. 'Our friend's magery was very powerful. He was a servant of the Eternal Flame, the Lamp of the Sun, which normally burns on the altar of the main temple in Oaxacu. The Emperor has snuffed it out, sucking its energy into himself. There was talk that perhaps Mulib Nati would try to get to the Forbidden City on the night of the ritual to rekindle it. The Emperor sent out a decree, therefore: if the Mulib would give himself up, the Son of Night said he would free all the others held in his traps.' His fir eyes when they turned to me were troubled. 'It was a cruel choice. Master was much tormented by it.'

Twelve days, on the day of an eclipse. Without thinking, I sent a kenning: *I'm coming, Small Brother.*

'Thee has a thundercloud on thy brow,' Imlaud observed quietly.

We picked our way on the raised heads of coral until the lagoon was shallow enough for wading, and then we went ashore. 'I am thinking that I should not involve your folk, Imlaud, but I need help.'

'My folk are already involved, Dragon Fish. On all fronts, the Tchlaxi try to force their way into the forest, slashing and burning the trees. They capture our friends, the birds, and the ones they do not eat they keep tethered for sport, making them hunt because they are starved. And then, worse than these offenses, they keep Nilarion, subjecting the tree to their foul practices. It is a heinous thing they do, truly. I would gladly give my life to see Nilarion growing once more by the healing pool.'

There was an unearthly light in his eyes. I've seen it once or twice dancing off the masts of a ship in a storm. I was not yet sure that the Eldest of the Yoriandirkin could be accounted a close friend, but I knew I wouldn't want him for an enemy.

Silently we gripped arms. 'Do we know which way they went, Imlaud?'

'Assuredly. There is only one way to the Forbidden City: by proa down the coast to the mouth of Amindrin, then up the great river to Oaxacu which lies on the shoulder of a fire mountain. It is a large city. It was a beautiful place once, a place of tinkling crystal bells and carefully tended trees with golden fruit tied in them, but I think it unlikely the Tchlaxi will have kept it up so well. They have no place in their hearts for beauty.' He seemed embarrassed that he had spoken so openly.

To take his mind off it, I asked, 'There's no other route, you're sure?'

He hesitated. 'There is the fen way.'

'Tell me about it.'

'It is a bad place, Kinu, a wild place that does not know whether it wants to be water or dry land. T'ings once bred there,' he added to convince me it was impossible. 'The rinnun would avoid it.'

'Just to be sure, would you send someone to ask the trees whether the rinnun went by the fen road?'

'It shall be done. What else? I have not conducted a war before.'

I did not look at the rows of dead lined up on the beach. 'I know your people find it painful, but the Anazi send their dead by fire. I must see to it, if I am the only man of the village left here.'

He swallowed. 'Then let us use driftwood only. Most of it has been so long in the sea that it has no memory.'

Like me, I thought. I nodded. 'The sooner this is done, the sooner we are at liberty to make our plans. How long will it take us to reach Oaxacu going by the overland route?'

'Three days. By sea and river the journey would take nearly a week.'

We were thinking along the same lines. 'Right,' I agreed. Then I regarded his green-leaf skin and shock of flaxen hair. 'Are there forests near Oaxacu?'

'No woods, but there are groves of fruiting trees and some gardens.'

I shook my head. 'Probably not cover enough. Then your folk, however willing, cannot help me much there. Your green skin would get you all killed. No, please, be sensible.

I will be better off doing this job alone, I have some experience at this kind of thing.' The words had come out of me naturally, with the force of the truth. Not just a fisherman, and not just a sailor, apparently.

'But thy red hair and skin will be as dangerous for thee,' he argued. 'Unless . . .' The Yoriandir looked full at me. '*Are* thee Marner?' he asked quietly.

I snorted. 'Not me, mate.' Then I grinned with my crooked jaw. 'But with a little bit of luck, we may be able to make them think so.'

He looked away, then walked a few steps up the beach. I thought he was put off by what sounded like a bit of cheek, but when he turned and regarded me steadily I knew it wasn't that. 'Then if thee's a man like any other man, these people who have been murdered are not thy people, nor are their children. For my own purposes I should not say this now, but it is only honesty to give thee a choice. Kinu, if thee could find thy way back to thy own land, would thee go?'

My heart leaped like a porpoise flashing in the sun. Before I could decide what to say, he had seen it.

'Imlaud, I didn't mean—'

He held up a hand. 'Do not say, not yet.'

I set my jaw. 'I'm going after Tiwi. I'm his Elder Brother.'

The warden measured me and nodded. 'Thy will. But do not set thy hope on saving the boy's life. The Emperor is subtle and very dangerous.'

'I know. But I have one advantage over him.'

Imlaud paused, the surf tugging at our legs. 'What is that?'

I grinned. 'I'm a pirate. He isn't.' I didn't know where the words sprang from, but the instant I said them, I knew I was right.

I left Imlaud to the grisly task of bringing the bodies to the beach and began to direct the building of the funeral hut. The Yoriandirkin helped erect it, using only dead wood fallen in storms, though even that made some of the green men queasy, and Grumahu piled driftwood under the long structure. I had decided to send all the dead in one hut, as one family. I didn't think they would mind being treated that way.

It was the babes – aye, that was the hard part to it. I did not know which one was Smallest Brother, son of Rafan and Wainoni, but really it was no matter. They were all my smallest kinfolk. I put the babies who had been found with a woman into their mother's arms; others, dragged off by the jag'hars for sport before they were spitted on stone lances, I put in any woman's arms. Again, I did not think they would mind.

The Yoriandirkin could not bear to be on the beach when I fired the hut, so I sent them on ahead with Imlaud. Grumahu heaped leaf platters with fruit. I found a few necklaces in the rubble of the huts, a few hairpins, a grinding stone, a griddle, some fish-hooks, a shovel with a blade made of thick shell, and put it all into the common hut. Then we rolled down and tied the sides. Grumahu stood back, hands clasped behind him, because I was the man of Anazi, and it was mine to do.

Pausing for a moment with the torch in my hand, I told them, 'There is no funeral feast, brothers and sisters. My cooking is not as good as yours; it would not make you feel happy. If I can bring the children of Anazi back to fish with me, then we will eat. Please excuse the haste, but I know you would rather have me go after them than linger here. Peace to you, therefore, people of Anazi. Fly straight to Mother's lap.' I stuck in the torch, ducking back as the gout of flame caught and roared up. I circled the hut, setting the pyre alight at several points, and then backed off. A fountain of sparks shot high in the air, carried by the leaping flames. It was a pretty effect, but I was glad none of the Yoriandirkin was about to see it.

I sat on the sand, and Grumahu set to work to shave my

mage-lock with a shell razor. I pressed my lips together a couple of times to stifle an unseemly curse, but the third or fourth time he nicked me I winced and hissed, 'Codswallop! Why don't ye just take the whole damned scalp and be done with it!'

He spat through the gap in his teeth. 'Used to shave master all the time. Never complained.'

'He was an enduring man,' I managed to say levelly. It does not do to insult a big man with a knife in his hand.

Finally it was done. I dabbed some of the water from my gourd onto the stinging spots and washed the one long lock, while Grumahu made a package of the rest wrapped in a leaf. I carried it to the white-hot pyre.

'This is Kinu's gift to his brothers and sisters and their children.' I threw the package on the funeral fire, then went back to sit on the sand and watch the pyre fall in on itself, while Grumahu fanned the night insects away from my shaven scalp and hit me with the frond just often enough to make me wonder whether he was doing it maliciously.

Such a vigil under such circumstances – the dark night sky, the fire with its noisome smoke, the occasional shower of sparks – encourages confidences, and I had done some thinking. I gave him the privacy of not turning my head to look up at him. 'Grumahu, do you mind very much that Bai Nati's gift of magery came to me, rather than to you, the man who had earned it?'

The fan went on with its steady swishing. 'Bit,' he said after several moments.

'I'm sorry I stepped between you and your hopes, then. I didn't mean to do that.'

A b'mbu pole settled in the pyre. The moths were beginning to dive into it. I did not call to them to tell them not to; they could not have explained their compulsion to me, and I could not have explained my sadness to them. The Walking Thunder said, 'Not your fault, Runt Mage. Master didn't know.'

No, he wouldn't have. Who'd expect such a thing, that this huge, silent man would secretly long for ears to hear and a voice to speak? After some time of silence to honor his confidence, I said carefully, 'You know, I can't stay here for ever. I have to go back to my own land, someday.'

He got it immediately. There was a slight break in the swishing rhythm of the fan and then he grazed my scalp, just a small thump to let me know he'd take no one's cast-offs. But all he said was, 'Why?'

'Well, it isn't that I don't like it here, don't get me wrong,' I told the fire. 'It's just that I'm a fish out of water.'

Thump. 'Kinu don't swim so good on land, eh?'

I gritted my teeth. 'Something like that. The people will need a protector, Grumahu.' I thought his pride might let him take it on that way.

'If you kill all the cats, they won't need one.' Thump. Thump.

My temper snapped. I grabbed the fan out of his hands, hurled it into the fire, and whirled to face him, my hands flashing up, poised.

He grunted a laugh and folded his arms on his massive chest. 'Thought so.'

'Thought what?' I said, my scalp stinging, my pride stinging.

'You're one like me.'

'You've lost me, Giant.' I stayed ready, in case his relaxed stance was a trick.

He kept his arms folded. 'Got a thick part along the edges of your hands, haven't you? Got a bigger right arm than a left one. Got a wicked temper. Got that.' He touched the corresponding place on his own head, though there was no dent in his skull.

He was gloating, no doubt of that. I supposed he felt vindicated in pointing out all my oddities. Still, he was not a man given to using many words – in truth, his little speech just about equaled the sum of what I'd heard him say previously – so he was telling me something important. I dropped my hands. 'What's your point?'

Grumahu walked the couple of steps until he was standing in front of me. He held up his hands. It took a moment to register, but then I easily marked the calluses. Then he put his forearms together. Even in the smoldering firelight I could see the difference in size. I looked up at his face. 'Giant, my head's as empty as one of these snail shells. Explain it to me, please.'

What he saw in my face sobered the big man. 'I don't say you're not a mage, but you're a w—'

Kinu! The mind-call cut through the night. *Escape to the trees!*

'There's trouble!' I began to warn.

The first slingstone bounced off Grumahu's hip, and then one caught my shoulder a stinging slap. The giant took time to snarl down at me, 'Got me talking, look what happens,' before he hurled me ahead of him towards the verge of the wood.

But it was strictly no-go there. We saw the other proa full of them breaking for us at a dead run from that direction. Our eyes went to the funeral pyre at the same instant. 'Grumahu!'

'Right. Here's my knife.' Without a moment's hesitation he jumped for one of the still flaming corner posts, landing it a flying kick. The wood snapped, and the remains of the fire spewed down the gentle slope of the beach. It wasn't much of a barrier, but it gave us a few seconds while the lead rank of them broke stride in their surprise. One man was speared by the man running behind him.

I whirled to face the attackers running at us from the other direction and put my back to the giant's, dropping into a defensive crouch. 'Run for the trees,' he rasped calmly. He began hurling flaming brands at the jag'har knights.

'I won't leave you,' I said stoutly, though my heart quailed at the sight of all those eyes shining in the firelight.

He spat a curse, whether at me or at the slingstone that had found him with a solid thud, I didn't know. Desperately I kenned out over the water, though I did not know their true-names: *Please, brothers of the sea, if thee could help us?* And then, nearly in the same thought: *Moth Folk, Moon Wings, can help, friends?*

The spear throwers were nearly in range, and suddenly I saw Grumahu's strategy: the two bodies of cat-soldiers were rushing towards us, but they were also running directly at each other. I got ready for his signal. The lead rank of spearmen stopped and poised, arms cocking nearly in unison. We held an instant.

The sand rose under their feet, hundreds of six- and seven-inch razor edges opening. The moths hit them at the same moment, flying through the flames, setting their wings alight, and then descending on the feather and pelt armor of the cat-soldiers.

I don't think the jag'hars ever knew what had hit them. By the time they might have realized that their feet were being cut to ribbons by the bivalves in the sand, they were already burning like torches, encased in flaming carapaces of armor. I was stunned myself. A spear landed quivering less than a foot from my sandals.

I looked up from it to the man who had thrown it, who was writhing now inside a sheet of flame, trying to lurch towards the water. I took a step to help him.

Two massive hands plucked me from my feet and hurled me bodily across the fire pit towards the forest verge. He landed beside me, hauled me upright, and we ran towards the sanctuary of the trees, away from their terrible screams.

Stop, a voice commanded in kenning. There were weights on my ankles suddenly, but I gritted my teeth and managed not to break stride. How had that bastard escaped a second time? I cast a quick look over my shoulder. I could just see a dark form in one of the proas drawn up on the beach at the water's edge. So the shells couldn't get him, and the moths, not perceiving him as a threat because he had raised no weapon, had sacrificed themselves on his men and left him alone. Denjar was very much alive.

'Don't listen to him!' I panted to Grumahu.

'Never did,' he replied, breathing easily.

We darted through the ruins of the village and gained the first slope of the hillside behind it. The shriek of a hunting jag'har came from the direction of the beach. I had an impulse to laugh. If he thought a war cry would stop us when kenning hadn't, he was arrogant to a fault. 'Stupid arse,' I panted.

'Shut up and run,' Grumahu rasped.

Then I heard what his sharper ears had already detected: behind us, and gaining over the soft sand of the beach, were soft running footfalls. *Four feet.* Denjar had loosed a hunting cat on us.

I labored up the incline, Grumahu beside me. *Tao-ti, close on that cat*, I begged the path, but this path had been cleared by the villagers' stone axes. It was not a space with life of its own. So my kenning had no effect, except that some of the trees to either side tried to lean in a little, and a beach rose threw out a thorny cane.

We gained the fork in the path where the righthand branch led up to the cave. I had a passing thought to go there – it would be easier to defend against the hunting cat – but Grumahu made the decision for me, helpfully shoving me round the turn towards the woods where Imlaud's folk awaited us. So desperate was our plight that the Yoriandirkin, who would not even burn wood, much less sacrifice other life, had sent out two archers to cover our backs in case the beast caught us outside the verge of the wood. The archers waited, arrows notched, one to either side of the trail, motionless as the trees themselves in that still night.

Seeing them gave me fresh hope. The weights on my ankles seemed to drop off, and I raced towards the leafy archway that seemed to open before me as Imlaud pronounced the word to make the space.

I heard the cat, I heard its paws scrabble a bit on the loose stones at the fork. It bounded after us, its footfalls a muffled gallop on the moist soil of the path. And then I did not hear it, and there was no hope at all of the Yoriandirkin getting off a shot at the springing animal because we were in a line with it. I twisted and dropped and got Grumahu's knife in its outstretched throat, but one of its paws striped my side and its fangs were clicking next to my ear. Then my bodyguard reached down, grabbed the jag'har by the scruff of the neck and one hind leg and flung it crashing into a tree trunk. I heard its backbone snap. It snarled and tried to raise its head, and one of the Yoriandirkin shot it through the eye for mercy's sake.

I dropped my cheek to the moist path.

The next moment Grumahu's hands were searching at the damage the claws had done. 'Graze,' he reported with what sounded like relief. A moment later he regained his composure. 'Damn fool.'

'Thanks, Giant, I'm glad it didn't rip your head off either.'

'Huh,' he saluted my sally. 'You walk?'

He pulled me to my feet, and we went under the branches into the forest, with the Yoriandir archers following watchfully. Denjar was still out there somewhere. I was nearly angered into the rashness of hurling my own voice back at him, but some instinct told me not to reveal myself. He would see the razor clam cuts on his men's feet; he might have seen the moths flying through the fire, a sudden cloud of them. He would know neither his kenned command nor his hunting cat had stopped us. He had certainly seen by the firelight that my build was not a skinny old man's.

Let him wonder whether there was a new mage in the valley.

I did not sleep well at all that night. It wasn't the pain of the clawing; Grumahu had seen to it that I went in the healing pool straight off in what amounted to a virtual ducking, and that had taken most of the soreness out. No, it wasn't the clawing. It was the eyes.

Every time I drifted off, they were there in my sleep, eyes like hundreds of cold bluish fireflies. They made a sound that set me to grinding my teeth in my sleep, a sound like a gigantic game of tiles, a sound like bones walking. Then would come the paws, heavily padding, and the panting breath of some beast, whining a little as it quested. I could not move, frozen in fright of its sapphire eyes gleaming in the dark. Then its jaws would stretch, red and dripping, and I would vault up out of sleep to find the pilgrims' shelter around me, and Grumahu snoring loudly enough to rouse every mage who ever slept in a cocoon.

It was a long night. I forced myself at least to rest my body by lying there in the darkness, not getting up to sit by the pool or wander the skellig, though it was a temptation. Not many things try the patience more than listening to someone else snore when you yourself are wakeful. I considered having some sport by calling on the moths again – his open mouth would have been a cavern they could have navigated easily at very little risk – but decided against it. At length, I turned on my side, jammed a finger in my exposed ear, and managed to drift off.

The next time I woke, rain was pattering on the frond thatching, and I could hear Grumahu's pipe out by the pool. I sat up gingerly, testing the extent of my hurts. No more than some stiffness remained, and when I peeked beneath the leaf dressing, I was astonished to find the claw marks virtually closed. I wrapped my kilt round me, slung on the cloak, and stepped out into the morning's steady rain, which in this land was warm.

The big man broke off his piping at my approach but did not get up from where he was dangling his feet in the pool. 'Warmth of the Fire,' I bid him, dipping a hand for a drink.

He nodded, but did not reply. I was beginning to get the hang of his system of sparing speech. To Grumahu's way of thinking, if one was able to get off one's sleeping mat, it was a good morning and needed no words of his to acknowledge the fact. Actually, it made sense, and I supposed if you were a man who didn't much care about having friends there was no need at all to pass the time in idle chat.

For some relief, I kenned across to Butterfly Bark, *How are thee this morning, pretty one? What does the air tell thee?*

I am well. Walking Thunder is sad, though.

I looked up at her in surprise. *He is?* I stole a glance at the impassive face. He had stuck his flute in the waistband of his kilt and was leaning to fill the water jug. *How can thee tell?*

By the song he played. He always plays that song when the rain is like this in the morning, but I do not think it is the wet that bothers him. Don't tell him I mentioned it. I like to hear him play, and he would stop coming here if he knew.

'Breakfast in a bit,' he told me over the sound of her last word in my head.

'That would be good, I'm hungry. Do you want me to collect some fruit or something?'

'My job, Runt Mage. Sit. Think.' He headed for the hut, unhurried as always.

'Anything in particular you'd like me to think about?' I muttered when he had disappeared into the doorway.

He had extraordinarily keen hearing. He reappeared beneath the thatched eave. 'Weapons,' he suggested. Then he went back to preparing breakfast.

Now there was a first-rate idea. Last night on the beach we'd been caught naked except for his knife, and that was useless against spear throwers. Reflecting that my hands seemed to know more about this business than did my empty head, I got to my feet, moved onto the terrace until I was clear of the pool and the long roots of the trees, and tried to relive the previous night's scene. I closed my eyes. The darkness, the pyre's light. Imlaud's mind-shout of warning, the proas full of bristling spears. One of the cat-soldiers came at me out of the darkness, spear raised over his shoulder. What if I'd had a weapon, what would I . . .?

My hand flowed into motion of its own accord, and I drew my sword from its sheath, dropping into defensive stance.

I opened my eyes to find myself crouching over an imaginary blade, free hand out for balance. In the doorway of the hut, Grumahu nodded. 'Right. Swords.' He held up a bowl. 'Come eat.'

I went in to find a stack of cakes, thin as La-lini's, set ready for me. In the bowl was a mash of fruit and nuts to spread on them, and he had the pilchu jug heated. He served me and sat back on his heels. Munching, I waved at the food. 'Come, have some. This is terrific. You're a good cook.'

'Eat mine later.'

I wiped my mouth. This was getting uncomfortable. 'Oh, codswallop, mate, join in, will ye?' I said impatiently.

'Mage gets served first. I have mine later. Mate,' he repeated woodenly, dark eyes warning me off.

I grabbed the pilchu jug and took a drink to give myself a moment to get my voice under control. 'Does it have to be that way?'

He nodded.

Walking Thunder is sad . . . He'd already lost his beloved master. There was no reason why I should make him lose the discipline he valued so much as well. I reached for another cake, spread it with the fruit and nut mixture, and ate while Grumahu busied himself around the hut, rolling the sleeping mats, brushing crumbs from his griddle stone, and dousing the fire.

'Any idea where we could get a couple of swords?' I asked, pouring myself another cup of pilchu.

'The beach.'

Of course. The beach. Simple. Should have thought of that. 'That's a good idea. We'll go back down as soon as the breakfast things are cleared up.'

Walking Thunder snorted. 'You sleep late.' He reached up into the thatch. 'I went already.' He handed me the trophies of his early-morning foray.

I stared stupidly. 'These are swords?'

They were wooden, shaped something like the paddles with which fishermen propel some of our smaller curraghs, the little leather boats one sees on every estuary and river in the country. (*What country?*) The wooden paddle blade was edged with thin, wedge-shaped pieces of what looked like black glass, sharp enough, as my cut thumb testified. The effect was of a canoe paddle with rectangular teeth.

'Swords,' he said, as to an idiot. A frown drew his heavy brows together. After a moment, he held out his hand. I passed him one of the paddles, and he took it outside. I stood in the doorway to watch his demonstration.

Grumahu tossed up the sword end over end, catching it out of the air. He cuffed an imaginary assailant with the butt end of the paddle, whirled to catch a second a skull-cracking blow with the flat of the sword, then raked the edge in a vicious hack at a third. His movements flowed surely one into another, his eyes darting everywhere, his weight poised on the balls of his constantly moving feet. He finished the bout with the paddle-sword extended in front of him, free hand out for balance, black eyes gleaming. 'Come. Try it,' he invited over the sword.

I laughed and made him the palms-together gesture of respect. 'Not against you, mate. What, were you the Emperor's master-at-arms or something?'

He straightened slowly. For a moment there was a flash of something in his face – pride? honor? – and then his habitual impassiveness came down like a visor. 'Maybe.'

'Sorry, none of my business,' I felt impelled to say. 'It's just that I respect your skill and wondered how you'd come by it.'

He measured me, dark eyes watchful under his straight-cut hair. He spat through the gap in his teeth. 'Same way you did, Kinu.'

'That's what you started to say on the beach last night, isn't it?'

Grumahu nodded once.

'I'm a soldier like you? Do you know of any red-headed cat-soldiers?'

'Didn't say you were a cat-soldier. Foreign soldier. You've had training like ours.'

'I have?'

The obsidian-edged sword made a heavy whup-whupping sound as it spun towards me through the air. Without thinking, I shot up a hand to catch its handle.

'You have,' he said laconically.

I was still staring at the thing in my hand. Then, as he had done, I went into a training exercise, parrying, striking, thrusting. At least, my body knew that was what I was doing, but the unwieldy weapon wouldn't co-operate, and I damn near sliced my calf off with it. I straightened, shaking my head. Looking over the paddle, I said to him, 'I can't have been a very good soldier, then. A child could get through my guard.'

He was studying me with an arrested look. 'No, that's not it. Your footwork is fine, and so's your timing. It's the sword that's throwing you off.' If he realized he was speaking in complete sentences, he took no note of it, but I did. He pulled at his lip, thinking. Then he cast an eye about. The branch that had broken off the tree above me on the day of the earthquake still lay where I had dragged it to the back of the terrace by the pool. The big man went to it, lopped it clear of side branches with a couple of practiced slices of his hands, then cast an eye at me to measure, and whacked off a length of reasonably straight pole. He advanced over the pavement to me. 'Here, try this.'

At once, the feel was different. I put one hand round the end of the pole tentatively, then took a surer grip, nodding to myself. Again I went to guard stance and began my exercise. The 'sword' flicked surely in my hands, blocking an overhead blow, disengaging and spinning on the out foot, sword held chest high in a horizontal slice to catch my imaginary enemy across the backbone, then the thrust away and the return to guard.

Grumahu grinned, the first smile I had ever seen on his face, and waded in. He carefully kept control of his edged weapon, parrying my thrusts, whacking me gently enough with the flat on the hip, never threatening my flesh with the black glass blades. As we both warmed up, the pace became quicker, the delight in the sport keener. I caught him a solid belt under the ribs with the pommel of my sword, he cuffed me with his free hand. I showed him an unprotected side for a moment, but he was too canny for that, and I found the paddle-sword coming in from the other side. I switched hands, ducked out of his swing, and then deliberately caught a space between the wide teeth of his sword on my stick. I had a good two-foot reach on him with my longer weapon, and he couldn't disengage. I levered the paddle-sword out of his hands and grinned at him. 'Bad luck, ma—'

He was as fast as that damned snake had been and his momentum carried us both into the pool to land with a splash that soaked poor Butterfly Bark. We surfaced sputtering and laughing. 'Cacamalu, that was fun!' he exclaimed, whipping the wet hair out of his eyes. 'I haven't had that much fun in a long time!' He chuckled reminiscently, then the memory seemed to stick in his throat. 'Long time,' he repeated more quietly, blowing a bit. He swam to the side of the pool. 'Was the sword, like I said.' The giant heaved himself onto the coping.

'Aye, you were right.' I followed him, swinging myself out to sit next to him. 'I need a longer sword, with a continuous edge on both sides of the blade. And I think it's much heavier than wood.' I nodded. 'Metal.'

He mulled it, then said, 'Wait.' He trotted across to the hut and returned with a bit of burnt stick. 'Draw it.'

I crouched, closed my eyes for a minute, and the image flowed surely from the charcoal: a long, low room, sunlight streaming in the window off racks of burnished weapons; the long slim lances; round bucklers, nail heads glinting; the sword rack, each iron weapon polished free of rust, long shining blades, weighted pommels, wire-wrapped hilts.

'Ah,' Grumahu said quietly.

There was something else I strained to put in the picture, something else that belonged there, a man's shape, dust motes shining right through him—

'I see,' the giant said, and water dripped from his forefinger onto the charcoal as he traced the sword's grip.

The image vanished from my mind, and I had to duck my head to hide my bitter disappointment.

'Why doesn't it snap off?' he wanted to know.

I swallowed. 'Because the blade is layered. The smith works it in layers, hot and cold.' I tossed down the charcoal stick. 'It makes the sword both supple and strong.'

Grumahu had his tongue stuck in his cheek, thinking hard. He nodded slowly. 'Make you one.'

I missed it for a moment, because I was trying to get back the image of the man I had almost seen in the armory. I swung my head to look at him. 'You'll make me one? Powers, are ye a smith, too, weaponsmaster?'

The visor of his impassivity came down, but there was a crack in his armor now: his eyes weren't giving me that flat stare. In fact, he was downright approving, if I read him right.

Grumahu rubbed his nose and got to his feet. 'A mage that's a warrior, too. Well, that'll be different. Rest awhile.'

'Where are you going?'

'Get some rock.'

CHAPTER EIGHT

He set up his forge in an angle between the walled garden and one of the tumbledown storage sheds. We'd had to work at it a bit to free the heavy anvil from the tumble of wreckage in what had been the skellig's forge, and when we finally wrestled the damn thing to its new home, it was so covered with rust I feared it must be unsound. We made a bellows out of some huge ballooning plant, and Grumahu stoked his fire not with wood but with a rock that looked like glassy peat. It took a long time to catch, but then it burned for hours with a steady white-hot heat. We had stripped bronze torch brackets and hinges. The amalgam Grumahu would make of these wouldn't match up to the best iron but should be fully adequate to take on the paddle-swords of the cat-soldiers.

The big man flipped the huge hammer in his hands, flexed the tongs that had been de-rusting in a bucket of the white grease of a spiny plant, and struck a resounding clang off his reclaimed anvil. 'Huh.' I think it meant, Good enough.

The smithing began, the blade growing quickly under his hands. I pumped the bellows until I thought my shoulders and back would give out from the strain. Grumahu, as any master craftsman, was oblivious of his suffering apprentice. The hammer rang, the fire roared. He was so totally consumed in the smithing that I could do no more than force water and the left-over cakes on him. I slept once, but

Grumahu bent over his anvil and kept at it.

Watching him, it came to me that he was not making the bronze sword for me alone, and not even for the sake of the Anazi children or their murdered families. There was much of Grumahu himself in that weapon.

Finally, he quenched it for the last time and drew it dripping from the trough. Our eyes met. Even unedged, it was an impressive piece of work. It needed no flashing jewels in the hilt to betoken constancy, valor, and purpose.

The giant sat down to the whetstone and carefully began honing the blade. I went outside to the pool and floated there awhile, washing away the sweat and soothing my aching back. The day was so warm and the shade of the trees so wonderful that I could have fallen asleep if it weren't for the fact that I'd have drowned if I had.

'That about right?' He stood on the pool coping, holding the weapon across his palms.

I dried my hands carefully on my cloak and took the sword from him. It felt beautifully poised in my hands, the grip fitted naturally to my fingers, the cross hilt thick enough for protection but not so wide as to catch on leather armor in a tight place. The pommel was rounded, heavy, no silly spike on the end of it. I can't abide those things; one good shove and your opponent has it in your guts. Grumahu had known that. I let out my breath in a whistle of satisfaction, spinning the sword in a flashing arc in the air.

It sang.

The best of the best blades do have a kind of keen hum when they slice the air. In the old tales, such a sword is the mark of a hero. I looked over it at him. 'Powers, man, I can't take this.'

His brow darkened. 'Why not? Something wrong with it?'

'No. It's fine. Too fine, for me.' I held it out to him. 'You take it, I'll learn to use a paddle-sword.'

I knew then why they called him Walking Thunder. The

black storm gathered in his eyes. 'Told you I'd make *you* a sword.'

If I pushed the issue, I was likely to have to draw blood with it. 'All right,' I told him evenly. 'I'll take it for now, on loan, you might say. When you want it back, just say so.'

'Huh.' It was good to have that settled. I wove a few practice figures in the air with the singing blade.

'We have to work now,' he said, watching me. 'Your timing's off. Practice.' He picked up his paddle-sword, flexed his huge shoulders once to work out the knots of the smithing, and poised.

My heart sank. The beginnings of something that might have been a grin appeared at the corners of his eyes, and he sprang into a charge.

We fought all over the terrace. He pushed me this time, forcing me to get back my footwork, hardening the hurt muscles of my damaged leg. 'It's like a skinny cat-soldier sword with a spear on the end of it,' he observed at one point, parrying my overhead blow easily with a cross block that made my hands sting.

'Huh,' I grunted, dodging as his paddle-sword hewed air. I caught his blade with my hilt, and for a moment we strained arm to arm, locked.

'You're pretty strong, Runt Mage,' he laughed into my eyes, then good-humoredly disengaged with a thrust away that put me on my butt halfway back to the pilgrims' shelter.

I leaned back on my hands, puffing and sweating. 'Thanks. You're strong as a dwarf yourself.'

He mopped his shining brown face with his hand. 'As a what?'

'A dw—' I stopped, the pit of my stomach suddenly cold. 'As a dwarf,' I repeated. 'They're short men, but broad, and strong as three stout lads put together. Most of them are pirates.' My breath was short in my chest. 'Good folk, until you cross them.'

'Here, Kinu. Drink,' he was saying.

I squinted up at him, dazed. 'What?'

'Drink.'

'Oh. Yes.' The water made a road down into my dusty heart. 'Charcoal,' I ordered quietly.

Without question, he jumped up and got me a stick from last night's fire. I fought to hold the image in my mind until my hand closed on the black stick, then sketched quickly, lest I should forget again. On the pool terrace appeared a ship. Not a proa, not a dragon-prow, this was a ship built for speed, lean, with a raked bow and a full press of sails catching the wind, a curl of wave at her bow, foam in her wake, and the men in her rigging like spry spiders. I drew him on the quarterdeck, malice and mischief in his eye, braids in his beard, crutches, the right leg gone, the other a stump that ended in a wooden leg. 'Ti . . .' I strained to name him, and a bright pain lanced across my head, deep under the dent in my skull. I gasped and tears sprang to my eyes. The image dissolved.

I rocked, holding my head.

'Hey,' Grumahu said, giving a tug at my mage-lock. 'Come. We have work to do. You promised that lady back at the cave. Right?'

'Damn it, why can't I *remember*?'

The Walking Thunder was silent for a moment. 'Not so bad, sometimes, not being able to remember.'

We crouched together over the sketch I had made. I reached to flick away a leaf that had fallen on the dwarven pirate's face. 'Maybe, friend,' I told him, 'but I do not know it.'

He rose. 'Wardens will be coming to collect us soon. Eat now.'

I wiped my face. 'It'll be good to eat something tasty again.'

'Huh. Want something tasty, try Tchlaxi brains.' He smacked his lips and went into the hut, whistling through the gap in his teeth.

Don't get your bowels in an uproar, he was only joking, I told myself sternly. These folk aren't, they can't be . . . 'Grumahu,' I called through the open doorway, 'do the Tchlaxi eat their enemies?'

The big man reappeared, stirring dough. 'Only on feast days,' he said and went back to his cooking.

Even with the word to open the path before us, it was still not a journey to be undertaken lightly. Imlaud admitted that, given other circumstances, he would never have tried it. In terms of distance, it was not so far, being perhaps fifty leagues from the ruined skellig to the place where we would emerge on the Amindrin River; but as I soon found, nearly all of it was through swamp, and we were carrying heavy pack baskets. These contained not only provisions for the journey, but the jag'har knight uniforms we would wear to penetrate the city of Oaxacu as well. Imlaud's folk had salvaged as many as possible from the troops on the beach and repaired the pieces that had been burnt.

The village of Anazi lay on a narrow coastal strip only about fifteen miles deep. Our route was characterized by the lush vegetation I had already noted around the village and through the woods where Imlaud's folk were wardens. It was warm even at night and, as I found on that first day's walk, the further we walked from the sea's moderating influence, the hotter it became. In fact, the whole place fairly began to steam as the sun beat down upon the canopy of leaves. Rising off the ground, out of the tree trunks, from the luxuriant flowers, the steam brought out the flying and stinging insects, clouds of them. I swatted and danced as if demented, but Grumahu just broke the leaves of some shrub and rubbed them over his skin. I tried it. The stuff was rank enough to make your eyes water, but it worked fairly well. The bugs did not seem to bite the green-skinned Yorian-dirkin, probably because they took the wardens for trees.

'Bad, eh?' the giant asked.

Stumbling ahead of him, panting for breath that seemed to be drawn through a hot, wet wool robe, I snorted and did not bother to answer.

'Wait till this afternoon,' he said with what sounded like relish.

I looked back at him, shifting the pack on my shoulder. 'Why? What happens this afternoon?'

'Rain.'

'Rain would be great. It might cool it off a little.' I thought for a moment one of the stinging insects had gone up his nose, but then I realized he was laughing.

Two hours later when it began, I saw why. At first, the sound was as though huge rodents were chasing each other across the leafy roof above us. The vegetation was so thick it actually took several moments for the rain to find it way through it. Then, all at once it seemed, the roof sprung leaks. If a friend for a jest tipped a barrel of water on you from the ridge pole of a barn, you'd get as wet as we did, and just as quickly.

As if the volume of water coming down wasn't odd enough in itself, there was the added peculiarity of the sunshine streaming right through it. I'd seen that happen sometimes at sea (*How do you know that?*), but never without at least some clouds being visible to account for the rain. Here, the sky never darkened at all.

Of course, even the moist jungle couldn't absorb that much water so quickly, so the open space apologized to Imlaud and promptly lost its footing. The mud came up and, with it, a new menace.

I first became aware of them when my left sandal suddenly began to feel tight. Stumbling, my pack rubbing holes in my shoulder blades, the mud above my ankles, I cursed and reached down to run my finger under the thong to loosen it. At once, I found my hand imprisoned in Grumahu's grip. He called shortly to Imlaud, 'Mismin!' A sharp pain as of a bite or sting shot through my foot, and I cursed in earnest, trying to break the big man's grip to get to the place.

The Yoriandir warden hurried back towards us from his position at the head of the column, an expression of dismay upon his face, while around us the other men began ripping open their pack baskets to take out pouches of what looked to me like sea salt. Further up the line someone else stifled a yell and slapped at the back of his calf. Immediately several of his mates went to help him. Others took up defensive positions, peering intently into the jungle on all sides and overhead.

Grumahu directed the sluicing run-off from a broad leaf onto my foot to wash away the mud, and I got my first look at the thing that was fastened to my ankle. My first impression was that it was a short, stout snake or worm, pale in color like the top of a toadstool, but then I realized it was an impossibly huge slug that was dining on my flesh as though I were a rotten cabbage. Already there was a jagged wound the size of a gold sovereign which bled copiously, and I could actually see the thing's rasping mouth gaping for another go.

Imlaud quickly spilled some salt from his pouch on the carnivorous slug. It tore free of me, doubling back on itself, snapping its teeth at the salt burning its mucus-coated skin. Grumahu whipped out his sword and clove it in half, while the Yoriandir fought my hands away from the wound – into which some of the salt had gone – and washed it with water from the skellig's healing pool.

I was a little barmy by this time and kept trying to climb the nearest tree to get my *other* foot out of the mud, but then Grumahu took me by the shoulder and shouted in my face that the damned things were in the trees, too, so did I really want to go up there? While I debated this, he hacked off some broad leaves with his sword and threw them down on the mud until we had a place to stand that didn't sink. Around us the Yoriandirkin were quickly doing the same thing, though another one of them was attacked in doing it. Imlaud went to him immediately. The wardens were still aligned in defensive positions, back to back on their improvised mats.

I grimaced, shifted my weight off my throbbing ankle, and looked around. 'Why—?'

'Listen,' Grumahu answered.

The downpour was lessening. The jungle was still rustling with it, though, so at first I thought I was still hearing the rain on the leaves. Then it struck me that the sound seemed to be closing in on us.

Up the line, Imlaud called urgently, *Tao-ti, thee must show thyself!*

The path began to re-emerge, the trees drawing back once more. I drew my sword. 'That sound can't be—'

'Yes, it is,' the big man said. His dark eyes flicked to mine for a moment before they returned to the jungle. 'Drawn by the smell of blood. Get your salt pouch out, Runt Mage. Here they come.'

I would rather have faced down an attacking force of cat-soldiers than those damned slugs. The path had opened for us, but the tao-ti was having trouble maintaining its hold; although the trees and vegetation were drawn back a man's length in most places, there were still a couple of trees leaning in and some vines looping overhead. 'Salt!' Imlaud ordered quickly.

Following Grumahu's example, I sprinkled sea crystals in front of me, only belatedly realizing I probably shouldn't have used up so much of my supply. We might be attacked by the damned things somewhere further ahead. I tucked my pouch, took hold of my sword, and waited with my back to Grumahu's. 'Imlaud, what's the true-name for these slimy bastards? Maybe if you and I together—'

'No, Kinu. The mismin have no minds to reach. They—'

The slugs broke from the jungle right in front of me, drawn by the slow ooze from my ankle. I shuddered, but kept a firm grip on my sword and planted my feet, getting ready. 'Got a lot over there?' I asked the giant over my shoulder.

'Fair number.'

They travelled faster than you would have thought. The first edge of what was nearly a solid carpet of pale slugs as long as a man's forearm oozed their way into the salted area. Immediately they recoiled, spewing slime to cover the salt. 'Start chopping,' Grumahu advised. I needed no urging. My sword went eagerly to work as though I were chopping bait for a day of fishing, heads and tails flying, slime everywhere.

I had forgotten about the trees overhead. A yell broke from me when the damned thing dropped on my shaven scalp. Grumahu helped me dislodge it before it could bite, and his sword hacked it in two pieces, which he nonchalantly flipped one after the other into the jungle. I shuddered and turned back for more sword work, but there was no longer any need. The slugs weren't interested in me now; they were feeding on the dead carcasses of the other mismin. We could hear them chewing.

Imlaud craned to catch my eye. 'We should make our escape now, while they are occupied. Can thee run?'

'Open the path ahead, mate, and you'll see how fast.'

He spoke the word to tao-ti, and the path fought its way through the last of the mud and rolled itself out before us, the trees obligingly leaning out of our way, though they jeered a little, and not all of it was good-natured, for we were in wilder territory than the valley of the skellig now, and besides, when the slugs were done dining on each other, they would turn to the vegetation around them. It is a great advantage to be mobile at such times, and of course the trees weren't.

The revulsion of the whole episode powered my legs, and I fairly flew down the path. Even then, I was no match for the Yoriandirkin, for they ran as lightly as the wind itself, and only the two green men who had been bitten like me seemed to tire at all. Grumahu was stolid as ever, though I took a perverse pleasure in noting that he was puffing a little as we breasted a tight little hill and gained the dryer land above the swamp. Here Imlaud called a halt to tend the wounded.

I leaned with my hands on my knees, getting my wind, and glanced over at Grumahu. He was wincing and, as I watched, reached over his shoulder with his salt pouch. The creature let go, and he calmly speared it on his sword and flung it down into the swamp. Blood streamed down his back, and when I spun him to see, there was a wound as big as a cryl fruit and as deep as half the nail on my forefinger.

'Damn it, Giant!' I exploded. 'Why didn't you say something?'

He barely changed expression when Imlaud first plastered the wound with salt to draw out the slug mucus and then rinsed it quickly with an entire gourd flask of spring water. 'Had a bigger one than that attach itself to me when I was a lad. It's part of a cat-soldier's training.'

Imlaud packed off the bite with a poultice of leaves from his healing stock, binding it in place with a strip of material like that from which our kilts and cloaks were woven. I sat with the other two wounded, and an older man saw to our hurts at the same time. All of us drank some water, and then the Eldest of the Yoriandirkin cast a glance up at the westering sun. 'We should try to push on a bit further today, Kinu. There are still some hours of light left, and I for one would feel easier with more distance between us and the mismin.' He gestured down the slope behind us. 'As thee sees, the next valley is drier, and over on that hillside we should find comfortable shelter for the night without being exposed to watching eyes as we are here.'

I turned to look at him. 'What watching eyes? I thought you said the cat-soldiers don't venture out here – which, by the way, seems remarkably sensible to me now.'

' 'Twas not I who underrated the intelligence of the jag'har knights,' he reminded me quietly. 'As for who or what may be watching, how can we know? The forest into which we venture now is far older than our friendly trees of the valley. Indeed, they are so old and so wild that even we Yoriandirkin do not know all of their true-names, nor all the names of the creatures who inhabit them. And, because the land is more passable than that swamp, some few cat-soldiers may man the hilltop forts where the fire signals are made for great events in the empire.'

Grumahu made the horizontal motion with his hand. 'I know those forts. Punishment to be stationed out here. Only soldiers you'd get here would be thieves and drunks.'

'Likely enough, but that might make them eager to get back into the good graces of their officers,' I said thoughtfully, 'and we can't afford to have these packs inspected. Better to be cautious, as Imlaud suggests.' I looked at Grumahu, and he nodded.

We rose, shrugged into the straps of our pack baskets (Grumahu simply brushing aside the two Yoriandir who wanted to share his out between them to spare his back), and began the descent into the next valley.

I kept expecting slugs, but as Imlaud had predicted, the land here was evidently too dry for them; I saw none of the creatures themselves, nor did I see any slime trails to indicate that they came out to hunt at night. I began to relax, but once when a bird startled from cover a few feet away, my hand whipped to my hilt before I could master the impulse. Behind me Grumahu chuckled, and I felt my ears grow hot.

The trees here were not as tall as those in the forest of the coastal plain, but they were broader and leafier, some with huge flowers that emitted a cloying perfume. These drew clouds of bees, and we were careful to go quietly round them, Imlaud murmuring a soothing word to the banded workers who responded with self-absorbed hums. Grumahu stalked stiffly past the trees, and I noticed sweat on his brow. His back must be bothering him more than he'd admit.

At the bottom of the valley we found evidence that others had, indeed, passed this way, though they must have followed the small stream, since for them there would have been no path. When it came my turn to vault the stream, I made damned sure not to land in the muddy verge on the other side, then knelt with Imlaud and Grumahu to examine the kill.

I recognized it as some kind of deer, but I had not seen one with the black stripe down its backbone or the tight, twisted antlers of this doe. Grumahu called Imlaud's attention to the thin shaft protruding from the carcass's shoulder, and the warden nodded. 'Yes, I saw it. Umlisi, probably. The poison must have made the poor creature mad with thirst, and she wandered down here for water.'

The Walking Thunder scratched reflectively. 'Didn't know any of the Umlisi were this far south.'

'The Umlisi are a tribe?' I asked.

Imlaud nodded. 'The name means Mud-Heads. No one knows what they call themselves, but this is the way others refer to them.'

'Fierce little bastards,' Grumahu ruminated. 'Wouldn't want to run into them.'

Imlaud looked faintly disapproving. 'They are a very ancient people who guard themselves well from outsiders. It is true they are not friendly, and they do not follow the Way. Still, they have no traffic with Oaxacu either, so they cannot be accounted enemies.'

Grumahu grinned and spat out of the gap between his teeth. 'Unless you come between them and their kill.'

We moved away from there in a hurry after that, Imlaud forcing the pace a little. 'Isn't going to do him any good to walk faster if Umlisi are after us,' the Walking Thunder muttered to me. 'You saw the print?'

I nodded. Someone with a very small foot had forded the creek *since* the rain. That being so, there was only one reason that person would not have begun butchering the deer. I looked around as unobtrusively as possible. 'Hear anything?' I asked the giant.

'No. But you never do,' he said certainly. 'Wrap your cloak round your neck, Runt Mage, and let the end of it trail down. Favorite spot to bury one of their rotten darts. Baskets will protect our backs; it's everything else we need to worry about.' He pulled some leaves off trees as we marched quickly after Imlaud. 'Tuck the tail of your cloak inside the band of your kilt, then stuff it with these. Might be enough padding to stop a dart.'

'It sounds as though you've met up with the Umlisi before.'

'No, only come along afterwards.' He was so grim that the Yoriandirkin walking ahead and behind us looked at one another, and then began to copy our motions. They were so rattled that I don't think any of them remembered to ask the trees' permission to take the leaves. At a time like that you tend to forget the niceties.

What with the heat, the rain, the mismin attack, and the nervous apprehension of wondering whether any fierce little man with a poisoned arrow was suddenly going to pop out of the trees, we were all more than happy when Imlaud led us up the hillside and we broke through into a grove of the familiar nling-ling trees. 'Excellent!' the warden exclaimed. Courteously he kenned our intention to share the grove for the night, and the perfumed trees murmured delightedly, expressing surprise that any two-leggeds should speak to them.

I spoke before Imlaud could: *Are other two-leggeds about, Sweet Dews?*

A few, Mage. Those little ones with the odd-color faces.

'Paint,' Imlaud explained in an aside to me, then added to

Grumahu, 'She says the Umlisi are about, as thee thought.'

'Huh. Better ask the tree if we can sleep up there, then.'

At first I thought he was joking, but Imlaud was already kenning the question to the nling-lings. The trees answered with lovely, roundabout phrases that boiled down to everybody being welcome to climb up carefully, but that they did not think any of their branches would hold the biggest two-legged. Imlaud argued earnestly that Grumahu had been an apprentice mage at one time (a nice touch, I thought, and all but true), and he would be very careful.

'Taking so long?' the giant wanted to know.

I put it as delicately as I could. 'They're a little worried about getting hurt.'

He looked down. 'Oh. Wouldn't do that.' The big man fiddled with his sword. 'Tell them I wasn't going up anyway. Somebody's got to stay down here with the packs, or there won't be anything left of them by morning.'

I dismissed this with a gesture and turned my kenning to the trees: *Sweet Dews, this biggest one is surely not a bigger threat than a small storm, yet thee's stood many a year in the wind. Could not one of thee undertake to bear him? He will be hurt if singled out for thy displeasure.*

I had thought they might share the characteristic of quick sympathy in common with the females of other species, and it proved true. A nling-ling nearby said in a sweet, low voice, *Master Almost-Mage may perch in my branches*. She rustled to show which one of the trees she was.

I nudged the giant. 'That one's spoken for you specially. She sounds nice. "Master Almost-Mage" she's named you.'

He'd been Bai Nati's man too long to be surprised at the dialogue, but I did notice a slight reddening of his face. 'Said I have to mind the packs.'

'The packs will come up with us, and you damned well know it, so quit mucking around,' I growled. 'I'm hungry, and I don't much fancy being caught on the ground.'

The Yoriandirkin were already passing up their baskets

to others already in the trees of the grove. Walking Thunder looked around. 'Oh, cacamalu, all right. Which one's yours?'

'That one, next to yours. The branches interweave, so if anything happens, I should be able to cross over them.' In truth, I didn't think any such thing because the branches looked very limber to me and I didn't think they'd bear a man's weight near the end of them. But I had to get him into that damned tree somehow.

Without another word he walked to the foot of my nling-ling and waited. I went over, unslung my basket, put my foot in his hands and he vaulted me up into the branches. I apologized to the tree at my hasty alighting, she tittered a little, and Grumalu handed me up my pack. 'Cakes and pilchu in the gourd. Too bad we can't heat it, but the trees would be too afraid of a fire, I suppose.'

'Not to be thought of,' I agreed. 'Thanks for the pilchu. Hot or cold, I like it. Get yourself up now, will you?'

His tree now fully sympathetic to her two-legged, she ducked her stoutest bough a little to make it easier for him, and even allowed him to haul his pack up on a rope. A few moments later, I marked him peering through the leaves at me. 'All right over there? Got enough to eat?'

'Fine. You've packed enough for a full crew. Have *you* got enough?'

'Like a couple of these nling-ling fruits, if mistress can spare them.'

I kenned his request, and the tree dropped two into his hands.

'Thanks. Listen, when you've done eating, be sure to put your pack basket across the branches beneath you.'

'I'd thought of that. Relax. We're as well off as we're going to be for the night. The trees will warn us if any of the Umlisi come near,' I told him, 'and Imlaud's folk have their bows.'

I knew from his silence that he was unconvinced, but I

was tired enough to take the time on trust. The tree and I exchanged some chat, then I made myself as comfortable as possible – helped by the nling-ling, who insisted that she really didn't mind moving this branch so, and that one a little this way – and fell into a light sleep.

I was awakened in the night by the music of a flute, a quiet, monotonous piping coming in no song that I could follow, only runs of sighing notes and then silence. My first thought as I surfaced out of sleep was that Grumahu had taken leave of his senses and might as well shout out our location. Then, as I readied a blasting mind-yell to him to knock it off, I realized in the same moment that my nling-ling had a gentle securing limb about me and that the piping wasn't coming from the neighboring tree.

Imlaud, is that a bird?

Nay, Kinu. Umlisi, outside the grove.

A second pipe began to play nearly opposite this side of the grove.

'Awake, Runt Mage?' came a soft whisper.

I kenned, *Of course I'm awake. Those little bastards out there are good at tactics, aren't they?*

'Huh. Wish they'd learn some new songs, though.'

Aye. Quiet, now. He stopped whispering as a third flute joined the first two. It was not long before we were ringed with small piping sounds in the pitch darkness. It was more unnerving than drums and purposeful chanting would have been, because the Mud-Heads had a knack for knowing just when you were about to drowse off again. Then a flute would sound its note from somewhere round the circle outside the grove. The nling-lings murmured sleepily about it, but darts were no threat to them, so they merely rustled a little, assured us that the little men were not in the grove and went quiet once more.

I think it was probably only after the welcome grayness of pre-dawn light penetrated the grove that most of us slept at all. Somehow, the fluting wasn't so bad with the approach of daylight. That relaxation of vigilance could have cost us dearly, but nothing untoward happened, except that when the dawn breeze came up, the Umlisi increased the volume of their 'music' to greet it. I cursed, buried one ear in the shoulder of my cloak, and snatched a few more minutes of sleep.

What woke us all, sweating and starting, was the cry.

It pierced the chorus of bird calls, a sharp, bitten-off cry that came from some distance away. So compelling was the sound of that agony that I wriggled free of my nling-ling's protective limb and was about to climb higher to find a vantage before I recollected that it might be a trick designed to flush us from cover. I froze with one hand to the trunk and the other gripping the hilt of my sword, praying that the rustling I had made might be taken for the natural tossing of the branches in the breeze.

Imlaud kenned an odd thing: he asked the trees to make the tao-chi, the 'way of the air', as nearly as I understood it. At once, my nling-ling began to weave her branch ends with those of Grumahu's tree, and as I looked about, I saw that the network of boughs was forming pathways among the trees of the grove. The green wardens ran lightly across these narrow bridges thirty or forty feet above the ground, scattering to the outside ring of trees, where they took up stations with their bows.

Imlaud himself appeared in Grumahu's tree, showed his head at the opening of the leaves for an instant, and kenned, *Come over, Kinu. The nling-lings will undertake to bear thee.*

I looked down, and I shouldn't have done that. Taking a breath to steady myself and telling myself it was no worse than rigging sail on the mainmast, I stood up on the thick bough my tree extended, clutched a branch above for balance, and shuffled out the length of it until I reached the interwoven twig tips. There was a tricky bit where the 'bridge' bounced disconcertingly, but I trusted the warden's word and crossed it. I think I wasn't supposed to have seen, but Grumahu let out his held breath when I was safely on the other side. I grinned and made the horizontal hand wave, and he shook his head, busily digging in his pack to come up with a couple of curled and crisp cakes. Even stale, they tasted good.

Imlaud was peering along the tao-chi, checking in with his archers. 'Do they see any Umlisi?' I asked, accepting a swig from Grumahu's water gourd.

The warden carefully let the branches he had been holding back fall closed. 'No.' Grumahu silently offered him a corner of a cake, but he declined, asking the tree for a fruit instead. All around us, beyond the circle of Yoriandir archers taking their frugal breakfast, the piping of the Mud-Head flutes whistled through the bird calls and twittering.

The giant took a gulp of water to wash down the last of his cake, corked his gourd, and wiped the back of his hand across his mouth. 'Got an idea. You stay here,' he ordered me, and before I could stop him, he climbed down the tree.

'Grumahu!' I called in a hoarse whisper, preparing to go after him.

Imlaud put a hand on my arm. 'Wait, Kinu. Let us see what our large friend has in his large head.'

I shook him off, stood up on the tao-chi, and began tailing the giant across the grove. Grumahu was taking his time to move from tree trunk to tree trunk, always out of the patches of sunlight, always with a stout nling-ling bole between himself and the outer edge of the grove. At first I thought he was exercising caution and mentally applauded, but then I realized he was listening for the fluting, homing in on one flute in particular, and he was having to wait for its occasional notes to guide him. He was trying to locate the last flute we had heard join in the Mud-Heads' band.

'Left a little,' I called down.

'Know that. Shut up.'

It was a good thing he wasn't really my servant, I

reflected, crossing another of the bouncing twig-tip bridges to keep up with him as he slanted left where the grove began to thin, the nling-lings interspersed with other trees now. A Yoriandir archer turned his head to me, nodded, and I took up a station beside him. This was as far as I could go on the tao-chi.

We watched as the giant eased round a tree trunk, sword drawn. Taking a look around, he crouched, fingered some sign in the leaf mold that the Yoriandir and I could not see from our vantage, and stood up. He abandoned caution and walked into the forest. *Giant, get your arse back here!*

We heard his sword hack at something, and I was almost fifteen feet down the tree when Grumahu reappeared, blade casually over his shoulder, holding up something small. 'Wind flute,' he called. 'Tied in the bushes. Neat trick, eh?'

I sent my sword to quiver in the turf, dropped down beside it, and went to meet him. The Yoriandirkin tumbled out of the branches like green apples. I snorted, examining the notched reed. When I held it up to catch the wind through the barrel, a low fluting note emerged. 'Well done,' I saluted our adversary. I looked up at Grumahu. 'How many of them do you think there actually were?'

'Only the one. Tracks are clear enough.'

Our eyes met. 'The scream came from that direction,' I said, turning to scan the trees.

'Right,' the giant agreed, and Imlaud flashed a hand signal to his men. We fanned out, each man staying within sight of the people on his right and left, and began to search. The tracking was quick enough; under cover of night and with us safely treed, the Umlisi had used a fairly well-trodden game trail, probably the deer track leading down the hillside to the stream. To save the tao-ti from wearing itself out needlessly, Imlaud signaled his team in, and we began to trot. Grumahu caught my eye and reminded me by a gesture to keep my cloak wound about my neck. It might, after all, be an ambush, more of the Mud-Heads waiting for their scout to lead us onto their spears and bows.

The trap had been perfectly placed. Only Grumahu's superior hearing kept us from running right up on it, and even then he had to grab Imlaud's arm and haul him back. I suppose if the tethered fawn had not suddenly bounded to its feet at our approach, we'd have been caught as neatly as the Umlisi had been, and tumbled into the pit on top of him.

The giant clamped a hand on the warden's shoulder, forcing him to crouch. 'He's alive, I can hear him moving. Show your head, he'll put a dart in your face. Jag'har trap. Cat-soldiers get pelts for uniforms this way.'

The fawn was trembling, its long knobby legs twitching. *Peace, little Bounding Hoof*, I told it, and it turned its head to study me with one large dark eye, but did not answer.

Imlaud was kenning to the man in the pit. *Peace, friend Umlisi. We know thee's hurt and want to help, but we are afraid of thy arrows. Will put down thy bow?*

A shaft whizzed into a tree above the pit for answer.

'Keep back,' I told them quietly. 'I have an idea. Grumahu, do you have your salt pouch still? Good. I have some kalan-kalan leaves here. Now, please, don't show yourself, Giant. You'll scare the hell out of him, and if you scare him, I'm dead.' I moved before he could figure it out and raise a row.

Hiding my knife, I went in a crouch round the tree at the foot of the pit. The fawn flicked its long ears at me and started a little when it saw me suddenly appear. *Be easy, little one. I'm only going to untie the rope so thee can go free*, I told it, making sure to direct my mental voice at the Umlisi as well. I wanted him to see this and know what I was doing.

The knot was stubborn, the frantic little creature having pulled it tight, and finally I had to help the strands part with the blade, which I showed to the Umlisi, but not to the fawn. When the last tough strand of vine rope parted, I stroked the delicate neck and poured out a little salt as a treat for the fawn. It nuzzled my leg a moment, stamped once, and splayed its feet to lick the salt. I raised my eyes to look over the edge of the pit.

The little man's blue eyes were cloudy with pain, and shock had left him pale even under the terra-cotta colored paint that covered his face and neck. His blond hair must have stood up proudly in quills before his sweat had loosened the bird lime. I looked down at the first pale skin apart from my own that I had seen in this land, and then my eyes traveled to the bronze jaws of the trap that had bitten nearly clean through his lower leg. I think it was only then I realized that the short bow was bent, and that he was holding it reasonably steady. I froze.

Master Umlisi, I am no cat-soldier, as thee sees, and the folk with me are tree wardens from beyond the swamplands. Thee's in a bad situation here. Will thee not trust us? The fawn butted against my knee for more salt.

I really thought he was going to fire when I saw his fingers move, but then I saw with immense relief that he was easing off the string. The bow went slack, and he unnotched his dart. I smiled and moved a step to go down and help him.

The Umlisi reversed the dart and stuck it in his own neck. His body convulsed, the breath left him with an explosive sigh, and then he lay still in the pool of blood at the bottom of the pit.

[illegible]

[illegible]

[illegible]

[illegible]

[illegible]

[illegible]

CHAPTER NINE

'Kinu.' Grumahu had to say my name twice before I heard him. I was crouching on the edge of the pit, Imlaud beside me.

I shook my head. 'I should have realized that's what he'd do.'

The giant shook my shoulder again. 'Look up, will you, Runt Mage? We've got a problem.'

When I followed where he was pointing, I saw nothing at first. Then the breeze caught the red pennant. I traced the rope down the tree to the bronze trap. 'So whoever set this knows it's been tripped.'

'Right. Won't let a valuable cat chew its paw off, either. They'll be coming soon. Should go.'

The tree wardens were a well-disciplined troop. At Imlaud's nod, three of them moved out up the trail as sentries, while several more took up guard positions off the trail, protecting our flanks. The odds were that the cat-soldiers would use the easier trail to come down from the hill fort that must crown this height, but it was just possible they'd approach through the woods.

Meanwhile, Grumahu pulled the peg that secured the chain of the trap, motioned back the two Yoriandir who made to go down into the pit, and went down himself to prise open the bronze jaws single-handedly. There had been no discussion among us, because there had been no question. The Umlisi would not be left for the cat-soldiers, not even dead.

The giant lifted the little man carefully and laid him on the matting that had covered the pit. 'No, give me that,' he said as I bent to pull out the dart and throw it back down into the pit so that none of our men would step on it by accident. While the Yoriandirkin wrapped the Umlisi in his funeral mat, the big man put the trap back in the bottom of the pit. He left it sprung, but slipped the dart along the chain, just where someone would pick it up. None of the wardens noticed what he had done, but I did, and I approved wholeheartedly.

The fawn was watching from a covert not far away. While Imlaud directed his folk in brushing out our tracks, I walked over to Bounding Hoof. *Thy dam is not coming*, I said as gently as I knew how. *And thee cannot follow us, little one, as far as we are going. Thee knows the grove of Sweet Dews yonder? Go there, and do not stray far from the trees till thee's grown. Tell them the mage sent thee*. It was as much as I could do.

By the time I had seen her on her way, Grumahu was standing with his fists on his hips waiting for me, but he said nothing when I rejoined the group. Two of the Yoriandirkin picked up the body in the mat, another two stayed behind to wipe away our trail, and Imlaud spoke to the tao-ti. We hastened away from the pit, the lookouts falling in as a rearguard.

Not a moment too soon. We were no more than a quarter of a mile on the path when the urgent mind-whisper came from the rearguard: cat-soldiers at the pit. Imlaud raised his hand to stop us all lest some stray sound should carry through the trees. The Yoriandirkin sat down upon their packs to wait. Grumahu rubbed his nose and looked at me blandly, but he was anticipating the news as much as I was.

One of the cat-soldiers goes down into the pit, a sentry reported.

Imlaud gave it a couple of minutes. *Well?*

The soldier has not come out of the pit, and now another

has gone down there too. Their leader looks angry. He is shouting now.

I smiled at Grumahu and winked. The big man nearly broke a grin, but then his eyes went to the rolled mat, and the satisfaction died out of his face. 'Cacamalu,' he grated quietly. He struck Imlaud on the arm and silently pointed.

Blood was dripping from the mat.

The Yoriandir warden struck his hand against a tree trunk in a rare display of anger, then kenned to his rearguard to hold the cat-soldiers as long as they could if they should pick up our trail. 'Bind the wound tightly and leave the mat here,' he ordered tersely.

Grumahu ripped the strip of material that held the dried poultice to his back. 'Here, use this.' His knife flashed to cut away the mat.

'I'm sorry, lord, I don't understand,' one of the mat bearers was telling Imlaud as they quickly uncovered the body. 'I did bind the wound, as thee sees, and we made sure to hold the Umlisi's feet higher than his head so that the body would not drip.'

There was something about the bandage they had tied, something about . . . that explosion of air . . .

'Kinu, what is it?' Imlaud asked in a low voice.

'He isn't dead.'

They have found thy trail, Lord Imlaud! Fly!

'Have to leave him,' Grumahu said to me, ignoring my statement as just another of my peculiar spells. He hauled me to my feet, but I chopped a blow at his forearm, not enough to damage, just to stun the nerves for a moment. The giant stared blackly, numbed fingers trying to seize his hilt.

'Look!' I said. 'None of that blood has clotted, it's all fresh. That's not how a corpse bleeds.' Heedless of my danger, I gestured Grumahu down again. 'You've the best hearing.'

Glowering, he put an ear to the little man's streaked chest.

For several moments he did not stir while the Yoriandirkin looked at each other nervously, and Imlaud listened to the reports from his rearguard. One of the men went down with a mind-shriek terrible to hear, and the leader of the wardens paled.

'Right, alive,' Grumahu reported. 'Loses more blood, he won't be, though. Put compresses on that,' he directed brusquely to the green litter bearers.

I dropped my gourd of spring water by them and followed Grumahu back through the trees at a run, our swords in our hands. I heard Imlaud assign a couple of archers to stay with the wounded man for protection against prowling jag'hars, and then the Yoriandirkin were closing the gap behind.

'No survivors,' I instructed the giant.

'Know that,' he said impatiently. 'Others in the fort, though.'

I glanced back. The tao-ti was closing behind Imlaud, so even if they got past us, the cat-soldiers would have a hard time following the blood trail.

They might have been drunks and thieves at this outpost, as Grumahu had said, but they kept their wits when the first rain of arrows whizzed through the trees, scrambling to flatten behind a huge downed trunk off the deer trail. From here they kept up steady fire, and they were fair bowmen. Another of the Yoriandirkin was hit, the shaft impaling his hand to the tree where he had his perch. He clamped his lips on the cry, and his mates pulled him free and propped him in the tree while they continued firing.

I tapped Imlaud's shoulder. *Flank them*, I told him. *Drive them to flee up the path towards the fort. Grumahu and I will deal with them.*

Imlaud nodded.

I opened a branching tao-ti, and the giant and I made our way up the deer trail towards the fort. When I judged we were out of bowshot of our own forces, we stood sheltered by trees and waited, one to either side of the path.

Thee's ready, Kinu? Imlaud sent.

Aye. How many are left?

Four or five, I think, but we will be able to pick off a couple as they break for the path.

'As many as five headed this way,' I told the giant. He spat through the gap in his teeth, raised his sword in a two-handed grip and poised.

Now! I kenned to Imlaud.

We heard the additional twang of bowstrings, an outraged bellow from one of the cat-soldiers, and then they sensibly took to their heels. They were running bent over and flat out by the time they reached us. Grumahu crushed the skull of the first, and I beheaded the second before the other two were even aware they were under fresh attack. It was not much of a skirmish, and it made me feel sad and dirty. We cleaned our blades and went back to Imlaud's group. 'Let's get out of here,' I said to him.

'Minute,' the giant said. He hopped down into the pit, rummaged around until he extracted the Umlisi's dart, quiver, and bow, and handed them up to me. 'No sense making trouble for the Mud-Heads,' he explained as he levered himself out of the hole.

The tao-ti opened back to the place where we had left our rescued little man. We followed it, supporting the injured men. The man with the shaft through his hand would be well enough, but the other was hit in the neck, a serious proposition. I walked beside him as others carried him, and kept a compress torn from my cloak pressed against the wound, while Grumahu took up the rear, listening for any commotion from the fort.

They took us completely unawares. I heard one of the men up front grunt, and then there was a hail of darts raining into our ranks. The litter bearers went down, the man with the neck injury cried out as he was dropped, and I found myself looking down our fallen line across the still form of the Umlisi we had rescued from the trap into the intelligent brown eyes of a Mud-Head with crisp chestnut-colored curly hair. Grumahu leaped in front of me with a roar and seemed to run into a tree bole, for he dropped on his face. *If thee's hurt my friends* . . . I said to those calmly watching eyes.

'Marner,' he said clearly, and then he raised his bow and shot me.

At some indefinable time I became aware of the lapping of water, a chill breeze blowing dankly in my face, and dim silhouettes around me, small men leaning on their bows, alert but not apparently alarmed. They spoke in quiet voices, only a word or two at a time in a language I did not understand, though my head seemed so stuffed with wool I wasn't sure I was capable of understanding anything anyway. There was an almost overpowering smell of pitch.

I rolled my head to the sound of muffled snoring next to me, and relief washed through me in a wave, though he was bound and gagged. Somehow if Grumahu was all right, things could not be so bad.

One of the Umlisi nudged another, and I saw his head tilt towards me. The second crouched over the giant's bulk, his eyes a faint sheen in the dimness. 'Sleep, Mage. No time – not time for be awake now,' he whispered in barely intelligible Anazi.

My tongue felt swollen. 'Not tired.' That was a lie; I was weighted with sleep like a net with anchor stones, but I have an aversion to being asleep while any man is standing over me with a bow.

He clicked his tongue impatiently and said something over his shoulder to the other man. I recognized the shape of a gourd bottle when he pressed it into my tingling fingers, but I couldn't summon enough co-ordination to pull the stopper. It was probably poison anyway. The Umlisi must have known what I was thinking, because he took the bottle back, wrenched out the stopper, and let me see him take a swallow. Then he held it out to me. 'Thirst?'

I fumbled for it and managed to get enough to wet my lips. Most of it watered my ear. 'Thanks anyway,' I told him, my voice emerging a rusty-sounding croak.

At once he put a hand over my mouth, pressing lightly. 'Shh! Not to make . . . um . . . make loud.'

I nodded against his hand, and he withdrew it. I had to know what he was looking at so anxiously. Gathering myself, I hunched up on an elbow. So quickly that I never saw his hands move, the other man notched an arrow and had his bow fully bent on me, hissing a warning to my water carrier.

'*Pei!*' my man whispered hoarsely, flinging himself between me and the bowman, arms outstretched. All three of us froze, and so did the other dark shapes around us. I was aware of the dull thumping of my heart, of Grumahu's snores, of the sudden sweat that gleamed on my water man's half-averted cheek. 'Hyssop, pei!' he repeated urgently, following this with something rapid and guttural.

My arm was twitching with weakness, but I didn't dare move even to lie down again. I watched the tip of the dart.

The archer suddenly made a sound of impatient disgust and swung up his bow, releasing the tension. He snarled something that sounded like a curse and turned his back on us.

I let my breath out with a sigh and, as slowly as I could, lowered my head once more. My man swallowed and looked down at me. 'I just wanted to see where we were,' I whispered in explanation.

He regarded me with an expression I couldn't read in the dimness. All I could really see was the poise of his head. He nodded after a moment, and his hand lifted to beckon me up.

I got as far as a sitting position, but the horizon kept swinging as though I were on deck in a heavy swell, so I contented myself with merely leaning against the bulwark at my back and looking over. That we were on a boat I already knew, but I wanted to know what kind of craft this was, and what I could see of the passing shoreline.

'Powers, it's a cave!' The whisper escaped me before I could check it. The surface of the water was only inches below my semi-reclining position; I was on some sort of raft or shallow-drafted barge, and to either side arched far walls of stone. These gave back a faint echo, the gurgling of our slow passage magnified, and I could see why the Umlisi kept themselves so quiet. The barge was powered by a stiffish wind blowing from our backs, a dark sail showing as a curved billow above my head. There was a tow rope, too; I traced it from the iron ring at the bow down into the water, but the odd thing was that it did not seem to angle towards either shore where I should have expected to hear the clopping of the draft animal's hooves. Instead, the rope led straight ahead. I squinted, but I could see no vessel ahead of us, nor did I hear the splash of any oars. 'What's pulling us?' I asked the water man.

His eyes swung to me, and he shook his head. I didn't know whether he meant, don't talk now, it makes too much noise; or, I don't know; or, I'm not about to explain it to a prisoner. Maybe the answer was all three.

'Where are you taking us?'

This, it seemed, he would answer: 'Go Il Numator,' he whispered.

My head was beginning to pound. He'd been right when he counseled more sleep. I put a hand to my temple. 'Il Num—?'

'Hyssop, aya!' one of the Umlisi nearby suddenly said, and everybody whirled to look where he was pointing.

'Hyssop!' came another urgent low call from the stern. 'Aya!' He was pointing at the opposite shore.

I held my head and looked ashore. At first I could see nothing but a faint break in the grayness where the cavern met the water. But then I saw the brief wink of eyes, eyes like the flicker of distant heat lightning, and terror shot through me. 'Walkers!'

All around me the Umlisi were quickly fitting into place overlapping panels of wood, raising a sort of wooden tent over our heads. In order to do this, they had to lower the sail; I heard the creak of a pulley, and then the yards of dark cloth billowed down around us while the last of the protective shields went up. The boat's forward motion decreased a bit, but we still made headway, so we were definitely being towed by some much bigger craft ahead.

The bulwarks had gone up not a moment too soon. Something thudded off the one above my head, and then another thud came from the other side of the barge. The Umlisi who had nearly killed me with his bow stepped to the viewing port that had been built into one of the shields. This seemed to be made of glass, and I thought it ingenious to have a port, but dangerous to have covered it with glass if the missiles from the walkers were as heavy as they sounded.

I struggled to my feet. 'Can I have a look, mates?'

To my surprise, they made way for me. The port was set at their height, so I crouched and peered through. 'What are they hitting us with?'

My water man, whose name was Barberry if I had understood them correctly, held up a dart for answer. 'But be bone here,' he told me, indicating the arrowhead.

I nodded. Once he said it, I knew it was right, as though I remembered it from some other life. 'And walkers can't cross water, right?'

'Can't. But can . . . um . . . put net – net, eh? – net in water catch us. Then spirit trap waiting.'

The pounding in my head got much worse, but it wasn't from the drugged barb with which they'd shot me back in the forest. It was from fear. A pain had knotted my right hand in a cramp, and I raised it before my face as though it belonged to someone else, someone who'd had one of those bone points go through it once, just there, where the ring finger met the palm . . .

Suddenly out of the darkness on the other side of the viewing port fangs leaped at me, fangs and wings and jet-bead eyes. I jumped back, stumbled in the folds of sailcloth, and went down heavily, rocking the barge. 'That was no damned arrow!'

'Erechthoi!' Hyssop called warningly.

'Be bats,' Barberry turned from the window to tell me.

'That was no bat,' I said positively. 'Its bloody head filled the porthole!'

No one paid me any attention now, however. Instead, the Umlisi were jumping to what must have been their assigned stations, some making haste to fold the sail out of the way so that no one else would get fouled in it as I had done, and some forming two ranks down the sides of the boat – this with difficulty because Grumahu and the sleeping Yoriandirkin were blocking most of the deck. Hyssop, who seemed to be the leader among them, flipped up the lid on a box built into the bow and began passing objects over his shoulder to the two waiting lines. The men handed them rapidly down the lines to two stations amidships. Because it was so dark inside the shields, I could only see what they were passing when they were right in front of me.

I gestured for one, and without breaking the rhythm Barberry handed one to me. By touch I explored it. As nearly as I could tell, it was a joint of b'mbu about a foot long, stoppered with a twist of some fibrous rope or twine that seemed to be dipped in pitch. 'What—?'

A flint struck sparks down the line to my left. I craned for a view. By the small glowing light of a wick, I could see one of the men crouching in a slate-lined pit, like those sometimes used by daring or foolhardy captains to provide a fire for the men on voyages in cold seas. The dwarves rely on flotjin rather than open flame to warm the watch, and as a result they very rarely lose a ship to fire, but it is not uncommon among other folk. I didn't like the idea of fire here on this small barge with walkers waiting on shore and bats swooping around our boat, but the Umlisi obviously knew what they were about, so I bit my knuckles and forced myself to stay out of their way.

The man in the pit was fitting one of the b'mbu tree sections into a cradle of some kind. When the wick flared as his mate touched it off, though, I got a clearer look. 'Auwe!' the gunner said, and the other pulled the lever. The catapult released with an airy whir, the lighted b'mbu missile arched out of sight through the firing port, and the gunner immediately slammed shut the hatch to prevent any of the bone arrows or creatures of the night from finding their way in. A moment later the firing team on the other side of the barge let go their own missile.

Even through the cracks in the shields and the limited views offered by the portholes, I saw the flaring brightness as the things hit. A moment later there was a smell of pungent smoke, sharp with resin, and echoing from both shores the sound of hoarse coughing and snarls of rage. Hyssop nodded with satisfaction, straightening from one of the viewing ports.

The barge stopped dead in the water.

I was on my feet before I remembered the bulwarks were made for much shorter men. It might have been funny, except that I instinctively tried to duck away from the hatch and so wound up belting myself a mean one just over the deep scar in my head. I groaned and dropped like a sack of cabbages, huddling on the sailcloth and rocking with pain, while gem-colored rockets arched over the sand floor of my mind and exploded in myriad rainbow sparks of fire that winked out as they sifted down, leaving naught but a charcoal ash on the swept sand.

Hyssop spared me a glance, smiled maliciously, and then stooped to uncover a bright lantern. I closed my eyes against it, but a moment later it dimmed, and I risked a squint. He'd put the lantern into some kind of revolving metal holder that must have been highly polished on the inside, because from the crack between the holder and the bow I could see a brilliantly white light streaming ahead of us to push back the darkness. It was very like a signal beacon or a miniature lighthouse. My estimation of these Umlisi warriors went up another notch. Grumahu might have thought them savages, but judging from the sophistication of their devices, they were far from the primitives I had expected.

The Umlisi leader was looking ahead of us for a net, I guessed, as he peered intently forward and put one hand on the towline. Now that I could see this better, I noted that it was not the rope I had thought, but rather a stout metal cable. Whatever had been towing us must be a monstrous big boat to haul so much weight, and I wondered why its crew had not fired some rockets of their own to make our passage safer.

At last Hyssop nodded to himself, selected a pane of what seemed to be amber glass (though I could hardly credit this, glass being precious enough to make this one sizeable pane worth a middling inn's income for a half year), and slipped the flat sheet vertically into a frame fitted before the lantern. The searchlight out over the water turned to a pure yellow, and at once the barge moved cautiously ahead. Hyssop kept his hand on the towline, shielding himself against a dart out of the dark shore by crouching a little behind the searchlight's metal housing. Still, it was a dangerous position.

'He should be wearing a pot helmet,' I muttered, feeling my throbbing scalp for blood. There was a smear on my fingers when I brought them before my eyes, but I judged the cut couldn't be too bad, a scrape at most, or the bleeding would have been much worse. Holding to the mast for support, I managed to sit up.

One of the other Umlisi nudged my arm, and I found he was offering a gourd bottle. I unstoppered it and tilted it to my lips thankfully. To my surprise and delight it was mead, and damned good mead, too. I took a second, longer draft, and wiped my hand across the mellow tang it left on my lips. 'Thanks, mate. Owe ye one.' As he did not seem to understand, I nodded in friendly fashion, tapped the gourd, and smacked my lips. 'Good stuff, this.'

His expression cleared, and he nodded in turn.

My brain did a slow turn, still recovering from the effect of the drug and now of the thump. 'Powers, *mead*!' I leaned towards him, forgetting their bows, forgetting everything else in my urgent need to know. 'Where did you get this? Is there a port at the end of this waterway, eh? A port, d'ye understand? A place with a lot of foreign sailors, people who look like me?' He was absolutely blank, my tumbling words obviously meaning nothing to him. I seized the gourd and held it up. '*Where get?*'

Barberry's small arm came between us, restraining me. I shook the gourd in his face, the mead gurgling. 'Barberry, where did this come from?'

He took the gourd from me very deliberately and handed it back to the man who had offered me his ration. Then my water man raised a thumb and jerked it towards the bow. 'Home. Il Numator,' he said as if it should have been obvious even to a mage who didn't know enough to pass out when he was supposed to and stay asleep until they had him safely imprisoned.

'Yes, all right. I guessed it came from your port city,' I said impatiently. 'But where did your folk trade for it? There must have been a ship with sailors who weren't from Il Numator, right?'

'Pei, no strangers at home. Be only us there. Never any strangers for long time ago.' He touched the bottle. 'Umlisi make honey-drink. Bee folk share.'

I gave it up, my head throbbing. Bugger it. I'd see this

Il Numator of theirs soon enough anyway, and then, by the Four, no pack of little painted men would stop me from getting a berth with an outbound ship. Well, after I set things to rights in the Forbidden City, anyway.

Be serious, mate. Ye'll never leave this mucking land alive, and ye know it, my dark voice said. *And even if ye did, ye wouldn't have a clue where to go, would ye?*

My eyes stung for a moment. I told myself it was just because my head pained so badly. 'Could I have another sip of that mead, Barberry, just for old time's sake?' I don't think he understood any word but mead, but that was enough. Moodily I slugged down another swallow, nearly emptying the poor lad's bottle. 'Never get home at this rate, or if I do, me beard will be white and down to my knees,' I muttered. 'And her asleep all this time with a babe coming and no way to wake. Powers, he'll be grown before I ever get to see him.'

Barberry leaned a little. 'What Mage say?'

'Nothing, nothing. Don't ye worry your little round head about it, matey. It's my problem, not yours. Here, have a go. We'll get roaring old drunk at this Il Numator of yours and bugger the whole mess, what d'ye say to that, eh?'

Even to me, my voice sounded thick, slurred with drink, though I'd had a relatively small amount of mead. *Concussion*, a calm voice told me steadily, a voice I almost knew. *And what are the indications for concussion? Let's see how well you remember your lessons.*

Come on, Nestor, quit mucking about. I have a whacking headache and you know it.

The indications, prentice mine. Read it from the herbal there if you can't remember.

Oh. Oh yes, the herbal. I always loved the illustrations in it much better than the text.

Your own sketches were better, my prince-medicine master told me fondly. *I always meant to speak to Master about letting you make us a new book, but there was never time in those days.*

Those days.

Aye, Aeng—

There was the sound of wings and a thin, high screech suddenly right next to my ear. Before I had comprehended, Barberry cried out some word of warning and tackled me to the side, using all his wiry strength to drag me a couple of feet from the mast. Hyssop had whirled round at Barberry's shout. He snatched up a bow from the man leaning next to him in the bow, notched an arrow, and let fly down the center of the crowded barge. The bat fluttered wildly, transfixed against the mast by his dart, red mouth and fangs gaping no more than an arm's length from my face. There was more than animal ferocity in its ruby eyes, there was positive malevolence, and it was glaring straight at me.

Quickly I threw down a cross-hatching of charcoal, my arm tracing surely above the sands of my mind, a net, a net to hold it, no, a net for us, meant for us*!*

'Stop, Hyssop!' I shouted, my arm coming up to point. 'They've laid a net!'

Miraculously, Barberry understood immediately. '*Thangoi!*'

To give him credit, Hyssop stared for only a split second, and I read that look for what it was: could he trust the lives of his men to the tallfolk stranger? Whatever he saw in my face must have decided him, because he yanked the amber pane out of the searchlight and dropped a red one in its place, heedless of dropping the yellow glass. I had no time to be amazed that the amber glass did not break before the barge halted in the river once more.

Immediately, Barberry tugged me away from the mast over towards the side of the boat. I thought for a moment the dead bat had come back to life and made a move for me, and so I moved quickly enough for all that my head was splitting. But a moment later, when they cleared away the sailcloth, I realized the men needed access to the hatch upon which I had been sitting. This hatch was built up a foot or so above the level of the deck, plenty to keep the waveless river water from flooding up through it, and now somebody lifted back the hinged cover. The b'mbu hurlers had jumped to their weapons once more, and now at a signal from Hyssop they fired simultaneously. From the outbreak of snarls and choking onshore, they had again managed to find the enemy with their smoke tubes.

Now Barberry rose from his crouch by me and quickly stripped off his weapons and clothing: another man from the other side of the barge did the same. Each holding a dagger in his teeth, they let themselves down through the hatch into the black water. The men in the boat waited tensely. Hyssop centered the searchlight a little to make the work easier. I watched the bat's blood drip into the river.

'Is there anything in there that could hurt them?' I questioned a man next to me in a low tone.

'Cold,' he answered.

Of course, I thought. It would be, here underground, here in Earth-Below.

When Barberry's head broke the surface in the middle of the hatch, all of us drew nearly as big a breath as he did and, like him, we grinned. Then the second diver was beside him, and the mates reached to haul them both aboard. Barberry said something through chattering teeth that drew a general laugh, and even a smile from Hyssop, and then the troop's leader changed our signal lamp to yellow once more, and we moved off.

I reproached myself for drinking most of their mead, because the two lads who'd cleared the net really needed the warming liquor now. Both of them sat under a pile of the sail, shaking with cold that only gradually yielded to the warmth of the crowded barge.

Hyssop handed over the lookout's task to another man and made his way back to us. I made a place for him to crouch, and he took a silver flask from the pouch at his waist and handed it to Barberry. Hyssop asked a question (by the inflection and tone perhaps it was something like,

Better now?), and when the lads nodded, he smiled a little again and reached to grasp them both by the hair in a playful roughing up. I gathered they'd done something a little against regulations out there, something he'd seen in the lantern light, or maybe it was simply that they'd been submerged so long they'd scared him, too. Then he turned to me, and the smile left his face. Whatever he asked, there was nothing playful about it.

Barberry looked past the silver flask at me. 'Captain Hyssop say, how Mage know net in water?'

CHAPTER TEN

He was not a man to be trifled with. Besides, he treated his men well and acted as a commander should. He'd earned enough trust, but I didn't think he was going to like this. I spoke to Barberry, but I held Hyssop's eye. 'I saw it in my mind,' I told him quietly.

When my reply was translated for him, his expression remained impassive. We stared at each other for a long moment. Then he rose, pulled his arrow from the mast, and dropped the dead bat in my lap. As clearly as if he'd spoken, it was a reminder and a warning. A moment more he stood without saying anything, and then he went forward to the bow again and took up his station.

Barberry leaned to whisper, 'Be smart Mage give bat to Cockleburr.' He indicated the other diver.

'Why?'

'Be like . . . um . . . thing to bring back from fight.'

'A trophy, you mean?'

'Aye, be trophy. Also, bat good to eat and Cockleburr have wife, childs.'

'You *eat* them? Well, I suppose it is meat, after a fashion.' I tapped the other man's arm and offered the carcass gingerly, Barberry supplying the few necessary words to accompany the gift. Cockleburr smiled and nodded his thanks, and the Umlisi troop murmured approvingly. Grumahu drew a snorting breath, champed at the gag for a moment, and relaxed again into sleep.

'Big Fella sleep loud,' Barberry observed.

'Big Fella does everything loud, my friend,' I agreed. He translated that for the crew, and I could guess what they made of it by the guffaws. Hyssop quieted us with a look, and the men settled around me, stretching out their legs over the sleeping Yoriandirkin. By this I guessed we must have quite a little time yet before we reached their Il Numator, so like them I made myself as comfortable as I could, put one arm over my aching eyes, and composed myself for sleep.

Someone fell over my knees and woke me. I murmured an automatic apology for being in his way, gave him a hand up, and then rubbed my eyes. 'About time, Runt Mage. Sleep longer than anybody I've ever known.' His words were bantering, but the look in his eyes was a clear warning. Of course, he had no way of knowing that the Umlisi and I had already come to our own understanding.

'How did you get them to take off the gag?' I asked, raising a careful hand to my head. The throbbing wasn't bad, and my eyes seemed clearer than they had before.

'Chewed through it. Want to watch the little bastards, they're all edgy as a female t'ing guarding a clutch of eggs. Don't move too fast.'

'Maybe they just don't like your snoring,' I needled and sat up carefully to test my head.

There was much more light than there had been, though as I was beginning to discover, brightness in these watery halls was a highly relative thing. Right now, for instance, it was about as light as a moonlit night. Still, after the absolute blackness it was a welcome relief to be able to see the shore clearly from the porthole.

I straightened and spied Imlaud sitting on a coil of rope near the stern. *Thee's well, warden?* I kenned to him.

Well enough, save that my head hammers like Grumahu at the forge. And thee?

Fine. You missed all the excitement last night. We came

under attack from walkers on both shores. They'd dropped a net across the channel to stop us, but the Umlisi took care of it.

Ah, as long as they took care of it, I find it surpassing hard to care at the present moment.

I grinned at him. The poor bugger had probably never had a hangover in his life, while I had found myself surfacing from a good many black dreams in my time. (*How do you know that?*)

The Yoriandir raised his head. *Has thee revealed to the Umlisi that thee knows the kenning, Kinu?*

No. That's our secret until the poor fellow we got out of the cat-soldiers' trap wakes to tell them. I'm not sure they take kindly to mages at Il Numator.

Imlaud looked at me sharply, trying to focus in the silvered darkness. *Il Numator? That is where we are going?*

We're nearly there, unless I miss my guess. See how they're making the lines ready?

Il Numator! Even through the kenning, I heard the excitement. *I know not what we will find there, but once it was a name out of legend, Kinu. 'The Kingdom of Earth-Below' our old songs name it.* He met my eye. *I am amazed they take us to it. To my knowledge, no one has seen Earth-Below since my grandsire's father's time, though there was once a flourishing commerce between the Umlisi and we Yoriandirkin. Then times grew dark, and friend could not trust friend. Foul things came to make their home in the swamplands, mismin and t'ings and such, so there was not much travel back and forth, and then there was none.* He glanced at the small men around us. *The Umlisi have been a hard-pressed folk bearing the brunt of the Emperor's hatred. I myself thought they had dwindled to a small forest-dwelling tribe. I had no idea they still maintained their old ways, or I should have made it my business to seek them out ere now.*

Well, I'm still going to keep my own counsel, I told him.

Help me manage Grumahu, will you? One wrong word to someone like Captain Hyssop up there and the giant will get us all killed. They'll have marked him for a cat-soldier, no doubt.

Possibly, he agreed, *though a cat-soldier traveling in company with a mage and a troop of Yoriandirkin must be something of a novelty even by Umlisi standards. Still, I think precautions are in order.*

I swung my gaze back to Grumahu, who was regarding me impassively, having guessed what Imlaud and I were about, for he questioned, 'He all right?'

'He says he has a headache.'

'Huh. Takes Yoriandirkin a long time to say things, doesn't it?' The giant looked around, but made no move to try to rise. Unlike the troop of green wardens and myself, Grumahu had been left bound hand and foot.

I could see the burns on his wrists where he had been working the ropes. 'Don't break those,' I warned him quietly. 'There's no need, we're safe enough, and you'll only put us in a bad light if they feel threatened.'

'Sure? Took our swords and bows.'

'Wouldn't you in their place?'

'No,' he answered promptly. 'I'd have killed us out there in the woods. No sense to this, except to get information. Still sure you don't want me to break these ropes, Runt Mage?'

He was right, of course. To avoid having to answer, I rose from my crouch and straightened thankfully, working the cramped muscles in my back. The flat roof had been folded open for ventilation and light, and to allow the setting of the mainsail once more sometime while I had slept. We were making spanking speed; in fact, the combination of towline and sail drove us along so swiftly that the flat hull of the barge sent up a curling bow wave that held steady just below the level of the low deck.

By the growing light that seemed to be coming from

somewhere ahead, I could discern the tow cable stretching tautly out ahead of us. As far off the bow as I could see, however, there was no other vessel, though it seemed to me that I could hear something. I looked down at Grumahu. 'What does that sound like to you?'

The giant cocked his head. 'Humming,' he said finally. 'Like bees.'

Mead . . . *bee folk share*, Barberry had told me. But what in hell would bees find to feed on down here?

While I was still wondering about that, Barberry made his way to me across the diving hatch. 'Captain Hyssop say tell Mage and other strangers stay still, not hit bee folk.'

'That is hives that we're hearing, then?' I asked.

He nodded and went off to relay the message to Imlaud and the wardens.

'Don't like bees,' Grumahu said unexpectedly. 'Got stung once, nearly died.'

The physician in me was instantly alerted. I had seen only one other such case; I had a clear image in my mind of a child gasping in a field where goats cropped the prickles unconcernedly, and I knew this was no trifling matter. Quickly I began covering Grumahu with extra coats, sacking, anything that might deter the insects from landing on him. As always, he was stoic, but already a muscle was jumping in his firm jaw, and I saw the bunch of his biceps as he tore apart the ropes round his wrists. If Grumahu was that afraid . . .

'Barberry!' I called urgently. When he looked up and came scrambling over the hatch, I told him, 'Big Fella must not get stung by the bee folk, do you understand? It will make him very, very sick. I don't want that to happen. Tell Captain Hyssop.'

When he was gone, I turned to find Imlaud settling himself by Grumahu's side. 'I heard,' the Yoriandir warden said. 'We should begin kenning to them now, Kinu.'

I heard him begin a gentle mind-chant, but before I could

join him, Barberry returned with Hyssop's terse advice. Tell Big Fella not to move and he won't get hurt. Yes, the Umlisi thought my friend was a cat-soldier all right.

My instinct was to bellow a warning to the bees to stay clear of us, but, mindful of that first blast that had bent poor Butterfly Bark nearly to the ground, I restrained myself and matched Imlaud's quiet, almost dreamy chant. A small black shape banded with a single wide stripe of yellow zipped over my head. Grumahu made a small sound in his throat and pressed himself into the ribs of the barge.

The black bees began to investigate the barge, only a few of them at first, but then in such number they might have been working a sweet pea patch on a summer's morning. Their flights took them quite close to us, though they seemed to take little, if any, note of the Umlisi, except once or twice to land on the very rim of someone's ear. At this, the Mud-Heads grinned as though it tickled, though they were careful not to wave the bees away, I noticed. Imlaud met my eyes, but we kept up our monotonous drone of kenning.

I fixed my eyes on Grumahu and broke my kenning to the bees long enough to tell him, *Steady, lad. It will be over soon. They just want to see what we're about*. He did not dare move to nod, but he blinked, and I took that for an answer.

One of the insects landed on my ear, and despite all I had just told the giant, I flinched badly. A light voice giggled. *My, my, dearie, ain't you the ticklish one, though. A mage, too.*

Sorry, mistress, I apologized stiffly.

Mabel, Harvey, come see this one! she called. *Let's give him a buzz down his drawers, what?*

My heart sank as several more of them landed on me, and Grumahu's eyes slammed shut, whether in fear or because he'd been stung I didn't know. *By thy leave, bee folk*, Imlaud's calm voice said in my mind, *we'd appreciate thy not teasing this large one here. He has great fear, and we would wish harm neither to thee nor to him.*

Belatedly, I remembered Bai Nati's teaching the night he opened my ears and lips in the Way. *Dew-Sippers*, I said, calling the bees by their true-name, *thee's seen we mean no harm and are here with the Umlisi. Would let us pass now?*

Oh, piffle, Mage, can't you take a joke? I swear, mages are the somberest, most unlaughful folk!

You're right, Isabelle, another voice chimed in busily. *Why, only the other day I was chatting with Hank from over at Nearer Here Than There Hive – you remember him, he's such a kidder, black with a gold band round his middle? That's the one – and Hank says, Louella, he says . . .*

The silence when they left us was deafening. 'Are you all right, Giant?'

'They gone?'

'Yes. You can come out from under the sack now. Are you all right?' I demanded.

Powers be thanked that he didn't nod, because one of the Dew-Sippers was crawling out of the sacking under his chin. The giant felt it and froze, and a moment later it buzzed off to join the others. His sigh was eloquent with relief. 'Don't like bees.'

'That's too bad,' I told him, 'because a couple of them thought you were really cute.'

Imlaud's fir-green eyes were dancing. 'Louella?'

'And Hank, you remember him, the black one with the, the . . .' By that time we were both sputtering with laughter. I had never seen Imlaud laugh before, and it was as much that as the chat of the insects that made me laugh until I had to wipe my eyes.

From across the boat Barberry grinned and called, 'Bee folk pretty funny, eh?'

Imlaud regained his composure. 'Indeed, Master Umlisi, they are that. Entertainment fit for a king's hall, I warrant.'

From the expression on Barberry's face and the anxious look he darted at Hyssop's back, we knew instantly it was the wrong thing to say. 'Make much trouble say that another time, Sir Tree-Talker.'

Immediately I kenned to Imlaud, *Ask him in mind-talk if it's because the Emperor of Earth-Above is after the bee folk too, as he is after the Umlisi. Barberry will expect kenning from a Yoriandir, but I don't want to show my tiles yet.*

After a moment the Umlisi lad nodded in reply to Imlaud's question.

Interesting, Imlaud kenned to me. *Is the Emperor so desperate for spirit elixir now that he seeks to enslave even the poor folk of the air?*

One part of my mind noted that Grumahu's hands were moving under the piles of garments we had dumped over him. He was retying the frayed ropes into some semblance of bracelets, I surmised, through which he could slip his chafed wrists and thereby cause no problem when they eventually took us off the ship. I gave him an approving nod and told Imlaud, *Every knowing thing, it seems, is fodder for the spirit traps. The Emperor must be sinking fast. What's even more interesting, though, is that no one except Barberry reacted to what you said or to his warning to us.*

None speaks Anazi save the boy, thee means.

Aye. But they all understand kenning: the bees are funny, he says.

Imlaud's green eyes swung the length of the ship casually as mine were doing, both of us looking for any sign we may have been overheard and understood. *We must have a care now*, Imlaud finally concluded. *For we do not know, not for certain, that none here understands. I shall tell my men.*

'I think I'll stretch my legs,' I said aloud.

'Stretch mine, too, while you're at it,' Grumahu grumbled

as I stepped over him. I gave him a wink, and stepped up on the diving hatch, one arm round the mast. This took me above the level of the shields, but many of the Umlisi were similarly perched, so I didn't think the danger from the walkers or the bats could be so great. Probably the bees patrolled both shorelines, though what they could do against walkers I didn't know.

Ahead I could see that this channel took a turn, and coming from beyond it was a bright illumination that seemed dazzling to me after so long in the darkness. We must be very near Il Numator now. The Umlisi around me began folding down the rest of the shields, and Hyssop blew out the lantern and straightened thankfully, flexing his shoulders. I could guess that the passage had been a tense one for him, too.

Barberry came to stand beside me, whether out of friendliness or on the captain's orders, I didn't know. Unobtrusively Imlaud got up, too, though I saw him give a hand signal to his troop to settle back down. If we were all on our feet, the Umlisi might regard it as a threat. I glanced down at Grumahu. The giant raised his brows, then closed his eyes, and gave every indication of trying to doze off again. I hid a smile.

The channel widened, and we shot down it, the wind from behind us much stronger now, as though the cavern ahead were sucking all the air into itself. The bow wave slopped over into the barge, and the Umlisi whooped, obviously urging their boat on as one cheers a racing horse. The cable sang ahead of us, the low lintel flashed by overhead, and we shot out into the moat protecting Il Numator. Beside me, Barberry cheered, and the other men raised their fists. I myself was so stunned I could not have moved if I'd wanted to.

A peninsula lay dreaming within its sheltering cavern walls, a patchwork of fields and flowers dimly lit by a system of lamps that burned with flickering light as though clouds of fireflies danced there. The roof of the garden cave was smoothed, I might have said plastered, and painted with dark blue clouds behind which just a crescent of rising moon showed. As I watched, the moon drew clear of the cloud silhouette with subtle, precise jerks, and a silver light cascaded down to illumine the garden. As if by magic, the night-blooming trumpets of moonflower opened, perfuming the air with their heady scent.

I let out my breath in a whistle of awed surprise. 'Powers, that's beautiful.'

Barberry stood beside me, nodding. 'Pretty, aye. But sun no comes up any more. Broke. Marner come to fix, aye?'

'Fix the sun?' I repeated, squinting up at the cavern roof for the opening to the sky – the real sky – that I was sure must be there, but there wasn't one. The boat full of little Mud-Heads had quieted to hear, earnestly intent. In the silence I became aware for the first time of a regular mechanical sound, like wooden gears meshing on a waterwheel, though not nearly so loud. 'Oh, I see. Your "sun's" broken, is it? Well, certainly I'll—'

Barberry whirled, throwing out his arms to his mates, and rattled off something in his own language. There was an approving murmur.

'Steady on, now,' I began to object, but he patted me familiarly on the butt, then went to help with the landing preparations.

That may not have been the best strategy, Imlaud kenned worriedly; at the same time Grumahu sniffed and rolled his eyes.

'Thanks,' I told both of them. 'Next time you make a mistake, I'll be sure to rub your nose in it too.'

Our barge had floated nearly to a stop by this time, and now one of the Umlisi unhooked the cable that had towed us, then straightened to give a wave to the crew of the strange structure that loomed ahead. It looked something like a lighthouse, in that it was a tallish tower with windows at the top facing the four quadrants, but mostly it looked like a windmill with the biggest sails I had ever seen, yards of canvas that would have done a dwarvish pirateer proud. Here, however, rather than grinding corn, the mills were employed in turning huge sprocketed drums of cable to draw boats up the channels which entered the moat from various points round the roughly circular perimeter. The stiff underground wind was efficiently employed, and I was impressed again by the level of sophistication evident everywhere my eye rested.

Unhooked from the cable, our barge now proceeded under oars, making way slowly towards one of the short wooden piers which ran out from the waterfront like caterpillar's legs. Though there was easily room for a large merchant fleet and the docks appeared in fine condition, very few vessels were actually drawn up to the moorings. Most of these were barges of the type we were on. I surmised that Il Numator, having declined from its days of glory, hosted far fewer visitors than it might have in happier times. To my disappointment, I saw no single flag of any country I recognized.

'I make it eight,' Imlaud said quietly.

'Eight what?'

'Eight channels leading away from the cavern, though I am not sure of my count on the far side; it seems much darker over there.'

I shifted my leaning position against the mast, elaborately casual. 'Aye. Either there are no ships coming up those channels, or the walkers have taken over those waterways and they are never used.'

'Move, please.' Barberry smiled. 'Make port now.'

We moved aside, going to sit on the edge of the barge near Grumahu. 'How about untying my friend?' I called to Hyssop. Barberry relayed my question over the creaking of the oars. The captain shook his head. 'You're going to have a job carrying him,' I warned. When Barberry translated this, the Umlisi leader simply shrugged. That told me he expected our ship to be met so that someone other than his own men would have to carry the giant's bulk.

The barge nosed into a slip at the dock, and two of our Umlisi troop stepped up onto the wharf to secure the lines. The sound of tramping feet drew my attention, and I got to my feet to see better, Imlaud rising beside me. 'Soldiers,' Grumahu said impassively, though he could see nothing from his position in the bottom of the barge.

Soldiers indeed. An armed troop, smartly turned out in leather and mail tunics, coiffed in mail, armed with spears and bows. They wore short surcoats over their armor, and these showed a cluster of yellow sunflowers blazoned on a field of green.

'Women warriors?' Imlaud murmured.

'One of the best pirates I ever knew was a woman,' I told him, the words coming naturally, though I had only the faintest image to accompany them: a large woman with dimples like a dairy maid's and a cutlass in her hand.

I was beginning to know the Yoriandir warden's looks fairly well, but he had no time to comment before the contingent on shore drew up alongside us. The woman in charge of the cohort asked Hyssop something sharp, staring at Imlaud and me.

Hyssop answered levelly enough, and whatever he said served either to mollify her or to remind her that he might have had some higher orders than hers, because although she clearly was not pleased to find us free of restraints, she nodded once, shortly. Then she pointed with her chin at Grumahu. And him? she seemed to ask.

I thought I saw the faintest of smiles on Hyssop's face when he gestured her to feel free to take the prisoner. Not a man of Hyssop's troop moved to lend a hand.

The woman soldier knew what game was being played here. With a sudden movement she jumped down into the barge and strode up to us. After a look at Imlaud and me, she dismissed us for the moment and crouched to Grumahu. 'Walk?' she asked.

The giant nodded. 'Try. Feet are numb, though. The ropes.'

We could see her translating this for herself. Barberry started to explain what Grumahu had said, but she cut him off with a dismissive wave. She drew a bronze dagger and held it loosely poised over the giant. 'Make trouble, I kill Mage. Understand?'

Powers, she'd read him like a book. As my sworn protector, Walking Thunder would do nothing to endanger me.

Grumahu measured her eye to eye. 'Make trouble for Mage, I kill *you*. Understand?'

She raised her chin and smiled proudly. 'Not so easy, Big Fella.'

'Not so easy, Little Miss.'

She cut the ropes away from his ankles, chuckling. The two warriers understood each other very well, it seemed. I breathed a sigh of relief, which was cut off midway through when she flipped back the sacking and discovered the loose rope bracelets. She gave Hyssop a look of derision and easily slipped the rope off Grumahu's raw wrists. 'Why did not do for feets too, Big Fella?' She snorted. 'No man on this boat to see.'

I had to save the situation somehow. We might need the barge crew as allies to speak for our good behavior. 'We did not wish to make Captain Hyssop angry. He had much to think about last night when we were attacked by the walkers. It was a good fight.' I had deliberately spoken in simple enough phrases for Barberry to catch. As I had expected, the lad went forward to tell Hyssop what had been said in the exchange. By the time feeling had returned enough to Grumahu's feet for him to be able to stand, Hyssop's angry flush had faded, and he had regained his composure.

As we followed the woman soldier off the barge, I nodded

civilly to Hyssop, and he nodded back. 'I remember the bat,' I said. Barberry murmured the translation.

'I remember the net,' Hyssop told me through the boy. I smiled, and the captain nearly matched me.

Grumahu leaned from the pier to pull me up, though I could have done it perfectly well for myself. He was making his position clear to all the cohort now, as he had done with their commander: this is my mage, understand? The Umlisi women in their chain mail looked up at him in disciplined silence, and if they were at all awed at his immense size, they didn't show it. 'Be quiet,' the commander told us. 'Folk be sleeping now.'

'Sounds like a good idea,' the giant grunted.

I belted him in the ribs. 'Lead on, miss.'

The commander of the cohort motioned us to follow her. I glanced back once to see how the giant was doing on his numbed feet and noticed that the Umlisi had very neatly divided up the Yoriandirkin troop, several women marching between a few of the green wardens. Imlaud was at my shoulder, and Grumahu kept station his usual three steps behind. None of us ventured to speak.

She led us at a brisk walk up a pleasant lane bordered with rock walls and flowers. There was a thick mulch of evergreen bark on the path, and at the time I thought it was to provide a carpet over the rock that must underlie most of the garden.

We passed several darkened houses, homey with thatch and vines winding about the windows, and then the commander stopped before a low gate. Through it we could see a small courtyard surrounded on three sides by a substantial structure of squared stone with galleries running the length of the sides on both stories. I judged it an inn, or at least a house that might have been an inn at some time.

'Big Fella, green men stay here. Wait. Mage come with me.'

'As prisoners?' Imlaud asked stiffly.

'Green men friends of Il Numator long time ago. This place for them to stay. Be . . .' She searched for the word, but it eluded her.

'An inn for tallfolk,' I supplied.

'Aye, by Five! Inn. Place so can stand straight up in. Food, sleep.'

'That is most generous,' the Yoriandir leader said. 'I wonder if thee can tell me, miss, how long we shall be staying here.'

Her eyes slid from him to Grumahu. 'Go in now, please.'

The giant folded his arms on his chest. 'No. Stay with Mage, told you.'

Before I could do anything about it, her hand whipped to her mouth. Grumahu fell and it was only then that I saw the dart.

'Damn it!' I exploded. 'That had better not be bee venom!' My angry shout rang out over the garden.

Kinu, be still! Imlaud kenned urgently. *We need the Umlisis' help!*

'Big Fella sleep now. Did say was sleepy,' the young woman soldier reminded me. She gestured to Imlaud, and he ordered several of his men to carry the giant into the inn. I made sure his pulse was strong as I helped lift him. I nodded to the warden, and Imlaud went in with his men.

'Come, go Auntie's house now. She be wakeful, wait for Mage.'

I was still angry at the casual way she had felled Grumahu, and I stalked off down the path. Who did these bloody people think they were, to lock up the Eldest of the Yoriandirkin and the giant? By the Powers, it was rough treatment for travellers who only—

'Mage.'

I heard her low call and stopped some way up a branching path.

She gestured down the other lane. 'Auntie's house be this way.'

My head was aching again. 'Quit pissing around, Commander,' I told her roughly. 'It's down here, second lane on the left after the sun mill.' I must have spoken more loudly than I had intended. Lights were coming on in the houses around us as people turned up their lamps to see what was the matter. *The sun rose suddenly, flooding the garden with a rosy glow of dawn, and bees hummed in clouds over tansy and phlox. The mill clacked busily. Sage Tanglefoot the lamplighter went past me, whistling merrily, to take the fireflies from the nightlamps to breakfast. 'Morning, Mariner,' he said. 'Morning, Sage. Another nice one.' 'Yes, sir, aren't they all!' I continued up the path towards home, where the breakfast bacon popped in the skillet . . .*

There was a golden glow beyond my closed eyelids and a warmth on my face that felt like sunlight. The aroma of bacon filled my nostrils. I surfaced out of sleep, pleasantly refreshed. 'Mmm, smells good,' I murmured, stretching and opening my eyes.

I was in a small cottage with whitewashed stone walls, a snug thatched roof and bright curtains covering a shuttered window. The golden light came from a lamp sitting on a table by the bedside. I turned my head towards it and flinched badly till I realized it was only a mouse sitting on my pillow. I cursed under my breath – I can't abide the kind of inns where you have to share with the resident vermin – and readied a stealthy blow to squash the cheeky little bastard.

Tiny bright eyes regarded me and long whiskers twitched. 'Right-o, you're awake, m'lord! We thought you might sleep a bit yet. Auntie will be back directly, she's just gone out for a word with Master Lamplighter. She's left the kettle on for your tea.' The mouse made a bow like a courtier's and invited me with one paw to the hearth at the other end of the house.

I lay still. Yes, I was awake, not dreaming. Yes, the mouse

was talking to me, not kenning. Yes, undoubtedly, I was mad. Cautiously I kenned, *Thanks, but I don't fancy tea much. Ye wouldn't happen to have any flotjin, would ye?*

He clasped his hands across his stomach. 'I'm afraid I don't know what that is, sir, but if you care to explain I'll certainly have a go at obtaining some for you. Oh, and by the way, you needn't wear yourself out kenning, m'lord. Plain speech will be quite good enough for the likes of me.'

'Will it?' I asked stupidly, staring in fascination at his tiny moving lips.

'Indeed it will. About the flotjin, sir?' he prompted.

Rubbing crusting from my eyes, 'It's a kind of liquor,' I replied automatically. In the next moment I found an image against the sand floor behind my eyes: wooden mugs lifted in a salute, and beneath them were grinning bearded faces. The beards were braided. 'Pirates drink it.'

'Pirates, m'lord?'

I sighed. 'Another life, mouse, another life.'

At once he stiffened alertly, grasping the end of his tail and twirling it. 'Yes, just so, sir! I told her you'd remember!'

I rose to an elbow and looked down at him. 'Remember what?'

'Who —'

The latch of the door lifted and an elderly female voice said, 'Theodore Thaddeus Chaff-Chaser, I thought I told you not to wake him!'

The mouse clasped his paws behind him and responded virtuously, 'Nor did I, madam. He woke up nice as you please and I invited him to take tea. We were just having a bit of chat.'

'And now he's got a thumping headache from having you chattering in his ear before he's even had his breakfast! Honestly, what must he think of our manners?' The small Umlisi woman was shrugging out of her green hooded cloak and hanging it on a peg on the back of the door. She turned and regarded me for a moment, smoothing her apron.

Her white hair was neatly plaited on top of her head and her cheeks were as red and wrinkled as late winter apples, but her eyes were as bright as a girl's and blue as two delphinium blossoms. She smiled warmly, and I found myself smiling back. 'Teddy T.'s not usually a nuisance. He's just excited,' she explained. 'We all are. I'm Tigerlily. You'll be wanting breakfast, I should think. Come, I've got it ready for you.' She indicated the round table already set for one.

'They call me Pel Kinu,' I said, though she had not asked my name. The mouse obligingly made way as I pushed back the covers and swung my legs over the side of the bed. Slippers were set ready for me, just my size, and much more importantly, a woollen robe since the air was chilly. The single spiral woven at the left breast of it momentarily gave me pause. I had the feeling it was familiar and touched it, frowning.

'Don't try to force the memories just now,' advised the elderly lady, who must be the 'Auntie' to whom Theodore had referred. 'There will be time enough for that later. Here, sit down. Do you take milk in your tea?'

'No, no thanks.' I scuffed across to sit at the table while she poured a bowl of steaming amber tea. I sipped it cautiously; the stuff had a curious flowery taste, not unpleasant, but not the kind of thing that would keep you awake on a long watch. I found I was thirsty and sipped again, blowing on the bowl to cool it a little. Meanwhile, Auntie served me rashers and thick slices of toast. Until I began to eat, I didn't realize how hungry I was. 'Where are my friends, Mistress?' I asked through the steam of the bowl.

She was scrubbing up the frying pan. 'Snug as bugs in their beds at the inn. You needn't look so worried. We'll not mistreat them, I promise you. A simple sleeping potion is all it is. They'll be better for the rest, and we don't want them out trampling the garden.' She wiped her hands and settled herself in a rocking chair, taking her spindle from its basket of wool.

I finished the tea and set down the bowl. 'I don't think the Yoriandirkin would hurt anything in your garden. That's not their way.'

She glanced up. 'No, of course not. The wardens wouldn't knowingly hurt a fly, but accidents happen. The giant seems a good enough fellow, too, but we just can't have him rampaging about. And then,' she paused to tend to a tangle of fibers for a moment, 'we'd rather they didn't remember much about Il Numator when they return to Earth-Above. It isn't safe. The enemy is everywhere.'

The memory of the bat's red eyes and gnashing fangs fluttered across my mind, and I suppressed a shudder, cupping my hands around the still warm tea bowl. Tigerlily saw this and quietly got up to pour more of the aromatic brew for me. The light scent of the flowers put me in mind of a summer day's dreamlike peace. 'Drink it, now, all of it. It will do you good,' she urged.

'What is it?'

'A herb we have here. We call it starflower.'

She returned to her spinning while I lingered over my tea, more awake now and suddenly realizing what I should have known before: the substance in the bowl might very well be a drug. I was alert for numbing of my lips and tongue, or for a change in my vision, but so far there was nothing. Still, I drank more of the tea. If Tigerlily was aware of this, she said nothing. To make conversation, I asked, 'Il Numator: what does that mean?'

She pursed her lips briefly, thinking. Then she looked up.'I suppose it might be translated as The Lamp.'

'Imlaud, the Eldest of the Yoriandirkin, tells me your place here used to be quite well known. You had many visitors, and folk spoke with awe of this place to their children. I can see why,' I added honestly.

Tigerlily smiled. 'Your friend was being circumspect. He didn't tell you that Il Numator once was the loveliest valley in the Empire. Our poems remember the smell of the breeze; the songs say the mist from the river used to fill the valley and then double rainbows would appear.' Her eyes sparkled, but the animation in them died as she came back to the present.

'The reekers came,' I guessed.

'Indeed. The Lamp oil draws them, you see. They know it could give them life. Real life, not this—' She grimaced. 'Not this half life they have now.'

I had no real idea what she was talking about, but I listened closely, both to her words and to the tone of them. If my friends and I were ever to get out of this cavern, it would be by this woman's leave. Therefore, what was important to her had better damn well become important to me, if only for the length of time it would take me to find and free Grumahu and the tree wardens. She was musing now, nodding with compressed lips at some thought or memory. Cautiously I probed. 'So when the reekers invaded your valley, your folk moved down here and built this place as a sanctuary?'

Her eyes fixed on me and she was silent for a moment, so that I wondered whether she would answer. 'No,' she said finally. 'When the reekers came, we moved down here, and our friend Marner built this sanctuary for us and taught us how to live in it. But he did not forget that we Umlisi are made for open sky and sunshine. He said he would come back when he had figured out how to drive the reekers and their master off the face of Earth-Above.'

Suddenly the floor swooped under me and the walls rocked . . . *the floor of the garden thick with narcissus under its dappled canopy of green light . . . the Power standing under the laden cherry trees with Rose by her side, beckoning. 'I can't stay, can I?' I asked. Ritnym smiled kindly. 'No, I'm afraid not. He is up in Earth-Above, son, and you must drive him from there . . . drive him from there . . .*

'Drink,' Tigerlily urged, holding the tea bowl for me. 'That's good, sip some more now. Starflower is sovereign for disturbances of the mind. It will clear your memories.'

I was sweating. 'Nothing to clear,' I denied roughly, gulping the tea only because it was warm and I was so cold.

'You're afraid of what you see, aren't you?'

'Yes!' I flung away from the table to warm my shaking hands over the fire. 'And don't look at me like that! You'd be seeing things, too, if people around you were as barmy as everybody in this bloody empire, and all you wanted was to get out of it and go home!'

'Where is home?' she asked quietly.

'Inishbuffin. Or at least to Jarlshof. That's where my mates live, that's where Timbertoe will be, now that he's Guildmaster and he and Brunehilda—' The words had come sluicing through my mind, the flow of water from a suddenly opened dam, but just as quickly the waters were stopped up again. I became aware that my palms were burning and snatched them away from the fire. 'Bugger me! I almost had it there for a minute!'

Tigerlily smiled, the apples in her cheeks bobbing as she nodded. 'Starflower.'

I reached for the bowl, drank, and licked my lips. 'Mistress Tigerlily, I'm not Marner. I know I look like the old painting of him back at Bai Nati's skellig, but that was made lifetimes ago. Obviously—'

Teddy T. scrambled up on top of the teapot, shifting from one foot to the other because it was still hot. 'But, sir!'

Auntie put a finger lightly on his snout, and the mouse subsided. To me she said, 'Certainly you are Marner. You're undoubtedly someone else as well – someone just as unique and wonderful – but you *are* Marner come again, exactly as he promised.' She took my hand gently and with a thin finger tapped the dull silver signet. 'This is his ring, you see.'

My crooked jaw locked, as it did under stress. Out of the corner of my mouth I forced the question: 'You recognize this?'

'Oh, my, yes! The Rainbow Ring is well known to us.' She folded her hands across her apron. 'In fact, Marner made it here from a stone he found—'

Her voice hummed in my ears like the wind over wing feathers, and the sands spread onto the painting floor . . . *salt smell and wet wool and a boat rocking under me. His voice, Bruchan's deep storytelling voice, rich but held low just now, guarding our secret from inquisitive ears . . . His eyes, one blue, one brown, watching me . . . 'I am not the guardian of the ring. It is mine by right of birth. When I die, it will be thine, grandson.' Then the sands becoming purer colors, undulled yet by years of use . . . the chalcedon's pearled sheen emerging from the node of lesser rock, molten silver for the band itself and then sparks of rainbow fire twinkling against the gloom of the chamber . . . the Fire of the Ring, red, indigo, and emerald strands arching to form a rainbow of light against the painted clouds of the ceiling, where the sun was a blindingly bright gem . . .*

The dazzle cleared from my eyes. I was staring into the crazed surface of the ruined stone. 'He made your sun with this, didn't he?'

'Aye. 'Twas Marner's magic,' the old woman confirmed.

The last few spangles of light in my eyes winked out. 'Is his workshop still here?'

She caught her breath, and Teddy T. did a somersault off the teapot to land in the crumbs of my toast. 'He remembers, he remembers!' the mouse exulted, leaving buttery footprints as he capered about the table.

I held up a hand. 'Not all of it, not yet. But you're right: something to do with this ring. I remember that I got it from my grandfather . . .' My voice trailed off as I tried to follow the memory back, but all I accomplished was to start the hammering in my temples once more. Hurriedly I reached for the tea bowl and drained it to the dregs. 'Maybe if I see the tools, I'll be able to figure out how he did the job,' I ventured, though without conviction.

The same thought seemed to occur to both Teddy T. and Auntie at the same instant, for the mouse suddenly sat still, twitching his whiskers, and Tigerlily's hopeful countenance fell. 'It's dark over there now,' Theodore murmured. 'The reekers . . .'

I regarded the ring, rubbing my fingers over the gem absently. 'I'll need my sword, then. It was in Captain Hyssop's boat last night. And I'd like Grumahu, the giant, wakened.'

Tigerlily said thoughtfully, 'Your friend will sleep for some hours yet, but the sword we shall certainly bring. Teddy T., just nip down to Barberry's cottage and ask him if he would accompany us himself. Then I'll need the key from Philomel.'

Theodore snapped off a salute, leaped from the table, and slipped out under the door. Auntie insisted on rinsing the teapot and cleaning the table before she would let me take her cloak from its peg and hold it for her. When I laid it across her shoulders, she reached to pat my hand. I could feel her trembling, but nothing of fear showed in her face. I put her arm on mine and led her out like a queen.

Outside, the little yard was dark, the borders of clove pinks turned pale white like moths in the lamplight behind us. The mouse was just coming under the front gate. 'Got it!' He had a key wrapped in his tail and was dragging it with some difficulty. 'Barberry is fetching your sword and his own kit, sir,' the mouse panted. 'He'll meet us at the Stoneway Gate.'

Tigerlily stooped to relieve him of his burden. 'You should probably stay here,' she told him.

'And miss an adventure? Not likely!' Theodore replied stoutly.

'Come on up, then.' She cupped a palm. He hopped in, and she lifted him into the pocket of her apron.

Beyond Auntie's front gate, the lane ran between low stone walls. Flowers peeped over these, but many were limp and yellowing. Tigerlily saw the direction of my gaze. ''Twill be so nice to have the sun again. We've missed it, truly. It's been horrendous work to take the plants – the sunflowers, that is, the ones we *must* save – topside every day and bring them back down each night to keep them safe from the enemy.' She reached to straighten a spire of foxglove that had fallen limply over the wall. 'We've saved the sunflowers, but these . . . these are just for pretty, you know, so of course we can't risk a plantsman's life to send them topside.'

I was hurt to see the sheen of tears in her eyes. Their gardens were all of life and of color that these poor folk had left to them, and I glimpsed how hollow their lives would be without them. Eventually, of course, to keep from going mad in this darkness, they would bolt and flee to Earth-Above, where the Emperor's creatures would be waiting.

By the lamp at the end of the lane, Barberry was waiting for us. My sword was propped against the stone wall, and my friend from the barge was dabbing on his face some ointment from a clay pot. It appeared brown in the lamplight, and I suddenly understood why other folk called the Umlisi 'Mud-Heads'.

'Ho, Marner!' he saluted me. He bowed to Tigerlily and offered the ointment pot to her. She dipped her fingers and made a spot on her forehead. Then he offered it to me. 'Do smell like mountain trees. Make reekers cough; go away,' he explained.

I lost no time in anointing myself with the pungent stuff. While I did, he lit the torches, more pine pitch, of course. I took up my sword and one of the lights, and Barberry led the way across a drawbridge over the moat that protected the gardens on this side. In the wall of the cavern beyond was a door, its heavy timbers soaked with creosote. A pair of sentries were posted here. They bowed to Auntie and spoke quietly with Barberry for a moment. One of them shook his head. 'Be no alarms all last night,' Barberry translated for me. 'Maybe reekers go 'way back in caves, eh?'

Tigerlily stepped around him to fit the key to the lock. He motioned me to one side, out of the way of anything that might come through the door when he opened it, and tugged the portal wide. Pitch blackness spread before us, and I was seized by an almost overwhelming sense of menace. 'They're out there,' I said between gritted teeth.

'Aye, Marner,' Barberry replied. The little man settled the bag hanging over his shoulder, handed his torch to Auntie, and strung his bow. Then he walked on ahead, just inside the pool of light thrown by our torches.

Not far down the tunnel, we stopped for a moment at a silver torch, and Tigerlily lit it. I looked at it closely, feeling sure that I had never seen a lamp made in the shape of a torch before. The wick was neatly trimmed, and the thing burned with a steady silver light like that of the 'moon' over the garden cavern. This Marner must have been a hell of a craftsman.

Barberry checked and halted. 'Walkers,' he said quietly.

Far down the tunnel, I could see a momentary gleam of eyes. I lifted my sword, but the Umlisi warrior took a short length of b'mbu stoppered with a twist of rough rope from a pouch hung at his waist. This he lit at the torch Tigerlily carried. Immediately the wick caught and began to sizzle down towards the tube. I could see his lips move, and he held his arm cocked, so he must have been counting. He uncoiled and threw the missile down the tunnel. We heard it clatter on the stone floor, and then there was a bright flare and roiling smoke.

The walkers coughed and snarled. The noise they made receded, and my sword chuckled to itself and went back to sleep. Barberry picked up his bow, and we went on, the Umlisi as matter-of-fact about the episode as a fisherman cutting a blundering shark off his line. I promised myself that if I managed to fix their sun machine, the first thing

I'd ask for as a gratitude gift would be a couple of dozen of those smoke tubes.

Not much further on we came to a door set into the tunnel wall, stout wood cross-banded with bronze. It, too, was painted with creosote, and there was a stout lock, too. Tigerlily fitted the same key to the lock. It stuck for a moment, but then opened, and she swung the door wide, gesturing for me to enter. Barberry made preparations to stay outside, crouching to lay a row of smoke tubes ready to hand. Then he unslung his bow, notched a dart, and took up his guard station.

Auntie lit the silver torch in its bracket, and the room was flooded with light. It was a workroom, with a long table down the middle on which were various clamps and tools that resembled chisels and engraving tools, together with mallets curiously covered with leather heads, buckets, long-handled tongs and other pieces I couldn't even begin to guess the uses of. I moved past the table towards the wide space at the back. The circular fire pit was easy enough to distinguish, half filled with the same kind of fuel Grumahu had used, but the two deep, wide basins set into the floor at the very back wall were a mystery. 'Mistress, what are these?'

In answer, she went to a square of stone incised with wavy lines and stepped down on it. The basins began to fill with water, and one of them was hot enough to steam. I gaped.

''Tis all still good. We have kept the walkers away,' she said. She waved a hand at both walls, which were lined with dusty wooden boxes. 'These were left by Marner.'

I reached to wipe away the cobwebs and read the label that had been burned into the crate with the tip of a hot iron: 'Spare partes: mille.' I shook my head, still baffled, and moved to the one next to it. 'Spare partes: rigging.' I turned to the table, snatched up a hammer and chisel, and prised the top off the crate. Inside were neat coils of smooth rope, the rigging line for the sails of a small ship, like a dragon-prow.

Now that I knew what I was looking at, the room's arrangement became clear. Marner had secured his cargo just as though he were aboard ship, each crate balancing one across the hold from it, each nailed shut to protect the booty, each carrying its label for the storemaster. (*How do you know that?*)

I went to the hot water basin and dipped my hand, but drew it back with an oath and hurriedly plunged my hand in the cold one. Then I went looking for a label that might guide me, Tigerlily watching all the while, quietly perched on the high stool at the table. Teddy T. crept to her shoulder. Spare partes: caulking. Spare partes: nayles. Spare partes: wickes.

Come on, mate, give it to me.

Spare partes: candle mouldes, pegges, more nayles, hookes.

I snorted, crossed the room impatiently, and began wiping labels clear on that side. Silvern torches, firefly lamps. Closer; he must have put his own ship's stores on one side of the workroom, and the crates on this side held the things he had crafted for the Folk. I caught a splinter from a box, but scarcely noticed. Plumbing, Paynt, Sunne. 'Got it, by the Powers!'

I shifted the boxes above it, not easily. The plumbing box was as heavy as pipe fittings could be; the paint box oddly light, but shifting awkwardly in my hands so that I nearly dropped it. Finally I got down to the large crate and tugged it out into the middle of the workspace near the fire pit. 'Hand me the mallet and chisel, would you?' When Auntie handed them down, I prised the nails loose all round, set the tools aside, and tugged at the lid of the wooden box. It let go with a rusty screech of nails, and I lifted it off.

Nestled in straw was a hunk of raw crystal so big it would easily have dwarfed even Grumahu's huge head.

No, it can't be, I thought, it must be glass. I wet a finger and gently drew it round the misshapen gray lump. The crystal gave forth a beautiful, unearthly music. Like an echo of it, my sword sang from the table where I had left it, not the warning song it had used for the walkers, but a soft whisper like a lover's caress.

I sat back on my heels.

'Can you fix it, Marner?' Tigerlily asked. She sounded tired, but hopeful.

'I don't know, Auntie. Here's the spare part, right enough, but I still don't know what's broken. I need to see the workings.'

She slid off the stool heavily. 'Aye. Will show.'

I hammered the top back on the crate and, though it cost me a squashed finger, tugged the crate back to its original place along the wall, moving the plumbing and paint boxes on top of it once more. The Folk were above suspicion, but if the walkers broke through that door, there was no sense in making it easier for them. I did not stop to question how I knew walkers would be attracted to the crystal, just as I did not wonder how I had known they could be beaten back with a sword. I was learning to trust my instincts, echoes from my other life beyond this land.

I blew out the torch, and the Umlisi woman and I rejoined a relieved Barberry. He had seen nothing, he said, but he could hear them back there in the darkness. Tigerlily locked the door and handed me the key. I listened carefully to my sword, but it was quiet.

It was a relief to walk over the drawbridge into the garden again and find ourselves awaited by many of the Folk. The rumor of my arrival had traveled like wildfire. The Umlisi children had clambered onto the wall and their elders were gathered beneath the lamp hanging over the entrance to the village alehouse. They were dressed in their work clothes, canvas smocks over their woolen robes, and many had set down by their feet the potted sunflowers they were moving up to the surface for the day. Apparently they were just waiting for a glimpse of me and maybe a hopeful word from Tigerlily.

'Warmth of the Fire,' she greeted them.

'Morning,' came back the chorus. They were staring openly.

Auntie Tigerlily took my arm. 'He's going to try to fix it.' There was a glad murmur. 'Meanwhile, let's keep up with our work.' The people bent to retrieve their plants or gardening implements, nodded in friendly fashion, and filed towards the slips where the barges were moored.

She turned to me. 'I'm afraid the steps are too much for me now, but Barberry can be your guide.

'You'll want to take a couple of the other warriors with you,' she said to my Umlisi friend. He had a surprisingly grim look on his face.

'I'll ask Cattail and Withee, shall I, sir?' Teddy T. ventured, and Barberry nodded.

After the old woman had left by one path, and the mouse by another, Barberry motioned me to one of the benches outside the tavern. I deduced we would have some minutes to wait. The warrior drew a marvelously carved pipe out of his kit bag and packed it. When he lit it, the leaf gave off a burly-smelling aroma that nearly counterbalanced the pine incense. He held it out to me. 'Marner smoke?'

'No, thanks. The skipper would like that, though.'

'Skipper?'

His image flashed across my mind again as I had drawn him for Grumahu. 'Timbertoe,' I said, the name rolling off my tongue now with no effort. I wrote it with a glowing iron across my mind, burning in the label so that I should not forget him again. *Timbertoe*.

Come on, Giant, I heard him say. *Arni's got the accounts hopelessly mucked up, the Guild's acting like a pack of regular fools, and Brunehilda's locked me out of the house.*

Bugger it. Let's go hunting again, hey? Old terms, of course, seventy-thirty split, my favor.

'Sixty-forty, or piss off, you old pirate,' I told him laughingly.

Barberry paused in drawing on his pipe. 'What say?'

I made the horizontal wave with my hands. 'Nothing.'

I looked up at the ceiling. Even if the 'sun' Marner had made for them was a crystal lamp of some sort, the garden still needed real sunlight. There must be a way to open a section of the roof, and this must have jammed, otherwise the Umlisi would not need to carry their plants topside each day to put them in the sun for a few hours.

Our crew appeared – two young Umlisi who must surely be the tallest and heaviest among the folk. Barberry knocked out his pipe, glanced once at the ceiling, and strode off down the path mulched with evergreen chips.

We passed among the dark cottages, small buildings, snug enough, stone, thatched. In the center of the garden was a windmill. Rather than canvas, the sails of the mill were shiny. I peered up at the still arms incredulously as we got closer. 'That's cloth-of-gold!'

'Aye,' Barberry confirmed. 'Do be pretty with sun all shining down. Mill go round, clack-clack, make much oil.'

Pressing as our business was, my curiosity wouldn't be denied. 'Could we go in?'

'Aye, Marner. Door always open. All Folk but littlest go in.' He held up the lantern and ushered me in, the other two lads crowding in behind, hands respectfully clasped behind them. If Marner wanted to inspect the mill he had built, why not?

The workings inside were well maintained, but there was yellow pollen or chaff caught in every possible nook and cranny. I bent to look under the millstone. 'What sort of grain do you grind here?'

'Sunflowers, Marner,' he said, sounding wounded, as though I took him for a simpleton.

I managed to avoid a show of surprise. They obviously had no way to grow barley or oats for bread, and in truth the sunflower meal must make a passable enough flour, because the bread I'd had was just fine. I nodded as though I'd known the answer all along, and motioned the lamp down to peer into the huge vat under the grindstone. 'So the sunflowers give you oil for your lamps?'

'Nay, Marner!' he said, shocked. 'Not to use gift that way! Oil only for garden, to make grow green!'

I straightened. 'Let me get this straight, matey. You're telling me you water your garden with this stuff from the mill, and your plants grow underground with no sun.'

'*Be* sun, only broke now, so carry plants—'

'Topside every day. I know. Auntie told me that.' I led them out of the mill and pointed up at the ceiling. 'That opens, right? And the sun shines in on good days.'

The three looked at each other, patently confused. Barberry undertook to answer me. 'If roof open like door, cat-soldiers find, walkers find, anything find. Why make roof open?'

I bit back the first three things that sprang to mind to call him, rubbed my nose, and said, 'You've got a damned strange boat here, mate, you know that?'

'Marner make,' he whispered, hurt.

'Aye,' I sighed. And I wished I knew what the bugger was about when he did it. 'All right, me buckos, show me the sun.'

Silent now because of what they perceived as Marner's bad mood, they led me on through the garden, through a small stand of dwarfed fruit trees, to the back cavern wall. Here one of the other boys held up the lamp, and Barberry opened a door to reveal a flight of steps spiraling upwards. Now we were getting somewhere, I felt.

We climbed one hundred and thirty steps without a landing. I know, because I counted them. The stairs were carved out of the rock itself, not overly wide, but adequate, defensible by one man with a sword. (*How do you know that?*) At the top of the stairs, a door stood in the wall. It was locked.

Barberry took the key from round his neck, but he wasn't expecting any walkers, I noted, because none of the lads had smoke tubes with them. I surmised this room had no other entrance than the one through the garden. The door hinges creaked a bit, but yielded easily enough to Barberry's push. 'Careful, Marner. Do be broken pieces,' he warned me over his shoulder as we went in. The other boy held up the lantern, and a myriad droplets of rainbowed light chased each other round the room, mirrored surface to mirrored surface. In the middle of the floor, dark, tumbled from its moorings and with its tip broken off, lay the sun. With my first glimpse of it, I knew I was in serious trouble.

'A deck prism set in a lighthouse,' I said aloud. 'Marner, you canny old bastard, you.'

CHAPTER ELEVEN

'I've no glasscraft at all,' I murmured to the watching boys. 'I've never seen it made. Powers.' The lads were silent, but my sword hummed a little. I was beginning to know its language, and this was definitely a small sound of commiseration, but whether for me or for the darkling crystal prism, I couldn't tell.

I stepped carefully among the fragments. Though the idea to unite a mirrored lighthouse with a deck prism was ingenious, Marner had used fairly standard engineering for both, and this enabled me to make some sense of what I was seeing. Like all the lighthouses I had seen, this room was rounded, the outer circumference composed of alternating panels of window and mirrored surfaces. The window panels were covered just now by heavy hatches. These were fitted with gears, so I assumed they were winched open each sunny morning to catch the sunlight – the real sunlight. So the lighthouse was a simple enough affair, as I say.

The difference was that, where the huge lamp with its multiple wicks would normally sit in the middle of a stone floor so that the mirrors would cast the light outwards at night, this lighthouse was fitted with the biggest deck prism I had ever seen. Normally these prisms are small glass fixtures, flat on one end and cut into a flat-sided cone on the other. The flat side is set flush with the deck of a ship, and the prism extends down through the planking to focus sunlight into the cargo spaces. This provides a dim illumination, enough to work in the hold without the need for lamps on a clear day. It saves using lamps, and that saves fires, the bane of any deepwater sailing ship.

Marner had fashioned a huge deck prism and set it into a kind of sprocketed cradle, meshed with the same gear that controlled the window panels and another protruding through the floor that must turn the cradle so that the prism tracked the sun across the sky. There must be another gear underneath us that opened the cavern's 'sky' too, I thought, so that the 'sun', though stationary in the center of the cavern, would direct its brilliant swath of light in a slow path across the garden below, simulating the passage of hours.

In essence, he had made a huge timepiece.

I finished my inspection back at Barberry's side. 'There was an earthquake not long ago.' I remembered Butterfly Bark's uneasiness and the taller tree shaking his damaged stump. 'Is that when the sun broke?'

'Aye, Marner. Look. Rock back-forth, break.'

The whole superstructure must have shifted just enough to jam the gears. As one of the other boys held up the lamp, I could see something dull white down in the gear well, about thirty feet below the platform. 'What's that, Barberry? Something's stuck in the gears.'

'Aye. Be Burdock, my brother. Was Servant of the Sun, Marner.' His dark eyes held mine, wanting me to know the depth of the Folk's devotion to their charge of keeping this garden alive. 'When shaking came, Burdock go down there on rope to look for other piece of sun. Then slip. Auntie say no other Folk go down there.' He looked away, and his sudden silence when Tigerlily picked him to be my guide was explained. He'd been given orders that he couldn't come up here to retrieve his brother, but now he could come up here because Marner needed someone to hold the light for him. 'Not right.'

'She was only doing what she thought was best.' I stood

and began stripping off my clothes. 'We need a couple of ropes, lads, good, strong stuff. Nip off and get them, would you?'

They hesitated. 'Auntie be mucking angry, Marner,' the boy with the lamp said.

'Right. Which is why we won't tell her. Go on, now.' He handed the lamp carefully to Barberry and raced out. I feared more for his safety on the stairs than I did for my own in the gear well. The structure itself was sturdy, and the gears were jammed solid. I didn't fancy being down there with a dead man, but I had to go down in any event to see what damage there was. Also, I wanted an idea exactly how the ports in the ceiling of the cavern worked. On the way up, I could certainly bring what was left of the little Servant of the Sun.

In less time than I would have believed possible, the runner returned with the rope. I tested it carefully, noted approvingly that it was twisted tightly and seemed durable, and quickly tied in some regularly spaced knots to fashion myself a climbing rope. I secured it to the gigantic hewn timber that formed the shaft of the main gear, then tossed the coil down into the gear well. 'Light that torch and keep it up here with you, then lower the candle lantern beside me as I'm going down.'

I shinned down easily and the boys paced me with the light, so that I got a good look at the broken teeth of the wheel. Taken all in all, the repair job didn't look so bad, at least regarding the few missing cogs. The shafts and footings seemed fine.

When I reached the bottom of the well, I clung to the rope, gesturing the Umlisi to lower the lantern until it was resting on the giant sliding door that must be where the 'sun' shone into the cavern. Burdock's body lay on this, head tucked half under his shoulder as he had fallen. The body was bloated, and the smell fair made my stomach turn, but there was no help for it: I'd told his brother I'd bring him up, and besides, if I did manage to fix the damned machine, those doors were going to open and drop him right down into the garden.

So I kept hold of my rope and cautiously tested my weight on the door. It proved to be as solid as a deck. Still, the dead man was a caution not to be too cocksure, and so I took the precaution of fashioning myself an Old Maid's Goose, a kind of rope seat used to lift drunken sailors from a dinghy up to the mother ship. It wasn't comfortable, but it would do. I drew the lantern nearer and looked up at the watchers above. 'Throw down my cloak, please.'

The balled-up material landed in my outstretched hands. The smell of corruption was making me gag. Quickly I shook out the cloak and laid it over the corpse, hoping his brother wasn't seeing too much up there. Then I gingerly tried to roll him in it. The body was exactly the consistency of one of those damned slugs. Involuntarily I recoiled, jostling the corpse roughly. The air whistled out of the bloated lungs with a tortured groan that was matched with one from me. My stomach lurched as the mangled head untucked from the separating shoulder.

The walker grinned and bit me.

I stared down stupidly at the long raw strip torn from my leg, at the drops beginning to patter on the wooden door, and my eyes came up to meet the shade's bottomless black stare.

Then I dived for the lantern, but the rope harness brought me up short, and the walker got me a good one this time, fangs ripping into my shoulder to tear away another strip. 'Walker! Throw down my sword!' I yelled hoarsely, snatching up a sliver of the broken deck prism. I whirled with this in my hand and managed to block the thing's ripping nails. 'MY SWORD!' I bellowed, trying to slash myself free of the rope harness, but it was no good, the rope was too thick and I was only cutting my hand with the glass. My bare feet were cut on the shards, and I lunged with the crystal point to catch the walker's eyes, but missed, and it snaked in again, flaying a strip from my ribs. *Sword!* I kenned desperately, slashing with the crystal fragment.

From the lighthouse rose a hum that mounted to a chant.

The walker looked up while flesh – *my flesh* – began to grow on it. The sword above bellowed an attack and dropped over the edge of the well, point downwards.

Instinctively I dived away to the side to avoid the cleaving blade, and the walker threw itself on the lever for the trap door. My sword severed the rope, and the floor dropped out from under me.

Kinuu . . . hear me?

Not very well, for a fact. You sound like you're at the bottom of a well.

'. . . alive?'

Of course I'm alive. Either that, or you're all dead like me. How about it, mates, go hunting, sixty-forty split, my favor? See this pouch of chalcedons, pirates? Know where the skipper and I got them? Aye, ye've heard the story, haven't ye? Of course it's all true, look at his missing leg if ye think it's not. Me? Well, no, nothing serious, few strips off my hide, few dreams about their damned eyes. Course, I had the Swan then to keep them off, lovely Lady with the music in her wings. Yes, it was, very beautiful. Much like that music, in fact. The music that's . . . *that* music – hear it?

Runt Mage, his flute said, *Kinu who took the gift that I so wanted, come on, wake up. My wife is in a trap up there in the dead city, and I'll rip the place apart stone by stone until I find and free her, but you can talk to her mind and I can't. I won't ever be able to, now.*

Walking Thunder is sad today, he always plays that song when it rains. Aye, lad, I know the feeling well. I loved, too, in my time. She was a witch. No, a real one, I mean. Kenned the dead, she did. Wish she'd ken me. Like her to know it's my child she's carrying. I *am* sure. When we were in the labyrinth at Cnoch Aneil, to make the paintings on Vanu's Eve. The paintings. *You* know, like Brother Ru taught me. Don't be a twit, of course I never made my own set of colors. Because I had those other pots, the ones Bruchan got for me. Colin M—

'Marner, sun no be fixed this way! Wake up!'

Colin Mariner, see there? Barberry said it, that's the name. Colin Mucking Mariner, Mage and Pirate, and a hell of a stout mate. Stowed his cargo well, good captain, all shipshape, all labeled. All those spare parts: nayles, rigging . . .

Paynt.

Bugger me.

'Timbertoe?'

The sound of the pipe broke off suddenly, and he leaned into view, dark hair cut straight above his black eyes, a smile breaking from that gap-toothed mouth that was so unused to smiling that one half of his mouth had forgotten how and remained a tight-lipped line.

'Oh, Grumahu, it's you. The paints . . .'

'Pains, eh? That little Umlisi woman gave you something. Knew it wasn't going to be enough. Wait a bit, I'll get Imlaud.'

I turned my head to follow him, and the pain lashed me like a whip cracking. My breath caught at my ribs, and I put a hand to the dressings.

Barberry was watching by the door. 'I'm sorry about your brother,' I told him.

'Be all right, Marner.'

'How much did you see?'

He knew what I was asking, because his face went grim under its evergreen bark paint. 'Walker take Burdock, do try take Marner.'

'It did take part of me, mate.' I winced.

'Aye. But Marner take back Burdock's rock. Make brother proud again.'

I couldn't lift my head yet to focus very well. 'Burdock's rock?'

'Servant of the Sun rock.' He gestured. 'Be in thy hand when fell. All time sleep, Marner hold to rock. Even Big Fella can't get from hand.'

I inched my clenched fist up on my chest and tried to open the cramped fingers. At first the hand would not obey, but then my muscles let go and dropped something small on the bindings.

Imlaud came through the door, Grumahu hard on his heels. The green warden smiled with relief. 'I thought surely our large friend must be joking, but I am glad to find thee once more in thy senses.'

'As much as ever.'

'Having pain, he says, green master,' my big bodyguard cut in impatiently. 'More spring water.'

'No, some of Tigerlily's tea. It helps clear my head.'

Barberry knew what I was talking about and moved to the hearth to get it for me.

I gritted my teeth. 'I'll take kalan-kalan, though, if you've got it.' While Imlaud was getting it out of his pouch, I asked Grumahu, 'Are you all right?'

'Fine. Slept late. Sorry.'

The Yoriandir warden handed the pain-deadening leaves to me. 'My men are out in the garden. It is a wondrous thing to see.'

I tucked the kalan-kalan in my cheek and sucked on it thoughtfully. 'What day is it? How long have we got to get to Oaxacu?'

Grumahu rubbed his nose and looked down at me. 'Tonight, tomorrow, tomorrow night. Then the Day the Sun is eaten.' An expression of pain came and went in his face so quickly that Imlaud, who was shoulder to shoulder with the giant, never saw it. But I did, and I knew Walking Thunder was thinking of his wife. He made the horizontal gesture. 'Rest. Heal up, Runt Mage.'

I sipped some of the starflower tea that Barberry had

brought. 'Grumahu, have you ever smithed glass?'

The big man and the warden looked at each other, and a message as clearly writ as a paper scroll passed between them: *Humor him.*

The giant folded his arms on his chest. 'Smithed glass? What, like the sword?'

'A dagger, actually. A little one, slender as a sea urchin spine, but immensely strong. It's got to be strong.'

He frowned. 'Why?'

The idea unfolded itself in my mind as I picked up and rubbed the Servant of the Sun stone between my thumb and forefinger. 'Because we're going to build a spirit trap for the Emperor.'

Imlaud swallowed. Grumahu clenched his jaw. Barberry turned to look at me from the hearth where he had been stirring up the fire.

'Crazy idea,' the giant growled. 'Never work.'

I swallowed some of the kalan-kalan juice and the throbbing of my walker stripes eased a little. 'Well, it's a lot crazier just to walk into the Forbidden City looking for a little boy and a tree, and expect the Emperor just to sit on his thumbs while we do it. Even if he let us escape for sport, how long do you think any of us can last without the sun? Because that's what he's going to do, you know: he's going to make sure that there is no dawn on the Day the Sun is eaten. *That's* why he needs so many spirits to feed his damned traps. He has to build his strength to the point that he becomes like a Power.'

The Eldest of the Yoriandirkin was horrified. 'By the Tree, could this be true?'

Barberry was nodding as he approached my cot. 'Be true,' he said with assurance. 'Emperor has done this before.'

All three of us stared at him. 'Umlisi folk know much of old, old days. Did talk to t'ings when valley was still peaceful, before walkers came. Dragons always said

Emperor had brought the Great Dark twice before. Did trap sun itself, they said. Make earth cold, white. No gardens grew then. T'ings have to sleep in caves deep under to live.'

Fascinated, Imlaud asked, 'And how was the earth made warm again?'

The Umlisi looked at him as though he were a simpleton. 'Sun came up, green man.'

Not without help. The thought came unbidden, almost like a kenning, but it hadn't sounded like Imlaud's voice. I drained my bowl of starflower tea. 'This is the way it is, mates: we have to fix a machine that Marner made for these folk, a sun machine. Don't look like that, Imlaud, the thing's been working for a long time. Didn't you wonder how they kept a garden down here? Marner left spare parts for it, and I'll bet my last farthing that one of them is exactly what we need to make some sort of dart or blade that will trap the Emperor in his body, that will achieve the reverse of what one of his skinwalker blades does to other people.'

They were thinking it through. 'He's very old, they say,' Imlaud mused.

'Dying,' Grumahu agreed.

'If body die, and Emperor trapped in it . . .' Barberry's voice trailed off.

'He won't be able to lay down his old body and take up the new one – even if the priests already have some poor sod prepared to be the Flayed One,' I finished for him.

Imlaud paced to the fireplace and back. 'What makes thee think a piece of crystal will hold him, Kinu?'

I held up the small red stone. 'This. It belonged to Barberry's brother, who held the title of Servant of the Sun. Look.' I brought my broken ring alongside the stone.

'Huh, same kind of gem. Kind of milky-looking,' the giant observed.

Imlaud looked over his arm. 'And, since it was from Marner, thee thinks the ruby may work magery?'

'I hope so. I intend to try it. Grumahu, get me up.' It

hurt fully as much as I expected, but he steadied me with a grip round my arm that was nearly as bad as the walker stripe on the other shoulder. I hobbled a couple of steps and nodded. 'Passable. The one on my leg is the worst. Help me get some clothes on, would you?'

'Don't know where your cloak's got to, here's the kilt.'

I knew where the cloak was and didn't really want it back. To take Barberry's mind off it, I asked, 'How badly did I damage the sun mill when I fell on the sails?'

'Sails be ripped, but Folk already sewing from spare parts. Be fixed jig time.'

'First rate. Now, Barberry, my lad, lead on with the smoke tubes. We're bound for the spare parts room.'

'Aye, Marner,' he answered sturdily. He made to lift my sword, heavy for him and awkward, to hand it to me.

'No,' I said. 'Giant, would you? I can't use it with these stripes.'

He looked down at the sword the Umlisi put across his palms. 'Carry it for you for a while if it's too heavy,' he agreed.

I smiled.

'That one.'

Grumahu shifted the top one, then pulled out the crate, putting it up on the table. 'Open it?'

'Yes, please.'

' "Spare partes: sunne"?' Imlaud read, puzzled, as the giant began prising off the top.

I left them to it and began prowling, rubbing off dust, reading the labels Marner had so laboriously burned into his cargo. 'Ah,' I murmured as behind me Grumahu got the top off the sun parts crate.

When I looked over my shoulder, the giant had the glob of crystal in his huge hands, turning it this way and that. 'Cacamalu, it's heavy!' He sniffed and looked up at me challengingly. 'Makes you think I can make something strong enough to hold the Emperor?'

'The crystal's the right substance. It only needs a mage to work it. You're the one.'

A thundercloud gathered on his brow, a deep wash of angry shame so red it was nearly purple under his dark skin. 'Not funny, Runt Mage.' He put the glob of crystal down on the worktable only a little too hard.

'I wasn't needling you, Giant.' His smoldering eyes came up from the crystal and I told him, 'The sword you made kens, Grumahu, it has a living spirit. You put that into it when you forged it, and that's nothing a mere craftsman could do, no matter how skilled he was. It may not be Bai Nati's kind of power or mine, but have no doubt – you're as much a mage as I am.' I read the silent set of his features and hazarded a guess. 'And you know it.'

For a moment, I thought he might hurl the mallet he was fingering but then he glanced at Imlaud, who wisely had stayed out of it, remaining silently sitting on the stool. Grumahu raised an eyebrow. Imlaud slowly smiled. The giant sighed and cleared his throat. 'Always wanted to be. But even as a lad I was big and strong, so I was picked early for the army. No choice about it. Got to be a cat-soldier, got to be in the imperial guards stationed in Oaxacu. That's where I met my wife.'

He was silent a moment, rearranging the engraving tools. He nodded at some private thought. 'She was a beauty, and all the men were interested in her.' His jaw clenched. 'Denjar wanted her, but she couldn't stand him. On our wedding day, he swore he'd make trouble.' Walking Thunder thumped a fist on the table, and the tools jumped. 'He did. I was the Emperor's cupbearer in those days. Denjar poisoned a cup one night, and I fed it to the Celestial One. Only his magery saved him. Denjar was there to call me a traitor and howl for my execution, but the Emperor wanted to make my death slower, so he sentenced me instead to the arena. I became a gladiator.'

'I'll bet nobody wanted to meet *you* in the ring!' I ventured.

'Huh. Was pretty good,' he allowed. 'Only can last so long, though. Bound to get killed sometime, so one day when they took us down to the river to build up our wind by swimming, I just went under and let the river take me. Was in the water a long time. Long time, like an old log.' He looked over at me. 'Was Bai Nati who fished me out. When I found out he was a mage, I stayed with him. Hoped he'd teach me enough magery to go back and free my wife.' He rolled a blow tube under his hand, the wall of his self-imposed exile solidly in place once more.

'Make me that crystal blade, and we'll do it,' I promised. 'Or die trying. I don't particularly care which. Do you?'

He measured me for a long moment against what he knew personally and at great cost of the Emperor's power, and then the giant rubbed his nose. 'Right. Where's the fire, then, to melt this stuff?'

'Marner,' Barberry called quietly from the open door.

I moved too quickly for my skinwalker stripes and the room momentarily spun, but I clutched the door jamb and stayed upright. The Umlisi had a smoke tube ready in his hands, but he had not yet lit the fuse. I stepped out into the corridor and looked up it into the darkness. I saw no eyes, but someone up the tunnel laughed a sly, sinister, repulsively intimate laugh.

'Piss off, you,' I growled, though the gooseflesh covered me.

Grumahu hauled me into the spare parts room and went out himself to take the smoke tube from Barberry. 'Light.' The little man touched off the fuse, and the giant hurled the missile. There was a chorus of howls and curses amid the coughing.

'Oho!' chortled the Umlisi. 'That stink up walkers good!' He patted the giant's forearm. 'Big Fella pretty mucking damn good!'

I think it was every word of praise he knew. Walking Thunder rubbed his nose, squinted through the smoke drifting down the tunnel, and said, 'Huh. Come on in here, now, little fellow. One of them's likely to take a notion to send one of your darts back this way.'

When Barberry was safely inside, Grumahu took up station just inside the door, the kenning sword in his hand. I listened for the laughter up the tunnel, but heard nothing. I tapped the blade. 'Did it warn you the walkers were coming closer?'

'Didn't hear a thing till little master there called you.'

'Maybe it judged they were no particular threat this time. All the same, listen for it.' He nodded, stuck another smoke tube in his belt ready for quick use, and accepted some of Barberry's little pot of evergreen paint. This he dabbed on both cheeks, and I could tell he was doing it just to make the Umlisi feel better.

When I came to the worktable, Imlaud vacated the seat for me, and since my legs were a little wobbly with the tension of hearing that sinister laugh, so familiar to me though I didn't know why, I slid onto the stool. The warden kenned, *They make an unlikely pair of friends.*

Sometimes those are the truest ones.

Indeed.

'Help me get the top off this crate, would you?'

Imlaud stuck the chisel in at his side and tapped it with the mallet, working at the nails. 'Paint, Kinu? I fear I do not see how paint will help to fix this sun machine of the Umlisi.'

'I dreamed while I was unconscious from the fall.' I met his fir-colored eyes across the top of the crate. 'I want to see whether the dream was actually some of my memory coming back.'

'Ah,' he said, although he was none the wiser. I worked at my side of the crate, got the nails up, and together we lifted off the lid. I looked down and for a moment saw the shapes I had expected to see: clay pots, each marked with a single spiral, sealed with wax the way Colin Mariner had left his spare set.

Then I blinked.

'Stones?' Imlaud asked. 'What has this to do with paint?'

'Chalcedons,' I breathed. 'Powers, he made his pigments from ground chalcedons! That was the power in his sands, because the gems pick up kenning, that's what Rose told me. With her ring and mine, we're the only two who can hear our own aura—'

'Kinu!' the green warden was saying. 'Stop it!'

I became aware of the chiming, a clashing cacophony of sound. Barberry was holding his ears, and even Grumahu was wincing. I drew a breath and calmed myself in the way . . . Symon? Yes, that was his name – in the way Symon had taught me. The chalcedons responded to my mind, their discordant jangling dying to a hum like some huge hive. I centered myself more, and the hum became a soft murmur like the sea on some distant shore.

Across that murmur the sword in Grumahu's hands began to mutter, and then woke to stridency. 'Walkers,' I said calmly. 'They'll be after these colors. If they get them, everything you love will die.'

Grumahu followed his sword round the door jamb, and Barberry was right on his heels. 'Have your men protect Tigerlily and the mill,' I told Imlaud. He left at a run.

I could hear the clang of sword on sword, and the twanging release of the little man's bow. The giant and the little man were holding against the onslaught for now, but inevitably the tide of walkers would swallow them up if I could not do the next thing, and do it quickly.

I took several of the amber and topaz chalcedons and the ruby gem that was the Servant's stone, and strode from the spare parts room. 'Hold them, lads.'

'Mucking doing, sitting on our thumbs?' Walking Thunder grunted. They had managed to drive the snarling walkers a little way down the tunnel, and now he stooped quickly to hurl another smoke tube. A bone dart shrieked out of the darkness through the space where he had been. He didn't see it, so I merely plucked it out of my shoulder, cursed under my breath, and told them, 'Listen for my signal. When you hear it, get into the supply room and for Powers' sake stay there until I tell you to come out.'

'What Marner do?' the little man wanted to know, sighting down his shaft. He released, and one of the walkers shriveled, wailing.

But I was already running, stopping only to jam an amber chalcedon into the lintel of the tunnel opening. I pounded over the drawbridge across the moat and did the same with one of the topaz gems, jamming this one into a chink in the stones of the rock wall along the lane. When I looked back, the two gems seemed to line up all right.

'Everybody get down! Down, lie flat!' I shouted to the teams of stitchers. Confused, they watched me dashing down the mulched path towards the door at the end of the cavern, and then I heard Auntie Tigerlily's swift order.

The stairs were an ordeal, but finally I made it to the top. I would rather have done the thing properly and not spoiled so much of the craftsmanship, but I had no time for other than desperate measures, so I hacked at the winch rope with my dagger, and the huge door in the ceiling slid open with a resounding thud against its retaining beams.

Many of the crystal fragments broken from the sun prism had fallen into the gear well, and then into the garden when the walker had dumped me, so I knew the job would not be perfect. Words sprang to my lips, words that seemed to come from somewhere else. 'Lady, if thee's ever guided the way for an unworthy mariner,' I prayed, 'let me hear again the music of thy wings. These wee folk have been as faithful as they knew how to an imperfect command. 'Twas not their fault, and they ought not suffer for it.'

Clasping both hands round the ruby chalcedon of the Servant of the Sun, I summoned the Fire. It burst from it nearly out of my control, a red and amber shaft of light. I fought the individual colored strands of light into one tightly twisted fire, guiding myself by the growing harmony of the dual crystal chiming. When the light was a brilliant gold radiance so that my eyes were blinded with it, I kenned, *Fire?*

Painter, it tinkled, acknowledging me. *What would thee make of us?*

Our work is to bind this glass, Fire, supplying that which is missing.

And what is the true-name of this glass?

A voice I did not know answered through my kenning, *I called it Hearthglow.*

Thy will, the Fire acknowledged, and the music of the braided strands tuned in an instant to the Hearthglow prism's own aura. Through my slitted eyelids I watched the huge deck prism healing, its cracks melding, its facets shaping once more into sharp planes and angles, its harmony restored.

When Hearthglow rang true, the Fire queried, *And now, Painter?*

That the window shutters may be opened.

The Fire danced over the hinges, cogs, and gears, woodwind notes now in the crystal tinkling, and the window shutters of the lighthouse opened on morning in the world topside. The sun stood a handspan above the eastern horizon, glowing molten gold in a ruff of burnished clouds.

Hearthglow lit, the deck prism tuning itself as a fainter echo of the sun, and the sunbeam burst upon the garden below. With my Fire, I turned the prism until its light focused in a pure beam. *Now, Giant, get out of the way, here it comes.*

Right, his sword answered, delighting me with his kenned voice.

I gave him and Barberry a moment to get clear, and then I drew the focus to a sharp point and trained it on the topaz chalcedon in the stone wall.

Hearthglow's fire streaked through the sky of the cavern, deflected through the topaz gem to the amber one, and shot down the tunnel past the spare parts room.

I heard them, I heard them die a second time, those walkers, and it was a terrible thing, But I did not hit the one I had hoped to.

I knew that when he cried out with rage, *Painter, you're marked with my Sign!*

And you are marked with mine, my lord.

There is no place to escape, you fool. Give it up. Yield.

And there is no time to escape, either. Give it up. Yield, my lord.

For answer, he laughed, his good humor restored. *Ah, Painter. You're good for me.*

I would not, no, I would not say the same of him. I could still smell Burdock's oozing corpse.

He knew. I heard his laugh receding, echoing in the caves, until finally there was only the padding of his paws, walking away.

I eased the deck prism back to its intended alignment, allowed its brilliance to flood beyond the narrow focused beam I had made of it, and the sun came up on Tigerlily's folk. I extinguished the Fire that slept in the chalcedon, thanking it for its faithful service.

I was aware then of the cheering below, of the sweet growing smell rising from the garden, of the rich perfume of morning drifting in through the open window hatches to meld with it. I was aware of all these things, but they were removed from me a little. I was tired and moved slowly, probably because the blood was streaming from the skin-walker stripes which had grown much wider. 'Imlaud? I'll take that spring water now,' I called, but my call was only a whisper.

I sighed and started down the stairs. Not long after, I heard them coming up, so I eased myself down on the steps to wait for them.

I never got a chance to say a word. Grumahu threw me over his shoulder, bellowed at the Folk to clear the stairs, and we went down two at a time, with Umlisi tumbling ahead of us like peas down a scoop.

CHAPTER TWELVE

The gossamer golden sails whirled steadily in the bright sunlight, and the Folk were busy as bees all over the garden, giving their plants a good watering with the liquid sun they distilled. I sipped more mead, relaxing insofar as I was able while Tigerlily changed the dressings and Imlaud paced.

'The sun mill's pretty, isn't it? Think how your trees could grow with a bit of liquid sun diluted in the water of the pool,' I said to the Eldest to distract him when he came past me again. His show of nerves was making my own stomach flutter.

Imlaud glanced at me as though I had interrupted some private dialogue in his head, looked briefly out to the garden, and nodded. 'Yes,' he agreed and continued walking.

The old Umlisi woman finished bandaging me, patted my arm gently, and helped me into a padded, hooded Umlisi robe. She watched the Yoriandir's back as he prowled restlessly. Her wise eyes lingered on him a moment, and then she looked down at me. 'Are you very afraid?'

'Terrified, Auntie. We don't even know if Marner's boat will hold together when it hits the water.' That was the last secret they'd had to show me, preserved all these years even as the 'spare parts' had been. The dragon ship floated in a dark adjoining cavern, and seemed sound enough, even though it was so very old. I might have enumerated all my other fears, all those whose hopes rested on this fundamentally daft venture, but in truth I dared not let myself think on it too closely. Imlaud's mounting inner panic and Grumahu's dogged persistence in trying to learn to craft crystal in a few scant hours were already a weighty burden.

But I had no need to say any of this to Tigerlily. She knew. From her apron pocket she took a small, wrinkled seed and carefully placed it in my hand. 'It's good sometimes to remember how a garden grows. Folk plant seeds, flowers grow, and all are happy. But the seed is not a seed, then. Is the seed happy?'

Under the bindings, my stripes burned. I looked beyond the wispy white hair of her profile to the illuminated garden. Imlaud crossed my line of vision momentarily, a dark green silhouette, and then passed. I recognized Tigerlily's question for what it was. My blood ran cold, but there was unexpected solace, too, in her carefully worded phrasing. 'I suppose so,' I answered quietly. 'If the seed knows about the plant.'

She closed my fingers gently about the seed. 'Oh, it does know, Marner. It has joy to leap out of the earth and see the sun again. I think it's the same with people when the spirit passes from their old body to a new one.' It was all her life, that wisdom of the seed.

His heavy tread stopped near my head, and I raised a hand against the sunlight as he stepped round me and crouched. 'That about right?'

Imlaud had hurried to meet him, and I heard the Eldest's gasp of awe. I began one myself, but bit it off as the fire of my stripes lashed me. 'Powers, Giant!'

He rubbed his nose as I took the crystal knife. 'Never saw one before,' Grumahu reminded me. 'So will it do, or what?'

I found my voice. 'You're a master. How did you get the engraving *inside* the crystal?'

His skin was showing an embarrassed flush under its bronze, and despite his normal flat tone, I could tell he was pleased at the effect his masterpiece had made on us. 'Well, same as working one of your metal swords, Runt Mage. Made it in layers, hot and cold.' He shrugged. 'Figured it needed to be strong.' He frowned. 'Came out kind of small, though.'

'That's all right!' I hastened to assure him. 'The working probably compacted it and made it more powerful—'

I don't know how long I had been aware of the humming, but suddenly my head was a hive filled with startled Dew-Sippers. The sands spread quickly across the floor of my mind: *fangs and eyes that glowed like heat lightning, rope bridges whipping as the cables were cut, and yellow-banded bodies dropping into the dark waters of the caverns.*

'WALKERS!' I shouted.

The Umlisi working in the garden froze for an instant, hoes poised, hands piled with weeds they had pulled, listening for the bees. But there was no rising hum to indicate an attack on our faithful guards, and the Folk looked at each other, and then at me.

Heedless of the pain, I sprang to my feet, thrusting Imlaud aside. 'They're using poison smoke!' I cried. 'Stop the wind machines!'

Quicker-witted than the rest, Barberry threw himself on the levers. The machinery shrieked, and there were echoing clangs from the bargeways as the mills slowly wound down, but already the first drifts of noxious smoke were pouring into the garden cavern. Hideous shapes began to stagger into the caves from the bargeways, Umlisi guards doubled over with coughing and racked by convulsions. Their skin was the blue color of drowned men.

The Folk held their jacket sleeves over their mouths and noses, but men had still to hold a weapon and women had still to gather their children. Tigerlily looked once up at the 'sun' and her old lips tightened. 'We'll burn all the sun oil, then go topside.' She called the order in the Umlisi tongue, and the Folk began running for the docks.

'No, not that way!' I bellowed. 'That way,' I pointed.

'Head for the stairs to the sun tower: it's the only way out. Go now, Lily.'

'Blessing to thee, Marner.' Her hand rested on my arm a moment, and then she gathered her skirts and walked briskly down past the sun mill.

'Here they come,' Grumahu said quite calmly behind me and drew his chanting sword.

One of the Umlisi women who had caught a barge drifting over from the passages stumbled into me, her hands clutching in agony, her eyes white with the smoke that had burned them as it was burning her lungs. I grabbed the satchel of paint stones and took a firm grip on the dagger.

All around us the bows of the wardens twanged, and bone weapons hissed through our ranks.

'Which is the lane to the ship? I'm all turned around.'

The Eldest's bow sang, and the walker with the spear poised to hurl at my back shriveled. 'Third left.'

Of course, I silently berated myself as I followed him at a run, Grumahu covering my back: the Mariner would have built his storeroom within easy distance of the wharf where he tied up his ship. I should have remembered that.

Captain Hyssop had the rowers at their benches by the time we came racing past the last silver torch on the dock. The dragon-prow floated on the black water in a scum of dead bees and spent arrows. Half the little Umlisi crew tried to cover the rowers with their feathered shields, their eyes fierce and smarting above the cloths they had wound about their noses and mouths against the smoke.

The Yoriandirkin turned at Imlaud's barked command and let go a flight of their long silver-tipped arrows that drove the walkers back a little. That gave Grumahu and me time to cut the bow and stern ropes. The boat began to drift away from the pier, and Imlaud's men vaulted aboard amidships to miss the rowers, quickly fanning out to take over the shield wall from the Umlisi. I made shift to clamber aboard, and the boat rocked as Grumahu shoved us off, then landed on the deck himself. The coxswain's b'mbu drum thumped, and the oars splashed into the water, bit, and heaved us away from the dock.

'Hyssop!' I called urgently. 'Don't take us too far, just out of distance of their arrows. Then hold us in the channel.'

Barberry relayed my order. I saw the look that darkened Hyssop's face, and guessed what he said when he waved a hand at both shores lined with all those flickering eyes. I stowed the satchel under the foremost rowing bench, dodged an arrow, and wormed my way as far forward in the bow as I could. 'Be special boat, Hyssop. Do have magic of her own. Stand clear.'

'The hell you doing?' Grumahu demanded, grabbing up a spare shield as he strode over the thwarts.

'The rowers can't row us all the way down to the entrance. Besides, if the watchers have broken through the cavern's defenses, then so have the bats, and we have no bees to protect us. So,' I glanced at Imlaud, including him in my explanation, 'I'm going to try to close this passageway and open a tao-ti that angles away and downwards, so that the water drains into it and carries us along.'

The giant raised the shield by reflex to deflect an arrow that was mostly spent anyway. 'Through solid rock?'

I pulled the padded hood over my head. 'That's right.'

'Huh,' he snorted, but he held the shield to cover me while I inched forward on the carved prow. I spoke to the ship in kenning.

T'ing Kinu, I kenned, calling her by her true-name.

Aye, Mariner, she responded promptly in a lovely contralto voice that seemed somehow familiar.

At once the ship seemed to shake itself, a movement like an awakening, and although my hand had not touched it, the lens of ruby chalcedon slipped into place over the deck prism eyes. A pure garnet light swept first one side of the channel, and then the other, for all the world like a great beast lifting one eyelid at a time as it surfaced out of sleep.

I heard the walkers murmur, a rumbling unease that echoed across the water.

The shafts of light strengthened to brilliant ruby beams, the t'ing figurehead glaring balefully at its mortal enemies. I looked back along the length of the ship and saw that it was not merely my imagination: every plank, every water drop along the rowers' blades really was glowing with what seemed an inner fire, right to the tip of the fish tail. I smiled, mentally sharing Bai Nati's private amusement in that very odd moment when he had given me my Anazi name.

What is the true-name of the spaces underground? I asked my Dragon Fish.

Tao-dan.

I had guessed it might be this, Way Below, but I hadn't dared to trust to a guess. Now that I knew positively, however, the last fear left my mind. 'Sit down, everybody. You, too, Giant. We're in for quite a ride, unless I miss my guess.' I pitched my kenning out into the channel. *Tao-dan, that thee would gather thy waters to this spot.*

The last of my kenning was still whispering out when the river rose under us with a swift inrush. It must have been drawing from all the waters of that underground realm, because I had a moment of panic that we might actually be crushed against the roof of the hollowed passageway. *Stop! Hold, please.* I drew a breath to steady myself, closed my eyes against the stares of the other passengers and the withering steam of the walkers, and addressed my boat once more. *Stand by, T'ing Kinu.*

Course? she wanted to know.

When I open the new tao-dan, will thee navigate it to the great river Amindrin, please, taking care that our passengers shall be spared great fright? I thought it prudent to add this last bit, having learned a little wizardry from my experience of asking the tree back in Imlaud's forest for 'a few' fruit.

She chuckled throatily, and I knew my hunch had been

right: this was a ship that loved to race.

Tao-dan, open the new way!

Scarcely had I finished kenning when there was a sensation of darkness and immense pressure as the rock closed round us. My heart leaped to my lips in a scream that could not emerge because we were for that instant encased in stone. Then the walls leaped up and around to form the tao-dan, the waters roared in behind us, and *T'ing Kinu* lifted on the flood, her great dragon head proudly above the foaming bow wave.

I struggled to my feet, seized by a fierce exaltation. 'Up the mains'l, lads!'

They probably understood nothing but my gestures, but that was enough, for Barberry and two others jumped up to hoist the golden sheet. My ship took the bit in her teeth, and though there was no wind in that underearth place, the golden sail filled and we raced through the passageways of night, guided by *T'ing Kinu*'s flashing ruby eyes.

Only minutes it seemed, yet it must have been hours that we sailed so, until at last we came to the opening of the tao-dan into Earth-Above. Grumahu's keen hearing warned him first: 'Waterfall!'

I turned with one arm still hooked about the mast. 'You're sure?'

For answer, he merely pointed.

T'ing Kinu, you little witch, what are you about? I said to bear us care—

We shot out through the archway of the cave under the starry night-time sky, flashing through the rapids, caught a gust of moist cool air in the cloth-of-gold sail, and the dragon-prow leaped over the falls.

I had a sick sensation in my stomach, and my arm began to slip from round the mast, but Grumahu reached one massive hand from his seat and plucked me back as I began to fall free, and then *T'ing Kinu* touched down in the foam as easily as a dragonfly alighting on a lily pad and rode proudly to a halt in the broad river.

Course? she questioned archly.

I mopped my face on the sleeve of the padded jacket. Imlaud drew a sighing breath and straightened, letting go of the edge of the bench on which he sat. The Umlisi and Yoriandirkin looked around at each other, and then everyone began to laugh, the tall green folk and the little men with evergreen paint on their faces. Hyssop and I found ourselves looking at each other, and then up at the waterfall. Wordlessly, the Umlisi captain patted the rail of the ship. Good boat, nice *T'ing Kinu.*

I grinned, and Hyssop broke a smile.

Beside me, Grumahu released the three or four Umlisi warriors he had kept from falling as he had rescued me and leaned his hands on his knees, gazing up at the tumbling waters. 'Cacamalu, that's one to tell in the barracks,' he murmured. He shook his head once, snorted, and dropped his eyes to me. 'What now?'

They quieted to hear my reply. I looked around at my motley crew, and spoke to everyone in kenning, now that there was no longer any need to pretend. *Aunty told me your folk can become invisible.*

Hyssop caught his breath and immediately jabbed a finger at five of the Umlisi. I felt an odd sensation, a kind of muffling touch along my skin. The light from *T'ing Kinu*'s eyes grew suddenly much brighter. At first I thought her eyes had flared because she sensed danger, but then I realized it must be that the Mud-Heads' protective spell had built a sort of wall around us and the t'ing light was contained within it. When I looked towards the shore, I found this confirmed: the red reflection on the water only extended some four or five feet out from the boat. The rest was pitch darkness.

I nodded, satisfied. *For the rest of you, some food and then sleep in whatever watches Captain Hyssop thinks are appropriate*. This was a courtesy gesture, there was no need to set watches, the ship herself would warn me of danger, but I'd need Hyssop's support, and he'd feel more himself if he had the discipline of his men well in hand. He nodded.

Imlaud used the mind-voice from his bench as I had done. *I would suggest we be as quiet as possible, nevertheless. We do not know who, or what, may be abroad tonight. There will be merchants and families bound for the city, we should remember, and other parties not so innocent as they. Even now, our advent has probably been observed.*

I grinned. *I hope so.* The men chuckled. *Eldest, will you and your men help the Umlisi with their armor?*

Of course, but we will need Walking Thunder to inspect all afterwards, as he is the only one among us who knows at firsthand how these costumes should be worn.

Scrubbing off the evergreen paint was going to be the most difficult part of this night's preparations I soon realized from the hissed curses among the little men. Not only did the pitch take skin with it as it came off, but more importantly the Umlisi would feel naked and utterly unprotected against their age-old enemies without it. It could not be avoided, though. One whiff of evergreen to set the Emperor's walkers sniffling and we would be caught like sardines in a weir.

I began scrubbing off my own coating of the stuff. The giant folded his arms on his chest. 'Make you something to eat now, Runt Mage, or sleep first?'

'Not much of either, I'm afraid. I've work to do. How long till dawn, do you think?'

He glanced up at the stars. 'Three hours, little more, maybe. Why?'

I kenned, *T'ing Kinu, that thee will take us to Oaxacu, there to arrive no later than four hours before dawn. And please to keep thy lovely eyes concealed as much as possible. We have great need of stealth tonight.*

Indeed, Mariner? Perhaps we should go by the tao-dan-sui, the Way Below Water, then.

No, no, I told her hastily. *That won't be necessary, thanks.*

I heard her sigh. *Very well. To the Forbidden City, then, with scarce a ripple for fun.*

That's it, my pretty.

Her eyes flashed once, and then dimmed to the barest of running lights, a low glow of ruby in the velvet-black night. The golden sail settled to the normal breeze on the river, and we began to move. *You're a lot older than you used to be, Mariner*, I heard my ship murmur, and then she stretched her dragon neck and sailed silently on in the veil the Umlisi made for us.

Grumahu followed as I made for the bow where I had left the satchel of pigment stones. I eased myself down tiredly, my back to the sturdy timbers of the bow, and clutched the satchel to my chest. The giant sat down on the first rowing bench facing me and leaned on his knees.

One of the Umlisi tapped him on the shoulder to pass us a couple of the flat rounds of bread. Grumahu ripped at the food fiercely, forgetting for the moment his policy of waiting until Mage had his dinner first. 'Thought you were going to make paints out of those,' he said, waving the diminished round of bread at the stones I had spread out on a cloth. The dimmed eyes of my t'ing boat cast enough light still for me to work, and I was sorting them by color.

The stones claimed my full attention, and I merely grunted something in reply.

'With no grinding stone? Chips will be too big if you just smash them,' he objected.

'I doubt you could smash a chalcedon in the ordinary way anyway,' I murmured, holding a stone to the light from the bow to judge its color more accurately. The ruby glow made differentiating sapphires from deep amythysts difficult, and the greens were nearly impossible.

'Help you?'

'You can.' I handed him a stone. 'Tell me whether that's topaz or clear.'

He squinted, holding the stone up between himself and the ruby light, and then sighting through it up at the stars. 'Yellow.'

'Right, I thought so too.' I put it in the pile. 'Keep an ear cocked to your sword. If it tells you anything tonight, I want to know about it immediately. Just because the Umlisi have us hidden in their still spell we shouldn't assume nothing on the river can hear us, or sense us. We don't know what's under our keel even now, though I'm sure the boat herself would warn us of danger from that quarter. Still, as a master of mine used to try to drum into my head, never be taken unawares.'

'Hasn't said a thing,' he assured me. He cast an eye back over his shoulder the length of the boat. 'Pretty tough lot, the Folk. Wouldn't want to be going into Oaxacu without *my* weapons.'

'Aye, that's for a fact, mate. I just—'

The two things happened so closely together that I scarcely had time to register the wave of kenned evil that raced down upon us like a tidal wave, washed over us and swept down the river, before *T'ing Kinu*'s eyes flew open, snapping, and the beacon fire at Oaxacu caught and climbed straight up in a column of flame that was repeated closer and closer down the valley, flashed into light on the mountain under whose shoulder we were sailing, and sped on.

'By the Tree, he's dying!' Imlaud's voice was strained.

Grumahu stared up at the city. His lips moved, but no sound came out except for the gulp when he swallowed the cry he would not bellow into the night.

Barberry sat down on the nearest bench. 'Will pith all childrens now,' he said softly. 'Many childrens go to Emperor tonight.' He took off his feathered helmet and ran a hand through his hair tiredly. 'Too late, Marner.'

'No,' I said. Their eyes swung to me. *No*, I said to the Power scouring the land for me, *you don't win the game that easily, you mucking bastard.*

Do trust this boat not to founder? I questioned them. Hyssop nodded immediately, and Barberry put his head to one side, studying me. His eyes were dark and dancing in the ruby light from the t'ing ship's eyes. The other little men stirred uneasily, most nodding and shrugging. *Hold on, then*, I directed.

The giant got it right away, struck his hands together, and came to sit down in front of me, settling his sword and grasping the rail firmly with one hand. I knew the other would brace me if I needed it.

'Better sit down, my lord,' I told Imlaud quietly. 'I'm not sure whether this will work with no tree branches to twine together, but if it does, it's likely to be sudden.'

'I have learned that where thee's concerned, my friend, anything is likely to be sudden,' he said, and only half in jest. He motioned his men down and sat himself.

I turned and went forward into the bow for a private word with my dragon-prow. I took one last look around to see that everyone was secure, and then I said the mind words: *The tao-chi! Take wing, my pretty!*

Fiercely eager to be in action once more, my ship found the Way Above under her keel and leaped into the air, dragon neck outstretched, the planks of her sides flaring like wings, and we streaked towards the Forbidden City like a shooting star.

I was looking down on the black satin ribbon of the river as we flashed across the hinterlands of Oaxacu. Everywhere along the waterway I could see barges and boats of every size and description suddenly pulling up anchor stones or untying from saplings along the riverbank. All that swarm of water beetles had been agitated by the signal fires, and now they were jockeying for position in the current, frantic to arrive with their cargoes of tribute and slaves in time for the huge sacrificial ritual. After all, any village whose tributary offering was not noted down in the priests' book stood a good chance of being put to the flint knives; every man, woman, and child.

Things were so chaotic down there, that I told the Umlisi to save their strength. We didn't need to be invisible, only quiet. Even at this height, we could hear the cries of astonishment and fear following after us. I am sure that from the river we must have seemed a firedrake, a malignant omen, perhaps even the Emperor's spirit itself, returning upriver to its dark and silently cold fastness at the Forbidden City.

Grumahu tapped my arm and pointed to tangled flotsam where a long barge and a slaver had collided. As we watched, the slaver slipped beneath the surface and disappeared in bubbling foam. 'They'll be the lucky ones tonight,' I murmured. 'Help me tie this, would you?'

He grunted a little sound that might have been a derisive snort. 'Pretty bumpy cat-soldier. Looks like a jag'har with ticks.' He pulled another lacing snug, then loosened it slightly in consideration of the bandages I was wearing under it.

'I don't see any way round that,' I replied. 'I can't take the chance of bleeding through it.'

He turned from securing the last thong of my cat-soldier's uniform and hefted my pack basket. The hilt of his sword protruded from the top. Since these baskets were made without tops (and since the sword was far too long for it to have closed even if there had been a leather flap), the hilt of the sword was in plain view. The Umlisi back at Il Numator had done their best to disguise the shape with a feathered sheath and a bit of garland wound round the handle, but they had been constrained by my reminder that we might have to use the sword at any time and wouldn't be able to free it from anything much more substantial than a little of the white cloth and some feathers. Even then, I fretted that drawing the sword from over his shoulder out of a pack basket instead of a scabbard might cost the giant crucial instants. Grumahu, however, was unperturbed.

'Takes cat-soldiers a minute to get their paddle-swords out too, Runt Mage. Be quick enough, comes to it. Best part is, jag'hars still won't know what the hell they're looking at even when I've got it in my hands.'

Now I hefted my paddle-sword and rested it across my shoulder, wondering how accurate his prediction might be, and whether we would have to test it. The giant bent to pull on the jag'har claws of his own shin guards, and I looked down the length of the boat. We were so steady in the air that the Umlisi were balancing easily on the benches while the Yoriandirkin helped them dress in costumes like those the male children would be wearing, costumes intended to make them look like the littlemen themselves: gilded sandals inset with pieces of turquoise and lapis lazuli; woven headbands in bright colors; and feathered tabards, bright with designs of birds or flowers. At any other ritual on any other occasion, the outfits would have presented a very colorful sight, but of course the little feathered coats would not in any way impede the action of a flint knife, and the poor boys were going to be stepping in blood in their gilded sandals going up the long flights of steps to the platform atop the Temple of the Eternal Flame. I had asked Grumahu whether the priests gave the doomed children a drug of some sort to make them biddable on that last halting climb, and he had confirmed that the last thing any of those children would remember was eating a piece of honeyed fruit.

With luck, not one of them would have to eat it tonight.

With every mile of dark landscape that passed under our keel, my confusion became worse. I'd had no starflower for several hours and was trying to conserve the small supply we had brought with us. I looked up once from checking by touch through the small pouch on my belt for the wrinkled seed Auntie Tigerlily had given me. Grumahu was watching me with concern. 'Just keep reminding me who I am,' I said out of that confusion. 'Just keep calling me by my name, all right? Don't let me drift too much, or I'll drag anchor in this gale and never—'

He took me firmly by the arm. 'Easy, Runt Mage. No gale. See? Stars.'

'There's a gale,' I said grimly through my teeth. 'You just can't feel it.'

'Emperor whishing about, that it?'

It was so unexpected a word, and so apt a description of the emanations coming from the city, that I laughed in spite of myself. The confusion drew back, and I knew myself again. I was Kinu, a shipwrecked sailor, bound for Oaxacu to do battle with a dying emperor for the lives of a little boy, a tree, and a hostage wife. Right.

Settled.

I drew a breath of the night air. 'Phew! What the hell is that stink?'

The giant patiently drew me round to face the bow. 'Fire mountain belches smoke sometimes. Stinks then. Usually, the breeze carries it away, though, and you can smell the orchards and vineyards.' He gripped the rail beside me, leaning a little, and the dragon-prow's light betrayed him, illuminating the fierce longing he had probably thought was hidden by the night.

I looked away to give him his privacy, up to the black-against-black cone that rose before us, cutting a wedge out of the starry sky. We skimmed a high hilltop and streaked into the valley, *T'ing Kinu*'s wings flaring to cup the air and slow us for a landing. The city, jeweled and bedecked with bonfires, emerged from under a pall of thin, noisome smoke, and its broad avenues surging with thousands of torches became living arteries of fire.

'Oaxacu, Queen of Cities,' the giant murmured beside me.

I forced a compliment past the clattering confusion rising in my mind once more, past the sound of the raging gale. 'It's beautiful, Captain.'

When I opened my eyes, he was holding out the gourd of starflower. I accepted it gratefully and drank a sparing mouthful. The din was muffled enough now that I could think.

Course? my ship inquired. *Shall we blow aside a few of those barges?*

No, a quiet *landing, T'ing Kinu, if thee please. My head is pounding.*

I know, she murmured sympathetically in her musical voice. *It's thy ring, Mariner. The Dark One uses it against thee.*

I got it. For one brief moment, I had it, whole and entire, my life, my Self, *a man's heavy silver signet set with a single gem . . . 'You and I,' she said in her musical voice, 'are the only ones who ken the sound of our own auras' . . . 'Wake! The ring is endangered!' The heavy padding of the beast, flagstones sinking beneath his footsteps . . . fumbling now, fumbling through the bandages for the ring on the bedside table. Where the bloody hell was it? Where?*

Here!

'Aengus, you jackass!' I berated myself in joy.

A moment later I couldn't breathe, he was holding his hand over my mouth, he was strangling me, and I fought.

'Damn it, Runt Mage! The hell's the matter with you, shouting like that? That troop of cat-soldiers down there heard you!' he snarled.

My head fogged like a window pane breathed upon by some cold frost. The memories slipped past my reach again, all save one. I pushed his hand away. 'It's my ring, he's got my ring.'

Imlaud must have come up to the bow to help subdue me if necessary. He exchanged a look with the giant. 'Thee speaks of the Emperor, Kinu?'

My lip was a little cut where the giant had pressed the flesh against my teeth. I spat the blood over the rail. 'Yes. There will be a ring on his finger when they carry him into the tomb tonight. I've got to get it.'

Grumahu whistled low between his teeth and shook his head, looking up the fire mountain towards the silent city visible only as a jut of walls and towers some five miles distant.

T'ing Kinu touched down in a shallow paddy, one of a patchwork of growing fields that had been made by digging diversionary canals for the river water. She had chosen the place well: though near the harbor, we were screened from that busy centre of activity by high levee walls crowded with the huts of poorer farm families, deserted tonight for the lights and rare spectacle offered in the city. Here the ship coasted to a stop beside the earthen wall.

Hyssop whispered an order, and all the Umlisi except Barberry began hopping lightly ashore, careful of their costumes. Unexpectedly he reached up to offer me something I couldn't identify in the dark until my hand closed round the slim hilt of a cedar knife. 'Be good thing to have if must go 'mong walkers.'

The little bugger had understood every word I said. I rubbed my nose. 'Bye, Hyssop. If you ever take up pirating, let me know,' I muttered.

The Umlisi troop slipped away through the narrow space between one hut and the next. Hyssop flashed me a grin, waved, and they were gone.

The Yoriandirkin, too, were ready. Imlaud's men swung over the rail, crouched for a moment to listen, and went single file down the narrow levee as surely as cats and nearly as noiselessly. The Eldest looked after them a moment. 'We will take back as many of the trees as we are able,' he said, 'even if we cannot find Nilarion herself, for surely it would not be right to have come so far only to leave them in torment.'

I gripped his hand. 'Good luck, Eldest. Remember the tao-dan, the Way Below, if you have to double back to the river.'

He laughed a little. 'Nay! That is an adventure I shall leave to thee!'

The Eldest and Grumahu gripped hands, and then the tree warden followed his men.

The three of us were silent when they were all gone. 'Don't like leaving them, Runt Mage,' Grumahu said finally.

'Garn, ye'd think it was going to be for all time,' I snorted, but I got the tone of it all wrong, and both of us heard it. I looked up at the tall, rather heavily set young man with the shock of blackest hair and woodsmoke-gray eyes. 'Let us go to your lady, my lord. I'll set her spirit free if I can. And beware Jorem: the bastard's about, I can feel it.'

'Easy, lad, take it easy, calm down. Here, drink.' His eyes were worried beneath his shaggy brows as he stumped quickly over to me, flask in hand.

The flotjin burned delightfully all the way down to my stomach, and I sighed with pleasure. 'Thanks, Skipper. Been a long time between drafts.' I lowered the flask, wiping my lips, and his brows were drawn straight as a crowbar in a frown.

'Talking crazy again, Runt Mage.'

I swallowed the flowery taste of the tea. 'No, you just reminded me of somebody else for a minute there.' I made the horizontal wave with my hand.

'Tis time, Mariner, her lovely musical voice reminded me.

I nodded. *Thee feels the Emperor's kenning, T'ing Kinu?*

Aye, Mariner. 'Tis a gale with silent winds, and it is rising every moment we delay.

I would not risk losing thee to those winds. Hide thee among the clouds until our friends summon thee. On no account seek me in the city itself.

She was silent a moment. *I shall be waiting for thee afterwards. Thee has merely to call, as always.*

As always, I told her.

The giant gave me a hand ashore, and Barberry lightly

followed us. She took off and circled once about the paddy before setting her neck into the night wind.

'Pretty,' Grumahu commented.

I watched my ship's eyes fade in the night, kissed my ring for luck, and followed the giant and the little man towards the Emperor's city.

CHAPTER THIRTEEN

We were there when they opened the gates, two jag'har knights standing with a troop of others in a staging area to the left of the main road. The formation was a loose one; our time had not yet come. Grumahu leaned on his spear in the practiced save-the-feet posture of soldiers everywhere. I leaned on mine to keep myself from falling over. Beneath the fur uniforms, my walker's stripes were raging bands of fire at shoulder, back, and leg.

'All right?' the giant questioned. His eyes as he turned his head to me shone dark under the snarling upper jaw of the jag'har headdress.

I considered how best to answer, but gave it up, as my stock of curses in his language wasn't adequate to the job. 'Not bad. I wonder if our friend is still around.' I wanted to know whether Barberry was close by, as he'd said he would be. In the press, we might have become separated, and with all the priests about, I did not dare send out a kenning.

The spear nearly rocked out of my hands as the Umlisi waggled it. He could not touch either Grumahu or me without rendering us invisible too, and that would have been disastrous. In fact, that was the chief danger in this crowd. I felt better now that I knew he was in front of us and between the giant and me.

Grumahu had seen the spear move. 'Guess he is, still.' He smiled a little at his own clever phrasing. If he was nervous in the least, he didn't show it.

By contrast, my own nerves were twanging like harpstrings out of tune. Half of it was the sounds coming from beyond the gate. I wished I could have heard only the aimless chat of the men around us, the restless settling and re-settling of paddle-swords and spears, the occasional growled curse as one trod on another's foot. But I could hear the other noises as well, and they made the hairs rise on the back of my neck, because I knew that rattle and click, that shuffle, for what it was. There were walkers beyond that gate, a lot of them . . . *the sun red behind the walls of the skellig, fog growing out of the ground, the sea a distant booming that we could not hope to reach . . . the muck, the swallowing slime of the bog hole, and terror as I sank in past my shoulders . . .*

Timbertoe was holding me up by one of the straps of my pack, but it wasn't Timbertoe when I looked up, dazed, it was a darkly sunburnt man with fierce eyes in an animal's snarling face, and panic shot through me . . .

'No, he's all right. Leave him alone,' I heard a familiar voice explaining in its peculiar stolid way. 'Just got hold of some bad liquor last night. One of those cheap inns downriver.'

The other pair of hands was withdrawn. There was a reason I wasn't supposed to look at this other man, but I couldn't remember what it was. I kept my head down and managed to say, 'I'm all right now, thanks. Bit dizzy for a minute.'

The other cat-soldier said companionably enough, 'Well, I can understand that, brother. Those damned innkeepers are all alike. They'll sell you fermented dog piss and then turn round and tell you it's your stomach that's bad, not their brew. But you don't want to let your commander catch you looking bad tonight of all nights. Brace up.' He struck me lightly on the shoulder, right on the walker's stripe.

Had it not been for the spear propping me, I would surely

have gone to my knees. 'Thanks for the reminder,' I said through my teeth.

He leaned closer, so that we were shoulder to shoulder, while Grumahu moved hastily to circle round behind him. 'You're wearing armor under your uniform, aren't you? So am I. Hell with orders, I'm not walking into this place without some protection against one of their bone points either. Like to make a wager? I'll bet half the lads here are wearing it too, and the other half are wishing they were.' He snorted a subdued laugh.

Grumahu's vast hand gripped his shoulder, not hard, but enough to get the point across. 'Shut up,' the giant said very, very quietly, his eyes going meaningfully to other members of the troop, none of whom was looking our way. But they may have been listening, and the garrulous soldier seemed suddenly to realize he had said too much. He gave a tug to his headdress and moved away.

Grumahu turned his back to the road casually, rubbed his nose, and asked behind his hand, 'Stay on your feet? Or want to sit down awhile?'

'Is anyone else sitting down?'

'No. Could go further up on the hill, though. Not so many people there.'

It would mean picking our way through the troop, and likely enough I'd have to look up at least once. Someone might see the blue color of my eyes, that was it, that was what I was supposed to remember. 'No, better not,' I told him. 'We've got a good place here.' I slid my hands up on the spear shaft and tapped my right ring finger. I needed to see whether the ring was on the Emperor's hand when the bier was carried past our vantage.

Grumahu understood. He nodded. 'Sip, then.' He was uncorking the gourd when his head came up, and he paused. Then he finished drawing the cork. 'Coming,' he reported.

I trusted his ears, though I could hear nothing myself. I took two quick gulps of starflower tea, jammed the cork back in the neck of the flask, and began a centering meditation. I must have control. I must not ken. I must not let anyone see my eyes. I must not let the malignant, whishing spirit find me here in this crowd, only twenty paces away from the gates within which he was master. Above all, I must not jeopardize Grumahu, because it was incredibly stupid of me to have brought him here at all, and now it was too late to send him away. Not that he'd have gone. Walking Thunder would do what he damn well pleased anyway.

The other cat-troopers around us were unaware as yet. Through the calming waves of the meditation, I centered on one voice, unable to shut it out because he sounded as though he needed to clear his throat, and that if he did he'd hawk up gravel. I guessed him for a man who'd been hit in the throat with the butt of a spear at some point in his soldiering life.

'No, listen, I'm telling you, it was as clear as a breakfast gong, and right above us as we were marching up the road. "My thing!" this voice said. "He's got my thing!" And then there was this tremendous whoosh and a huge red eye, and then there was nothing.'

For a moment there was silence among the listeners, then one asked, 'So then what did you do?'

A slight hesitation before Gravel Voice rasped, 'We fell back to defensive positions.'

'Hah!' somebody else jeered good-naturedly. 'Is that what they call it now? Cacamalu, Ladrax, that was pretty good!' The teasing voice went melodramatic: ' "My thing! He's got my thing!" ' He guffawed. 'Never knew t'ings were choosy about—'

'It was a t'ing, I'm telling you!' Ladrax retorted in a flurry of gravel. 'And it had some poor bastard by the—'

'FORM UP!' the order came down the line.

The men hefted their spears, replaced their headdresses if they had removed them, and quickly moved into ranks.

There was a subdued chuckle and one final cough, and then we stood motionless, awaiting the passage of the Emperor. I held myself as straight as everyone else, but I had drawn my jag'har's snout forward over my eyes so I was in effect looking out through the mouth of a cave with two ivory stalactites framing the view.

At first there was nothing much to be seen, since it would not have been proper military decorum to look right, down the road where the procession was drawing near. I could hear the steady thumping of the drums and the jangling of a lot of hand bells, but it was not music of any kind, at least not to my ear, schooled as it was to the strumming of a harp or the fluting of a pipe.

The standard bearers were at the front of the procession, at the place I would have expected to see heralds or priests. Perhaps this was to signify that the procession and everything in it, every*one* in it belonged to the dead king. I doubt anyone had to be reminded. I centered my meditation further, and the pain withdrew, the confusion withdrew, until I was watchful eyes only, not a mind to be touched if the Emperor's spirit should suddenly screech a kenning to see who in the crowd jumped.

Priests formed the next rank in the funeral procession. They wore the only full-length robes I had yet seen in this country, and feather capes of brilliant red and glossy black. Their hair was oiled and pulled back into a severe knot at the backs of their necks, and the jade earrings they wore must have weighed several ounces apiece. Each priest had in addition a staff banded with more jade, surmounted by arching feathers. Their gaze was haughty, despite the blood dripping slowly down each man's cheeks; the gashes high on their cheekbones were apparently self-inflicted, the blood an offering to the Emperor. Their flint knives were thrust through their sashes, in plain view of the silently watching people, and the tips of them were red.

The high priest, distinguished by having a border of

heavy gold embroidery on his cloak and a necklet of gold disks not unlike the ones on the armor I had hidden under my jag'har uniform, stepped out in front of the standard bearers, held up the key to the city in the sight of all, and unlocked the gates. I think the sudden clearly audible rattle of delight from the citizens of the dead city gave even the priest pause, because he seemed to take a little longer at swinging the gates back to fasten them than was strictly necessary. Then he raised his staff, beat it three times on the road, and passed through the portal. I should like to have seen what happened to him on the other side, but I could not, not without turning my head. Obviously he was not expecting the walkers to attack him, though, and I wanted to know why not.

After the priests had gone by, the procession seemed to speed up a little. Possibly those to the rear were simply closing ranks, unconsciously seeking the protection of numbers. The eagle knights marched in next, the fixed amber eyes and vicious hooked beaks of their headdresses protruding above stern faces. I had understood from Grumahu that there was considerable rivalry between the cats and the eagles, but as nearly as I could tell, none of their eyes flicked to us, and certainly I heard no sound from behind me. The rivalry, if not put to rest with the dead king, was at least under control tonight.

There were nobles with jade and silver jewelry and high sandals to mark their class. There were more soldiers, some jag'hars this time, and then they marched the children past us.

Powers, what a sad thing that was. The boys and girls, ranging from about eleven or twelve years old down to five or six – just old enough to climb the temple stairs unassisted – each held to the shoulders of the child in front, so that they moved in undulating human chains. The coats of the boys were mockingly bright with feathers, and the little girls' dresses were of bleached white cloth heavily embroidered and dotted with precious stones. The children looked like a flock of birds, but their eyes were ringed with dark exhaustion bruises, and their mouths were open, their lips cracked. They had not been treated well in their captivity.

And, since the ceremony would last so long, they had not yet been given the drug that would have brought them oblivion. There is nothing so devastating as the look of a child who has been betrayed. I had to close my eyes to keep within my control meditation . . . *a boy no older than eight or nine years, with a blanket draped hastily about him, who stared at the twitching thing on the ground, unable to connect it with his father . . . his eyes, his eyes that followed me as I rode towards the sea . . .*

Tiwi's eyes, one puffed, both turned shocked and hard since the last time I had seen him. He straggled past with the other children, looking aside as though he could not face the gate looming before him.

Wild anger ignited in me, and I began to surface from the control meditation. At that moment, Tiwi stumbled against the boy in front of him and, in the process of sorting himself out, looked quickly behind him to see whether the priests who followed might have noticed his transgression. None had, and the boy's shoulders relaxed, his head turning front once more. In so doing, his gaze crossed mine.

I saw him suck in his breath. To make matters worse, the whole column drew to a shuffling halt, bottle-necked at the gate where one little girl and her twin brother had suddenly grasped the bronze bars and clung, wailing piteously. A couple of the cat-troopers to either side of me looked that way, and the attention of everyone in the column was momentarily diverted.

Tiwi dropped his eyes to the earth at his feet and with his gilded sandal drew the roughest outline of a fish I have ever seen. But I knew what it was, and he knew. A moment later when the procession resumed, the boy scraped out the sign with his foot, a faint smile on his face. He did not look up at me again, nor did he try to ken. He was a likely lad to be a mage, and I wondered whether Bai Nati might have given him his aura after all.

More soldiers, a few more priests of lesser rank, nobility.

Finally there was a long gap in the processional, an empty space in which only two people walked. The priest with the ritual drum I discounted, but the cat-soldier next to him was Denjar. I tightened my hand on my spear as though it was his neck, my control meditation wavering. You lousy, lousy bastard, I thought coldly, but I was careful not to ken it.

The powerful hatred in me must have attracted the Emperor's questing shade, though, because instantly the terrible shrieking noise in my head came back threefold, and one of my eyes – the one that drooped – streamed with tears of pain. I bit my lips, but I was not so stricken I did not know when Denjar raised his hand and stopped the procession. A scalding sweat broke on me under the uniform, and I hastily tilted the snout of the jag'har headdress a little more towards the ground.

'Well, well,' he said in the spreading hush as the procession clumsily drew to a halt. 'Grumahu. Do come down.'

The giant did the only thing he could to save the situation for me. In one fluid motion, he shucked off the pack, drew his paddle-sword rather than his bronze one, and shouldered me aside to leap down into the road. 'Denjar, you lying scum!' he roared.

The disruption was so unexpected that none of the troopers around me reacted in that first moment.

Barberry, hide the great sword from Big Fella's pack, I kenned as quietly as possible. Out of the corner of my eye, I saw the feathered sheath round the hilt disturbed, and then the sword vanished from sight. I drew my paddle-sword, held it down along my leg, and began to edge sideways towards the closed litter that had halted a little way short of the jag'har troop in which I stood. We had expected the Emperor to be carried on an open litter so that his subjects might venerate him, but the corpse was hidden within the curtains of the litter. I would have to part them to see whether they were sending him with the ring still on his finger. And if I had to get that close, this would be my best, perhaps my only, chance to snatch it.

Denjar and Grumahu were circling, each man readying himself, and this gave me another moment. I got between two cat-soldiers who were fumbling for their weapons and felt the touch at my knee as Barberry took hold of my jag'har shin guards. He had timed it so well neither of the other troopers noticed.

'Ring,' I whispered aloud to the Umlisi, whom I could see sharply against the paler forms of the people outside the stillness spell. He nodded, we slipped through the soldiers into the road, and then the giant and the butcher of Anazi swung up their swords at the same moment.

Denjar feinted suddenly left, but Grumahu was too canny a fighter and did not block there, meeting the obsidian blade as it came at him from the right. I saw him put some mustard into the countering block, and Denjar winced and fell back a step, recovering immediately and parrying Grumahu's attack. Barberry tugged at me impatiently, and he was right. Come whatever else might, I had to get to the litter.

We ran towards the cordon standing alertly round the Emperor's litter, their weapons bristling, eyes going everywhere. The paddle-swords clattered together further up the road, but I could not spare a look. Barberry looked up at me inquiringly. Careful to make no sound, I took off my pack. It was too bulky for this work, and though I hated to put down my color pots, there was no other way to draw off some of the guards around the litter. I drew Walking Thunder's blade, and dropped the pack near a bulge in the line of troopers at the side of the road where they strained outward to see what was happening in the fight. I gestured the Umlisi on.

The officer in charge of the honor guard surrounding the

litter barked an order at the jag'hars on the side of the road, and they immediately drew back to their positions, snapped to attention by his tone. My pack, now clearly visible, lay where I had dropped it in the middle of the road. The officer barked again, pointing at it; a man in the front rank started to deny it was his, and the officer stepped away from the defensive wall round the Emperor's litter. Barberry and I saw the opening at the same moment.

If I drew a full breath, I might touch the honor guards to left and right of the opening in the line. With Barberry clinging to my jag'har claws, I darted between them sideways and reached to part the curtains of the litter.

The darkness within was nearly complete, but the reflected torchlight showed me enough to know the priests had seated the shrunken form on his throne, and the ring with its broken stone was on his hand, a pale glimmer of chalcedon and silver. I snatched at it, jostling the elaborately robed figure, and the dead jaw fell open. *Not so fast, mate.* Shocked at the kenning, my eyes snapped to the face that now sagged forward into the torchlight.

It was like looking into a cracked mirror.

The visage was deeply lined, a leathery, ancient face still with the sun-blotches of the lifetime sailor darkening cheeks and nose even through the death pallor, but there was no doubt that his skin had once been light like mine, not earth-colored like Grumahu's, and the few wisps of hair escaping from under his elaborate golden headdress were rusty white, so he had in his prime been a red-headed man. I knew with certainty, too, that his eyes had been blue. It could not be, but it was. I was touching the hand of a man who should have been dead for five hundred years, not for five hours.

Only the good die young, boy. His chuckle was a sinister, repulsively intimate sound, and I knew in that instant Colin Mariner had never laughed so in his life. The Power of the Dark had taken the human man's skin and become an emperor here in Earth-Above.

He opened his eyes. 'It's the oldest pirate trick in the book, isn't it?'

I hurled myself backwards as the Emperor suddenly lurched off the throne, one skeletal hand reaching for me.

Barberry grabbed for me to hide me within his spell once more, but it was too late.

The Emperor of Earth-Above sprung the trap he had carefully prepared for me: the bone dart was in his hand, and he moved suddenly to plunge it deep into my neck.

Tch, tch, pickpocket, he chided. *You disappoint me. I expected a better game than this. You've had enough practice at it.*

It took me a long time to fall backwards to the dirt of the road. It didn't feel like dying, but I knew it must be death that the captain of the guard saw in my eyes to make him lower his paddle-sword slowly and back up a couple of paces to give me room to topple. He thrust out an arm, barring his men from crowding forward to finish me off with their spears, and looked up to the Emperor. 'This is the one, Celestial One?' His voice wavered curiously, and I thought maybe he pitied me until I realized it was my hearing that was going, not his voice.

The Emperor rasped, 'Of course this is the one.'

I did not feel anything when I hit the ground; in fact, I only knew I was down because the dust puffed suddenly around me, then drifted up to halo the torches. I heard a familiar voice bellowing. Save your breath, Skipper, I thought. It's too late. I've beaten you home to port . . .

'HOLD!' came a shout from the direction of the gate. 'Denjar, what is the meaning of this outrage! ON YOUR FACES BEFORE THE CELESTIAL ONE!' The head priest strode through the bowing crowd, the senior clerics in his wake, all of them with the flint knives in their hands. He made a deep obeisance, then whirled to the captain furiously. If I had had a stomach any more, it would have turned: the hem of his robe, sodden and already blackened with the blood of sacrificial victims, whipped me across my open eyes. I didn't feel it, but I could smell it. I wondered how much of it was Umlisi blood, and then I thought of Tiwi's little sketched fish.

Inwardly I screamed with rage, the sound bouncing from empty room to empty room in the ruined skellig of my soul. There was incredible pressure in my skull, in the wry bones of my jaw that opened in a primal cry against the Dark though no sound emerged, in my neck muscles down into my painting hand, *and the bone dart moved.*

The numbness was momentarily shattered by an icy pulse of agony that swept through me and died to nothingness once more, but I knew I had felt the thing move like a splinter squeezed. I could not afford to think that I might be driving the dart inward, so I lay in my body, gathering my spirit to try to move it again.

The high priest's voice pierced the fog in my mind. He must have been speaking, but I had not heard him in my intense inward preoccupation. '. . . jag'har guards fighting like two commoners in the marketplace? An unknown thug – ' here he spurned me with his foot, but it made as much impact as kicking a sack of grain '– allowed to disturb my lord's passage? The ritual itself—'

'Huacan.' The Emperor's dry-as-dust voice stopped him in full stride. 'This is the one.'

The priest kicked dirt in my face as he whirled. 'This jag'har knight, Celestial Sire?'

The Mariner sighed, and there was a rattle at the end of it. 'He's no cat-soldier. Expose his face. Let the people see what the Flayed One looks like; let them know what their Emperor will look like when he returns with the sun tomorrow morning.'

'You shall look like yourself, Celestial Sire. You shall not die,' the priest said strongly.

'Don't strive to be a twit, Huacan,' I heard the Emperor advise in an undertone. 'You don't have to work that hard.

Just pick him up – carefully, mind you, he has one of my darts in him – and let's get on with this.'

I struggled against their hands, but all I could manage was a feeble elastic flopping. My face was temporarily towards the litter, and I saw him watching me. *Don't try to move, lad. The dart's quite near your spine, I think, and we don't want any accidents, do we? Relax. The pithing won't hurt a bit, I promise.*

I tried to ken a rich obscenity at him, but only succeeded in setting up a crashing clatter within the crystal walls of my spirit trap that deafened me for a moment. When I became aware again, my head was cold and the ivory stalactites of my helmet were gone. They must have displayed me to the people, as I was on a level now with the Emperor's litter. I could see the shafts of the spear-litter that held me across the brawny shoulders of two eagle knights beyond my sandals.

'But Grumahu attacked us, Celestial One.' Denjar's voice, deferential, but confident.

The Emperor was weakening; I could hear it in his voice and in his ragged breathing. 'Did you think I didn't know it was *you* who poisoned my cup all those years ago, not Grumahu?' he asked, and the captain of the jag'hars froze. The Emperor fixed him with a stare. 'His wife refused you, didn't she? Yes, and you were so jealous you set out to ruin him.' He sighed again. 'Grumahu.'

The priest called sharply, 'Approach, traitor! The Celestial One would speak to you!'

I watched the dust puffs rising over the heads of the cat-soldiers as Walking Thunder approached. I smiled when I saw him, but Grumahu only swallowed hard when he saw me. I wanted to tell him it was all right, because I was going to work the bone dart out – if I had time before they sucked the spirit, the self, out of me and gave my body over to the Dark Fire that burned in the Mariner's rapidly failing one.

The Emperor's voice came now as a hoarse, rasping

whisper: '. . . only man I could ever really trust, Giant. I want you to know I was truly sorry when you were condemned to the arena.'

'Load of pure celestial cacamalu,' Grumahu said calmly.

The Emperor laughed. It went on and on and turned into an ebbing tide of breath. I strained to turn my head to see him. His lips were blue, and just when I thought the Dark One might have miscalculated and trapped himself in a dead body, he drew a huge breath and leaned back against the throne. A moment later his mind-voice sounded in my head, weak but acidic still: *You should see your eyes, the hope in them. Well, no such luck, I'm afraid. Actually you should be hoping I don't go down in the Mariner's body, because if I do, all those spirits I'm holding in my traps will die too. Yes, that does include Grumahu's bride, Painter. And you yourself, of course.*

He turned his gaze to Grumahu. '. . . execution of course, Denjar's right about that. But you merit a death by combat, if you choose, rather than going by Huacan's knife.'

'Thanks,' the giant said. 'Sire, I do choose.'

The Emperor lifted a feeble hand. 'See to it, Huacan. And let it be fair, on pain of your own death: three bouts, and if he survives, he's a free man.'

The priest didn't like it, but he bowed.

Watch your back, Giant, I kenned. I had not tried to force the words beyond the trap, and perhaps it was the very quietness of them that helped some whisper of my thought to escape. Grumahu looked down at me. I did not tell him that Barberry had his sword and must be about somewhere; I did not want my kenning to alert the Emperor, who thus far had not said anything about the Umlisi. To take my mind off it and shield my thoughts, I forced the splinter some more, gasping with the pain as I tried to work my muscles. There was an odd grating sound that I identified after a moment as the point of the dart scraping against the bones of my neck. Powers, if it was as deep as that . . .

I came out of the darkness to find myself looking down on a procession for a dead man. For a moment I heard the slow clopping of a horse-drawn wagon and I saw a green man with a banner in his hands leading the way, but then the dream dissolved, and I was looking between the toes of my sandals past two eagle knights.

We were moving across the sand-floored arena before the great stepped tomb. Though I couldn't really see them in the cold haze surrounding me, I knew hundreds of people were on their faces, paying homage to the malignant spirit that wanted to be reborn in my body. I strained to send my spirit beyond the trap, questing for Tiwi, but the dark crystal bent my kenning back upon itself until the chiming was too much to stand. I gave up, hoarding my small store of strength to spend upon the effort to rid myself of the dart.

Grumahu was allowed to fall into step alongside. I stared up at him, trying to blink, unable even to give him that much reassurance. Reading his dark eyes, I knew he was trying to use the kenning. I pressed myself against the black crystal of my trap and listened.

His voice was muffled, as though he was pitching his mind-voice to some other ear than mine: *. . . seed she gave him, hurry up. Ready? One, two, three.*

Abruptly, one of the front corners of the litter tilted as the soldier who had been carrying it stumbled in the loose sand, dropping his hold on the spear. I didn't feel anything as the cloak came unrolled from the shafts and dumped me unceremoniously. The Emperor cursed with exasperation and warned Grumahu back with a look, which the giant returned with a shrug of innocence confirmed by the nod of a priest behind him. The giant had not tripped the litter bearer.

Among the hands trying to lift my inert form back onto the litter, I could feel two small ones that grasped my crooked jaw gently and forced a tiny, round object through my frozen lips. 'Eat, Marner,' Barberry whispered close to my ear.

I tried. I concentrated every bit of will I had left on shifting that seed into my mouth, but I couldn't swallow it. It just lay against my teeth.

Spears flashed down to bar Grumahu's way. Something cracked in his eyes, and I saw wild panic there for an instant. Then he had himself under control. 'See you, Runt Mage,' he said, as they lifted me once more and began to climb the steps of the temple.

Aye, mate, and we'll laugh about this some day when we're in our cups.

I managed to lift a finger to him in farewell.

CHAPTER FOURTEEN

Red carpeted steps led up the side of the steep temple, and the litter bearers had some trouble negotiating them. Finally, though, they got us up to the platform safely. It was open to the view of the city. Over the two thrones set ready for us was a stone canopy supported by thick square pillars, deeply carved with the serpent and jag'har motif of the imperial court. I surmised this might afford shade for the royal box on hot days when there was some spectacle requiring the Celestial One's personal attendance. Behind the thrones, perhaps fourteen steps towards the center of the platform, was a low pavilion open to the four sides of the temple. Within, I could see the altar where the Eternal Flame should have been burning brightly. But the altar was dark, and if the Power who had taken Colin Mariner's skin had his way, it would forever remain so.

The Emperor cast an eye up at the moon. 'Two or three hours yet,' he reckoned. His smile turned to me. 'Time enough to enjoy ourselves a little before we must tend to business. This is an unexpected surprise: I find myself actually interested in this match, and it's been a very long time since I was much interested in anything.' He must have read the look in my eyes. 'No, I don't know how it will come out. Grumahu was the most skilled gladiator we've ever seen, and Denjar is the best jag'har knight.' He pursed his lips and lay back against the cushions of the jade throne. 'Of course, Walking Thunder is somewhat out of practice, one supposes, while Denjar is at the peak of his form.'

And if they kill each other, that will be two strong men fewer that might be a threat to you. Aye, I know what your game is, mate. I've played with crooked dice before, I thought.

Propped on my own throne, I surveyed the crowd through the smoky effect of the dark crystal trap. Now that the Flayed One had been found for the ceremony at midnight, the assembled nobles, wealthy merchants, and priests who lined the great steps of the temple could relax and enjoy the spectacle. They had brought cushions for the purpose and were now sitting on the steep steps where, after midnight, the blood would run. Slaves fanned away the night insects and served flat cakes and pilchu for snacks. Every once in a while, one of the nobles would toss a half-eaten cake down to the sandy floor of the arena at the foot of the temple, and bony little boys would fight and scuffle over it, silently and in deadly earnest. The nobleman would grin at his peers, his teeth and jade earrings gleaming in the light of the hundreds of streaming torches, and there would be general laughter as one of the children clouted the others and escaped with his morsel.

The spectacle disgusted me and, as I couldn't turn my head, I lifted my eyes so as to ignore them. Looking beyond the temple enclosure I could trace the broad avenue that looped back and forth as it descended through the city to the river. The torches that lit the great road still flared, a chain of fire that made the surrounding darkness all the blacker. Somewhere down there and off to the right of my vantage should be the Imperial Gardens, and somewhere nearer at hand would be the place where they were holding the children. I would not think about Imlaud and his team, or about the Umlisi. The bastard next to me might be able to read it from my mind if I did. I must possess myself in patience, work at the dart in my neck, and give them all time. I drew as much of a calming breath as possible and focused on the sand arena once more. Only then did I realize how quiet the crowd had gone.

Denjar was attended by an honor cohort of his jag'har peers. The knight was in his full regalia, the spotted pelt of his uniform rippling with every stride and a cockade of feathers adorning the snarling snout of his cat helmet. He carried a thickly feathered shield on his arm and even from high above I could see the light gleam on the deadly black edges of the obsidian blades in his paddle-sword. He strutted to his position directly below the Emperor's platform and bowed.

The Emperor weakly lifted a hand in acknowledgment. 'Announce him,' he ordered quietly, and Huacan stepped to the front of the platform.

The high priest leveled his jade staff to point down at the knight. 'Here is Denjar a Tchlaxi, captain of the Imperial regiment. See him!'

'Jag'har, jag'har!' the assembled guests cheered, and a shower of jade rings and gold or silver arm bands arched from the spectators to the sandy floor. One of his cohorts said something as Denjar withdrew towards the stone steps, and beneath the jaws of his helmet, I could see his smile.

I scanned the long length of the arena, looking for Grumahu, but the next men to appear on the arena's sand were three slaves, identifiable by their short kilts and shaved heads. They were rolling what appeared to be a stone wheel of some sort, knee high to a man, and pierced in the middle for an axle, and it was obviously very heavy, because they were having a devil of a time heaving it through the soft sand. I suddenly thought that it might be a sacrificial stone. If I could have gone colder than I already was, I'd have done it then. The crowd began to jeer impatiently, and the slaves hurriedly withdrew.

Finally, they brought Grumahu out. 'A fair fight,' the Emperor had ordered. Well, if this was their idea of fair, the giant might just as well have elected the high priest's knife. Walking Thunder was stripped to his kilt, and had no shield or helmet. In his hand he held a limber twig, a mock sword, that bent in the small breeze blowing through the arena. A length of rope was knotted about his waist and trailed as he marched between his guards up the sand floor. The crowd erupted with cheers and whistles, and I was amazed to see the cascade of jeweled ornaments they threw down. The cheers didn't sound derisive; in fact, had it not been for the glittering in their eyes and the bloodthirsty curls to their smiles, I might have thought the nobility of Oaxacu were solidly on Grumahu's side. Obviously they remembered him from his gladiator days and looked forward to some good sport before Denjar killed him.

His guards secured the trailing end of the giant's tether to the rolling stone. Then they left him to face the Emperor. Walking Thunder kicked the rope out of his way and touched one knee to the sand. Huacan intoned, 'Grumahu, slave and gladiator, who has elected the trial by combat. What is your will, men of Oaxacu?'

They roared, 'Fight! Let him fight!'

The Emperor lifted a finger, Huacan raised his staff, and instantly all was quiet. 'The Celestial One inclines to leniency on this, the eve of our great festival. The gladiator will be allowed three bouts according to custom. If he still lives at the end of them, he will be free.' The cheer swelled, but trailed away when Grumahu held up a hand for quiet. Puzzled, the nobles leaned forward to hear what he would say.

Grumahu remained kneeling, and I suspected this was because if he had risen to his feet, the match would have been on, and Denjar – who was whistling his paddle-sword about his head to warm up – would have taken off his head immediately.

Huacan glanced to the Emperor. 'See what he wants,' Colin ordered.

The high priest struck his staff on the edge of the platform. 'Speak, slave!'

Now Grumahu rose to his feet. 'Claim a boon, Sire,' he called. 'Saved the Celestial's life once.'

Nobles were nodding in their seats. Whatever my friend had done, they all knew of it. Now some were turning to look up to the platform. Beside me, the Emperor sighed. 'Have him name it.'

Huacan imperiously signalled Grumahu to continue.

The giant held himself proudly. 'Like my wife's spirit freed.'

Even through the distance of the black glass between us, I heard the gasps from the crowd. I doubt anyone else had ever accused the Emperor to his face of holding spirits in his damned traps. Inside my crystal prison, I was smiling.

I heard my amusement echoed beside me. The Emperor was quietly chuckling. 'Cacamalu, he's got balls. Tell him we remember his service to our person and will reward him appropriately.'

'But, Sire!' the priest began to object.

Colin turned his head to regard Huacan steadily. 'I'm in a good mood tonight. You wouldn't want me in a bad one, would you?' The question hung in the smoky air and the priest hurriedly bowed and relayed the message. It wasn't much of a promise, but Grumahu bowed again briefly and called up his thanks.

It was hard to see at this distance, but I thought his eyes might be on me. I tried to pitch my voice to carry outside the glass. *The rope, Giant.* The chiming inside the trap drowned my words and in frustration I clenched the muscles of my jaw, howling inwardly at the pain of the bone splinter. The darkness grew, a mist that thickened between me and the puffs of sand kicked up by Denjar's leaping attack and Grumahu's swift dodge, and colors spread across the painting floor . . .

. . . the figure was indistinct at first and small, so that I

thought it was a child. I had an impression of stone walls quite close on either side and then the figure checked and halted, raising one hand to signal those who followed. He craned to see ahead of us, then turned his head briefly. The red feathers of his mask showed black in the darkness. He held up two fingers and the man beside me nodded and brought out his blow dart tube. The Umlisi troop hardly breathed. In fact they went so still I couldn't see them at all, only the man with the dart tube remaining visible. He crept forward, taking it slowly. I went with him.

We were in a tunnel, or narrow passage, that ended in a stout wooden door. Positioned to either side of this were sentries, but they obviously were neither jag'har nor eagle knights. No, these were ordinary foot soldiers, dressed in uniforms of quilted cotton with only a few feather adornments. Their spears looked sharp enough, though.

The fellow on the left looked bored, but the one on the right was plainly worrying at some thought like a bone. He glanced at his companion. 'Do you have any children, Namet?'

'Don't think about that,' the older man advised. 'Just shut up and do your job.'

'But—'

'Shut—'

The darts flew in such quick succession that the two hit the floor in the same instant.

'Ho, well shot!' Captain Hyssop whispered fiercely in his own language, and I understood him. Working quickly, the Umlisi plucked the darts from the bodies, but they did not take the soldiers' weapons. We wanted to spread as much panic as possible, and it is hard to explain two dead sentries who have absolutely no marks of violence upon them. From the man Namet's body, Hyssop took the key to the door.

Before fitting the key to the lock, he examined the portal closely for traps. Then, satisfied that the Oaxacans had trusted to the security of their own Forbidden City to deter would-be thieves, he unlocked the door and inched it open.

The stench made him draw back and raise his bow against walkers, but then he recognized that it was only urine and excrement, not the foul smell of corruption. We had found the pit where the Emperor's troops had imprisoned the sacrificial children. Hyssop lowered his bow and peered into the darkness. 'Childrens?' he called quietly. There was no answer except a clink of chains and a muffled cry.

Hyssop flicked his fingers and two of his men crouched to let a third climb up on their shoulders and reach up for the torch which had been set at tallfolk height. With this in his hand, the captain looked down into the pit beyond the door. I moved to look with him.

Like so many starving fledglings in a filthy nest, the doomed children squinted up fearfully at the light, mouths a little open, eyes glittering with sudden tears of terror.

Beside me, Hyssop swallowed audibly. Then he handed the torch to another man and removed his mask before crouching at the rim of the pit. 'Not to fear,' he told them gently, 'Umlisi be friends of childrens.'

For a moment the silence remained unbroken. Then there was a rattle of chains beneath our vantage, and a boy's voice said wonderingly. 'Hey, it's a Mud-Head!'

At that, there was a general stir. A little girl, her delicate brown features blurred with dirt, stared up at the nimbus of golden torchlight. 'Did you come to take us home, Mr Mud-Head?'

Hyssop slowly smiled. 'Did so,' he confirmed. 'Umlisi always come when childrens need, eh?'

'I know,' she said solemnly.

'Shh, shh!' the captain cautioned when some of the boys and girls gave way to tears or cries of relief. 'Must be good childrens, be quiet till Umlisi take away from here. Not to wake up warriors or walkers, eh? Shh,' he repeated, and the children co-operated, though one or two could not help their sobs. I didn't think it would alert any guards; after

all, they must hear a lot of crying from this pit.

There was a ladder propped against a nearby wall and the Umlisi put this down into the hole. While Hyssop and another man stayed topside to guard the door, the others went down to free the children. All of the chains were locked, but Barberry had been right; locks were no particular problem for the Folk. Some of the children were so weak they could scarcely stand, so Hyssop ordered that each of the boys and girls should be fed a sip of mead strengthened with some of Imlaud's spring water. As I watched, the color came back into pale cheeks and big eyes regained their customary brightness. While that was pleasing, I fretted that the increased noise they were making might be dangerous.

The Umlisi urged the children up the ladder. When they were all safely topside in the glow of the torch, my heart leaped. Tiwi was standing right before me, hale as could be expected, and with a certain light of anticipation in his eye. He looked about, frowned, and then asked Hyssop, 'Isn't Kinu with you, Mr Mud-Head?'

The captain was preoccupied with ordering his ranks so that they could protect the children if necessary and he would not have recognized my name, anyway. Cattail heard the question, though. 'Be tallfolk man, red hair, blue eyes, come from Anazi?'

Tiwi smiled proudly. 'He's my elder brother. I know he's here somewhere; I saw him out there on the road. He'll be wanting to find me, and I—'

Cattail caught Hyssop's glance. 'Kinu real name be Marner, boy. Marner be here, but have other thing to do. Did leave childrens for Umlisi to help. Will meet us later, eh?'

It wasn't exactly a lie, but it wasn't all of the truth, either, and Tiwi heard the hesitation. 'He's been captured, hasn't he?' he whispered.

Hyssop's hand chopped down at the same time one of

our sentries hissed, 'Walkers!' Cattail clapped a hand over the boy's mouth to forestall whatever he meant to say, and I knew in the instant what Tiwi would do. If he hadn't been so very new to magery, he would never have tried it, but the young Mage of Morning didn't stop to think of the Emperor's malignant, watchful spirit. All he knew was that Elder Brother was in trouble, and alone.

'Kinu!'

His kenned call rang like a struck silver bell, and the walkers homed in on it immediately. A couple of bone spears streaked towards us, landing short. The Emperor's creatures came boiling down the tunnel, roused and black. Hyssop did not hesitate. He dropped his bow, clasped both hands about the ring I had made of the Servant's Stone, and shouted, 'Il Numator!'

A powerful bolt of ruby Fire shot from the ring. There was a howl and a cut-off shriek, then a hiss, as of steam, and then nothing but some bronze from their swords dripping down the walls of the tunnel to pool on the floor.

'Whew!' Cattail sighed. 'That be too mucking close!'

Hyssop made a peculiar sound and went to his knees, hunching over the dull gray point protruding from his stomach. The little girl who had believed in him so backed up with her hands pressed to her mouth, holding in the cry because he had told them to be quiet.

Cattail was the first to kneel and get the injured man turned over onto his back. 'Go!' the captain gasped, the word coming on hard gulps of air.

'Pei, Hyssop, take you home!'

Hyssop was turning black with the congestion of the dart. He kept possession of his senses, though, working to twist the ring from his finger and press it into Cattail's hand. 'Take childrens home,' he ordered. 'Now!' He put all the force he had left into that command, and it drained him. He choked on a breath and did not draw another.

Cattail bit his lip, looked away for a moment, and then

touched his captain's shoulder in farewell before bounding to his feet. The ring slipped onto his finger. 'This way, quick!'

The branching tunnel seemed all right, but some instinct warned me even before I heard the tell-tale click of the trap. 'Net!'

Whether or not I actually kenned it, Cattail halted in mid-stride, ducked back from the spears that suddenly shot out of both walls, and calmly burned them with the ring to open a passage for the Umlisi and their charges. 'Do hear, Marner,' he murmured, looking into the ruby chalcedon as though he could see me there. Maybe he could. 'Will take childrens to great boat, then come back for Marner.'

'No, don't!' I said, but my shouted warning only crashed and jangled inside the black crystal where I was imprisoned, and the pain spun the colored sands until I was so dizzy that I slid down the curve of the trap . . .

A long, sustained animal sound like a wolf pack howling roused me. 'Not too much, you'll choke him,' the Emperor was saying over the shouting of the crowd. He was leaning forward on his throne, looking past Huacan's arm. I heard a weak cough and recognized it as my own. I couldn't taste whatever they had fed me, and that was probably just as well, because it smelled like nothing should. The Son of Night saw that I was aware once more and he smiled a little. 'Huacan, I hope you have the elixir ready to feed him later. I don't want to wake up with the taste of that stuff,' he flicked a contemptuous finger at the ornately carved gourd, 'on my lips in the morning.'

'I shall see to it personally, sire,' the priest assured him, straightening in front of me.

I couldn't control my movements, but I could flop, and by chance I landed a pretty fair kick square on the bastard's knee. Huacan hissed and drew back his arm, but then he mastered himself. He contented himself with baring his teeth at me and limped aside. I strained for a look down to the sand floor.

The Emperor was following the action down there, too, but he glanced at me. 'Who were you calling, by the way? "Kinu," you kenned while you were out. Who is that? Grumahu, maybe? He isn't much of a fish. A whale, maybe, but not a fish.' Colin chuckled. 'Well, no matter. The fact that you can ken at all in your condition merely confirms what I already knew, Mage of Morning.'

I knew he was watching my eyes, so I gave him what he was looking for, a hard, flat stare like that of an angry, defeated man. It wasn't a difficult part to play.

He laughed, coughed suddenly and reached for the cup Huacan offered. Free of his attention, I looked down at the arena.

I had dreamed for quite a time, apparently, for there was a long rent down the side of Denjar's jag'har uniform and he no longer wore his snarling helmet. Grumahu's skin glistened with sweat in the torchlight, but I couldn't see any wounds on him and he was moving well. He had a knife in his hand now.

'They played one bout while you were unconscious,' the Emperor informed me. 'Grumahu won. By the rules, the challenger gains a knife at the end of the first match and a sword at the end of the second if he survives it. The champion loses first his helm, then his uniform or armor. By the end of the second bout, assuming both are living, they are fairly evenly matched, except of course that the challenger remains tethered.' He smiled. 'The rock is the champion's other weapon, you see. The exhaustion of dragging it around will wear down even the strongest gladiator in time.'

He sounded so smug that I wanted to spit, but I couldn't help Grumahu even that much.

He suddenly leaned forward intently. 'Ah, there! You see what I mean!'

The giant had stumbled. Much of the crowd rose to its

feet, screaming. Walking Thunder fought for his balance, free arm up to ward off Denjar's upraised paddle-sword, knife hand in the sand to keep himself from falling backward.

The paddle-sword whistled down.

Grumahu suddenly sprang aside on his 'injured' ankle, raking the point of his knife in a quick slash across Denjar's chest and armpit. The paddle-sword thudded into the sand as the jag'har knight gasped. The giant had his knife poised over Denjar's undefended back when the game steward hurriedly rang the gong. 'Two bouts to Walking Thunder!' he proclaimed.

Inside my dark crystal trap, I shook my head, wincing at the pain of the splinter. *Cacamalu, Giant, that was too damned close.*

Perhaps it was just my imagination, but I thought I heard his mind-voice answer calmly, *Not to worry, Runt Mage.*

'Bring up the trap of Grumahu's wife,' the Emperor ordered Huacan quietly.

The priest was visibly staggered, but he dared say nothing. With a bow and a flurry of feathers, he hurried off. The entrance to the inner chambers of the temple must be in the small structure behind us, where the Fire altar sat cold and dark. In the deepest bowels of this stepped mountain would be his treasury, his traps. I forced my eyes sidewards to stare at Colin; it was too easy to see the Emperor as Colin in that fading body.

'Yes,' he answered to my look. 'I believe I *will* actually free her if Grumahu wins. It's a fit gesture for an emperor's re-birthday, don't you think?' He cocked his head, regarding me. 'Of course, he has to win first, and somehow I don't think that will be easy, even for our giant.'

So it was all a rigged game, a little taste of blood to warm up the audience for the night's foul ritual. I wondered if Grumahu knew what trick would give Denjar the final, fatal advantage. Surely an ex-gladiator must have fought in a few rigged matches of his own, and he would be expecting the Emperor to play him false. I wondered, too, why the Emperor was even bothering to have the trap brought to him if he meant never to have to unseal it.

The arena slaves were raking the trampled sand while the steward and his assistants supervised the stripping off of Denjar's uniform. The bloody gash shone in the torchlight, but the cat-soldier bounced on the balls of his feet while they bound some strips of cloth around his chest and arm, then he pushed the slaves roughly away and brusquely signaled over the cupbearer.

In the middle of the arena, tethered to his stone, Grumahu carefully dried his hands with some sand and took the paddle-sword offered to him. A cupbearer, a different one, approached him, holding out—

Don't take it, Grumahu! I kenned, setting off a deafening clanging inside my trap.

I was sure I heard him this time: *Cacamalu, know that,* he sent disgustedly as he waved the cupbearer away. He inspected the sword carefully, walking to the furthest extent of his tether to get nearer a torch. I saw him peer, then stride to the round wheel that had half buried itself in the sand. The voices of the crowd quieted as they turned from their wagering to see. With unhurried deliberation he raised the sword above his head and brought the flat of it down upon the stone. The paddle sword broke vertically into two perfect halves.

The Walking Thunder looked straight up at the Emperor's pavilion. 'Lousy sword, Sire,' he called.

The Celestial One murmured, 'Ah, clever fellow.' To the priest who had jumped to fill Huacan's place, he said, 'Tell him he may have another of his choice.'

I thumped a fist off the black crystal in my mind and wished I could nip back outside the gate of the city and retrieve the giant's bronze one. But it was impossibly far away, even if I had been free to move.

Grumahu was careful about his selection, but he didn't push the Emperor's patience, for he knew well that the old man beside me could arbitrarily end the contest any time he wanted to do so. Finally the giant signaled that he was ready, and Denjar came out to meet him.

At once, I knew that whatever had been in the cup they'd given the jag'har knight to drink from, it had been a powerful stimulant. Denjar fair sprang across the sand. He was glistening with sweat although the match hadn't yet begun, and even from my vantage I could see the veins bulging in his neck. A man in his condition can take a deal of punishment and never feel it. A wordless groan of dismay ran round the walls of my trap.

Grumahu braced himself. The steward raised his staff, looking up to the imperial box for the signal to begin.

I heard a step on the pavement behind my throne, and Huacan's arm appeared between the Emperor and me, holding a palm-sized globe of jet-black glass. Colin took the trap and held it before my eyes for a moment so that I could see the terrified eyes and soundless scream deep in the heart of it. 'Yours looks just like it,' he needled maliciously. Then slowly he sat forward and placed the crystal on the carpeted step, pushing Huacan away when the priest would have helped. When Colin straightened, his color was bad, but he pressed a hand to his chest and called, 'Here's your boon, Gladiator.'

Grumahu looked up and went rigid.

'Of course,' said the Emperor of Earth-Above, 'you'll need to catch it before it shatters on that bottom step down there.' And quite deliberately he gave the crystal trap a nudge with his foot. Every eye in the arena followed the black ball as it dropped over the edge of the first step, thudded softly to the carpet, seemed to pause, and then began rolling slowly across the carpeting towards the edge. Every eye in the arena lifted first to the Emperor in disbelief, and then down to the crystal trap.

And while we were all watching, Denjar attacked.

Duck, Giant! I screamed in the kenning, but it was already too late, because the jag'har was a crazed man, hewing with his paddle-sword like a woodcutter. Grumahu leaped back to avoid him and caught his foot in the rope. He managed to partially block the stroke that would have crushed his knee, but one of the obsidian blades on Denjar's sword bit deep into his calf before he could fend the cat-soldier off with his knife.

The trap with his wife's spirit locked inside it dropped over the edge of the second step. I dived for it.

At least, that's what my mind told me I had done, but Huacan's assistants easily controlled my lurch forward and slammed me back in the chair, and not gently. I opened my mouth to scream at the pain and the black sand came up to swamp my senses and drag me under . . .

As our sleeves brushed the foliage of a low tree, the night air was perfumed with a spicy scent. In the darkness, Imlaud smiled. 'Beriath,' he murmured. 'Take it.' One of his men gently tugged the dwarfed tree free of its pot and placed it securely in the large collecting basket strapped to another's back. They had been at it quite a time; I saw foliage peeking out the tops of most of the baskets. Only Imlaud's seemed empty, and I knew that he was looking for Nilarion.

The Emperor's garden of potted trees rustled in the wind around us. I saw Imlaud lift his head and sniff, then stifle a cough. 'Truly, the fumes make it difficult to scent any tree tonight,' one of the Yoriandir company muttered disgustedly, nose wrinkling at the odor of rotten eggs that wafted down from the mountain top.

'I do not like this wind, either,' Imlaud answered. 'There is something unnatural about it.' He went on exploring each tree by touch and sight, working steadily across the center of the garden. At this rate, it was going to take them all night, and I knew Grumahu didn't have that long. There

was nothing I could do, though. I could only observe.

'Shall we not try the kenning again, Eldest?' one of the wardens asked. 'Surely Nilarion could respond enough for her voice to carry if we were close by.'

Imlaud shook his head. 'I doubt it. We have found not one tree, tonight, that still has its spirit. He has pithed them all and Nilarion has been held here longest. I wonder if we shall find her living at all,' he whispered dispiritedly.

One of the Yoriandir had walked on ahead by a few steps. Suddenly he stiffened and halted, holding up a warning hand. He was looking down at the ground. Immediately the Yoriandirkin troop froze. 'What is it?' I heard Imlaud ken.

The man turned his head to look back at us. 'This track,' he pointed, 'I think—'

A dark shadow about a foot long and very narrow swooped low over the potted trees, snaked its head towards the Yoriandir scout, and ejected a stream of its venom into his startled eyes.

'T'ing!' a man behind me cried aloud. 'Look, there's another! Guard thy eyes, brothers!'

The poor fellow who had been sprayed crashed into the potted trees, clutching at the agony in his eyes. There were already blisters rising on his green skin. Imlaud grabbed him and did the only merciful thing there was: with one touch on the back of his neck, he knocked him unconscious, the same way Bai Nati had put me under on the night of the snake. 'Spring water to bathe his eyes, quickly!' he snapped, wincing and scrubbing his own hands with dirt. 'Melion, do thee try to keep them off us.' Scarcely had he ordered it when the master bowman unslung his weapon and dug into his quiver.

'Eldest, that's not the Way,' I chided, and though I was fairly sure no words of mine reached Imlaud, some of the feeling behind them must have.

'Wait, wait, I have bethought me,' he said. Another of the

t'ings swooped low, and we all guarded our eyes with a fold of our hoods. The venom splashed harmlessly off the foliage. 'Lurion, thee knows the Evening Peace song? Sing it with me, then.' Together, the wardens began a gentle chant that rose and fell like an evening breeze, like a baby's sleeping breath, like a moonlit sea. So beautiful were their clear voices, held low and quiet for safety's sake, that pressed as we were, all of us found ourselves eased. Terror faded out of the night.

One t'ing alighted in the branches of a potted tree about twenty feet away, cocked its serpentine head, and regarded us. We held our cloaks ready to cover our faces, but otherwise made no movement. Lurion and Imlaud sang on, ancient words in some language immeasurably older than any I knew. A pair of t'ings landed on the tree closest to Imlaud's head and I held my breath. The Eldest closed his eyes, but he kept singing, and I marveled at his courage. Finally there were over a dozen of the tiny dragons perched all around us. I had heard about them in fable and song, but never seen them, and despite the dangers of the night I was thrilled.

Finally the song ended. Would the t'ings attack now?

The Yoriandirkin peeked at the creatures from under their hoods. The t'ings stared at the green men out of small bright eyes, the moon reflected in them like the sheen on the surface of a chalcedon. Just when I thought someone might sneeze or the injured man might groan awake, a dry voice said softly in our minds, 'Thee's much a singer, Eldest, and this one beside thee also knows the Song well.'

'We thank thee,' Imlaud answered. 'I know well that we have not the right to ask thy true-name, old master, but would give us a thing to call thee?'

'Indigo Star will do. It has been long since anyone talked to us, Eldest, much less sang the Evening Peace song. How chances it a troop of Yoriandirkin wardens comes here now?'

Imlaud bowed his head. 'We should have come earlier, in truth. I have long neglected my duty out of fear.'

Indigo Star, distinguished by the deep blue line down the ridge of his hackles, raised his head to look up the mountain at the city. It looked dark, except for one torchlit area. The arena, I guessed. 'I can understand why thee's afraid of him,' the t'ing said dryly. 'See what he has done to us.'

'I did mark it, master. He has thy spirits partially entrapped, then?'

'Indeed.'

Imlaud and his men were furious, for all learned men know that the t'ings are the most ancient beings on earth. To do them this villainy was beyond comprehension. Even a demented emperor-mage should have some threshold he will not cross.

The Eldest of the Yoriandirkin straightened and, as a sign of trust, threw back his hood. The moonlight gilded his golden hair. 'We come in peace to thee, Master Indigo Star. Had we known thee were held in bondage here we would have spoken to thee sooner. This night may be the turning of a thousand old injuries if all goes well.'

'Thee's looking for Nilarion, then, are thee not?' the t'ing asked.

'She is the key,' Imlaud acknowledged, 'and time is running out. We come to rescue her and take the Tree to her rightful place.' On a sudden impulse, he asked, 'Would thee come as well? There is room in the valley for thee and thine, and we would be glad to have t'ings among us once more.'

Indigo Star said sadly, 'It is too late, I fear. Even if we could escape, he holds us. We will never grow to our full stature and fly free.'

Imlaud held his eye. 'Master, we did not come to the Forbidden City alone. Even now, friends labor on all our behalves.'

'My word! Thee's brought a mage with thee!' The t'ing

bobbed up and down on its branch in a most undignified way. 'By all means, then, let us attempt to get the Tree out of this vile place! Tell thy mage the word of unbinding is—'

'Is *what*?' I shouted, beating my fists against the crystal in frustration.

'Ah, you're awake. Good. You'll want to see this.' The Emperor reached a helpful hand to jerk my chin up off my chest. The dart grated. I kicked convulsively, but this time I pushed the darkness back and managed to look down the steps to the arena.

The first thing I saw was the black crystal trap. It was on about the fifth step up from the arena, rolling faster now as it picked up momentum, and landing with a thunk I could hear all the way up here. When it dropped off the temple onto the stone paving below, it would surely smash.

My eyes flew to the sand floor. At my first sight of him, I knew we were going to lose. What I could see of Grumahu's back was streaming with blood.

Denjar had got between the giant and the wheel, and pushed Walking Thunder back to the full extent of his tether, so that the gladiator could not possibly employ the rope as a weapon to trip his opponent. Instead, Grumahu was being forced to drag the wheel back with him just to stay out of reach of Denjar's lunging swings.

The giant's huge thigh muscles bunched and strained, and he heaved himself a step closer to the temple stairs. But Denjar swiped at his head, and Grumahu ducked and stumbled, his bad leg giving out on him. *Sword!* I kenned desperately, but there was no rising powerful chant, only the cacophony of jangled crystal.

Grumahu tiredly hewed with his paddle-sword. His swing caught the jag'har knight a glancing blow on the ear. Denjar backed off a pace, shaking his head, and the giant smashed him in the mouth with one cut fist. They went down in a tangled heap.

'Boo! Foul!' yelled the crowd, and the stewards hurried to drag them apart.

Denjar threw off the officials as soon as he had regained his feet. Grumahu took the moment to look back over his shoulder.

The crystal spirit trap rolled off the edge of the next-to-last step.

The giant's jaw was slack with exhaustion, but now he drew a huge breath, pushed back the officials, and swung his paddle-sword. At the same instant, Denjar whistled a blow towards his midsection. The two weapons collided and Grumahu's flew out of his hands. The cat-soldier let the force of his swing carry him around, and landed on guard. His eyes widened as he realized what had happened, and he straightened, grinning. At his leisure now, he walked to the giant's sword, picked it up, and sent it spinning a long way down the arena. Then he turned glittering eyes to my friend.

For an instant, the whole arena was silent as the two enemies stared at each other. Then Grumahu dived for the temple stairs, twisting to land full-length, fingertips desperately stretching.

The black crystal ball rolled off the last step and shattered on the pavement four inches from the giant's grasp.

The Emperor laughed. 'It wasn't hers.'

Grumahu surged up, forgetting the tether, grasping Denjar's descending sword as if it had been no more than a child's toy. *Sword!* he bellowed in kenning.

From far down the avenue there was an answering sound like that of marching men who sang as they came onto the battlefield. The nobles stood up to see. The guards leveled their spears. The merchants clutched their gem pouches. The Emperor struck Huacan's arm. 'Up! Get us up into the temple! Hurry, you fool!'

The high priest beckoned others and they bent to lift us. Suddenly a bronze shape streaked in the torchlight straight to the hand of the mage who had warded it. Grumahu swung the hero sword and cut the rope tether. On the same stroke, he felled a guard who had been rash enough to stumble towards him. Then the giant turned to Denjar.

The jag'har knight still did not comprehend that the thing in Walking Thunder's hand was a sword. Grumahu blew aside the paddle-sword and thrust the bronze blade right through Denjar. He kicked the body off his sword and started up the temple steps.

I saw a wink of ruby light in the dark sky away over the avenue, and my heart leaped until I remembered that half my ring was still on the Emperor's hand and I couldn't do a thing about it. *Go on, Giant, get out of here.*

'Get what I came for,' the gladiator snarled.

By this time Huacan had unceremoniously hoisted the old man out of his seat, and two of them were working on lifting me, having to be careful because they were afraid they'd drive the dart in too deep before it was time.

I may have been the only one in the Forbidden City who expected what happened next.

There was a roaring whoosh, as though some huge bird had swooped over the top of the temple behind us, and then everything was illuminated in a rich ruby light. Gigantic talons clutched Grumahu right off the temple steps and my dragon ship, *T'ing Kinu* circled with him. But she could not get near me because of the stone canopy over the imperial box. I heard her despairing cry.

Fly, my pretty! Straight back to Il Numator, thence to the valley! I ordered, and regretfully she lifted over the dark altar of the Fire.

The Emperor struggled to his feet, hands clasped around his ring – around my ring – and ordered, *Stop*. Simply that, as if he expected the ship to obey. I summoned all my strength and lashed out at him with my fist just as the weak Fire was beginning to kindle over the broken chalcedon's surface.

One of the guards leaped between us, and his dagger flashed down to impale my hand to the throne. I didn't feel it, I couldn't feel anything, but I seemed to *remember* feeling another blade there. It really was no matter. The children, the Tree, and the giant were safe. I raised my eyes to the Emperor, and my frozen lips smiled.

'You little bastard,' he snarled, and his fury set him coughing. 'Now, Huacan!' the Emperor gasped. 'There's no time to waste.' His bottomless, ancient eyes turned to me. 'And don't pith him first: I want that pleasure for myself.'

'As you command, Sire,' the high priest acknowledged, and he gave me a knowing, cruel smile.

CHAPTER FIFTEEN

As my litter was borne into the tomb with the measured tread of the Emperor's bearers right behind us, the canopy of the stars went out, and I was looking up at hewn stone blocks. That might be the last time I ever see the sky, I thought.

Panic threatened to overwhelm me. I began working my hand, feverishly trying to bring the jumping muscles under my control, since it was obvious that merely trying to move the dart by tightening my jaw wasn't going to work, at least not in time.

It seemed a very long way to wherever we were going, not that I minded, and I gradually realized we must be winding round and round and down. When we passed into the rather smallish chamber with the vaulted ceiling, I knew the place at once: sand floor; a hollowed alabaster lamp in one corner casting a steady warm light; the four low lintels, each carved with its own symbol: Leaf, Wavy Line, Jagged Line, Sun. The ancient sanctuary of the Four Powers. Only one detail seemed unfamiliar to me. I did not remember the hundreds of darkly gleaming chalcedon crystals that covered the sanctuary's every wall.

Then I realized. These were the spirit traps.

The bearers drew up before the small dragon-prow, its planks gleaming with gold plating and sail wired open to a wind that would never blow in here. 'Quickly,' the Emperor said. 'I'm tired.'

We were handed aboard, the eagle knights grunting a little to lift my litter over the side. While several of them removed me from it and laid me on the bier that had been bolted across the thwarts, Huacan and another priest leaned into the covered litter to lift the wizened old man out. They laid him next to me on the cushions.

'Fine,' the Emperor said. 'Leave us now.' Huacan began to say something, but Colin just shook his hand from side to side tiredly, and the priests hastily dropped to the sand, touched their foreheads to it in respect, and left.

We listened to their footsteps quickly receding. They went out considerably more quickly than they had come in, I noticed as I methodically clenched and relaxed, clenched and relaxed my twitching, wounded hand. Come on, damn you, I coaxed it desperately, you worked better than this even with a bone dart through you.

Far up above us there was a heavy echoing clang. They had shut the bronze doors. Though the tomb was not cold, I was suddenly frozen. I looked up past the golden sail straining from its yards in the silent gale of the Emperor's evil and wondered which of the dark crystal traps held my spirit, and which one held Grumahu's wife.

'I never could understand his fascination with the sea, all those salt blisters on one's hands, all the maggoty biscuit and the deck bouncing around in a storm,' the Dark Power that had usurped the Mariner's life said, regarding the sail. 'Ah well, I suppose I'll have to do it all again, won't I? You're a sailor, too. Damn. Once, just once, couldn't you come back as a fat innkeeper with a taste for bad ale and murdering pilgrims in their beds? Hmm?'

I thought I could oblige him about the murdering. In fact I'd get a head start on it right now, if I could get my hands round his neck.

He might have known what I was thinking, for he chuckled softly as he took a golden needle from the cuff of his robe. I knew then.

'Yes,' the Emperor told me. 'You've had quite a bit of experience with the Hag's Embrace on this voyage, haven't you? What is it, two times you've taken it? Three? Didn't you suspect there might be other effects besides the initial coma? My, my, and you trained as a healer even.'

I had been afraid, but now I was angry. Facing the end of his life, a man does not need some sniggering fool to tell him what he's done wrong. I clenched my jaw until the wry bones popped with an audible click. It had often embarrassed me in the past, but now I scarcely heard it above the grating of the bone point as it slid. I drew a breath, steadying myself against the pain to try it again, and was able to open my jaw a little. The seed which Barberry had put into my mouth was still there; I could feel it suddenly, resting against my teeth. Immediately I clamped my jaw again. Slide out, damn you! I screamed inside my mind at the bone dart. The pain was a hideous burning at the base of my skull that seemed to run through my body along the web of my veins.

I struggled back desperately, because I could not afford this blackness, not now, not when he had the drugged pin already in his hand.

He had struggled up on an elbow, but the effort set him coughing again, and he rolled to the other side, trying to catch his breath through the spasms.

I nursed the seed onto my tongue, tried to swallow it, and found my mouth was so dry and my throat so swollen that I could not. Near despair, I kicked one leg convulsively and discovered the slim crystal sliver still secreted in the kilt at my hip. I tugged at it with my fingers and got it free, holding it down alongside my leg with my left hand, while with my wounded right I groped for the bronze dagger at my belt. Even if I had not intended it, I made a lot of noise clawing at the leather sheath.

The Emperor, his breath jagged, struggled to turn. He saw the bronze dagger nearly free in my right hand and made a face, as though I were a child set upon being difficult. The Dark Fire leaned to wrest the weapon from my fingers, and I brought up the crystal point.

He rolled on it, and I felt the blade snap from the hilt. I wasn't sure it was in him, though, until his face contorted with fury and I saw the Power looking out through those ancient eyes, trapped in Colin's dying body as I was trapped in mine. 'Your mother was a whore who abandonded you,' he hissed, and the venom struck to my very soul.

I strained away from the drugged pin, grappling for it with my flopping hands, trying to turn it back on him. If I could catch him in the Hag's Embrace for the twelve hours the coma lasted, I would probably be able to work the dart in my neck free and wrest my ring from his finger. With it, I might free all these poor shades from his dark traps. I felt a flash of bright triumph as I turned the pin towards his skinny forearm.

But he was a Power, and I was only a mortal, and he knew all my weaknesses. 'Give it up, fool,' he rasped, our eyes close together as we fought. 'Don't you know if you go this way, you'll never see the maid again? *She won't be in the garden waiting for you!*'

For a moment, I wondered whether he was right. He felt my hesitation, grinned like a walker striking, and clubbed down with the golden goblet from the tray next to him just exactly on the thin place under the fissure in my skull. I gasped as pain exploded the color of the golden sail to dull gray bits, and his hand found the bone dart in my neck.

He pushed on it.

I jerked like a fish on a harpoon and heard him grunt. The drugged pin was torn from my grasp. I heard a gurgling rasp, an explosive cough, a bubbling sigh that ran out suddenly, and then it was utterly still and utterly cold.

It was all dark. I had never seen a painting floor with sand so black. It swallowed all my colors, like seawater draining from a beach. I put down a few sprinkles of garnet and watched them wink out and disappear.

'You see?' a familiar voice said, echoing a little. 'Give it up, Painter. You cannot win. Come, turn the last Tile.'

I gritted my teeth, sorrowing for my colors, sorrowing that all that might have been made beautiful would now be lifeless and gray. 'I only have one Tile, and Thee knows it, my lord.'

He laughed the laugh that people chuckle behind your back when everyone in the village knows who knocked down all your carefully stacked turf pile so that the rain ruins your winter's fuel, and the other half of it shows up missing. 'Oh, so-and-so's old brown cow must have got out again,' they say. 'Or maybe 'twas those damned thieving tinkers – take the feathers off a chicken and never wake it up, they will.' But you look in their eyes and you know what they're really thinking: 'Damn drunk. Take his turf. He'll never be sure how much he cut anyway.'

It was that laugh. It had brought tears once, when I was very young and overheard it. Now it brought a quick flood of anger. For a moment, the black sand stretching before me gave up a little of the color I had put into it: blue-gray, hard as slate.

He saw. 'Still trying to paint.'

I felt the mockery like a whiplash. 'I can't give up.'

'I know. It's a great burden, isn't it? I always thought it grossly unfair of my exalted Siblings to have given you this Tile to play, and only this one. The Fifth Tile, as it were.' Tydranth chuckled. 'Confidentially, Mariner, I may say none of the rest of us would be stuck with it. That's how the lot came to you.'

'Don't call me that,' I said.

'What?' He sounded surprised, the Power off there in the darkness somewhere.

'Don't confuse me with Colin Mariner. I'm . . . I am . . .'

'Yes?' he prompted maliciously.

My hand knew. I stretched it out over the sand and quickly let the colors trickle . . . a lad crouched outside an alehouse, the hunched line of him a compact coil of restless energy over the painting he was making with some crushed peat . . . then the worn boots of a stranger that stopped suddenly at the border of the picture, the travel-worn robe, silver beard threaded with black, the deep, wise eyes, one blue, one brown. Bruchan, my grandfather.

'Yes,' the Power agreed. 'I knew him. Incidentally, he was never sure you actually were his grandson, you know.' The black sand swallowed the silvered line of him grain by grain until only his eyes remained, watching me steadily with some question in them I had seen but not registered before. Then they, too, vanished. It seemed much darker when he was gone.

'Thee lies,' I said sullenly.

'No. What I said about your mother before was true. Think about it: what king's daughter would go with a drunkard commoner like your father? How likely is it that Bruchan's daughter Breide ran away for love with a good-looking wastrel? No. Bruchan saw in you what he wanted to see, and he taught you to believe it, too.' He sniffed. 'The old man might have spared you much agony if he'd left well enough alone outside that alehouse that day.'

It was true about the agony. My hand flew over the black sand, throwing down the colors in broad strokes: here the skellig, still smoking, the gouts of blood disfiguring the faces I had loved; then the high cliff and the raven that had flapped past, beak open, and I had fallen, a slip that perhaps I would not otherwise have made; the grays that were all that were left to me, except when, as now, I let the poppy take me just to see the muddy colors bloom and swirl across the wall of my cabin . . .

He kicked me with his pegleg, and I rolled, protesting. 'Again,' he rasped, and the mute boy dashed another bucket-

ful of stingingly cold seawater in my face. I gasped and lashed out, and the lad fell heavily to the deck, the bucket bursting its bands. 'Get up, Giant,' the pegleg rasped. 'Your watch.'

I bit back the groan and dragged myself to my feet. I was looking out over the rail into a sea of flickering eyes. I felt the blood drain from my face. 'Powers, Timbertoe! How the hell did they get so close?'

He looked up at me, his dark eyes glowering. 'Tell me, Pilot.' He drew his cutlass, motioned the boy back, and we jumped together to beat back the first wave of them as they swamped our rail.

'Give me the chalcedons!' I said urgently.

He thought I was going to leave him, I saw it in his eyes, but he passed me the pouch of gems. I fumbled for a huge one and tossed it in a high arc, but the walkers still came on, getting their fangs in past our whirling blades, until finally the skipper reached down, ripped off his good leg, and threw it to them. They snarled and fought like wolves wrangling over a kill, and that held them for a time at least.

I turned to him. The blood was pooling on the deck, and he was regarding it thoughtfully, balanced on his ivory pegleg and a crutch. 'I'm sorry, Timbertoe,' I said, horrified.

He lifted his eyes to me. 'Codswallop,' he said . . .

The black sand absorbed the red blood. The Power said quietly, 'You asked too much of him, Painter.'

'I know.'

'Did you really think a chalcedon mine was recompense?' His voice was no less acidic than the taste of guilt in my mouth.

I lifted my head. 'No. But it was all I had to give, that and my son.'

He snorted, a sound of derision that festered immediately in my ear and dripped poison into my brain. 'What son? The only son you have, Painter, is the one that's growing in your jolly girl's belly back at Inishkerry.'

I was chilled. 'Sweet Pegeen is pregnant?'

He sneered. 'Yes, and the poor little whore is happy about it, because she loves you. Too bad you've eyes only for the witch.'

'Thee lies,' I accused again. This time, he did not even bother to deny it. My hand scattered the colors, a bulwark against the gnawing doubt. Her sea-green eyes, that's what I needed, her sea-green eyes resting confidently on me, full of love . . .

The sand is cold under my naked back, and her lips taste only faintly of strawberry. The surf crashes ceaselessly somewhere near at hand. 'Be time go, Marner,' she whispers.

'Nay, lass. I promised ye I'd come back every time, and I will.'

She holds my face. 'Marner. Be time. Even stars do fall when fire goes out. Get tired. Time for make big sleep now. Please?'

I look at her. 'I'll paint for you one more time. After that, I'll go.'

Her long hair sweeps the sand, and she follows it with a hand to smooth the surface. 'Tell story, then.'

I draw the satchel to me, set out the color pots and begin.

I put down the wash of the sea first, restless and blue, crested with white, hazy in the distance where it becomes the sky and then the deep midnight of stars, the great Arch beyond which no one can pass.

Then a dot of land on the surface of the sea, fringed with a green canopy and a pink reef. A pretty place, warm. I was happy there with Tanu, and I made the voyage a couple of times.

Then I stayed away, I stayed with my wife and my sons, because she loved me and I owed them that much at least. My brother gave us poison; this dark blot is it, only you can't see how it burned, and you can't tell the scars it left. I could paint that, but maybe it would make no sense to you. Everybody has different scars.

So I couldn't face my wife and tell her I had killed three of our sons for vainglory, and I couldn't die because I am the Fifth, the Timekeeper, the only one of the Tiles we mortals are given to turn, so there I was. I went where my heart, at least, could still be alive. I went to Tanu.

She was gone. He had got there before me, and taken her for spite. I went after him, but he caught me in his damned trap, and there I stayed eons it seemed, withering until I couldn't even remember what 'blue' was. Eventually I knew I was dying, and at first I welcomed the idea because this gray and white and black was all I knew. You see how drab it is, I'm sure.

Then a lad like me came and I saw a chance to see the world again through fresh eyes, and I wanted that, just once more before I went, just once more to see her, really see her, but the boy died and that chance was lost. I came back here, but—

No, I said, taking out my pots too. This is my story, Colin, and it doesn't end that way.

Look, here's the tomb they sealed us in. It was black in there all right, because it was lined with hundreds of spirit traps, most dull and lifeless, some few with a spark still flickering inside. Spirit traps you *set.*

I didn't, he protested. 'Twas him, the Dark One.

You should have kept painting, I told him coldly. You should have done that much, at least, to save them. Look, have you forgotten how? Here's the ship, ruby eyes flaring through the night, seeking us on the Way Above and the Way Below, and every place in between. Remember how proudly she rides the currents?

I remember, the Mariner said.

Now, here's the Arch.

I never sailed there, he objected.

But I did. You forced me to, when you sent the ship for me.

Cacamalu, lad, ye had a voyage, didn't ye?

I showed him my voyage, knowing we had an audience, knowing the Dark was interested too, because he had never been beyond the Arch either. The Zones Outside were no domain of the Powers . . .

First I quickly sketched the Tower, chiming in the sea wind, crystal battlements appearing suddenly out of the mist above the cataract. I filled the picture with the white foam and the roaring at the edge of the world. The prow of my boat tilted over and down and we fell at first, fell a long way. I painted them the terror of it, the fingernails I ripped clutching the tiller, and when that went, sliding until I wrapped an arm round the mast, the stars streaming past, my foot finding purchase against a thwart. Then the dragon-prow's wings unfolding to try to cushion the impact, and the geyser of water that rose up and smashed me under the waves so that my leg snapped when the bench did.

Then the picture that flowed from my hand became confused: an old man, white mage-lock blowing softly above his eyes, one blue, one brown, a tall man, brown as the earth, arms folded on his chest, his carefully braided beard gray but his eyes still shrewd and his balance good despite the ivory pegleg, and the picture skewed just a little and he was on two firm legs, a king's son, proud of glance, with a yearning heart and a notion the child might be his; a small picture, woven through the larger one, a little man with a chipper grin and sandy hair and evergreen paint on his face above his old clay pipe; a woman with glossy black hair that tumbled like a waterfall and smelled of nling-ling flowers, watching me from the depths of a dark crystal trap, watching me confidently, with love in her sea-green eyes . . .

'You misunderstood,' the Power interrupted. 'It was pity you saw there, not love.'

'No,' Colin and I said at once, in unison. The Mariner said, 'She loved me, right enough, you bastard. Try as you might, you can't take that away from me.'

The Power said nothing for a moment. The colors sank

into the sand, and I was alone, facing the blackness.

'And you, Painter? Did she love you?'

No, my heart whispered. She never even knew you, Aengus. We never had the time for love to bloom.

The two of them were waiting, the Power and the Mariner, and I knew I was a poor third. I stood up on the dark sand.

'Go on, lad, paint her once more. 'Twill ease your heart,' the Mariner counseled, not without compassion.

'Go on,' the Dark Fire challenged. 'Paint her. Find out.'

'It doesn't matter,' I told them quietly, and I headed for the surf of that vast beach.

'Wait! Where are you going?' the Power demanded. 'We're not done yet! Turn the Tile.'

I summoned my ship, and from afar Pel Kinu answered, trumpeting like a swan, the wind a music in her wings. 'No,' I told him. Simply that, and then I waded into the curling breakers.

'Well played, Aengus!' the Mariner called after me.

'You can't do that, you sniveling little wretch!' the Fire sputtered.

The other Powers refuted him from the darkness: 'Of course he can,' Aashis of the Winds said, and Tychanor the Warm agreed. 'He may elect to quit the game at any time,' Ritnym's musical voice added. 'There is nothing in the Rules to say he must turn the Tile and be reborn.'

'But . . .' the Dark One still objected.

I paused in the surf, the warm waters foaming around my knees. I considered it a moment, then bent my neck quite deliberately, straining against the bone dart until I heard it crack. I hawked up the pieces and spat them into my hand. 'Thee desired mortality so much, my lord, to touch her, to make her thine. So, here I give it to thee.' I flung the bone shards at him in the darkness.

I heard him grunt, and then a flare of red light lit the black cavern at the edge of the World Sea. Tydranth looked down at the stub of bone protruding from his chest. When he raised his head, his eyes were shocked and furious. 'Let's not forget the Rules here, mortal.'

'You were never a pirate,' I sneered.

Our hands shot up at the same instant, but I had only half a ring and he was a Power, so I dived for the water. His Fire turned it to steam that scorched me. I swam deeper, seeking cooler water for my burns, but of course I could not breathe and he was waiting for me when I came up. At the moment my head broke the surface, he saw me and raised his hand once more.

'Go home to Ilyria!' Colin Mariner shouted.

That made me angry. At least he could have got my homeland right. 'I'm from the Burren, not from your damned Il—'

He threw me the other half of the ring. Tydranth threw his Fire. I caught them both.

I groaned at the pain in my neck and raised a hand to touch the place. It came away bloody. What the hell? I thought. The golden sail fluttered a little above my head, drawing my eyes. It was movement that had fluttered the sail, not wind, movement of this funeral ship. The tomb itself was moving, the rumble more a feeling in the bones than a sound. Beside me something else stirred.

Memory flooded back. I rolled, grabbing for his hand to wrest the ring from it, but the signet, its chalcedon intact, was glimmering from the deck some distance away, having apparently rolled there. I staggered up, but the Power caught my ankle. His strength wasn't much, but it was enough. I fell, cracking my head painfully against the gold-plated deck, which now bucked strongly under my hands, as though we'd been hit underneath by a whale. My head cleared a little, and I realized the tomb really was moving and that there was a rotten, sulphurous stench. And here I was, on the flanks of a fire-mountain.

I kicked free of him, grabbed my ring, and cleared the

rail of the ugly gold ship to land on the sand floor. Jamming my ring on my wounded hand, I raised it and the rainbow Fire crackled on the surface of the chalcedon. In answer, the crystal traps lit. The sand floor rocked, and a fissure opened in it, steam boiling out of the vent. My senses reeled. What would be the word of unbinding?

Desperately I raked my mind over all I knew of the Power and of the Mariner, and then I realized what Colin had tried to tell me. On the impulse of my joy, pure streams of indigo, emerald, and ruby shot from the ring on my hand. 'ILYRIA!' I cried.

All around the walls of the chamber, the dark crystals snapped and tinkled to the floor. I saw their eyes, the eyes of the dead, and I saw the peace in them.

'Fly, shades, straight to Mother's lap. She waits for thee.'

The sweet breeze of their passage momentarily cut the foul vapors of the tomb.

He jumped from the rail of the ship above me, bronze dagger in his hand. I dodged the blow, aimed my ring at the sealed door, and exploded it. The floor heaved, the gold ship rocked off its davits, and I scrambled back up the winding passage towards the entrance. The beast's running paws clicked on the stone behind me.

There was no magery about the doors, so I simply blew them back off their hinges with my ring and paused an instant to look back. I could see his sapphire eyes gaining on me. I couldn't kill a Power, of course, but I could slow him down. I aimed my ring at the stonework of the tunnel ceiling and brought it down on top of him. By his howl of rage, I knew I had done no more than madden him.

I sprang to the Fire altar in the unnatural darkness. *Il Numator*, I said, calling the crystal by its true-name, the only one that made any sense. *Be thou healed. Here is my* *wn small Flame to help*. My rainbow danced over the kling crystal, and the cracks fused.

The sun lamp coalesced, its natural pearlescent surface restored. *And now the light, Mage, if thee please?* Her voice was a soft contralto, giving promise of warmth.

Aye, mistress. The light. I heard the tunnel behind me blasted open, and a furious scrabbling as the Wolf tried to free himself from the narrow aperture he had made. I stepped clear of the altar, looking towards the narrow line along the eastern horizon where the barest sliver of the sun's orb crept above the earth, but could not rise because the Dark's power held the earth in shadow. I hoped that narrow gleam of Light might be enough, though, if Colin Mariner had been the craftsman I thought.

I raised my ring once more, and threw my kenning across the miles of dark jungle to the Umlisi, who would be waiting for my call. *Kindle!*

Immediately there was an answering ruby gleam that shot into the sky as a signal, and then a piercing beacon of sunlight grew from the far valley as the Umlisi used the Servant of the Sun stone to swing their deck prism in its huge gears. 'Come on, lads,' I urged in a murmur, 'come on!'

The crescent of sun reached over the dark horizon. Caught and magnified by the Hearthstone of Il Numator, the brilliant golden rays shot from the tip of the deck prism straight to the sun crystal on the Fire altar. With a whoosh of indrawn air, the eternal Flame kindled.

At the eastern horizon the sky turned peachy gold, and the sun came up on the first day of the Third Age of Oaxacu, in the year 1 T'ing.

I crossed my arms over my head as the heavy squared blocks of the ritual enclosure began to cave in around me, the flagstones sinking at the weight of the beast's paws. 'Next time, Painter,' he snarled. I had my mouth open to tell him what he could do next time, and all the times afte but then a stone crushed me to the floor. I saw the bloc dripping down the temple steps.

How odd, I thought. *I've always heard . . .*

They say that at the moment of death, one's life flashes before one's eyes. Is that what happened to me?

It is true that a beam crashed down on me where I lay in the house of healing during the earthquake that rent the Vale in two and allowed the sea to rush through the narrow saddle of land between the arboretum of the Yoriandirkin and the terraced hill on which the hospital of the siochlas sat. Evidently I was trapped in the rubble for some time, because so many of the siochlas were killed and there was so much devastation that it took the survivors days to dig us all out. By that time I was, to all appearances, dead. Neilan affirms this, and I have surpassing faith in her abilities as a healer. That I woke some time later on my funeral ship does not detract from the truth of Neilan's testimony.

They say, too, that dreams can be more vivid than waking. That much is certainly so: for a long time after I sailed my battered ship into port at the Vale, I kept asking how Grumahu was doing at teaching Tiwi his magecraft, hoping he knew his beloved was now free, and whether the Umlisi had moved topside to their valley, and did the Yoriandirkin delight in talking to Nilarion? The siochla nurses made soothing talk, and Neilan herself spent as much time with me as she could spare, but only the sound of Dlietrian's harp eased me. Sometimes, in fact, it was the only company I could stand.

When I was strong enough, I used to sit in the sun in a warm corner of the hospital's terrace – which was slightly tilted now towards the new channel that cut us off from the arboretum on the other shore – and watch the boats go to and fro. Like any old salt sunning himself on a bench, I would think that I could make a smarter entrance to the piers, or clear the harbor more quickly. After all, I was quite a mariner, with or without a dragon-prow with ruby eyes. Finally, Timbertoe got tired of seeing me sit about, and he stormed up the hill one day to physically haul me down to board the *Inishkerry Gem*.

Rose was delivered of a son in due course of time, but she did not wake from the Hag's Embrace, not at Berren's birth, nor at his naming day, nor when King Beod sent the boy he believed to be his own to the dwarves for fostering. We're doing a good job with him, if I may say so. Is he my son? I do not know. I hope so. I like the lad.

So it was all a dream, thee may say. Yet there is talk of a tree in Yoriand of a kind the green men have not seen before. The leafkin appeared by a bubbling spring which forced its way to the surface there after the earthquake. It grows steadily to maturity, and seems as though it may bloom and set berries this year or next . . .